INNOCENT LIES

A gripping detective mystery full of twists and turns

CHRIS COLLETT

Midvale Community Library
P.O. Box 127
Midvale, ID 83645

Revised edition 2017 by Joffe Books, London.

First published by Piatkus in 2005 as "Blood of the Innocents."

www.joffebooks.com

ISBN-13: 978-1-912106-11-0

For Joe and Beth.

Author's Note

This is the second mystery featuring Tom Mariner. It is set in the early 2000s, when the internet was in its infancy, mobile phones had yet to evolve into smart phones, and people still read print newspapers.

CHAPTER 1

Striding to the window, Tom Mariner pulled the metal frame shut with an irritable bang, before releasing the venetian blind. It jerked down notch by notch, snagging on its tangled cord as if in the final throes of death. The immediate problem was solved, reducing the hammering and banging from the extension work in progress below to a series of muffled thuds, but neither action did much to alleviate the heat or glare from the midday sun that beat relentlessly in through the south-facing window. His was not an office designed for heat waves. It wasn't designed for cold snaps either, but right now the prospect of a biting frost or a raw wind was as distant as the Outer Hebrides and the sting of icy rain on his face would have been a refreshing relief. He needed a drink.

But when he got there, the water cooler was empty and there were no replacement bottles, forcing him to sift through the loose change in his pockets and head for the soft drinks machine on the ground floor. He joined a long queue, then when his turn came, the machine greedily swallowed his money and refused to cough up the can. He was poised to give it a hefty kick when probationer PC Liam Grady intercepted, calling down the stairs to him.

'There's a Miss Streep on the phone, sir. Claims she has some new information on a city-centre armed robbery you dealt with back in March. I did ask if she could come to the station, but she insisted that you'd want to go out to talk to her. To be honest, she sounded a bit of a fruitcake. Do you want me to deal with it?'

Mariner slammed his open hand into the side of the machine in frustration. 'No, it's okay. I could do with a break. I can get a drink while I'm *out*!' He glared at the machine. 'And if she is a time-waster it won't take me long.'

'Right, sir,' said Grady uncertainly.

* * *

In fact it took Mariner less than ten minutes to get from the station to the address given: a house on a small but exclusive, newly built estate in leafy Bournville. Four- and five-bedroom executive homes set in several immaculately landscaped acres among mature oaks, their combinations of colonial and mock-Tudor fascias rendering each one marginally unique. Number eighteen stood towards the end of the winding cul-de-sac. Mariner walked up a block-paved drive, past a gleaming new BMW convertible and pressed the doorbell. After a moment the door cracked open a couple of inches and behind it, out of sight of the street, Mariner saw Miss Streep.

Young and pretty, her thigh-length, burnt-orange silk shirt complemented the colour of her eyes. As he watched she let it fall open at the front, revealing that underneath she was wearing very little. 'Please come in, Inspector.' She smiled.

Mariner swallowed hard, his professionalism on the line. No contest really. With a furtive glance around to check that he was unobserved, he stepped into the hallway and immediately the door closed on him, she grabbed his tie, pulling his face down to her level and kissing him full on the mouth, while her other hand sought out his already expanding crotch.

'You have to stop doing this, Anna,' Mariner said, sometime later, lying back on the pillows, his pale skin glistening with perspiration, while she sat astride his abdomen now wearing only the silk shirt. 'Someone at the station is going to catch on to these women all specifically asking for me to make house calls when I'm meant to be working. I can't always just drop everything on a whim.'

Anna was pragmatic. 'This is only the second time, and you're entitled to some kind of lunch break, aren't you?'

'In theory yes, but you know how that works.'

'It's the only time during the week when I can guarantee that Jamie's not here. It seems a shame to waste the opportunity. Besides,' she added, artfully. 'You do always have the option of turning me down.' She slid down over his thighs and started work again.

Mariner's gaze swept over her exquisite body as he felt the blood flowing back to his groin. She'd put on a little weight since he'd first known her, rounded out a little, but all that had done was make her more irresistible. 'Oh, yes,' he said, as if she'd pointed out something new.

In truth he was a little afraid of what might happen if he did decline these invitations. Anna had saved his life, well, his sex life anyway. Single-handedly, as it were, she had resuscitated his seriously ailing libido and now, to paraphrase Harold Macmillan, he'd never had it so good. Added to which, she was bright, she was great company and he . . . well, he liked her . . . a lot. It was too much to risk. Except at times like this, when he felt guilty knowing that he should be somewhere else; his mind on other things. Fighting his natural urges, he propped himself up on his elbows. 'I really should go.'

'Okay.' Anna stopped what she was doing and climbed off him, eliciting another sigh. Her casual acceptance of the demands of his job disconcerted him.

3

His ego would have liked the occasional protest, except that wouldn't have worked either. It never had with previous girlfriends. And Anna didn't have time to get hung up on what may or may not be commanding his attention. Since assuming sole responsibility for Jamie, her autistic younger brother, she'd been presented with a whole raft of needs and demands that had to take precedence. Mariner understood that — most of the time.

Before dressing, he ducked under the shower for a few minutes, putting on Anna's shower cap to keep his hair dry. He didn't want the other detectives on the squad thinking he'd developed a sudden fetish for showering in the middle of the day, even during a heat wave.

'Lovely,' said Anna when he reappeared still wearing the cap. 'And there's a pair of French knickers in the drawer—' Mariner snatched off the hat and threw it at her, spraying her with water, making her wriggle and shriek and giving him the overwhelming urge to re-join her on the bed. 'What shall we do on Friday night?' he asked instead, pulling on his boxer shorts.

She wrinkled her nose. 'Actually I fancy a quiet night to myself. I've got stuff to do.'

Mariner curbed his disappointment. 'Saturday then?'

'If you feel like coming begging with me.'

'Begging?' Mariner repeated, checking that he'd heard correctly.

'Look in the small bedroom.'

Mariner walked through, buttoning his shirt as he went. He pushed open the door, or tried to. After a few inches it jammed and when Mariner poked his head through the gap, his eyes lit on an Aladdin's cave piled high with consumer booty: a wine cellar, electrical store and toy emporium all crammed into one tiny confined space.

Letting the door close, he went back to Anna. 'If you've started shoplifting again I'll have to turn you in, you know that.'

4

She ignored him. 'It's for a tombola stall at Bournville festival next month, to raise funds for Manor Park,' she said, proudly. 'Don't you think I've done well?'

'Manor Park's nowhere near Bournville,' said Mariner. The festival was a local event held in the grounds of the chocolate factory, not two miles away, whereas Jamie's respite care facility was located a good six miles out of town, in the wilds of the Worcestershire countryside.

'It doesn't matter, apparently. We're a registered charity, so they're happy to accommodate us. All we have to do is find a day's worth of prizes.'

'We?'

'Simon's helping me.'

'Oh great.' Mention of Jamie's care-worker forced out the response with more sarcasm than he'd intended.

Anna was oblivious. 'That might look like loads in there,' she chattered on. 'But it'll be nowhere near enough to keep us going for a whole day. This Saturday we're targeting Harborne and Bearwood, asking all the shops if they've got anything to donate.'

'Is that legal?'

'We're only asking them. They're at liberty to say no.' She smiled one of her most persuasive smiles.

'Same as me then. Hobson's choice.' Mariner sat on the edge of the bed to tie his laces.

'You could donate something,' she said suddenly as the thought occurred. 'Granville Lane, I mean.'

'What, like a CS canister signed by the chief superintendent? That would be a coup for an adventurous five-year-old.'

'How about a weekend for two in the custody block? Or a set of handcuffs. I can think of a few couples who'd go for that.' Her smile was pure mischief. 'There must be something. What about a tour of the nick?'

'I'll give it some thought,' said Mariner. 'In all the spare time I'll have on Saturday.'

'Poor old you. Look, this is the least I can do. Manor Park has been a lifeline for me.'

'I know.' God, she was gorgeous, even with a face like that on her.

'Shall I give you a call when we've finished? We could go out somewhere to eat.'

'I suppose it'll have to do.' Fully dressed, he leaned over and gave her a slow and tender parting kiss. 'I'll talk to you soon.'

* * *

But driving back to the station Mariner couldn't shake off a creeping sense of dissatisfaction. He hadn't meant to sound so aggrieved. His reaction was especially ironic given that Anna's independence was one of the things that had attracted him to her in the first place. It had been liberating to be with a woman who had as many obligations as he did, and who therefore wasn't constantly checking up on him. But somewhere recently the balance had shifted and increasingly the relationship was on her terms only.

To begin with that had been inevitable because of her commitment to Jamie, and Mariner had waited patiently while Anna did what she felt was right by her younger brother. But now with regular respite care Jamie was becoming more independent and Mariner had always assumed that in consequence he and Anna would spend more time together. Instead, she just seemed to find other things to occupy her, such as this latest round of frenetic fundraising. The fact that she was completely open and honest about her intentions, giving him absolutely no reason to feel threatened and thereby casting him as the selfish one, only salted the wound. It was a new experience. Accustomed to being more needed than needy, Mariner didn't much like the reversal.

* * *

The air conditioning had made his car just about tolerable by the time he pulled into the station parking lot, and he'd have liked to have lingered a while in the relative cool. But glancing up he caught sight of a familiar figure pacing the pavement outside the main doors, pulling anxiously on cigarette. He got out and walked over to her.

'Colleen?'

Turning, the young woman flicked ash onto the pavement. 'You took your time.'

'I was out on a call.' *Shagging my girlfriend*, but we won't go into that. 'What's up?'

'It's my boy: Ricky,' she said. 'He didn't come home last night.'

Here we go again, thought Mariner, but he said nothing and hoped that his face had stayed neutral. Mariner had known Colleen Skeet for more than ten years, since back when he was in uniform and her husband used her as a punch bag on a regular basis. She must be in her mid-thirties now, though she still looked little more than a kid herself, small and painfully thin, her mousy hair pulled back from a pale, freckled face into a tight ponytail. Today, only the dark circles beneath her eyes betrayed her age and the extent of her anxiety.

'Have you reported it in there?' Mariner nodded towards the station.

'They said I could talk to someone. But I wanted to wait for you.'

'Well, here I am. Let's go inside, out of the heat.'

'I can't smoke in there.'

'Maybe I'll bend the rules a little.'

'You don't like it though.'

'Christ, Colleen. When did you start considering my sensibilities?' It raised a weak smile. 'All right. Finish up and then we'll go in.'

CHAPTER 2

'So tell me what's happened.' The interview room was eight feet square, with a tiny window, and even without Colleen's cigarette smoke the air was heavy and stale.

'Ronnie turned up,' she said, chewing on a fingernail. She was sitting back in her seat, the other hand cupped beneath her elbow. 'He was there Saturday afternoon when I got home from work.'

Mariner shook his head in disbelief. 'Why do you let him in?'

'He's the father of my kids.' She was petulant. 'Whatever he might have done, he's still their dad. He'd brought Ricky the new Man U shirt, which really annoyed me because I'd already said he couldn't have another one.'

'All the choices around here and he's still a Man U fan?' said Mariner. 'That lad's got no sense of loyalty.'

'Ronnie was spinning all sorts of yarns, you know, all the usual crap about how he'd sort things out and one day he'd come home and we could all be together like before.'

'I hope you didn't fall for it.'

'What do you think? He'd already had a drink. Ricky knows it's all rubbish too, but I think underneath it all he really wants to believe him. Ronnie might not have been the best husband but he was good with Ricky, taking him fishing and to the football. Ricky would love to have his dad back and us be a happy family again.'

'Wasn't all that happy as I remember it,' said Mariner.

'You know what I mean. Anyway, Ronnie stayed all day Sunday, took Ricky down the social club with him, stopped the night. On the sofa.' She emphasised those words. 'When we got up Monday morning, Ronnie had done his disappearing act. Ricky was upset but I thought he'd get over it. I mean, it's not the first time, is it? When he was little it didn't seem to matter so much. He had me. But now he's growing up. He sees his mates going off to the match or down the pub with their dads and he knows he's missing out.'

'How old is he now?'

'Fifteen, the kind of age where he needs a man about.' She looked up at Mariner, catching him off-guard. 'You must remember that.'

Mariner had forgotten how well Colleen knew him. A moment's indiscretion in the dead of night, once when she was going through a bad patch — the second beating within a fortnight. 'My dad used to hit me too,' she'd told him. 'I must deserve it.'

'That's rubbish,' he'd said. 'Nobody deserves this.'

She'd laughed, a short, bitter laugh. 'Yeah, I don't suppose your old man ever laid a finger on you.'

'No,' he'd admitted. 'But that's only because I've never met him.'

She'd looked at him differently after that.

'It's too long ago,' he lied now, though in his case there had never been any question of his dad turning up. He wondered if having a disappearing dad was worse than having one who's non-existent.

'Anyway,' Colleen went on. 'Ricky went off to school as usual Monday morning a bit quiet, but I never thought anything of it. He wasn't there when I got home from work that night. He must have come in after I'd gone to bed. Then last night he didn't come in at all. His bed hasn't been slept in.'

'Ricky has done this before,' Mariner reminded her gently. 'Gone off.'

'Not like this. A couple of times he's stayed out all day at the weekend, and sometimes late after school, too.' She leaned in towards Mariner, urgency written all over her features. 'But he's never been out all night. First thing I knew, I got a call from the school asking where he was because he hadn't turned up. When they talked to his friends — and that didn't take long — they hadn't seen him since yesterday afternoon. They got let out early because of the heat. Ricky hasn't stayed out this long since before Ronnie left us.'

'No.' Whenever Ricky had disappeared before it was because he'd been an unwilling witness to his dad laying into his mum. As gentle as his dad was violent, Ricky had done his best to intervene but he hadn't stood a chance. The last time he'd run away it had been in shame because he hadn't been able to protect his mother when she'd needed it. He'd been ten years old. Afterwards Mariner had spent some time with the boy trying to reassure him that it wasn't his fault. They'd got to know each other a bit.

'When Ricky stays out all day, have you any idea where it is he "goes off" to?' Mariner asked.

Colleen shrugged. 'It's not with his mates. And when I ask him he just says "around." Typical teenager.'

'How's Kelly?' asked Mariner. In the past it was Colleen's older daughter who'd been the real headache, going AWOL for days at a time.

'Kelly's settled down now.' A brief smile played across Colleen's lips. 'She's got a baby of her own and a nice fella.'

'Are you sure Ricky hasn't taken a leaf out of her book?'

'Ricky's different: he's quiet, sensitive. He's never stayed away all night. And he never misses school. Something's happened to him.'

No, that was another thing — Ricky didn't miss school. The boy's genetic makeup was a mystery. Against the odds he was a studious kid with big ambitions and the common sense to know what he had to do to achieve them.

'Is everything all right there? Anyone giving him a hard time?'

'No.'

'He hasn't fallen out with his mates?'

She snorted. 'He hasn't got many to fall out with. You know Ricky. He keeps himself to himself.'

'Any girlfriends on the scene?'

'No.'

'What about you?' Mariner asked. 'Are you seeing anyone?'

'A guy called Steve. He's a friend.' A touch of defiance crept in. 'A good friend. We've been together nearly a year.'

'Does Steve get on all right with the kids?'

'Yes. No,' she conceded. 'He finds Ricky hard work because he's always got an answer for everything, always coming out with these long words. But Steve wouldn't be enough to make Ricky stay out all night. I know it.'

'All right, we'll ask around and see what we can dig up,' said Mariner. 'But I'm sure Ricky will turn up with a good explanation for all this. I want you to go home. Let me know if you hear anything and we'll keep you posted. And try not to worry, eh?'

'Easy for you to say.'

* * *

Mariner walked Colleen out, and the instant she cleared the automatic doors, she snapped a Zippo and sucked the weak flame into a desperately needed cigarette.

11

Mariner stood for a few moments, watching her go, and taking advantage of the cooler air while he was out there. Ricky Skeet was a puzzle. The disappearing act was out of character, but then he was at a difficult age with a pretty tough home life. Colleen was right to be worried, but the chances were that seeing his dad again had stirred up emotions that he couldn't handle and that in the fullness of time, when he'd got over the turmoil, Ricky would turn up. The lad probably just needed some space. Mariner heard the doors behind him slide open. It was Delrose, the civilian receptionist.

'DCI's looking for you,' she called. 'And he seems to be getting a bit impatient.'

Well, wasn't this developing into a perfect day? What a shame Anna's stall at the festival wasn't the wet-sponge stall. He could think of a prime target for all the punters . . .

* * *

His mood deteriorating with every pace, Mariner went straight to the DCI's office and knocked on the door.

'Come.' The request was barely audible but Mariner went in anyway. As Acting Detective Chief Inspector Gavin Fiske looked up from his desk Mariner was reminded of a lizard emerging from under a rock, blinking lazily with a brief smile that didn't hang around long enough to reach his eyes. His movements were slow and calculated, like a reptile conserving energy in the heat. A fly was buzzing around the room and it would have been no surprise to Mariner to see the DCI flick out a long tongue to catch it.

As smooth as regular DCI Jack Coleman was rough, Fiske was at least ten years younger than Mariner — all designer suits and Samsonite briefcase, with just the right amount of gel styling his hair. Doubtless he had a bathroom cabinet full of 'male grooming products' at home. His gym bag sat conspicuously on the floor of his office, a habit reflected in the toned muscles yet unhealthy, pallid complexion. Mariner never had been able to understand the logic of paying hundreds of pounds for the privilege of walking on a machine in a room full of sweaty bodies when the same effect could be achieved in the fresh air and changing landscape of open countryside. How could MTV ever seriously compete with the stunning view over the Vale of Evesham from the top of Breedon?

In the three weeks that Fiske had been in the station covering while Jack Coleman was seconded to the Independent Police Complaints Commission on an internal investigation, he'd already acquired a nickname. The first time Mariner had heard him referred to as 'Fido' he didn't get it.

'It's because he thinks he's the big I Am,' a staff sergeant had enlightened him. 'You know, like the dog food.'

'Ah,' Mariner had replied. 'So not because he thinks he's the dog's bollocks?'

'Glad you could find a window,' Fiske said. It took a couple of seconds for Mariner to work out what he meant. The consensus was that Fiske had risen so quickly through the ranks because of his snappy vocabulary. He could ring-fence like no other and he was the first man Mariner had come across who regularly diarised, something that sounded to him more like a painful medical procedure. What Fiske didn't yet appreciate was that, where buzz words might impress interview panels, in the real world they had the potential to make him a laughing stock. He'd walked into his first briefing at Granville Lane deporting a shield of ignorant self-confidence that had protected him from the sniggers that greeted his lexical repertoire, but that wouldn't hold for long.

'Interesting afternoon?' Fiske asked, his unfortunate nasal inflection adding value to the patronising tone.

'Yes, sir,' said Mariner. 'I've been following up on a missing juvenile.'

'And prior to that? I've been trying to raise you on your mobile.'

'I'm sorry. The battery must be flat, sir.' Mariner hedged, suppressing the slightest twinge of guilt.

'Do I look like a complete prat, Mariner?'

What a question, thought Mariner, wondering if there was any way he could get away with the truth. Luckily the DCI saved him from himself. 'Where were you?' he demanded.

'I was responding to a call, sir. PC Grady can conf—'

'Oh yes, from a "Miss Streep." Would that be Meryl by any chance? Fitting you in between filming commitments, was she?' Mariner was annoyed to find himself colouring in response. How the hell did Fiske know where he'd been, unless he was checking up on him? Fiske didn't wait for a reply. 'Not exactly the example we want to set for junior officers, is it?' he said mildly. 'If you've ambitions to become Granville Lane's answer to Peter Stringfellow, I suggest you wait until the end of the working day like the rest of us.'

'Thanks for the analogy, sir.'

But for all that, Fiske's irritation was carefully controlled. I'm on your side, said the knowing smile. We're all lads in this together. Failing to realise that Mariner didn't wish to be a member of Fiske's exclusive club – or anyone else's.

The dressing-down complete, Mariner started towards the door. 'I'll take more care in future, sir.' In more ways than one.

But Fiske hadn't finished. 'Talk me through this missing juvenile,' he said.

Stupidly Mariner mistook the command for interest. 'Ricky Skeet, aged fifteen, went out yesterday morning but didn't come home.'

'Where's home?'

'Nansen Road. It's on the—'

'Oh, I know where that is.'

Mariner wasn't surprised. Long and winding, Nansen Road took its name from the grim council housing estate through which it ran, and whose reputation was notorious. Built in the sixties when housing was cheap and shoddy, the development comprised rows of boxy white stucco houses, interspersed with more space-efficient low-rise flats and maisonettes. During the seventies the local authority had made it their policy to re-house 'problem families' on estates such as this, in the hope that they would learn from their more socially conscientious neighbours. Of course that wasn't the direction in which osmosis had occurred. Instead, what had subsequently developed was a ghetto of problem families living alongside those like Colleen Skeet who couldn't afford to move on. It was also one of the crime hot spots of the locality. And for all these reasons, Fiske had clearly already passed judgement.

'Why wasn't this just reported to the duty sergeant and passed to uniform?' he asked.

'I have a history with this family.'

'Oh? Would that be personal or professional?'

Mariner hardened his voice. 'Colleen Skeet's former partner was violent. Over the years I got called to the house a number of times—' Where he'd spent numerous hours trying to persuade Colleen to go into a refuge. He'd succeeded once, but she hadn't stayed long.

'Was?'

'Ronnie Skeet did everyone a favour and cleared off a couple of years ago, with another woman.'

'And is that the sole basis for your relationship with this family?' Mariner hesitated. 'I can look up the case notes,' Fiske reminded him.

'The older girl has been in trouble; truanting, shop lifting, that kind of thing. She's run away before, too.'

'Not what you'd call a model family then.'

'Colleen's had her share of problems over the years, yes sir. She's a woman on her own trying to raise her kids and keep them from being poisoned by the influences around them. It doesn't make her a bad person. And I thought that was what we were here for, sir. To help people who are in trouble.'

'Don't lecture me, Tom. Are we sure that this is a genuine disappearance?'

'I'm sorry, sir?'

'Are we sure that this boy wants to be found?'

'His mother wants him found. That's why she came to me.' Mariner made to leave. 'And if there's nothing else sir, I need to get started on the risk assessment paperwork.'

'Someone else can do that. I need your expertise on something else.' *Expertise.* Good choice of word. Mariner should have been flattered. He wasn't.

'With respect sir, this mother has approached me directly. I know the family and I think I'm the person best placed to—'

'And as your commanding officer I think *I'm* the person best placed to determine your priorities, don't you think, Inspector?'

'And they are?'

'Another missing teenager.' His face said that the irony wasn't even lost on him. The OCU covered only one small area in the south of the city. What were the chances of two kids disappearing on their patch in the same day? 'In this case it's a seventeen-year-old girl,' said Fiske. 'I want you to handle it.'

Mariner had a premonition of a poisoned chalice heading his way. 'But I'm already—'

'Charlie Glover can take that on.'

'So that I can look for another missing kid? That makes sense.'

'Playing the smart arse won't get you very far either.' Fiske's voice was icy. 'This case is not the same as Ricky Skeet.'

'Oh, really?' Mariner was unconvinced.

'I want you to follow it up. You can take that as an order.' The pulse at Fiske's temple throbbed. 'I think you'll find the risk assessment profile on this one rather more urgent.'

'Yes sir.' *And fuck you, too.*

Fiske handed Mariner a picture of a young Asian girl smiling cheerfully from a standard school portrait. She looked younger than seventeen. She wore the uniform of the girls' high school located in a middle-class residential area, several miles from Kings Rise comprehensive where Ricky was a pupil. Middleham Road ran between the two, parallel with the Birmingham to Bristol railway line. The two kids were quite literally from opposite sides of the track. 'Yasmin Akram,' Fiske announced, importantly. 'Last seen by her friends getting her train at Kingsmead station yesterday afternoon to go home. It's worth bearing in mind that her parents have some influence within the Asian community.'

So that was how this one was different. Yasmin Akram had hit the jackpot. She was young, female and respectable middle class. At one time being Asian might have counted against her, but not any more, not in the wake of McPherson, the enquiry into police institutional racism that had, quite rightly, followed the bungled investigation into the murder of black student Stephen Lawrence. It meant that these days, sometimes, being from a minority ethnic group could be a positive bonus. Mariner bit back his objections. On that score Fiske was right, it wouldn't do him any good. The pretty teenager smiling up at him had to be found. She was vulnerable and at risk. It just didn't mean that Ricky Skeet wasn't.

'Yasmin's parents, Shanila and Mohammed Raheem Akram, run an independent Islamic prep school, *Allah T'ala*, in Sparkhill,' said Fiske. 'And until we've established that this is a simple missing persons, we need to keep our options open.'

Mariner picked up the inference immediately. For months now right-wing nationalist groups had been taking advantage of the growing public fear of Islamic fundamentalists to stir up unrest, and in recent weeks a number of Islamic institutions had themselves been under attack, from the eighty-six mosques in the city to businesses, large and small. Muslim schools in the city were among the obvious targets, mainly because of the threat posed by their academic success and the perceived potential for indoctrination.

'If this does turn out to be politically sensitive,' Fiske went on 'I need someone on it who knows what they're doing and will cover all the angles right from the beginning.'

Coming from Jack Coleman, that would have been a compliment, but Mariner wasn't naïve enough to take it as such from Fiske. The DCI was simply covering his own back. Mariner had the distinct impression that Fiske was out of his depth already. His previous posting in rural East Anglia had been poor preparation for a city as huge and culturally complex as Birmingham. And while he might have read a few textbooks and attended a couple of seminars on equalities, Mariner doubted that Fiske would have any real grasp of the issues involved.

At the turn of the millennium Birmingham had become the first European city to no longer have a single ethnic majority and Mariner had lost count of the number of ethnic groups that made up the million plus population. The whole spectrum of racial integration was represented, from communities that remained relatively closed and self-sufficient, to those individuals whose physical characteristics were the only indication that their ancestors weren't of Anglo-Saxon origin. Over the years Mariner had worked with colleagues and members of the public from every background imaginable, but he still would never presume to understand all the nuances of living inside a different coloured skin.

Added to that were the infinite configurations of family life, regardless of ethnicity, culture or class. He also wondered how much the DCI understood about handling the press on a case as potentially high profile as this. If Yasmin's disappearance should turn out to be racially motivated, then they would be queuing in the wings to join the dots and draw their own conclusions.

Fiske buzzed through to his PA. 'Is PC Khatoon here yet?' In response the door opened and a young Asian woman entered. Almost matching Mariner for height she was generously proportioned, and Mariner couldn't help thinking how unflattering the police uniform could sometimes be.

'This is Jamilla Khatoon, a family liaison officer who's going to be on loan to us from Operational Command Unit 2. She'll be working with you on this for obvious reasons. Jamilla, this is DI Tom Mariner.'

He didn't hang about, did he? As they shook hands Jamilla's smile was guarded and Mariner was left wondering how Fiske had prepared her for this introduction. Mariner forced a smile. 'Nice to meet you, Jamilla.'

The tentative smile stretched to one that was broad and white. 'It's Millie, sir.'

'Okay.'

'I want you to keep this low key,' Fiske intervened. 'Just the two of you on the preliminaries until we know what's going on. Talk to the family, friends, the usual. If this does develop into anything, we're going to have the media and the politicians crawling all over us. So let's get it cleared up quickly and cleanly, whatever it takes.'

Then if I do screw up, at least not too many people will know about it, Mariner tacked on, in his head. It was Fiske's dismissing remark.

CHAPTER 3

Mariner was seething with resentment on the walk down to his office. For the second time that day he was leaving an encounter feeling manipulated. First Anna and now Fiske, working him like a puppet on a string.

Although there was a strong possibility that Fiske could be right, he resented the assumption that Ricky Skeet's disappearance was routine and entirely down to the kid's chaotic kind of home life. Never mind that he was a bright lad. He didn't stand a chance. Colleen wasn't going to like this one little bit. And added to that was the clumsy assumption that, as a white, male officer, he needed help to handle the Akrams. Mariner would be the first to admit that he was far from being an expert on Asian convention, but the initial interviews would be standard stuff, establishing the facts. This was just too much too soon.

'Congratulations on being hand-picked by Mr Fiske,' he said to Millie, not without sarcasm. 'The press would have a field day with this — prejudicial use of resources so early on. We haven't even filled out the risk assessment yet.'

'With respect, I'm not sure that it's—'

'How long have you been in the job, Millie?' Mariner ploughed on.

'Just over a year, sir.'

'Something you might want to remember. If you want the police and media to sit up and take notice when you disappear, you'd better be female and from a "good" family. Don't ever be male and from a broken home, with a dodgy dad, like Ricky Skeet because then the media aren't interested and the police won't give a fuck.'

'Girls are more vulnerable,' she pointed out.

'Which doesn't mean that boys aren't,' Mariner replied, with feeling.

'No, sir. Who's Ricky Skeet?' Millie asked.

'He's another kid who disappeared yesterday. I know the family so his mum contacted me. I've just been pulled off it. Not a good use of an inspector's time, as he's probably just a runaway. No fanfare of trumpets or special resources for Ricky Skeet, but then he's the wrong kind of MisPer.'

'I'm sure the officer it goes to will give it his best shot.'

'The officer it's gone to doesn't know the family and is up to his neck in other unsolveds.'

'And you're not? Sir?'

Said so innocently, Mariner couldn't help but smile. 'Let's get a drink Millie. And then we'll see who knows anything.'

* * *

Fresh-faced PC Robbie Thorne knew more than anyone, having been the uniformed constable who responded to the initial missing persons call for Yasmin Akram. Summoned to Mariner's airless office, he sat down to form the third corner of a human triangle with Mariner and Millie, and read from his notebook.

'Yasmin was last seen yesterday afternoon at around four thirty, when she left the girls' school with a group of friends to go home,' Thorne said. 'She took her usual route: travelling three stops on the train to the university station where she gets off and walks several streets to her house. Her friends last saw her running for the train at Kingsmead.'

'And no one's heard from her since?'

Thorne shook his head. 'She carries a mobile, which as far as we know is working, but she hasn't used it. That's partly why nobody was panicking at first. She wasn't even reported missing until this morning.'

'After she'd been gone all night?' said Mariner.

'The father is away and the mother thought she'd gone to stay with a friend. It wasn't until the school called her this morning to say that Yasmin hadn't turned up that she realised that wasn't the case. That's when she contacted us.'

'Since when did schools start ringing up parents to ask where their kids are?' Mariner asked, remembering that Ricky had been subject to the same checks.

Millie supplied the response. 'Since the truancy rates went through the roof and school attendance became a government issue,' she said.

'Hm, back in the day if you wanted to bunk off, you just did it. The teachers were grateful to have fewer kids in the class.'

'That was before results and league tables got to be so important.'

'Shanila Akram, Yasmin's mother, seemed worried about her husband's reaction to involving the police, too,' Thorne added, 'though I couldn't work out why.'

'Where is he?'

'Away on business, she said. He's due back later this afternoon.'

'Do we know if Yasmin's ever done this kind of thing before?' asked Millie.

'Only the usual. Once when she was little, she threatened to run away to her auntie's, but only got as far as the end of the street.'

'This auntie has been contacted?'

'Yes, sir. Mrs Akram has been in touch with all other family members she could think of.' Thorne glanced at his meticulously taken notes. 'And the only thing Yasmin had with her was her school bag. She didn't even have dinner money.' He glanced up. 'The school operates some kind of credit card system so no cash is exchanged. All that we know she had on her was her travel card that covers West Midlands buses and trains.'

'So theoretically she can't have gone very far.'

'Tell us about the family set up,' said Millie.

'The family is Pakistani Muslim. Yasmin's the second of three children. There's a sister in her twenties who now lives abroad, and a ten-year-old brother. Paternal grandmother also lives with them. The home language is a mix of Urdu and English but the mother speaks English fluently.'

'How did she seem?' asked Mariner.

'About what you'd expect: anxious.'

Mariner looked over at Millie. 'So, let's go and see for ourselves.'

* * *

Yasmin may have disappeared on their patch, but both the family home and her parents' school were some distance away. The city's foundation grammar school system meant that hundreds of kids travelled such journeys every day.

The drive over to the inner-city suburb of Sparkhill was about as uncomfortable as it could have been. In the mid-afternoon sun Birmingham smouldered, heat shimmering up from the roads, melting and splitting the tarmac and condensing the air to a stinking, exhaust-laden smog. In the last few weeks the city had become noisy and overcrowded, too small and cramped for its one million inhabitants causing more than the usual friction and conflict. There had been an increase in the number of domestic and common assaults, and road-rage incidents this month had risen by a quarter.

Even the trees looked as if they'd had enough, their leaves limp and lacklustre. Traffic on the outer-circle route this afternoon had virtually ground to a halt, leaving drivers to stew impatiently in their vehicles. Despite the full-on air conditioning, Mariner could feel his shoulders beginning to prickle and itch. He glanced up in despair at the cloudless blue sky. After five weeks the heat was showing no sign of abating. News reports were full of dire warnings about hosepipe bans and forest fires. Ironic given that spring had been one of the wettest on record, submerging whole areas of the country beneath flood water for days at a time. Impossible to imagine now.

'What does it mean, *Allah T'ala*?' Mariner asked Millie, as they idled at yet another congested junction.

'Literally it means "god most high."'

'So this is the school of god most high?'

'That's right.'

'What do you think of segregated schools?'

Millie's response was measured. 'Lots of parents, white and black choose to send their children to private schools for many different reasons.'

'But these are primarily religious reasons. What kind of precedent are we setting for these kids? Already in this city we have Catholic schools, Jewish schools and Muslim schools, all telling children that their religion makes them special and different from others. Then they go out into the world and we expect them to forget all that and take their place in a multicultural society.'

'The good schools also teach tolerance and respect for the religious beliefs and customs of others, whatever they may be,' said Millie, reasonably. 'I don't think you'll find bigotry on the curriculum at many.'

As if to illustrate this crossover, the *Allah T'ala* turned out be housed in an imposing ironstone building with twin white spires and a high arched window — a former Anglican parish church that dominated a meandering street of Edwardian townhouses. As they drove up, a man scrubbed at an illegible slogan that had been sprayed in red paint along one wall. Approaching from the same direction, but on foot, were two women in full burkha, the black robes leaving only their eyes exposed. A less common sight in the southern suburbs, Mariner was well aware of the connection made by some between the mode of dress and the perceived oppression of women and was surprised to find himself mildly unsettled by the sight. As the women neared the door marked 'entrance,' it swung open as if by magic, just wide enough to admit them, and they were gone.

Mariner hoped that as a man he wouldn't have a problem gaining access. As much as he was prepared to trust Millie he wanted to be there himself to talk to the Akrams. And the school was co-educational, which presumably meant that male teachers worked here. Cars on the forecourt outside the school were of mixed vintage and power.

Despite finding a patch of shade cast by an ancient spreading beech, they stepped out of the car into what felt like a fan assisted oven set to 'high' and it was with reluctance that Mariner retrieved his jacket from the hook behind the driver's seat, slipping it on as they walked the few yards to the school. Millie rapped the door-knocker, simultaneously holding her warrant card up to the peep-hole below. Again, the door opened marginally, sucking them into a dim reception room before closing softly behind them.

Once Mariner's eyes had adjusted from the brightness outside, he could see that this was the main administration office, crowded with phones, computers and filing cabinets. The walls were decorated with childlike powder-paint creations annotated with quotations, most probably from the Koran. A small brown-eyed child fidgeted on a chair beneath the proclamation that: 'In the remembrance of God do hearts find satisfaction.'

Millie greeted the young girl behind the desk, whose face was now exposed to them, with a salaam. 'I'm Liaison Officer Millie Khatoon and this is Detective Inspector Tom Mariner,' she said. 'We have come to speak to Mr and Mrs Akram.'

The girl flashed a brief sympathetic smile. 'Of course. I'll tell Mrs Akram you're here.' Picking up the phone she spoke briefly in what Mariner surmised to be Urdu, before rising from her chair. 'Please come with me.'

* * *

She led them through into a small lobby then up two narrow flights of stairs, gliding with the kind of feminine grace that her flowing robes seemed to induce. Behind closed doors they could hear the insistent chatter of children's voices. Shanila Akram greeted them as they reached the door of another, tidier office — lighter too, thanks to the broad window that overlooked the street. As they entered she got to her feet and came towards them extending a hand. Mariner took it. It was delicate and as cool as marble. Small and slight, she was also dressed all in black, her hijab wrapped about her face like a nun's wimple. In ordinary circumstances she would be stunningly beautiful, with flawless olive skin, mahogany eyes and a full mouth, but today those features were clouded with tension and Mariner wondered how she was managing to carry on working.

'Our school must continue for the children,' she explained apologetically when introductions had been made, as if she was party to his thoughts. 'And I felt it better to keep busy.' Outwardly in command, she was struggling to maintain eye contact for more than a few seconds. The girl from reception had brought in chairs

26

behind them and Shanila Akram invited them to sit. 'Would you like tea?' she asked.

'Yes, thank you.' Mariner had expected this from past experience. He was no great fan of the traditional sweet Masala tea, but he knew better than to decline. Accepting the hospitality would make the atmosphere more conducive to open communication and trust. However when refreshment came, it was served western style, for which he was grateful.

'My husband should be back very soon,' Shanila Akram told them. 'I haven't yet been able to contact him.'

Good, thought Mariner, we may be here when the news is broken. We'll be able to judge the reaction. 'Meanwhile perhaps you could start by telling us about yesterday evening,' he said.

'Of course.' Shanila Akram cleared her throat. 'I arrived home at a little after seven. It's a busy time of year. There is such a lot to do here at the school, with all the preparations for the end of term. The children's amma, my husband's mother, is at home all day so is there to welcome Yasmin and her brother. Sanjit was at home at the usual time. I had allowed Yasmin to go and stay with her friend—' She broke off uncertainly, as if she was going to say more of that but then changed her mind.

'And the friend's name?' Mariner prompted.

'Suzanne. Suzanne Perry. The arrangement was that Yasmin would phone from Suzanne's house to let us know that she was safe, but when I got home she hadn't yet phoned.'

'Didn't that concern you?'

Almost immediately Mariner regretted the insinuation. Shanila Akram's eyes filled with tears. 'Not unduly. I thought that perhaps Yasmin had forgotten, that she was having a good time . . . I didn't want to crowd her, so I thought I would phone Suzanne's parents, but that's when I discovered that their number isn't listed. By this time it was getting late and I just thought . . . Of course I know

now that I should have persisted, but at the time I had no reason to think that anything was wrong.' With effort of will she looked Mariner in the eye. 'It was a mistake. Of course I realise that now. I was ready to scold Yasmin for not keeping in touch, but I was shocked when the school contacted me this morning to say that she had not arrived and that her friends had not seen her since yesterday afternoon.'

'So she didn't go to stay with Suzanne?'

'No. At the last minute she changed her mind and told her friends that she was coming home instead.'

'But she didn't do that either.'

'No.' The woman's voice had dropped to a whisper. Through the open window they heard a car pulling onto the forecourt below. Shanila Akram got up and went to look out. 'My husband,' she said. But her expression was far from relieved.

They heard voices below and moments later Mohammed Akram burst into the room, his face a mixture of anxiety and bewilderment. In his mid- to late forties he was unexpectedly dressed in a dark business suit with a crisp white shirt and striped tie.

'Moshi, this is Inspector Mariner and Constable Khatoon. They are from the police.'

Akram shook their hands, 'Fakhra told me you were here. What's happened now? Have there been more letters?' As he spoke Akram pulled up a seat beside his wife.

'It's Yasmin.'

'What about her?'

'She has disappeared.'

'What?'

Something subtly changed in the atmosphere. Something Mariner couldn't identify. Shanila Akram's fragile confidence had deserted her and she seemed to shrink away from her husband, as if he might be angry with her. Perhaps he would. She had been left in charge of the family, after all.

'It appears your daughter changed her mind about going to stay with her friend yesterday evening, but she didn't return home either,' Mariner said. Now Akram seemed confused.

'Yasmin was to go and stay with Suzanne last night—' his wife reminded him.

'She what—?' Akram's confusion turned to anger.

'They had to finish their project,' Shanila cut in. 'The presentation they were doing together. Yasmin was desperate to go. But she must have decided against it after all.'

'I don't understand.'

'The school telephoned me this morning to say that Yasmin hadn't arrived there this morning. That's when I called the police.'

Akram's full attention was on his wife, Mariner noticed. He seemed to have forgotten that they were there. 'Why didn't you wait—? Never mind.' Mohammed Akram's eyes narrowed as he tried to make sense of what his wife had told him, and Mariner tried to read the emotion. Shanila Akram's demeanour had completely transformed. No mistaking who was the dominant person in this partnership. Only, it seemed, when he had swallowed his anger did Akram think to ask: 'Where has she gone? Have you spoken to her friends, to the rest of the family?' He reeled off a list of names.

His wife shook her head. 'I've tried them all. No one knows where she is.'

'It seems the last people to see her were her friends yesterday afternoon,' said Mariner.

'So I'm to understand that she's been out all night? How has this happened?' The demand was made of Shanila, who visibly flinched. There was something else going on here that Mariner didn't yet fully grasp.

29

'I understand your concern, Mr Akram,' he intervened, in an attempt to defuse the tension. 'But the fact remains that it has happened, so we need to ask you some questions, so that we can find Yasmin as quickly as possible.'

At that, Akram seemed to get a grip. 'Yes. Yes of course,' he shook his head slowly. 'It's just so hard to take in. I can't believe it. What is it that you need to know?'

'We were just talking to your wife about the events of yesterday evening.'

'Well, as I'm sure she has told you, I have been away on business since yesterday afternoon.'

'May I ask where you've been, sir?'

'We are opening a school in Bradford. I went to meet with some of our staff up there for a planning meeting.'

'And you left Birmingham at what time?'

Akram thought for a moment. 'It was around four thirty in the afternoon. I had an appointment with the printer and went on from there.'

'This friend, Suzanne. Has Yasmin stayed with her before?' Mariner addressed the question to both parents, but it was Mohammed Akram who answered sharply.

'No.' The look he shot his wife was clearly one of disapproval and a frisson of conflict thickened the air again. They'd need to return to that.

'She has been to Suzanne's house for tea sometimes, but always comes home later in the evening,' Shanila said, softly.

'And what did Yasmin take with her?' asked Mariner.

'As far as I know the usual things: a change of underclothes, toiletries. Other than that it's hard to tell.'

'And you have no idea where Yasmin may have gone. Are there any friends or relatives she might have gone to stay with instead?'

'I've contacted everyone I can think of,' Shanila told him. 'We have family in London and Bradford.'

'What about your cousin Ameenah?' Mohammed Akram asked of his wife.

'No, I've called them.'

'I understand Yasmin's sister lives abroad.'

'In Lahore,' said Shanila Akram.

'Is there any chance that Yasmin would try to go there?'

'She doesn't have a passport yet, we are in the process of applying.'

'And where would she get the money for a ticket?' added Mohammed Akram.

'Mrs Akram, I'd like you to think back to Monday night; Yasmin's last evening at home. How did she seem then?'

'She was fine.'

'And nothing unusual occurred?'

'Nothing. Except . . . she was late home from school. There had been a problem with the trains, but that's always happening.'

'Does Yasmin enjoy school?' asked Mariner.

This was safer ground, easier to elaborate. 'Yes, she's a clever girl. Her teachers are always pleased with her.'

'It was a big decision to allow Yasmin to go to a school outside our own religion,' Mohammed Akram added. 'But the high school has an excellent reputation and we felt it would benefit Yasmin's career prospects to go there, even though it involved travelling.'

'And there was nothing bothering Yasmin that you can think of.'

'Nothing.' It was Shanila who spoke, but the glance between them was unreadable. It could simply have been a clumsy and belated attempt at mutual reassurance.

'Yasmin hadn't fallen out with any of her friends?' Millie asked. 'It happens all the time with girls that age.'

Mohammed Akram spoke up. 'If there is anything on Yasmin's mind she tells us. She's a sensible girl and we are very close. The family is important to us and we always encourage our children to be open and honest with us, so that we can support them.' Recited like a mantra.

'Anything could have happened to her. She's so young—' Shanila Akram's voice cracked with emotion.

Leaning across, Millie put a hand on the woman's arm. 'I know,' she said, demonstrating the value of her presence. 'But the vast majority of missing persons turn up alive and well within seventy-two hours, Mrs Akram. We'll do everything we can to find Yasmin.'

'We'll need to look at her room at home,' Mariner said, offering something practical to focus on. 'It's just routine, but the sooner we can do that the better.'

'I'll come with you,' Akram volunteered.

'That may not be necessary. You said that Yasmin's grandmother is at home? If she can let us in—'

'Yes, of course.'

'Then we won't keep you any longer,' said Mariner. He took a business card from his inside pocket and handed it to Mohammed Akram. 'If Yasmin contacts you, or you think of anything, however small, that might help, give me a call at any time. And we, in turn, will keep you informed.'

'I'll keep in touch,' Millie reassured Shanila Akram.

It was Mohammed Akram who got up to show them out. Signalling for Millie to go on ahead, Mariner waited until he and Akram had descended the stairs and were alone in the lobby before saying: 'Mr Akram, when you first came in you seemed to think that we might be here about something else. You asked your wife about some letters. Do these relate to the graffiti outside?'

Akram rubbed a hand over his face. 'And the rest. It's become a way of life for us: graffiti, bricks through the windows, dog excrement through the letterbox. Recently my car was damaged.' His eyes lit up as he seized on an idea. 'Do you think Yasmin's disappearance is connected with these occurrences? There are some sick people out there, Inspector,' he said, with growing fervour. 'After September 11, we went through a bad time.'

'We can't jump to any conclusions at this stage,' Mariner said. The incidents would have to be looked into, but it seemed a little premature to be making those kinds of assumptions, unless Akram knew something they didn't. 'Do you have any thoughts about who might be behind these attacks, Mr Akram? Or anyone who might have a specific motive to harm your family?'

'Apart from the usual?' Akram glanced up at Mariner. 'My wife and I built up this school from nothing. When we both left college as trained teachers we could see that the British education system was failing the children in our communities. Many of the children around here have little English when they enter the school system, so they are already at a disadvantage. We founded this school in an attempt to give them a better start. Now every year we are inundated with applications. We have expanded several times but still we don't have enough space to take all the children who want to come here.'

'And plenty of people resent success,' said Mariner.

'While others feel very threatened by Islam, as I'm sure you are aware, Inspector. Bad enough having the country overrun with Asians, let alone *educated* Asians.' He took a pamphlet from his pocket. 'We get these all the time.'

The red, white and blue pamphlet was being published by an organisation calling itself 'The Right Way.' Mariner had encountered it before, a far-right organisation led by Peter Cox, a known white supremacist based in the city. 'When was the last time?'

'It comes and goes.' Akram was suddenly uncomfortable. 'It's been worse since the letter.'

'What letter?'

He shifted uncomfortably. 'I belong to an Asian business consortium. We have all been targets of this kind of material, and we were sick of the constant harassment.

33

We wrote a letter to the local press denouncing the cowards who instigate race crimes and in particular The Right Way.'

'So you could well have inflamed the situation.'

'It was impulsive, something I now regret. It seemed like a reasonable thing to do at the time, but it probably hasn't helped.'

To put it mildly, thought Mariner.

'This came through the post at the end of last week.' Akram took from his pocket another sheet, this time of A4, word-processed on a computer, which he handed to Mariner.

> *Al-Fath* (The Victory)
> Punish the hypocritical men and
> the hypocritical women. For
> them is the evil turn of fortune,
> and Allah is wroth against them
> and hath cursed them, and hath
> made ready for them hell . . .

'It's from the Koran,' Akram said. 'My wife hasn't seen it. I didn't want to upset her, especially now—'

'It's powerful stuff. Do you know if anyone else has received anything similar?'

'I don't know. I haven't told anyone.'

'Not even the police?'

'What would be the point? It's completely anonymous. What could you do? It could have come from anywhere.'

'And the envelope?' Mariner asked, without hope.

'It was printed anyway, but I threw it away.'

'I'll take this to get it checked for fingerprints.'

Akram shrugged. 'As you wish.' But they both knew that it was a long shot.

'If you get *any* further communication like this from anyone, let me know immediately.'

'Please help us find our daughter, Inspector.'

'We'll do everything we can. You said you were away from yesterday afternoon? Where did you stay last night?'

'We have family in Bradford.' As he spoke Akram pushed open the door to the reception area, where Millie was chatting to the girl behind the desk. Seeing them she drew the conversation to a close and Akram showed them out.

Outside on the forecourt another car had been added to the collection: Akram's top-of-the-range black Mercedes with the registration MOH 1. It had a vicious scratch along one side. 'Yours is the Mercedes?'

Akram nodded.

'It's a distinctive car,' said Mariner.

A glint of irritation flashed in Akram's eyes and Mariner began to recognise him as a man with a short fuse. 'I work hard. I should be allowed to drive the car I choose.'

'Naturally,' said Mariner, calmly. 'I only meant that it makes it an easy target. We'll be in touch Mr Akram.'

CHAPTER 4

While they'd been inside the sun had moved round and their own vehicle was no longer shielded from its burning rays. The heat inside gusted out when they opened the doors. It wasn't until Mariner pulled out onto Highgate Middleway, where the traffic and the air moved more freely, making the car bearable again, that he asked: 'So what have we got here, simple absconder or something more sinister?'

'I thought it was interesting that Mr Akram made the point about his wife reporting Yasmin missing.'

'Implying that perhaps he wouldn't have? That she's overreacting?'

'Could be. I thought his response was unusual once he'd got over the initial shock. He seemed angry to begin with, then once he'd calmed down he was almost business-like.' Millie was perceptive.

'Maybe he's just a pragmatist,' said Mariner, '*Okay, this is the problem, so what can we do about it?*'

'There doesn't seem any obvious reason why Yasmin would have run away.'

'Not one that they're telling us about. But does there have to be one? It could be that even Yasmin herself doesn't know. Perhaps she just needed some time alone. It happens.'

Millie turned to face him. 'Does it? That sounds like experience talking.'

Mariner shifted in his seat. Now wasn't the time. 'Think about it,' he said. 'Yasmin's parents are both high achievers. It makes me wonder what sort of pressure they put on their children.'

'Without playing a particularly active part in their lives. They're "busy people." Sounds as if a lot of the parenting gets left to amma.'

'Even worse then: at seventeen, having an elderly woman breathing down your neck.'

'Yasmin might have a great relationship with her grandmother,' Millie said.

'Yes, she might.' But the ensuing silence signalled that they both had doubts.

'Have a look in the inside pocket of my jacket.'

Millie fished out the plastic wallet containing the sheet of A4. 'What's this?'

'It's the latest in a series.' Mariner took her briefly through his conversation with Mohammed Akram.

'So he was pretty quick off the mark to finger Cox's organisation.'

Mariner shrugged. 'If you'd been subjected to that kind of campaign it would be only natural. Though I did wonder about their knowledge of the Koran.'

'It would be a clever tactic though; turning someone's religious beliefs back on them.'

'Maybe.'

'Alternatively, this could have come from inside the community. Sometimes the infighting can be worse than anything from the outside.'

Mariner turned to her. 'You've got a reason for saying that?'

'Fakhra in the office was less than discreet. Competition to get into *Allah T'ala* is fierce. There are 46

37

places available for the new term, and they've already had 138 applications.'

'Mm, Akram didn't quantify it, but he said as much to me.'

'Did he also tell you that one family in particular was upset that their child didn't get a place for September?'

'Not specifically. But 46 kids for 138 vacancies doesn't make for great odds. Not getting a place is pure bad luck, no worse than losing on the lottery. Why take it personally?'

'This child is very disabled. The father seems to be angry about this anyway and has turned his frustration on the school. According to Fakhra he's also a religious fanatic and in her words a "bit of a nutter." The consensus is that he was the one who damaged Akram's car.'

'That's interesting. Did you get a name and address?'

'Fakhra was reluctant. She said she'd want to speak to Mrs Akram first. They don't want to make more trouble for this man's family. I think she already felt she'd said too much.'

'All we'd want to do is eliminate him from the enquiry.'

Millie wafted the letter in mid-air. 'In the meantime how seriously do we take this?'

'It's hard to say. After the quote, it all gets a bit vague, so I wouldn't want to automatically jump to any conclusions. And it's not much of a lead. It could have been written by anyone with access to a PC.'

'Even Mr Akram.'

'That had crossed my mind.'

'You didn't immediately warm to him, did you?' Millie deduced.

'That obvious? I agree with you that his reactions weren't quite right. Anger seemed to outweigh anxiety.'

'It's not always an indicator. People can be very good at covering their feelings, can't they? His wife is clearly not coping, so he may feel it's important to try and appear in control, even though he's not.'

'I felt it was more than that,' said Mariner. 'I thought he seemed annoyed with her.'

'She'd been left in charge.'

'But that shouldn't make her wholly responsible. There seemed to be some blaming going on.'

Millie didn't seem convinced. She turned her attention back to the letter. 'But if this is a genuine threat we might be looking at abduction.'

'Could be. Akram was quick to suggest that too.'

'Wouldn't we expect a ransom demand?'

'Not necessarily right away. The timing would have to be right.'

'And in the meantime?'

'We continue to treat this as a missing persons and talk to the people who really know what Yasmin might be thinking.'

* * *

In terms of location there could hardly have been a greater contrast between the Akrams' small Islamic school and the girls' high school that Yasmin attended. The Granville Lane patch was more familiar to Mariner. Purpose built between the wars, the red-bricked building nestled snugly in leafy suburbia, surrounded by ten acres of what at any other time of year would have been lush green grass, but which had by now been scorched to a crusty brownish yellow by the relentless sun.

Here Mariner really was glad of Millie's presence. Even as a teenager he'd found adolescent girls baffling, and that was going on for thirty years ago. In addition, these were likely to be anxious adolescent girls, given that one of their number had disappeared. The meeting with Yasmin's closest friends, arranged by phone, would be supervised by the head of pastoral care but even so, Mariner felt a certain apprehension as in the middle of the afternoon, he and Millie drove slowly along the winding, tree-lined drive.

They were a little early, so were invited to take a seat in the reception area to wait.

With its coffee table reading and rampant pot plants it was more like the lobby of a private corporation, though it lacked the comfort of air conditioning. The power of the connection between aroma and memory never failed to amaze Mariner, and the combined old-school smell of cleaning fluids and cooked food was one of the most potent of all. His lightweight suit felt suddenly constrictive as he made a conscious effort not to let his own experiences affect his perceptions. His own school days had been far from the happiest of his life when he'd been a square peg in a round hole at the boys' grammar school he'd attended.

Nearly six-foot tall by the age of thirteen, he'd stood out, literally at first and then socially too, when people had gradually discovered that his was a single parent family. Lone parents back then were still a relative rarity. In his particular stratum of the lower middle class, they were virtually unheard of. Throw into the equation his mother's eccentric mode of dress and outspoken views, and any attempt of his to blend in hadn't stood a chance. He and Anna had recently watched the video *About a Boy* and in the central character Mariner had seen shades of himself, from the bizarre dress code to the gross social ineptitude. He too had been a victim of hand-knitted pullovers and oversized homemade PE shorts. Even his lunches had been outside the norm, with sandwiches made from home-baked wholemeal bread at a time when white sliced Mother's Pride was all the rage. It was during those years, at the age when conforming meant everything that his relationship with his mother had begun to deteriorate.

Mariner wondered how Yasmin fitted in here. Looking at the most recent school photo, displayed on the wall ahead of them, there weren't many other brown faces.

Did this mean that Yasmin had a point to prove, or was she made to feel like an outsider? The staff line up was interesting too; the proportion of men to women more evenly balanced than he might have expected and Mariner wondered, not for the first time, what would make any man want to work in a school full of young girls, exposing himself to unattainable temptation.

Around the main photograph were displayed portraits, drawn, the label announced, by members of the Year 12 A-level art group. Some were pencil sketches of body parts. The most striking was of a male torso, from the waist to just below the chin, displaying a series of intricate tattoos on the biceps and shoulders. It was expertly drawn, the proportions exactly right.

'Robbie Williams,' said Millie, knowledgeably, at the same moment as the deputy head appeared. Small and trim, her powder blue suit and bright turquoise and yellow blouse, offset by shoulder length blonde hair, Mrs Darrow stood out like an exotic bird from the drab navy blues of the school uniforms. She apologised for keeping them waiting before setting off at a brisk high-heeled pace along endless corridors, leading them through what seemed to be an impossible number of left turns. From time to time, confident young women clomped by in heavy shoes and perilously short skirts, surreptitiously eyeing them up, perhaps thinking that Mariner and Millie were parents, although Millie was way too young. Mariner took the opportunity of the lengthy trek to draw out Mrs Darrow's opinion of Yasmin.

'She's a popular girl,' was the somewhat trite reply. 'She came to us from her parents' Islamic school, which is a big leap, especially socially, but she seemed to take it absolutely in her stride.'

'Her parents implied that she's had a closeted upbringing,' Mariner said.

'Relatively perhaps, but she's had the opportunity to spread her wings here,' Mrs Darrow replied. 'In many ways

Yasmin's background is very different to some of the other girls, but because she's friendly and outgoing, she gets along with people. She's also not afraid to express her own opinions. Don't be misled into thinking of Yasmin as a meek little Muslim girl.'

'Would anyone particularly resent that, an Asian girl being clever and popular?'

Mrs Darrow stopped and turned to face him. 'We don't tolerate racism or bullying in this school, if that's what you're implying.'

'That's not to say that it doesn't go on.' Mariner held her gaze. 'I can't imagine that there's any school anywhere that doesn't have a problem with bullying. Some establishments are just more aware of it than others.'

Mrs Darrow's colour deepened before she walked on. 'You're right of course, Inspector. Realistically it happens from time to time, but I've never known it to be an issue with Yasmin.'

'You have a good reputation in the area,' commented Millie.

Had she been a bird Mrs Darrow would at that point have preened her feathers. 'Mm. We had an eighty-four percent pass rate at A-C and a ninety-three percent pass rate at A level last year. It put us into the top ten in the national league tables and this year we're on stream to do even better.' The numbers, largely meaningless to Mariner, fairly tripped off her tongue.

'And is Yasmin keeping up?'

'Her GCSE grades were excellent: Six A stars, three As, one B.' Mrs Darrow frowned. 'Although as with most of the girls, she's finding sixth form a little more of a challenge.'

'Why's that?' asked Mariner.

'The work is harder,' she said simply. 'Added to which these are girls at the mercy of their hormones. They get distracted. It's not an uncommon thing to happen. They're under an enormous amount of pressure, to be clever,

42

pretty and popular. Some girls cope better than others. For Yasmin there's the additional conflict that what her parents want for her isn't necessarily what she wants.'

'And what does she want?'

'At present just to keep her options open.'

'And her parents don't?'

'Like many of our parents, Mr and Mrs Akram have fairly fixed ideas about what constitutes a worthwhile career. Often those views can be quite traditional.'

'Medicine or law,' Millie chipped in.

Mrs Darrow smiled. 'Exactly.'

'How have her teachers responded to the drop in standard?' asked Mariner.

'We encourage her to put in that little bit more effort.'

'And does it seem to worry Yasmin?'

'It's hard to tell, but I'd guess that it might unsettle her a bit. Yasmin's a bright girl and I know her parents have high hopes for her.'

'Are they adding to the pressure?' Mariner wondered.

'No more than any other parents who want their child to do well.' Mrs Darrow responded quickly.

'What's your relationship with Yasmin's parents like?'

'They're very supportive. Many of the resources we acquire these days are accessed through specific government initiatives, often through matched funding.' Seeing the blank expressions she continued. 'We put up half and the DfE matches it.'

'Ah.'

'Yasmin's father has been very generous in our endeavour to acquire language college status.'

'What about friends?' Millie asked. 'You said Yasmin is popular.'

'She's part of an established group.'

'And Suzanne Perry, the friend her mother thought she was staying with?'

'I was quite surprised about that I must say,' said Darrow. 'Their friendship has always been rather an unlikely alliance.'

'Why do you say that?'

'I'll let you find out for yourselves. Here we are.'

CHAPTER 5

They had reached their destination and Mrs Darrow pushed open the door of what seemed to be some kind of recreational room. Low, comfortable chairs were grouped around a couple of square wood-effect utilitarian coffee tables. At least she'd taken on board Mariner's request to keep this informal. There were five girls present. They had been talking, but quieted politely when the adults appeared. Unlike the girls Mariner was used to dealing with, this lot weren't cocky and streetwise. Even at this age, they seemed cool and sophisticated, and more than a little intimidating as they appraised their visitors. Mariner wished he'd checked his flies before coming in. Each girl had put her individual stamp on the school uniform, but one in particular stood out. She looked older than the others, not just because of her spiky red hair or the heavy black eyeliner that circled her eyes. There was something about her demeanour. She was the only girl in the room to return Mariner's gaze and some.

There were three vacant seats. Mrs Darrow offered one each to Mariner and Millie, before making introductions and taking the other herself.

As Mariner had agreed with her beforehand, Millie took the lead in the hope that the girls might be more relaxed talking to a woman nearer their age and therefore more inclined to open up. Mariner was pleased with the way she handled it, too: just the right proportion of friendly to professional.

'Hi,' she began. 'We're really glad that you agreed to meet with us today. If any of you has any idea where Yasmin might have gone, it's really important that you tell us now. It goes without saying that everyone's very concerned about her, and there's a chance that she may be in danger.' Silence. Time to be more specific. 'Yasmin told her mum that she was going for a sleepover with Suzanne. Is that right?' Millie scanned the room inviting a response from Suzanne.

When none came, Mrs Darrow intervened quietly. 'Suzanne?'

'That's right.' The sullen reply came from the spiky-haired girl, who addressed her answer to Mariner, at the same time shifting in her seat and conspicuously adjusting her tiny skirt.

'So what happened?' Millie asked.

'She changed her mind.' Her green eyes remained disconcertingly fixed on Mariner's, but Millie persevered.

'Why was that?'

'She said she wasn't feeling too well. And she felt bad about coming.'

'What about the project?'

Finally Suzanne turned to face Millie. 'What project?'

'The project you and Yasmin were working on, that you had to finish?'

Suzanne frowned. 'First I've heard of it.'

'Okay. Why do you think Yasmin changed her mind about coming?'

'Because of the row with her dad,' she said with exaggerated patience.

'What row was that?'

'About the sleepover.' Mariner could imagine her tapping the side of her head in despair. What kind of thicko was she dealing with here? 'Her dad wouldn't let her come.'

Understandably Millie was puzzled. 'I don't understand. I thought she'd had her parents' permission.'

'Her mum's,' Suzanne corrected her. 'Her dad had said absolutely no, but when Yaz found out he was going away, she talked her mum round. That's the whole point. That's why she changed her mind. She felt bad about going against her dad.'

So the Akrams were in conflict about Yasmin's sleepover with Suzanne. That explained a lot.

'And the two of you hadn't fallen out?' Millie asked.

'No. Yaz just succumbed to emotional blackmail, as she was expected to do.' Suzanne's voice was heavy with contempt.

'And as far as you're aware, Yasmin went straight home from school?'

'Yes. She said it would keep.'

'What would?' Mariner asked. Suddenly he was interested and Suzanne knew it, in fact, Mariner realised, she'd played it with exactly that in mind.

She fixed him with her gaze. 'Yaz had something important to tell me, but she said she'd know more by the next day.'

'More about what?'

'I don't know, but it was heavy. She was pretty wound up about it.'

'Wound up how?' asked Mariner. 'Excited or worried?'

Suzanne took her time. 'I'd say excited.'

'But she didn't give any hints about what it was?'

'No.'

'Who travels home with Yasmin regularly?' Millie asked. A couple of hands went up tentatively. Mariner had forgotten what a programmed response that was. 'Could you tell us about that journey, yesterday?'

At last a shrug from the girl called Emma, with dark hair tied back and an uneven, lumpy complexion. 'It was just the same as any other. We had graffiti club after school so we were late leaving.'

'Graffiti club?' said Millie.

Mrs Darrow smiled. 'We're not encouraging vandalism, Constable. It's just the trendy name for our art club.' A couple of the girls smirked at her use of the word 'trendy.'

'What time was that?'

'About quarter to five,' the girl whose frizzy hair was escaping from her ponytail spoke up. 'We had to go back into school because Yaz couldn't find her travel card. We had to retrace our steps, everywhere we'd been that day.'

'And did you find it?'

'It was on the floor in the art room. The last place we'd been. Typical.'

'Go on, Emma,' Millie encouraged.

'It was the same as usual, said Emma. 'We all walked down the road together. Some of us carried on along the main road to get the bus, while Yaz went down the side road towards the station for her train. We saw it coming in as she got there, so she had to run.'

'Is Yasmin the only one to get the train?'

Another girl spoke up as confidence began to grow. 'Some other girls in the school do, but none of our crowd.'

'At that time in the afternoon, most of the girls would have already gone,' added Mrs Darrow. 'The only ones left are those who stay for after-school activities. We've asked for anyone who might have seen Yasmin on the train to come forward, but they haven't as yet. It's quite possible that no one did.'

'And no one else lives near Yasmin?'

Shakes of the head, but that came as no surprise. They already knew that.

'And Yasmin didn't say anything about doing anything different or going anywhere yesterday evening? Could she have gone into the city, for example?' asked Millie.

'Suzanne?' Mrs Darrow prompted.

Suzanne merely shrugged and it was Emma who supplied the answer. 'We had a piece of English homework that was going to be hard. Yaz was going to phone me later when she got home.'

'And Yasmin was excited rather than worried about anything? Other than the disagreement about the sleepover, nothing recently had upset her?' Mariner asked Suzanne directly.

'She was pissed off with her parents, but what's new?' She glanced at Mrs Darrow to see if her language would be censured and was satisfied by a disapproving glare. Mariner could imagine Suzanne being pissed off with just about anyone. She behaved like a girl who was used to controlling adults for her own ends, and it was obvious why Yasmin's parents didn't want to encourage the friendship between their daughter and this girl. He wondered what it was that made her so angry. But then he remembered that most teenagers were like that at some point for no reason at all. He was just out of touch. 'Yasmin's old man doesn't give her an inch. She's always in trouble with him about something lately. He's a psycho.'

'Suzanne, that's going too far!' Mrs Darrow was looking not altogether happy about the way this was turning out.

Shooting her a look that would fell an elephant at nine paces, Suzanne's 'what would you know?' remained unspoken, but it reverberated around the room nonetheless. 'Look at the fuss they made about her staying late for graffiti club.' She quoted it as evidence, making Mariner wonder if this girl might have a career in law ahead of her.

'They were unhappy about that?' said Millie.

'Her dad's unhappy about anything that isn't work: "go to school, go home, do your homework." Yaz is expected to be a good little Asian girl.'

'Does she resent that?'

'Sure she does, but not enough to do anything about it. She's not allowed to wear makeup, but instead of standing up to her parents she just puts it on while she's on the train coming into school and washes it off afterwards. She just gives in to them all the time.'

'She comes to graffiti club,' Mariner pointed out.

'Only because sir stuck up for her.'

'Has anyone got anything else to add?' asked Millie after a respectable pause. More shakes of the head.

'Well, if there's anything else you think of, we'll be giving Mrs Darrow our contact number. And please remember, it's vital that you tell us anything you know, however small or unimportant it may seem.'

The head teacher nodded in agreement. 'I'll put the number on the common room bulletin board,' she told the girls, and as there seemed to be nothing else forthcoming, she dismissed them back to their lessons.

'I'm sorry that wasn't more helpful,' said Mrs Darrow, after they had gone. 'And I would take Suzanne's last comments with a pinch of salt. Some of the girls at this age do have this "whole world's against me" mentality, usually with parents and school at the top of the list. Added to that, their imaginations are fuelled by the constant confrontations they see on TV soaps. Suzanne in particular can be something of a drama queen.'

'Who runs this graffiti club?' Mariner wanted to know.

'The "sir" Suzanne mentioned: Mr Goodway. He's the head of D & T.'

Mariner turned to Millie for clarification. 'Design and Technology,' she obliged, with a sad shake of the head. 'I expect it was plain old woodwork in your day.'

'We could do with talking to him,' Mariner said to Mrs Darrow. 'It looks as if he may have been one of the last adults to see Yasmin yesterday afternoon.'

'We can see if he's free.'

* * *

Throughout the introductions Brian Goodway blinked rapidly at them through dense wire-framed glasses. Although school was in session, he had what Mrs Darrow referred to as a 'non-contact' period and they found him pottering about in the technology room, which Mariner discovered to be the home of wood and metalwork, textiles and art. Picking him out on the school photo, Mariner wouldn't have attributed anything artistic to Brian Goodway. He was too tidy, more maths or geography, with his neatly knotted tie and one of those ubiquitous tweed jackets that had gone out of fashion years ago with everyone except a certain generation of teachers, although this one didn't extend quite as far as leather elbow patches.

The classroom was a different matter entirely; a chaotic arrangement of workbenches topped by the skeletal frames of half-finished sculptures and interspersed with spindly easels displaying adolescent creations in various stages of completion. Goodway himself seemed surprisingly unmarked by the explosion, several pairs of overalls hanging on the back of the door took the strain.

Mariner's eye was caught by a particularly ghoulish design, not unlike those on display in the entrance hall. 'Body art,' Goodway volunteered, seeing Mariner's interest. 'If you're going to motivate the kids you have to operate on their level, tap into what's relevant to them. The days of sketching a vase of flowers or bowls of fruit are over. That particular effort was drawn by a young lady in class 9G. She's been working on it for three weeks now, mainly because of the problems she's had with the proportions of the eagle's head just here, getting those feathers to sit properly.' He ran a finger along the

51

offending area and Mariner had the impression that whichever of the creations he had picked on, Goodway would have been able to supply exactly the same amount of detail.

Goodway showed them some still life drawings that Yasmin had been working on. One was a pencil drawing of a hand, the veins and skin texture perfect. 'Yasmin is a very talented girl,' he told them. 'Art is a discipline like any other. Along with creativity you must have a precise eye.' He smoothed his sparse sandy hair over his scalp and took his glasses off, peering through them at arm's length before wiping them on a tissue. 'Occupational hazard,' he explained.

'I understand that you fought Yasmin's corner for her when her parents were reluctant to let her stay for the art club,' said Mariner.

'It would have been a criminal waste if she hadn't been given the opportunity to develop her talents. As it is she's been persuaded to give up art in favour of more academic subjects at A level. Graffiti club means that she can pursue both.'

'Would she make a living at it?' Mariner asked, wondering if this was the conflict of interest with what her parents had in mind for her.

Flattening his hair again, Goodway let out a sigh. 'As a freelance artist? Not necessarily. Art is such a competitive world.' He gestured towards a photograph of three teenage children — two boys and a girl — that was pinned to the wall above the corner desk. 'That's my daughter Chloe,' he said. 'She was gifted enough to get a place at the Slade Art College in London, but she still struggles to make a living as an artist. I try to ensure that the girls here have a realistic view of what they can achieve. Encourage them to get their academic qualifications too, looking at a more structured career within the art world, perhaps within graphic design or illustration.'

'How did Yasmin seem at your class yesterday afternoon?'

'Fine. The girls seem to like the club. It's a chance to relax and shake off the shackles of prescribed coursework.' A twinkle gleamed in his eye. Despite appearances maybe there was a rebellious streak in there after all.

'She hadn't fallen out with anyone?'

Goodway shook his head. 'You know what kids are like. Even if she had, I doubt that I would know. It may be a more relaxed class, but I don't fool myself into thinking that any of the girls would share much with an old fogey like me.'

Mariner wasn't so sure. 'Why do you think Yasmin's parents weren't keen on her staying for the graffiti club?'

'They're naturally very protective of her. The club runs throughout the year and in the winter months it can mean the girls getting home well after dark. Yasmin had a longer journey than most.'

'What changed their minds?'

Goodway shrugged as if it was no big deal. 'I had a chat with them and they're reasonable people.'

Not what Suzanne seemed to be saying, but then the adult perspective would be a different one. 'Thanks, Mr Goodway.'

They were nearly out of the door when Goodway called after them, uncertainly. 'Yasmin's a good kid. I hope she turns up soon.'

Mariner turned back. 'So do we, Mr Goodway. So do we.'

CHAPTER 6

'A committed teacher,' Mariner remarked on the walk back through the school.

'He's inspirational,' Mrs Darrow agreed. 'A real Mr Chips. We don't get many of those any more. I think having his own teenage children helps him to stay in tune with the girls.' She was full of admiration. 'We'll be sorry when he goes.'

'Goes? He seems a little young for retirement.'

'Mr Goodway wants to spend more time with his family,' was all Mrs Darrow would say.

* * *

From the art department Mrs Darrow took them to Yasmin's locker, opening it with a master key. It revealed little. The inside of the door was lined with the ubiquitous teen posters of pop stars and TV presenters, none of whom Mariner recognised. A wad of drawings fell out and scattered on the floor. The drawings were good. Some of the same 'body art' that they had seen in the classroom. On the face of it they'd learned little to progress their search, except perhaps to learn that Mr and Mrs Akram hadn't been entirely candid with them.

They were standing directly underneath the bell when it rang deafeningly, signalling the end of the day. Through the open door of the classroom opposite, they watched girls filing out, dipping into a bright red plastic crate on the way.

'Retrieving their mobile phones,' Mrs Darrow explained. 'The things are a nightmare. We tried banning them completely at first, but it was hopeless as practically all the girls have them. Parents complained too that they needed to know that their daughters were safe. Ironic given this current situation. So instead most teachers collect them in at the beginning of each lesson, to remove the temptation.'

'Couldn't the girls just put them on silent or switch them off?'

'I'm afraid they can't always be relied on to do so. With text messaging they can be holding lengthy conversations without staff even knowing. It's a distraction we can do without.'

'Do any phones ever get left behind?'

Mrs Darrow knew what he was getting at. She shook her head. 'Very rarely. It's amazing. These girls might lose everything else: clothing, books, you name it, but their phones seem to be surgically attached. The few that are get put in lost property. You're welcome to have a look.' They did, but neither of the couple of outdated handsets that were there could be identified as Yasmin's.

'Well, thank you for your time Mrs Darrow.'

'Not at all, Inspector. Whatever we can do to help.'

* * *

'I don't get it,' said Millie as she and Mariner drove from the school. 'How can someone just disappear?'

'If she wants to, it's easy.' Mariner knew from personal experience. He'd done it himself when he couldn't face another night of coming home to the Spanish

Inquisition. His mother had taken his popularity with girls particularly hard. Although he had vague memories of the occasional short-term 'uncle' early on, latterly it had just been the two of them and as Mariner grew, the dynamics of dependency had shifted as his mother discarded other facets of her life to concentrate on him. Her whole life became dedicated to her only child, and at the time when other parents were letting go, Mariner's mother clutched on with increasing desperation, until finally he had to take the initiative and break away completely. Instead of getting the bus to school one day, on an impulse he'd caught the train to Birmingham and gone to look for a job. Except for brief visits since, he'd never gone back.

'If what Suzanne told us is right though, it sounds as if everything wasn't as rosy in the Akram household as we were led to believe,' he said now.

'You think she was telling us the truth?'

'It would account for the tension between Mr and Mrs Akram, wouldn't it? I thought he was just annoyed that his wife had contacted us before telling him. And having left her in charge it may be natural to hold her responsible. But if she'd gone against his wishes as well . . . Let's go and see what we can pick up at home.'

* * *

The two uniformed officers who were to help with the preliminary search met them at the Akrams' house, which turned out to be a detached and imposing red-brick in Edgbaston, probably, like those around it, built at around the turn of the century. It was the home of a successful couple. With the shrinking of the nuclear family, these houses were normally too big to fulfil a useful purpose as a family home and several of the other properties on this street displayed boards to indicate their conversion to business hotels and retirement residences. The Akrams' property was set back from the road behind a five-foot high decorative wall, the entire front of the house shaded by a dense umbrella of chestnut trees, which created a cool oasis of relief from the heat. Grandma, an elderly woman in a white saree, came to the door, her eyes watery, whether from age or from weeping it was hard to say.

'*Salaam Allah Kouom*,' Millie smiled, knowing that she spoke little English.

The old lady nodded. '*Walaik um-asalaam.*'

Millie explained in Urdu the reason for their visit. Scrutinising Mariner's ID, the old lady nodded wordlessly and indicated that they should follow her. True to his word, Akram had phoned ahead to let her know they were coming. She led them through the house. Cool and dark with high ceilings, it was neat and tidy and deathly quiet in the absence of anyone else.

Leaving the rest of the house to the uniforms, Mariner and Millie focused their efforts on Yasmin's bedroom on the first floor. It was comfortably furnished, the décor in feminine pastels, but without frills or luxury. A giant desk dominated the room, beneath a solid shelf of reference books, but there was no CD player, TV nor any of the other usual electronic paraphernalia that most kids were reported to have these days. Cuddly toys were neatly arranged on the bed and a further shelf displayed a number of photographs including a formal family group, presumably taken at Yasmin's older sister's wedding. Millie picked up the photograph to verify this with grandma. The two women embarked on an animated conversation, during which Millie successfully shepherded the older woman back downstairs leaving Mariner to continue the search unobserved.

Yasmin's hair brushes were neatly aligned on the dressing table. If they were going to need DNA . . . Mariner refused to let his mind move along that track. A small jewellery box contained a few simple gold chains and bracelets. Checking in the drawers her clothes were neatly folded. The only hidden treasure Mariner found was a small pouch of eye shadows and mascara hidden under some T-shirts at the back of a drawer. Apart from the schoolwork there were no personal items: no diaries or letters to help them out.

There was the distant sound of a door slamming and moments later a diminutive figure appeared in the doorway, dark eyes watching Mariner intently while he fidgeted against the door frame. Yasmin's younger brother.

'Hello. It's Sanjit, right?' said Mariner.

A nod. 'You're a policeman?'

'That's right.'

'Are you looking for Yaz?'

'Yes. Have you got any idea where she might have gone?'

The boy shrugged. 'She doesn't talk to me, except for a bit of verbal abuse.' He made a quacking gesture with his fingers and thumb, and Mariner curbed a smile.

'What are you looking for in here?' Sanjit asked.

'Anything that might give us clues about where Yasmin is.'

'Have you found her secret box?'

'No.'

Without another word the boy dropped to the floor and wriggled on his belly under the bed, emerging minutes later with a small, cardboard shoebox. 'She thinks I don't know about it.' He handed it to Mariner. Inside were an ornately carved rubberwood chest and a ceramic moneybox in the shape of a teddy bear. Mariner lifted the lid off the first. It contained more makeup, a leaflet for the Tate Modern, illustrated with a Lucian Freud nude, and a couple of tickets for the London underground dated March of that year. 'Did you go down to London too?' Mariner asked.

'Nah, she went with her school.'

Zone One. Must have been a special trip if she'd preserved the tickets. And why two tickets? Yasmin and Suzanne?

The money box, when Mariner prised off the stopper in its base, contained three ten-pound notes and some loose change.

'It's her pocket money,' said Sanjit. And surely the sort of money Yasmin would have taken with her if the disappearance had been planned.

'Anything unusual happen lately?' Mariner asked, replacing the items. 'Yasmin fall out with anyone?'

Sanjit rolled his eyes, forcing Mariner to suppress a smile. 'She's always arguing with dad, stomping around and slamming doors. We have to walk on egg boxes all the time,' he said, getting the idiom almost right.

* * *

The uniforms had given the house a good going over but found no sign of Yasmin nor anything else unusual, and nearly an hour after their arrival, Mariner pulled out of the drive feeling frustrated at the lack of progress. He was hoping that Millie had been more fortunate. She shook her head.

'Not much to help us then. All we know is that Yasmin had a row with her dad about staying at Suzanne's, then apparently Mum gives in while Dad's away and says she can go. Did you ask Grandma about that?'

'Yes, and she has views all right, although she was shy about expressing them. Naturally she sides with her son and sees this as a direct consequence of Yasmin's mother flouting his wishes.'

'So she blames Shanila rather than Yasmin.'

'Not exactly. She just implied that Yasmin is no different from your average teenager and that it's her parents' duty to give her strict boundaries. "Righteous women shall be obedient. And those you fear may be rebellious admonish" — it's what the Koran says.'

'Then perversely, when her mother lets her beyond those boundaries, Yasmin decides not to go to Suzanne's after all, but for some reason doesn't make it home either.'

'Because she's had enough of rules and wants out completely?' Millie speculated.

'She didn't take her pocket money with her.'

'It's not necessarily long-term. It could just be a gesture. Giving her old man the finger because of the hard time he's been giving her?'

'Anything's possible,' conceded Mariner. And that was the whole problem. There was nothing to narrow things down.

* * *

Back at Granville Lane, DS Tony Knox had requisitioned the CCTV footage from Kingsmead railway station, where Yasmin boarded her train.

'What's it like?' Mariner asked as they settled down to watch.

Knox shrugged indifferently. 'See for yourself.'

The black-and-white image was crude and snowy. Knox perched on a desk behind Mariner and Millie as they watched a train draw into the station. A number of people disembarked while a couple further down the platform climbed on. The train waited. Then at the last minute, in the bottom right-hand corner of the screen, a figure could be seen running for and jumping on the train. A split second before, she turned and gave them a full facial shot. No question it was Yasmin.

Knox snapped off the film. 'The footage from the university station isn't quite so helpful.' This was the station at which Yasmin would have disembarked. 'It's harder to see Yasmin, there's a lot of movement.' He wasn't wrong. The platform was crowded and although several people left the train, they had to strain their eyes to pick Yasmin out as any of them.

'There,' said Millie eventually. Reaching out, she pointed to a figure moving across the bottom of the screen.

'Right height and build,' Knox agreed. 'Same colour clothing from what you can see, and a bag over her shoulder.'

'Like just about everyone else,' said Mariner.

'She's walking pretty casually, too. In no particular hurry.'

'That's Yasmin Akram?' They all turned. They hadn't heard Fiske come into the room.

'We think it might be.' Mariner remained cautious.

'Good, so we know that she followed her normal route.'

'We're not—'

But Fiske didn't want uncertainty. 'Which means that she must have disappeared somewhere between the station and her house,' he cut in. 'I understand that from there she walks through part of the university campus to get home?'

'Yes sir.'

'In that case let's do a search of the area between the station and her home. If that turns up nothing we'll do the railway track.'

'But—'

'You'll need to talk to university security, too,' Fiske went on. 'Are we absolutely certain there's no one she could be staying with?'

'Her parents have spoken to anyone they can think of,' said Mariner. 'Robbie Thorne is double checking that. And we're doing the usual phone round of hospital emergency departments. I think we should wait until—'

'So let's just get on with it, shall we?' Fiske rubbed his hands together. 'Organise the search for first thing in the morning. I'll make sure that there are uniformed officers at your disposal and we can bring in an additional search team.' He was halfway out of the door before he turned and added: 'That's good work, all of you. Well done.'

'He's easily impressed,' remarked Millie when Fiske had gone.

'He's just hoping that he might be able to stop shitting himself sometime soon,' said Knox.

'That's what I'm afraid of,' said Mariner, getting up from his seat. He caught up with Fiske just outside the DCI's office. 'Organising a search at this stage is a bit premature, sir,' he said.

'Nonsense,' said Fiske. 'We've got the CCTV footage. What more do you need?'

'It's not entirely clear. I'd like to get it enhanced to be sure.'

'But I saw it with my own eyes and your colleagues seemed pretty certain. What reason is there to delay? Superintendent Bourne is due to meet with community leaders later this afternoon and it would be beneficial to have something substantial to give them. Get it done, Mariner, first thing tomorrow.'

'I'll need to widen the investigation team,' said Mariner. 'Millie and I can't do this alone. And Charlie Glover's in the same boat.'

'Use whoever you need,' said Fiske. 'Charlie Glover's on a different inquiry. For the moment our priority is to find Yasmin Akram. If Charlie Glover doesn't like it he can come and talk to me.'

And giving Mariner no more opportunity to argue he turned and went into his office, resolutely closing the door.

So that's what the hurry was all about: Fiske's desperation to impress Superintendent Bourne with the efficiency of his leadership. More than anything Mariner wanted Yasmin Akram to turn up soon, alive and well. But he also harboured the hope that somewhere along the way Fiske would shoot himself comprehensively in the foot.

* * *

When he got back to the office he found that Knox had gone.

'Isn't he a jolly soul,' said Millie. 'Not one word to me after you'd gone out.'

At the time Mariner had barely noticed but now he thought about it Knox had seemed unusually subdued, and he hadn't been particularly welcoming to Millie. 'Promotion back to CID must be losing its novelty value,' he concluded, hoping he was right. After all it had been a couple of months since Knox had returned to the fold following a previous digression, so the initial elation must be wearing off.

'Anything else happened?' he asked.

Picking up the phone, Millie shook her head. 'I'll get on with the calls.' She'd be checking the usual: hospitals, hostels and women's refuges within a ten-mile radius. If that yielded nothing, they'd spread the net.

Meanwhile Mariner ensured that the photograph of Yasmin was being circulated citywide, including to the press, and arranged a TV bulletin for the ten o'clock local news.

It was close to eleven when they both resurfaced. Now they had to sit back and wait for the results. 'We've done everything we can for now. We might as well knock it on the head for tonight,' said Mariner.

Millie smiled. 'I'll see you in the morning, sir.'

CHAPTER 7

It being mid-week, Anna would have her hands full with Jamie, so there was little point in Mariner calling round to see her tonight. Despite the heat, the aromas of Sparkhill had lingered with Mariner and were tweaking at his hunger, so when he drove past Yasser's, his local Balti house and saw that it was still open, it was impossible to resist stopping.

Only when he was inside did he see that Tony Knox had fallen on the same idea. Nodding a greeting, Mariner placed his order and sat down beside Knox on the bench. 'Dinner's in the dog, eh?' he joked.

Knox looked momentarily blank. 'Oh yeah,' he said, eventually catching on.

'Tell Theresa it's my fault,' Mariner went on. 'Keeping you out all hours.'

'Sure.' But unusually for the otherwise gregarious Knox, he wasn't inclined to talk. Not that Mariner minded. He was tired himself and there had been enough talking today. So the two men sat in companionable silence until Knox's order was called and he got wearily to his feet.

'See you in the morning,' said Mariner.

'Right, boss.'

But ten minutes later, driving away from the restaurant, Mariner was surprised to see Knox with his carrier bag standing waiting at the bus stop. He pulled over and lowered his window. 'Want a lift?'

'Nah, you're all right, boss.' Knox glanced up the road hopefully, though it was late and Mariner could see in his rear-view mirror that there was no sign of any red, white and blue double decker.

Both men knew that Mariner would have to virtually drive past Knox's doorstep on his way home and by now Mariner was curious to know what was going on. 'This is ridiculous, Tony,' he said. 'Get in.'

Knox wouldn't meet his eye, but this time he concurred.

'I didn't know your car was off the road,' said Mariner conversationally as his own vehicle began to fill with the warm smell of cumin and coriander.

'The bus is fine.'

Drawing up outside Knox's house Mariner noted the complete darkness. Knox's kids were grown up now, his daughter living with her own children and partner, and his son away at university. 'Theresa not home, then?' Mariner said.

'She's up in Liverpool, has been the last few weekends,' said Knox. 'Her mother's not well.'

'I'm sorry. How old is she?'

'Seventy-two.'

'Well, I hope she pulls through.'

'Thanks.' Knox pushed open the car door. 'I won't ask you in, boss, the place is a bit of a tip. But cheers for the lift.'

* * *

Closing the front door behind him, Tony Knox bent to pick up the mail from the mat. He'd recovered from that first plunging disappointment he'd felt on seeing the empty driveway, but now anticipation rose again as he embarked on the emotional bungee jump that had become his end-of-day ritual. He sifted through the post, each letter stabbing at him anew as he passed over bills and junk mail, and found none bearing her handwriting. Disgusted, he tossed them onto the growing stack. She hardly ever wrote to anyone, so why would she suddenly take to writing him letters? Especially now.

For a moment he hovered by the phone wondering whether to check call minder now, or to wait, in the superstitious hope that patience would be rewarded with a positive outcome. Superstition lost out. Leaving his supper on the kitchen table he returned to the phone and keyed in the number of the answering service. Two new messages. His hopes soared again. 'Come on, come on!' he urged the recorded voice. But call one was from a call centre in Delhi, asking him to reconsider his mortgage arrangements and message two was a hang-up. Cresting the wave of optimism, he came tumbling down on the other side and the searing emptiness that had taken temporary residence somewhere above his diaphragm returned. The same black hole he'd woken up with every morning for the last two weeks.

Walking back into the kitchen, Knox stared at the plastic carrier bag, smelt the rich spices, and they made him want to gag. Ignoring them he went instead into the lounge and picked up the next in the neat row of Glenfiddichs that he'd stockpiled over the last few Christmases. For years they'd stood untouched in the cupboard. He didn't really even like Scotch that much, but Theresa's sister had got it into her head years ago that he did. Now it was coming into its own and in less than a fortnight he'd emptied all but two bottles. Still, they needed using up and if alcohol got him to sleep at night and helped him to face the next day, that couldn't be a bad thing, could it? The phone rang as he was swallowing the last dregs in the glass and he raced to pick it up.

'Dad? It's Siobhan.' Knocked back again. 'Mum told me. Are you okay?' Asked out of concern or sense of duty, he wondered.

'I'm fine.'

'Will you be able to sort this one out?'

'I don't know, love.'

'You have before.'

'This is different.'

'Well, if you need anything, you know where we are.' The offer was cool, the onus on him. The subtext: this is your fault, you stupid old git. Well, he didn't need his daughter to tell him that.

'Dave and the kids okay?' he asked.

'We're all good, just worried about you.' When did that about-face happen? So suddenly he hadn't even noticed it. 'See you, Dad.'

'Bye, love.' Cradling the phone Knox looked around the room at the depressing mess; the accumulation of soiled mugs and glasses, items of clothing discarded from the nights when he couldn't face the bed they'd shared and had opted instead to sleep on the sofa. He'd clean it up later. But first he'd have another drink. He couldn't find his glass so he swigged straight from the bottle, the first mouthful burning a path to sweet oblivion.

* * *

Mariner likewise returned home to an uncharacteristically empty house. His lodgers, Nat and Jenny, students at the university, were away backpacking in Eastern Europe for their summer vacation. After years of contentedly living alone he was surprised to find how much he missed them. The top floor of the canal-side house was almost a self-contained unit, so it wasn't as if they were under each other's feet all the time. In fact, Mariner had seen more of them since he'd invested in a decent DVD player — they used it more than he did. But they'd given him an insight into the student life he'd missed out on and he liked having them around.

Snug in the winter, in summer the house could get stuffy, so he threw open all the windows in an attempt to entice in some of the stagnant evening air.

The light on his answer phone was flashing, so he pressed the play button. Two hang-ups and his mother: 'How are you, dear? It's so long since you've been to see me. Give me a call soon, would you? There's something I want to talk to you about.'

Mariner sighed. What scheme was she hatching now? Something, no doubt, that would involve him in endless discussion and research on her behalf, which would come to nothing when she changed her mind, like her idea of selling up and moving to a retirement property in Weston-super-Mare. That one had kept him busy for weeks. Three times inside a month he'd even taken her down there to get a feel for different areas. Then, on a whim, she'd dropped the idea and that was when he first developed the suspicion that she'd concocted the whole thing just to keep his attention focused on her.

When he'd left home as a teenager, he'd hurt her. He knew that and had come to regret the fact, even though at the time his leaving had been an act of pure self-preservation. It was only a matter of four or five years before their relationship was re-established, but she'd never let him forget the digression. Since that time she'd demanded assurances that though they had their separate lives, as long as he was able, he would be there to support her. And she'd kept him to his word, ensuring that at regular intervals some project or minor ailment would occur that required his attention. Schemes which invariably failed to come to fruition, but were enough to keep him dangling. As she got older her demands had increased in frequency so that she seemed to be developing classic 'cry wolf' syndrome. With a stab of guilt he thought of Theresa Knox ploughing up and down the motorway to visit her mother on Merseyside. Funny Tony hadn't mentioned that before. How long had it been going on?

Cracking open a bottle of home-brewed Woodford's Wherry, kept cool where he stored it in the lowest depths of the old-fashioned scullery, Mariner took his dinner out onto the canal side. The water was silent and still, with hardly any sound from the surrounding city and no breeze to sway the birches on the opposite bank. In the cooling evening air the smell of vegetation was strong. Mariner even caught a hint of perfume from the single strand of wild honeysuckle a few feet away. Screaming swallows had given way to bats and crane flies, but even now the air was warm and sultry. If Ricky or Yasmin were sleeping rough tonight at least they'd be warm.

Usually at this time of year there would be a couple of narrow boats parked a few hundred yards up river where the two canals joined, but the low water level was discouraging most, forcing them to steer a central line or risk being grounded in the mud. In some areas of the country stretches of the waterways had even been closed. Fishermen had given up on the stagnant waters and even the ducks seemed lethargic in their quacking.

In the twilight Mariner could just make out the perfectly symmetrical silhouette of the guillotine stop-lock, beyond the junction with the Stratford-upon-Avon canal, put there more than a hundred years ago, to prevent the water from the higher canal escaping to the lower. His meal finished, Mariner took a long shower to wash off the grime of the day, before tuning in to watch the local news on TV.

'There are growing concerns for the safety of schoolgirl Yasmin Akram, who disappeared on her way home from school yesterday afternoon,' the anchorman said.

The same smiling photograph that Mariner carried in his pocket flashed up on the screen. 'She was last seen boarding a train for the university station and police are appealing for anyone who may have any information about the schoolgirl's whereabouts to get in touch.' The bulletin ended with the Granville Lane telephone number. Now they could sit back and wait for all the cranks. Some anorak was bound to have seen Yasmin abducted onto a spacecraft by aliens at the very least. An incident information centre had been set up at Granville Lane to pick out the genuine calls.

Mariner wondered if Colleen Skeet was watching too. If so, she'd want to know why there was no mention of Ricky. He'd deal with that one tomorrow.

He tried Anna's number a couple of times but strangely her line was engaged. A bit late to be canvassing for donations, he thought, but he didn't like to consider any other possibilities. And now he'd left it too long to think about calling his mother. That one would have to wait. Checking that his mobile was charged and switched on Mariner went to bed.

* * *

It was an undisturbed night and Mariner woke early to another blistering morning, the sun pushing up over the skyline already dazzlingly bright. He got to the office to find, among other things, a call from Colleen Skeet waiting to be returned. Millie was already at her desk deep in a phone conversation, trawling the hospitals once again, just in case. Mariner gestured 'drink' and got a thumbs up in reply.

On his way to the water cooler he had to pass DC Charlie Glover's desk. Glover too was on the phone, shirtsleeves rolled up, tie hanging loose and a thin sheen of sweat coating his pale features. He looked as if he'd been up for hours. Without breaking the conversation he looked on warily as Mariner sorted through his in-tray, finding the file he wanted two thirds of the way down the pile.

'That's great. I'll look forward to hearing from you soon,' said Glover, concluding the call. He replaced the receiver. 'Can I help you, sir?' he asked mildly.

Mariner was reading the top sheet of the chosen file. 'Not much progress,' he observed.

Glover leaned back in his chair. 'I'm doing the best I can with just the one pair of hands, one pair of legs and a desk full of other crap.' He wasn't being insubordinate, merely stating the facts.

It's not enough though, is it? Mariner wanted to retort, even now picturing Colleen sitting at home, poised by the phone, longing for it to ring. But he kept quiet, because Glover was right. It was just one case among dozens. And it wasn't Charlie's fault that it had been pulled from Mariner and given to him.

'I've talked to the lad's friends.' Glover went on. 'Not that he's got too many of those. He seems to be a bit of a loner. According to the school he's a bright kid with a promising future. Nobody saw him beyond Monday afternoon when he left to go home. He went off on his bike. And we've checked the places his mum says he usually hangs out.'

'Fido thinks he's done a runner.'

Glover shrugged. 'Could be. He's taken his life savings with him.'

'Has he?'

'All seven quid of it,' said Glover. 'Did you know he'd been talking to his mum about joining the army? Apparently she didn't take him too seriously.'

'I'm not surprised,' Mariner said. 'Ricky's not that sort of kid.'

'Maybe he wants to be that sort of kid: a hero.'

To make up for the times he hadn't quite managed it before, thought Mariner. 'Colleen's phoned me,' he said. 'Okay if I return it?'

'Sure.'

* * *

Colleen picked up before Mariner's phone had even rung out.

'Why have they taken you off it?' she demanded immediately.

'Something else came up,' said Mariner.

'Something more important than Ricky?'

'Something different.'

But she wasn't listening. 'Is it that girl? She went missing near here, too. I saw it on the telly last night.'

'Charlie Glover's a good bloke and an experienced investigator,' said Mariner, sidestepping the question. 'He'll do a thorough job. He's talking to Ricky's friends—'

'Huh. That won't take long. Why can't they put Ricky's picture on the telly?'

'They still might,' Mariner told her. 'They're doing a search of the places you suggested first. Plus we've issued a description of Ricky and his bike. We're doing all we can, Colleen.' But it wasn't enough, and it wouldn't be enough until Colleen had her son back safe and sound. That twinge of guilt returned, remembering what he'd put his own mother through all those years ago.

The knock on the door preceded DCI Fiske. Mariner groaned inwardly.

'Anything?' Fiske demanded. 'Any results from last night's appeal?'

'It's still too early,' said Mariner.

'But there's nothing? I thought not, which is why we need to push on.'

Tony Knox appeared at Fiske's shoulder.

'The search volunteers are awaiting your briefing, boss,' he told Mariner.

'What search volunteers?'

Fiske smiled knowingly. 'I've enlisted the help of the Operational Support Unit and their team of specialist search-trained officers. We need to up the ante,' he said. 'Yasmin's been missing for two nights now. As you so rightly said, you need to widen the investigation team, so I thought it would be helpful if I put in a word on your behalf. Uniform have rounded up some volunteers to help do the search, too. It seems they're awaiting your instructions.'

'But as I said yesterday, sir, we still don't know for certain where Yasmin got off the train. The last people with a definite sighting of her are the friends who saw her running for the train at Kingsmead. We don't have—'

'You have the CCTV footage.'

'I don't think it's conclusive,' said Mariner. 'I'd like to-
'

'It's enough.' Fiske's abrupt departure signalled that the debate was over.

'Crap!' Mariner flopped back in his chair.

'They're all out here waiting for the party to start,' prompted Knox.

'Well, we'd better get on with it then.' Mariner didn't like this one little bit. 'Either he lets me run this or he doesn't,' he muttered, on the walk to the briefing room. 'We don't have enough clear evidence that Yasmin even got as far as the university. Next thing we'll have finance on our backs telling us we've run out of money.'

'He has to be seen to be doing something,' put in Millie, who was trailing behind.

'Even if that something could be a complete waste of fucking time?'

'Look on the bright side, boss,' said Knox. 'If it is, he's the one who will get it in the neck.'

CHAPTER 8

As the main search area was on the university campus, a courtesy that had to be observed was getting permission from one of the deans. But before that, Mariner took Millie and Tony Knox along with him and parked by the university railway station. To get an idea of the general lie of the land, they then walked the route that Yasmin would have taken. Emerging from the station, a tarmac footpath took them through well-groomed park land that ran for several hundred yards alongside a piece of rougher untamed ground before climbing a slight incline towards the group of mock-Elizabethan buildings that was dominated by the university clock tower. The path emerged onto a network of roads, just along from the stripy arm of a security barrier. Some of the roads were public thoroughfares, connecting the main roads that ran either side of the campus, while others simply linked the different faculties of the university.

From there Yasmin would have crossed University Square and continued out through the east gate onto a well-used public highway. Looking back, it was plain that the most vulnerable section of Yasmin's journey would be between leaving the railway station and getting to the main body of the campus. That was where they would concentrate their search.

* * *

Dean Angela Woolley's office was situated on the first floor of one of the original university buildings that surrounded the impressive Chancellor's court and was overlooked by the 300-foot tall Chamberlain clock tower, named after industrialist and Lunar Man Joseph Chamberlain, and affectionately known as Old Joe. An information board in the courtyard told them that they were on the site of one of the original red-brick universities, built at the turn of the twentieth century with the intention of educating those who would manage the Midlands' burgeoning manufacturing industries. Not much call for that any more, thought Mariner. But its reputation lived on and now the university seemed to serve as many students from overseas as it did local youngsters and halls of residence to accommodate them were springing up all over the south city. Inside, the building reeked of academia, an atmosphere that Mariner found at once reassuring and intimidating.

'You ever wish you'd gone to university?' he asked Knox, as they stood cooling their heels outside Woolley's office.

The blank response seemed to indicate that the thought had never entered Knox's mind. He shook his head. 'You?' he asked.

Mariner wasn't so certain – it was definitely an opportunity that would have been open to him, in fact it was one he'd been under some pressure to take. Sometimes he wondered what the effect might have been on his chosen career path and on his life. People like Fiske met their life partners at university, or had a core group of friends left over from their college days. 'No,' he said. 'Don't think I do.'

* * *

75

Angela Woolley was sturdily into middle-age, her auburn hair set in rather an old-fashioned perm, the colour perfectly complemented by her beige silk blouse. They didn't need to explain their purpose in being there. She was fully abreast with current events. 'Anything we can do to help, Inspector,' she said. 'Though I'm sure nothing untoward could have happened here in the university without someone noticing. There are fewer students on campus now that the academic year has come to an end, but I'll make sure that word gets round to those who remain and ensure that the relevant departments to co-operate with your officers.'

Along with all the search team from the OCU, a handful of members of the public had also come forward to help, some of them students, mostly postgraduates. The summer exams were over and many of the students had gone down. The straggling line swept across the ground like an ill-disciplined advancing army.

* * *

After issuing instructions, Mariner left Sergeant Pete Welford to supervise the search. Taking Knox with him, he walked along to the hut at the barrier to talk to the security guards who had been on duty on Tuesday afternoon. This was not an area covered by CCTV so they were going to have to rely on the vigilance of the university-employed personnel. Not that Knox was much help. He seemed to be having problems focusing on anything today. One of the security guards thought he remembered having seen Yasmin on several occasions, but not every day, and he couldn't specifically recall seeing her on Tuesday.

Which didn't mean that she hadn't been there. The guards weren't compelled to stay in their hut all afternoon, especially in this sort of weather, when the flimsy structure offered little relief from the heat. And inevitably, with fewer students around, the rules were more relaxed. It was not unusual for them to leave the barrier raised for lengthy periods. Most people coming in and out at that time of day would have their own passes. Neither man had noticed anything out of the ordinary on Tuesday afternoon. Leaving the booth, having learned next to nothing, Mariner was immediately accosted by a young woman.

'Are you here about the girl who's gone missing?' She spoke with an upward inflection at the end of the sentence that placed her as a native of the Antipodes. She was dressed for a day out on Bondi Beach, in low-cut denim shorts that were a long way off joining company with the cropped T-shirt that stretched across her ample chest. All of which was offset by a rich honey-coloured tan. Instinctively Mariner glanced across at Knox for signs of awakening interest. On any other day his tongue would have been practically hanging out. But for once he barely seemed to notice.

Mariner nodded. 'We're the investigating officers.'

'They've told you about the flasher, right?'

Mariner glanced back at the security guard who squirmed uncomfortably.

She shook her head knowingly. 'I thought as much. A couple of months ago, back in May, one of my roommates, Lizzie, got flashed at.'

'Do you know exactly what happened?'

'Oh yeah. I mean it was a bit of a giggle, but it shook her up all right.'

'What time of day was this?' asked Mariner.

'It was early evening. About five, half-five. She was coming back over the meadow.'

'The meadow?'

'It's what we call that rough patch down there.' She pointed down the hill from where they stood to the area that the search party had just left — the area that Yasmin would have crossed immediately after leaving the station.

'Go on,' said Mariner.

'Well, the way she told it, Lizzie was just walking along the path minding her own when this guy jogged past her. She thought nothing of it, but then as she rounded the corner and into the trees there he was again, standing with his back to the path like he was taking a leak. But as she approached he turned around and it was all, like, sticking out there. He grinned this nasty little grin and mumbled something about getting "caught short."'

'Did Lizzie think that could have been genuine?'

She shook her head. 'Not a bit. She said: "no guy I know pees with a stiffy like that."'

'So what did Lizzie do?'

'She said something like, "get a life, loser", and got past him as fast as she could. She came straight home and told me all about it.'

'She didn't report it to the police?'

'When she'd calmed down a bit she thought it was a fuss over nothing. Just some perve getting his kicks. And I think she felt pretty stupid too, you know? I guess you always think if you're in that situation you'd be cool and just laugh it off, because it's so pathetic. But I think she was shocked and she knew that this guy could see it. So he got what he wanted, didn't he?'

'Did Lizzie feel physically threatened in any way?' asked Mariner.

'I don't think so. Like I say, she just felt stupid that something so harmless freaked her like that.'

'There's nothing harmless about flashing,' said Mariner. It was always the same. Despite the progress made in forensic psychology and the established principle that indecent exposure could, and often did, escalate to serious sexual assault, flashing had never somehow lost its reputation as one step up from a music hall joke. 'Did Lizzie tell you what this man looked like?'

'Not really. I don't think she got a good look. She'd come from the bright sun into the shade, and she said he was turned sort of sideways, with a baseball cap pulled low.' She gave a wry smile. 'And I guess his face wasn't the first thing she noticed, you know?'

'Did she tell anyone else about it?' Mariner asked.

'She didn't want to. But I made her write it all down, just in case, and she agreed to think some more about reporting it. In the end she chickened out and mentioned it to one of her tutors, who said she'd pass it on. They told her security would deal with it — issue a warning to students and let the dean know and, to be honest, I think that suited Lizzie.'

'And?'

'We heard nothing more. Then a couple of weeks ago there was this rumour going around that it had happened again to someone else, in practically the same spot. I wondered if it could be the same guy. I know Lizzie did too.'

Mariner nodded. 'Where's Lizzie now? We may want to talk to her.'

The girl pulled a face. 'I can't be very specific. She's backpacking round Europe with her boyfriend.'

Mariner was sure none of this had got as far as the police. Incidents like these would show up on the monthly intranet bulletin. There had been a spate of indecent exposure as there often was when the weather got warmer, but nothing that he could remember having been reported on or around the university. He turned to the guard. 'You knew about this?'

He shrugged. 'I'd heard something, but we were told not to make an issue of it.'

'It already is an issue,' Mariner pointed out. 'What makes it worse is that we weren't told.' Angela Woolley would have to be confronted about that.

'Do you know the name of the other girl?'

She shook her head. 'Sorry.'

* * *

Mariner knocked and walked into Angela Woolley's office, leaving the dean little opportunity to protest. She was on her feet, packing things into a briefcase. 'I'm sorry, Inspector, I'm due at a—'

'I think that might have to wait,' said Mariner coolly. Now he had her attention. 'Do you understand what we're doing here?' he demanded. 'That we're here searching for a seventeen-year-old girl who may well have vanished less than a mile from this very office? Why didn't you tell us about the indecent exposures that have been occurring next to this campus for the last two months at least? Of course, that's not counting any incidents that will have gone unreported because the victim is completely unaware that it's happened to anyone else but her. Ms Woolley, you have a sexual predator operating here and I think it's about time you told me what you know.'

In effect they'd had the better account from the student and Angela Woolley's version demonstrated that she'd barely attended to the facts. At least now she had the grace to be embarrassed.

'I'd really like to know whose idea it was to suppress this information,' Mariner said.

Woolley was defensive. 'It wasn't a question of suppressing it. We just felt it was better that only a limited number of people should know. What we didn't want to do was cause panic among the students, or deter any prospective students. Miss Greenwood was offered counselling, as were the other two young women—'

'You mean there are at least four?'

'Really, Inspector, this all happened months ago and I'm sure it was just a harmless student prank. There haven't been any incidents since the end of—'

'You mean, there haven't been any *reported* incidents. And why would students report it when none of this information is acted on? These incidents are far from harmless. Have you ever met any sexual deviants Ms

Woolley? Any convicted rapists among your acquaintances?'

'I don't know what—'

'Let me tell you something about rapists then, because in my line of work I've met one or two. And guess what? They don't wake up one morning and decide that today they are going to rape. Rape is just one stage in a progressive pattern of sexually abnormal behaviour. And that pattern starts, more often than not, with flashing; indecent exposure; an unsolicited demonstration of naked sexual power to an unsuspecting victim. Then when the buzz begins to wear off from that relatively harmless little pursuit — and believe me, it nearly always does — that's when things start to turn nasty. If you're so concerned about adverse publicity, I wonder what prospective students would make of the fact that, for the last few months, failure to disclose information to the police has exposed existing female staff and students at this university to the risk of being attacked by a potential rapist.'

Angela Woolley did not have a reply.

* * *

'Jesus. Since when did education become an exercise in PR?' Mariner boiled as they left the building. In the absence of any response from Knox, he answered his own question. 'Since it became a commercial enterprise, that's when. It's all about reputation and money.' He took a deep breath. 'We'll need to track down all the girls who've been victims of this flasher and take statements from them. It might not have anything to do with Yasmin, but they need to be investigated just the same.'

They had been given one other name. Helen Greenwood was a library assistant who fortunately remained on campus throughout the holidays.

'Take a detailed statement from her,' Mariner said to Knox. 'Then I want you to go back to the station. Follow

81

up on any other similar incidents there have been locally and see if there are any links.'

'Yes, boss.' Knox had about as much enthusiasm as a bloodhound on Valium.

* * *

Librarian Helen Greenwood, was thirty-three, so she said, but in Knox's eyes she could have been anything up to about fifty. Her mousy brown hair was held off her face by a tortoiseshell Alice band and her simple blouse and skirt could only be described as 'sensible.' All she was missing, Knox thought, were the horn-rimmed glasses. He really didn't want to have this conversation. Greenwood was already behaving as if she was afraid of him, but then, he was a man so perhaps she was. It was hard to imagine her having had much experience of the opposite sex. Knox found her as she was about to take her lunch break.

'I've brought sandwiches and I usually go out for a bit of fresh air,' she told him apologetically.

'Well, perhaps you could walk me to where it happened,' Knox suggested. 'Then you can tell me about it.'

'Oh, I don't know . . .'

'We'll take it slowly.'

'All right,' she said, sounding as if it was anything but.

It was going to be a waste of time, thought Knox. She was scared of her own shadow. They walked down the footpath, back towards the railway station until they'd almost reached the rough ground, where the path went briefly through an area of shrubs and there was plenty of scope for concealment. Then she stopped abruptly. 'It was about here.'

'So he could easily have been waiting over there on the rough ground until you came along, then hopped over the wire,' Knox surmised. 'Was there anyone else about?'

'Not here,' she said. 'I mean, the campus wasn't deserted, but there weren't many other people in this area at the time.'

'Do you take the same route every day at the same time?'

'I used to, yes, but not any more. If it's quiet I walk all the way round on the road now.'

'Can you describe to me exactly what happened?' Knox took out his notebook, partly because his memory didn't seem to be all that reliable at present, but also so that she wouldn't have to look at him while she went over the details.

'I was just walking down to the station to catch the train, along here,' Greenwood began, her voice reedy and thin. 'It was one of the first really nice warm days we had this year. It seems ages ago now.' She cleared her throat. 'He just stepped out from the bushes in that way that everyone says they do. I didn't notice at first. He smiled at me so I smiled back, but his smile was sort of . . . lewd, and then we were almost level when I happened to glance down. I don't know what made me do it and I saw that he had his, his . . . thing out.'

'His pri— his penis.'

She flushed scarlet. 'Yes. He was holding it. And it was huge and horrible. I just felt sick.'

'What did you do?'

'I just got past him, around him, as fast as I could and hurried down towards the station.'

'Did he follow you?'

'I don't know. I didn't dare to look back, but I don't think so.'

'So what was he like?'

'That's the silly thing. I can't really remember. I only glanced at him for a second or two.'

'Was he white or black?'

'White.'

'You're sure?'

'Yes, he seemed to have a very high colour, from the little I could see. He had this cap pulled down low so I couldn't really see his eyes, but his cheeks and his chin were—'

'What?'

'Sunburnt, I think. His chin was very red.'

'What colour was the cap?'

'Dark. Blue or green, I think. One of those that lots of men wear these days.'

A baseball cap. 'How tall was he?' Knox stepped back and stood up straight. 'Same as me?'

She made herself look him up and down. 'Slightly taller, I think. And thinner.'

Knox pulled in his stomach. This was better than he'd expected. 'You're doing well,' he told her. The other overriding impression, she said, was the powerful smell of his cologne '—or aftershave or whatever. It was too strong, and smelled sort of cheap and nasty.'

* * *

Taking the statement took around an hour. A couple of times Knox had to ask Helen Greenwood to repeat what she'd said because he'd missed it. Now, back in the office he was finding it difficult to concentrate on what was on the screen in front of him. He had some detective work of his own to do and he wouldn't be able to settle until he'd done it. The office was quiet, everyone taken up with the two investigations. Knox reached for the thermos he'd brought with him. He needed a bit of Dutch courage for this.

Minimising the programme he was in, he went online.

'It's someone I've known for years,' Theresa had told him during that painfully brief conversation on the phone.

'Do I know him?' he'd asked. She hadn't answered, which meant that maybe he did.

'Where did you meet?'

'It's not important.' But Knox had already worked it out. The only someone she could have known a long time who was also a mutual acquaintance must be someone from school. Theresa used the computer all the time. She'd been on courses and could find her way round it better than he could. He also knew that she visited the various school reunion sites that were springing up. Once she'd even urged him to have a look.

'It's fun,' she'd said. 'You get to find out what's happened to all those spotty oiks.' But Knox had declined. He didn't have the same enthusiasm for the past as Theresa did. Maybe it was a woman thing.

There were half a dozen sites offering to put people in contact with old acquaintances. Knox logged into the first and typed in the name of the secondary school that he and Theresa had gone to. Then the year they'd both left. By the time he clicked on it, his palms were sweating and his heart pounding. Would he know who it was? Would he recognise the name?

'Anything?' Mariner's voice behind him made him jump out of his skin. He hadn't heard anyone come in.

'No. Nothing yet, boss.' He shrank the screen but Mariner was already looking over his shoulder.

'Are we sure we're looking in the right place?' But it was curiosity more than anything else.

Knox fumbled for the notes he'd made. 'Checking back over indecent exposure incidents in the south of the city during the last six months, there have been two others as well as the unreported ones at the university,' he told Mariner. 'All occurred at different times of day, and on the surface there doesn't seem much to connect them.' He'd plotted the incidents on a map, which they now pored over. 'As you can see, boss, the other two happened in secluded areas, but then a flasher is hardly likely to strike in the middle of a busy shopping centre, is he?'

'Not usually known, no.'

'One common thread seems to be that a lot of them take place fairly near railway stations.'

'Like Kingsmead.' Mariner was thoughtful. 'Okay, we'll keep it in mind. How did you get on with Helen Greenwood?'

Knox reported what she'd told him.

'Sunburnt, eh?' said Mariner. 'That might be useful.'

CHAPTER 9

Calling in at the incident room revealed that the news bulletin had been less fruitful. Although there were a handful of possible sightings of Yasmin to follow up, the descriptions were vague and there didn't appear to be anything that held any great significance. Mariner could safely leave Knox to handle those. As the search of the university campus had turned up nothing either, apart from a handful of spent spliffs, the logical thing to do was to widen the search to the stretch of railway track between Kingsmead station and the point at which Yasmin left the train. That would be a much bigger operation requiring far more manpower, which Mariner didn't like to think about just yet. As far as he was concerned they were already jumping the gun. Instead he wanted to concentrate on the information they already had. On an investigation like this it was important to be systematic, starting at the core and working gradually outwards, making sure not to miss anything.

* * *

DCI Fiske, however, had other ideas and any decision on how to prioritise was all but taken out of Mariner's hands. Now that Yasmin's disappearance had been on TV the press were on to it and this was exactly the sort of case to capture the public's imagination. Always on the lookout for an 'angle,' the media were playing up the possibility of a racially motivated abduction and, ever helpful, Fiske was taken with this idea too. He was now making noises about a press conference with Yasmin's parents.

'What about this letter?' he asked, demanding that Mariner bring him up to date. 'If it's genuine, it was a pretty open threat.'

'Forensics have found nothing on it,' said Mariner. And it's hard to tell how genuine it is, given that it's such an undistinguishable note. And the Akrams have had similar stuff in the past.'

'But this follows the consortium letter to the press: a provocative act if ever there was one,' said Fiske. 'If the low-level campaign failed to subdue them — which it patently has — then the perpetrators might feel that it's time to do something more dramatic. And so far you don't seem to have come up with any other reason why Yasmin should have gone missing.'

'We're still exploring all the possibilities,' said Mariner.

'Like what?'

'Well, for one thing we've learned that everything in the Akram household wasn't as rosy as we'd been led to believe. Mr Akram and his daughter had disagreed.'

Fiske looked disappointed. 'I'm not saying you shouldn't keep the family under scrutiny, but you can do that while following up other avenues. The racist incidents have to be examined. Mohammed Akram has sent us a list of dates and occurrences going back over three years.' He held up some papers.

'I haven't seen that.'

'It was passed directly to the superintendent. This is a copy.'

Mariner took the sheet. The incidents were, as Akram had described them to him yesterday, fairly low level — excreta through the letterbox, windows broken, graffiti sprayed — sometimes happening weekly and usually at night. Up until now the school had always been the target. Attached to the list was a copy of the letter written to the local press by Akram and several other business owners in the area, denouncing what they called 'terrorism by stealth,' perpetrated by 'those too weak to reveal themselves.' It spoke about The Right Way being a club for cowards who indulged in covert petty crime instead of openly confronting the issues. The question was whether it was enough to prompt such drastic action from The Right Way and, if so, could they expect a ransom note at any time?

'And that, Inspector, should be your next line of enquiry,' Fiske said.

Mariner opened his mouth to complain, but stopped himself. It was a valid line of enquiry that would have to be pursued at some time. They may as well do it now and with any luck his deference would keep Fiske off his back for a few hours.

* * *

But before entering the lion's den Mariner wanted to arm himself with a bit more information about the man they might be dealing with. Detective Sergeant Bev Jordan came over from the racial crimes unit at Lloyd House to talk to him and Millie.

'What do you need to know?' she asked when they were installed in Mariner's office.

'Everything of any relevance about Peter Cox,' said Mariner.

Jordan grimaced. 'He's a nasty piece of work in every respect. He runs a very active cell of The Right Way who hold particularly strong views on immigration, repatriation, birth control programmes; you name it. He's denounced the BNP for being too moderate.'

'What a charmer,' remarked Millie.

'Absolutely.'

89

Mariner handed Jordan the leaflet Mohammed Akram had given him. 'Is this one of his?'

Jordan scanned the document and nodded. 'This is exactly the sort of stuff he churns out. In the past there have been various threats against groups and individuals. And Cox has his own little band of fanatically loyal followers in the south of the city and beyond, mainly recruited via the internet, though not exclusively. He spreads the word in local pubs too, particularly those on white, working-class housing estates, areas of high social deprivation where white kids are pretty frustrated with their lot and generally powerless to do anything about it. One of his favourite themes is the threat of Islamic fundamentalism to the British way of life. Muslims taking over jobs, local businesses—'

'And schools.'

'Particularly schools, because that's where it's all seen to be taught. He'd be encouraged by the current climate, too. Since September 11 and other terrorist incidents, and the rise of Islamic State there's been a resurgence of interest in the membership of these types of organisation.'

'And beyond the leafleting?' asked Mariner.

'Oh, the usual petty harassment: damage to property, disgusting stuff pushed through letterboxes and sent through the post. We have a couple of informants on the inside, but Cox is clever. He's very careful not to be directly involved. He relies mainly on the susceptibility and fanaticism of his recruits. He provides the ideas, they carry them out. So far we've only ever been able to charge a few individuals with criminal damage. There's one in particular, David Waldron, who's a real fall-guy for Cox.'

'Are you aware of the antagonism with the Asian business consortium?'

'Oh, yes,' said Jordan. 'It's been brewing for a couple of years and Akram's letter to the press won't have helped the situation, but again Cox is too smart to let something like that get to him. It was only a letter, after all. It's his followers who would be more upset by it.'

'Do you think any of them would go as far as abduction?'

Jordan frowned. 'Up until recently I'd have said no, but there has been a worrying trend lately, which is that, thanks to the internet, these groups are developing international links and being increasingly influenced by their counterparts across the pond.'

'In what way?'

'A spate of letter bomb attacks in the South of the US was followed weeks later by similar attacks here, in Manchester and Leeds last month — remember?'

'And?'

'You may not know this – there was a press embargo – but a couple of months ago the daughter of a black, US senator was abducted by right-wing activists in Savannah, Georgia,' Jordan said. 'The senator was proposing legislation to curb the distribution of certain right-wing propaganda.'

'And has the girl been found?' asked Knox.

'Oh yes. Strangled and dumped in a garbage skip. It's believed that there was never any intention to release her alive.'

Mariner was appalled. 'Do you think there's anyone in The Right Way who would go that far?'

'It only takes one nutcase,' said Jordan. 'Cox likes his followers to "prove themselves" by acting on their initiative, so it would only take one of them with a particular bent for this kind of activity, and we have our abduction.'

'And Waldron?'

'He's on remand at present, so effectively out of the picture. It might be worth a chat with Peter Cox, though. Find out if he's hired any new recruits lately. Yasmin was last seen at four thirty on Tuesday afternoon, wasn't she?

It would be interesting to know what Cox was doing then, too.'

'I can't wait to meet the animal who's caused so much misery.'

'He's not what you'd expect,' said Jordan. 'He might not put it to any great use by working for a living, but he's bright: a graduate. He just prefers to utilise his talents for stirring up trouble.'

* * *

The other surprise was that Peter Cox lived in a smart neighbourhood in a homely 1930s semi with bay windows and a porch. It was a neighbourhood for young families and, given what Jordan had told them, Mariner guessed that it was his parents' house, the one he'd been born and raised in. What set it apart from its neighbours was the jungle of a garden and the limp, discoloured curtains hanging behind grimy windows. As there were no garages, Knox and Mariner drove the length of the street looking in vain for a parking place and were eventually compelled to settle for a neighbouring street. Mariner craned his neck to concentrate on a reverse park, which he executed smoothly.

'Very neat,' said Knox. It was the only time he'd spoken on the entire journey. His words seemed to sweeten the air somehow, but Mariner dismissed the sensation as his own overactive imagination. They climbed out of the car and walked back to number forty-eight, where what prevailed was the smell of decaying refuse.

The doorbell showed little indication of being connected to anything, but Mariner pressed it anyway and beside them, at the bay window, the shabby curtain was pulled aside. A round white face peered out at them.

'Mr Cox?' Mariner called out, politely, holding up his warrant card. 'Could you spare us a few minutes?'

The face regarded them with distaste, but the curtain dropped back and moments later the door was opened.

'Can we come in?' Mariner asked. It was obviously the last thing Peter Cox wanted, but he nevertheless stepped back to allow them through.

What sprang out first at Mariner from the gloomy hallway were the framed posters on the walls. From his limited knowledge of the Third Reich, Mariner thought one of them might have been Rudolf Hess. The other was unmistakable — Adolf Hitler, eyes focused purposefully on something in the middle distance, one hand on his hip in a pose which, in Mariner's opinion, made the Führer look a bit camp. He thought it best not to mention this. Cox was not a friend of fresh air it seemed and, in the heat, the atmosphere inside the house was acrid with stale cigarette smoke and had a vaguely feral undertone. He took them into a small front living room that was piled high with books and papers, in the centre of which was an old and battered sofa. A lap top, its screen blanked, was wired up in a corner of the room.

Cox himself was small and weedy, as unhealthy as a plant starved of natural light, as if he never ventured out of his dark and dingy lair. Balding slightly, he was as pale as uncooked pastry and the amber coloured stain bleeding along the index finger of his right hand was consistent with the pile of home-rolled dog-ends in the makeshift ashtray. 'How can I help you, officers?' he asked politely, his accent unexpectedly refined.

'By answering a simple question for us,' said Mariner. 'Where were you on Tuesday afternoon at around four thirty?'

'Now why would you want to know that?' But before they could answer, he laughed out loud. 'This is about that little Paki, isn't it?' He shook his head sadly. 'Dear me, you must be desperate if you've come to me about that.'

'Her family seems to be on the mailing list for your enlightening pamphlets,' said Mariner.

'Are they? I really wouldn't know. We have an extensive target audience.'

'And David Waldron, one of your party members was caught inflicting damage on property in the vicinity of the Allah T'ala school.'

'As I think I told your colleagues at the time, I can't be responsible for the actions of all our members. All I do is provide a forum for like-minded people to share their views and concerns.'

'In the same way that the National Socialist Party of Germany provided a forum?' said Knox.

Cox's tone hardened. 'I repeat, Waldron was acting independently. I had nothing to do with any of that.'

'—until Mohammed Akram brought your name into it. He said some not very nice things about you publicly, some highly provocative things.'

Cox smiled. 'Do you seriously think a bit of name-calling's going to bother me? It's what you get when you're prepared to stand up for what you believe in. It goes with the territory; our territory.' He noticed Knox's gaze roving around the room. 'Want to have a closer look, do you?'

'It would help us to—'

'Well, you'll need a warrant and a fucking good reason,' Cox said, mildly.

'So maybe you could answer the question, just for the record,' said Mariner. 'Where were you?'

But disappointingly Cox did have a pretty unassailable alibi; at that precise time he'd been speaking at a meeting of 'like-minded people' in Walsall. He travelled on the train. And if, as he said, the meeting didn't end until five, it would have been practically impossible for him to have been anywhere near Yasmin Akram when she disappeared. It would be easy enough to verify.

* * *

'It still doesn't mean that he hasn't put someone else up to it,' Mariner said to Knox, as they traipsed back along the street.

'Mm.' Knox grunted.

Back at the car Mariner saw he had a missed call on his mobile. He rang back. It was Millie. 'I've got a name for you. The disgruntled parent we spoke about is a man called Abdul Sheron. Oh and another thing—' suddenly she sounded uncomfortable. 'DCI Fiske is organising a press conference.'

CHAPTER 10

'Police Constable Khatoon should get her facts straight before she comes bleating to you.' Pacing the floor of his office, DCI Fiske was angry. Extremely angry, if the twitching muscle in his jaw was anything to go by. Even so he seemed keen to defend his actions, Mariner thought with some satisfaction. 'I am not *organising* a press conference, I have merely indicated to the press that one is imminent, and asked the TV station to be on standby.'

'Which, with respect sir, is as good as declaring it where the media are concerned.' said Mariner, seriously wondering if Fiske was beginning to lose it already. More than accustomed to keeping the press at bay, he'd never had to fend off an over-zealous commanding officer before. 'The timing of press conferences is crucial and I'd have preferred to hold it when I was ready. If you want me to continue as SIO then I need to be able to do things my way.' His powers of diplomacy were being stretched to the limit.

'That seems to involve doing very little, as far as I can make out. This case is developing a high profile—'

Yes, and who do we have to thank for that, thought Mariner.

'We need to be seen to be acting,' Fiske went on. 'We should be looking at running a reconstruction too. People expect it.'

That was the problem with having all these bloody crime programmes on TV. The public thought they knew better how to do the job. 'It's much too soon,' said Mariner, firmly. 'We're following up outside leads, and after a week we'll get someone to walk the route to encourage any new witnesses to come forward, but we can't discount Yasmin's family and immediate friends yet. We already know that the parents aren't telling us everything.'

Fiske pounced. 'So having them in for a press conference would give you an opportunity,' he said. 'TV cameras are an excellent way of stripping away any pretence.'

'Not necessarily-' Mariner began, knowing that in some cases just the opposite was true.

'Right, that's settled then,' Fiske cut across him. 'As soon as we can.'

Mariner took a deep calming breath. 'Yes, sir.' He turned to go. 'And maybe sometime you could go over that egg-sucking thing with me again,' he muttered under his breath. By the time he'd walked back to the main office he was resigned to it.

'Let's bring in Mr and Mrs Akram,' he said to Millie.

'Any particular way you want me to steer things?'

'No, save that for afterwards. Keep it all light and conversational on the journey here. That way Akram's guard won't be up — if that makes a difference.'

* * *

As SIO, Mariner had no choice but to accompany Fiske to the appeal, which passed in a blur of flash-bulbs and quick-fire questions. Afterwards, he, Knox and Millie watched the playback. Mohammed Akram was calm and dignified while even his wife, holding on to her husband for support, remained composed despite the obvious strain. She seemed diminished since two days ago, as if she'd lost about half a stone and all of it from around her face where the skin was pale and sagging. Mohammed Akram did all the talking, reading from the prepared statement he'd been given by the press officer, appealing to Yasmin to come home, or to anyone who may be holding her to please let her go. Throughout, his voice was clear and steady, his gaze straight into the camera.

'He's a cool one,' Mariner conceded.

'Don't be fooled,' said Millie. She was right to be cautious. Even when parents made emotional public appeals for the return of their offspring, they couldn't be eliminated from the enquiry. Distress and guilt had the habit of manifesting themselves in very similar ways and in recent years increasing numbers of murderers had successfully, at least for a while, concealed one with the other.

* * *

Before being returned home the Akrams were taken into a side room and offered refreshment and after fielding the volley of questions from reporters, Mariner went to talk to them. Two sets of eyes turned pleadingly towards him as he went into the room. He shook his head, 'I'm sorry, there's nothing new. But I do need to clarify a couple of things with you.'

'Anything,' said Akram.

'We've spoken to Yasmin's friends and I understand that you were not entirely happy about Yasmin staying the night with Suzanne,' Mariner said.

Mohammed Akram responded instantly. 'It was nothing. It was the kind of thing every parent goes through with their child.'

'Is that why it didn't seem important enough to mention?' asked Mariner. 'I must impress on you that anything out of the ordinary, however small could help. Tell me what happened exactly.'

'Yasmin asked to go and stay with her friend, overnight. I said no,' said Akram matter-of-factly.

'Why was that?'

'It was a school night and she would have had homework. It was inappropriate.' There was more to it than that, Mariner was certain. But he wouldn't push it now. Was Akram just trying to be diplomatic about his dislike of Suzanne, or were there power games between Mum and Dad?

He looked from one parent to the other. 'So am I to understand that Yasmin was defying you by going to Suzanne's?'

'She was defying me, not her mother.' Akram glared at his wife. 'After I left the house on Tuesday morning, Shanila allowed Yasmin to go.' The accusation was there along with the obvious source of that additional tension.

Shanila Akram made a weak show of sticking up for herself. 'Yasmin was threatening to go to Suzanne's anyway,' she said to her husband. 'I thought it much better that she should go with our blessing than deceive us. I thought if she was allowed to go once it would be less of an issue — she would get it out of her system.'

'So you encouraged her to collude with you in deception.' Mohammed Akram's anger was plain.

But his wife was equal to it. 'I would have told you when you returned.'

'Do you approve of Suzanne, Mr Akram?' Mariner asked. There followed enough of a hesitation to confirm Mariner's suspicions. The antagonism simmering there was palpable.

'It's not a question of approval,' said Akram tightly.

'Then what is it?'

'You went to see Yasmin's friends. You've met Suzanne?'

'Yes.'

'Then you'll know that she is very different from Yasmin.' Full marks for tact.

'And that bothers you?'

'As we've already said, Yasmin is relatively inexperienced at life. It would be easy for her to be influenced by a stronger, more . . . worldly personality, someone who has different values.'

'So you've discouraged the friendship,' said Mariner.

'We have been realistic. We can't prevent Yasmin from mixing with whoever she wants to at school. Let's just say that we haven't done anything to encourage it.'

'How does Yasmin feel about that?'

'Kids get angry, you know, especially if they can't get their way,' Akram said. 'Have you got kids?'

'No.'

'Yasmin said—' Shanila Akram stopped abruptly.

'What did she say, Mrs Akram?'

'She said we might regret it if we tried to stop her from doing things.'

'So that was why you decided to allow Yasmin to go and stay with Suzanne,' Mariner concluded.

'Yes.' She addressed her husband. 'I was concerned that being too strict on Yasmin might push her away from us. I thought that once it had happened and you saw that no harm had come of it and that Yasmin appreciated the gesture, it would be for the best.'

'For the *best*?' Her husband snorted contemptuously. 'How can you possibly say that now? Look at what has happened. Now we have no idea where our daughter has gone.'

'Of course I can see that now, but at the time—' Mrs Akram's eyes filled with tears.

'How did Yasmin react when you told her she *could* go to stay with Suzanne after all?' Mariner intervened, keen to maintain the momentum.

'She was excited, happy. She hugged me. But I know she was mindful of her dad's feelings, too.'

'Mindful how? Do you think Yasmin really intended to stay with Suzanne, or could she have decided to get back at you for making life difficult for her? Could she have run away?'

'Yasmin isn't like that,' said Akram. 'Even if she was angry I don't believe she would take it this far. If she'd decided to punish us it would be a gesture, that's all. She would go somewhere safe, to someone within our family. I believe Yasmin thought of her duty to me and was intending to come home. Something prevented her from doing so. Something has happened to her, Inspector, and I really think your time would be better spent out there looking for her instead of dissecting our family life. I don't understand why you are persisting with this. I told you about the trouble we've been having. Why aren't you talking to Peter Cox?'

'We're following that line of enquiry,' Mariner assured him. 'But we do have to ensure that all possibilities are covered. Tell me about Abdul Sheron.'

'How do you know about him?' Akram stared.

'That doesn't really matter,' said Mariner. 'Just tell me.'

'Abdul is an old friend. Things have been a little strained because we felt that we couldn't meet the needs of his youngest child in our school. It can be hard to accept but it is for the good of the child.'

'I understand he was angry about that.'

'At first he was, yes, and that was to be expected. His daughter has lots of problems and it is hard for him. But our families have known each other for years. Abdul would not do anything to hurt us. It's out of the question.'

And on that note of certainty Mariner allowed Millie to take them home.

* * *

'What do you think?' Mariner asked Knox after they'd gone.

'He's working very hard at trying to steer us towards the racist angle,' said Knox with rare lucidity.

'And away from anything else? My thoughts exactly.'

As a follow up, Mariner had suggested a few directions for Millie to take with the 'informal conversation' on the way back. When she returned to the station, he was waiting for a debrief. 'What else did you find out?' he asked.

'About as much as I would if I'd been making a social call,' said Millie. 'But I do think Shanila is beginning to open up and talk to me more as if I was a friend of the family than a police officer.'

'That could be helpful.'

'Maybe. It depends on how much they decide to patronise me and how much they disapprove of my role.'

'What do you think?'

'They still hold a fairly traditional view of the female role. Not outright disapproval, but probably not what they'd want for their girls.'

'Yasmin's older sister lives abroad?' Mariner said.

'Yes, we talked about Amira. She was married earlier this year, apparently.'

'Quite recently then. And how often does she see Yasmin?'

'Often, according to Mum and Dad. Amira's husband is a successful lawyer and travels extensively. They were over here just a few weeks ago.'

'Was it an arranged marriage?' asked Mariner.

'Sounds like it, in that the two families already knew each other and the match was obviously approved by both sets of parents.'

'That's a scenario that Yasmin might have wanted to escape.'

'It depends on how strictly it's followed through,' said Millie. 'Arranged marriage is not always a bad thing. Usually these days the son or daughter has the right of veto. This couple are a mix, like their dress: her in traditional, him in western. On the one hand Shanila Akram seems very western and liberal, but at the same time I get the impression that Mohammed likes to keep Yasmin on a tight rein.'

'By not allowing her to stay overnight with her friend,' said Mariner.

'Although I can see why Suzanne might be viewed as a less than ideal playmate.'

'This kind of conflict isn't so uncommon, of course. Yasmin's parents want her to have all the advantages of growing up in western society, as they so successfully have, but within the confines of their religious rules. Problem is, the two are not always compatible and it's hard to find a balance. It can create a fair amount of tension. To Yasmin, at her age, it probably seems as if she gets the worst of both worlds. She gets to work hard to achieve what her parents want, but without the social life enjoyed by her friends.'

'So they limit her.'

'They'd say they're protecting her,' Millie said. 'Family life is important to them.'

'Doesn't make it any easier for Yasmin.'

Millie shook her head. 'You have no idea.' She spoke with feeling and Mariner realised for the first time how little he knew about his colleague's own background.

'I asked them again about Abdul Sheron too,' Millie said. 'Neither of them believes it would be him but they have at least agreed that we can go and talk to him.'

'No time like the present.'

Millie pulled a face. 'Sorry, sir. I've a few calls to make.'

'That's okay. Tony!'

CHAPTER 11

Sheron's residence turned out to be a hardware store down the Stratford Road from *Allah T'ala*, between a shop that sold wedding sarees and an Indian sweet shop. At ground-floor level was a family-run hardware business that flowed onto the pavement outside, with stacks of plastic buckets and storage containers arranged in neat rows, mops, brooms, cleaning cloths and tubs of cheap batteries. The family, Millie had been told, lived in the flat above. Mariner's opening words established that Sheron didn't speak English, so one of his brothers came to interpret for him — while Mariner gave himself a mental kicking for not having waited for Millie instead of bringing Knox, who was chewing grimly on some menthol-smelling gum.

They followed the two men through the shop and up a flight of dark, narrow stairs. The room at the top was grubby and dismal, the floor uncarpeted and strewn with piles of newspapers and a few broken toys. From one corner a huge wide-screen TV dominated the room, the sound turned down so as to be virtually inaudible. A long sofa was arranged directly opposite and beside it, on the bare floorboards sat a child of about three or four, pretty, with dark curls framing her delicate face. Her head wobbled as she balanced uncertainly and her limbs occasionally twitched, threatening to throw her off-balance. As they went in, their footsteps echoing on the wooden floor, she seemed to look up at them and smile, but Mariner could tell that her eyes were unfocused. A slender, transparent tube was taped under her nose, the other end draped across the sofa and connected to a tank leaning against the wall. Sheron and his brother completely ignored both the child and the elderly matriarch who sat at the TV end of the sofa, her eyes fixed on the giant screen, and the conversation was conducted with all four men standing in a corner of the room. Most of the communication was with the man who had introduced himself as Hasan, Sheron's brother.

'I'd like Mr Sheron to tell us about his involvement with the school, *Allah T'ala*,' said Mariner first.

The brother translated and for a few minutes there followed a jabbered exchange in their native language. Then for the first time Hasan acknowledged the child. 'This is his daughter, Shebana,' said, looking over at the little girl, who was now gazing intently towards them. 'He put her name down for the school two years ago. His other children go there and he has given them money. Now it's time for Shebana to go they are saying that they can't help her. It's because she has problems, but they say they haven't got enough teachers or enough room for her oxygen tank. All her siblings and cousins have gone to the school, but not Shebana. Now you see she is here, she will have no school to go to and it's the fault of the Akrams. They have been unfair and it made him angry.'

Still muttering, Sheron walked across the room and retrieved something from one of the piles of newspapers. It was a glossy magazine, a prospectus. He thrust it in front of Mariner, rapping a forefinger down on the page.

'He's saying: "Look at this. See what it says here,"' Hasan told them. 'It's written in this book, but the words don't mean anything.'

Mariner looked. The brochure talked about welcoming all children of all different abilities. He turned the brochure over in his hand. At the bottom of the last page was the name of the printer, presumably the one Akram had been to see on the day when Yasmin disappeared.

'It is an insult to our whole family,' said Hasan. 'That's why he's so angry.'

'Angry enough to damage Mohammed Akram's car?' Mariner asked.

'He knows nothing about that,' said Hasan immediately, without conferring, and Mariner suddenly wondered if that were true and if the deed had been carried out on Abdul's behalf. It was pointless to pursue it further, though. It would be impossible to prove. The significant thing was that this was clearly still an open wound, the situation unresolved. The question was how far would Sheron's demonstrable anger drive him? The Akrams had made a victim of his daughter. Would he want to do the same to the Akrams?

'Does Mr Sheron know Yasmin Akram?'

'Of course we do. She was friends with my daughter,' said Hasan.

'Was?' Mariner picked it up straight away.

'Going to that school has corrupted her. Now she thinks she is better than her old friends.'

'Does your brother know anything about her disappearance?'

Hasan spoke to Abdul. The response came back immediately, with more anger. He pointed a finger emphatically at Mariner.

'How would he know that?' Hasan translated. 'He doesn't care. Now they can know how it feels.'

It was a predictable response. 'Where was he on Tuesday afternoon at four thirty?'

'Abdul was here in the shop. We have a business to run.'

They thanked Sheron and his brother for their time and walked back out onto the busy street to the sound of voices raised in Urdu, the discussion continuing beyond their departure.

'Akram certainly seems to have got up his nose,' said Mariner.

'They don't like Yasmin much either,' said Knox. '"Corrupted" is a bit strong.'

'Maybe he just meant she's got too big for her boots. Yasmin goes to a prestigious school. Sounds as if she flaunts it.'

'Another reason to wipe the smirk off Akram's face,' Knox pointed out.

'But if they've abducted her, where is she and where are the demands?' Mariner wondered.

'There might not be any. The Akrams' distress might be enough.'

'But Yasmin disappeared a good six or seven miles away from here, near the university. Sheron would have had to be highly organised to operate in a part of the city that he's not familiar with. Where would he get the means?'

'That's where,' said Knox. His eyes were on the opposite side of the street as they watched Hasan Sheron emerge from the shop and climb in behind the wheel of the private hire taxi that was parked on the kerb outside. 'How convenient is that?'

* * *

Impulsively on their way back to Granville Lane, Mariner asked Knox to wait in the car while he called in on Colleen. The end of terrace house had been given a sparkling new coat of white emulsion since his last visit and the rotten windows replaced with uPVC, ill-disguising the fact that it was basically structurally unsound, riddled with damp and — along with the whole estate — should have been condemned years ago.

The front door was ajar so he called out. 'Hello. Anyone about?' She came to the door, her hair hanging lank and unwashed, the inevitable cigarette on the go. Her face displayed a mixture of hope and fear. It was a mistake to have come.

'I've no news,' he said straight away.

'So why are you here?' She was dressed unflatteringly in a loose white T-shirt over faded black leggings, her bare feet in cheap velour slippers, worn through at the toe. 'To tell me that you've found that missing girl?'

'I can't talk to you about other cases that we're handling.'

'How come her parents get to go on the telly?' she wanted to know. 'All they've done for my Ricky is put up a few posters. Why can't I go on to ask him to come home?' The belligerence in her voice belied the desperation.

'It's not always appropriate,' said Mariner. 'It depends on the circumstances.' How could he tell her that she just wasn't TV material? That the success of a press conference depended on the public identifying and sympathising with the parents, and that neither of those was likely for a single mother on her third partner in as many years. They would make the same assumptions that his DCI had.

'You think that girl's more important than my Ricky.'

'I think nothing of the sort, Colleen, and you know it.'

'Maybe not you, but the others do. Just because she comes from a posh Asian family. I'm not stupid, you know. I get what's going on here.'

'We're doing what we can, Colleen,' Mariner said. It was true . . . to a degree.

'So where is he?' She took a step back, her lower lip starting to quiver. 'Where's my Ricky? Come and see me when you've found him.' And then she carefully closed the door in his face.

If it did transpire that Ricky had run away, Mariner would personally lynch the boy when he turned up, for having put his mother through this.

* * *

The blatant hypocrisy of such thoughts was spelled out immediately he got home that evening, to find yet another message from his own mother on the answering machine. 'There's something I want to talk to you about,' she said again. 'I suppose it will have to keep until next time I see you.' Implying that this ought to happen soon. He wondered if this 'something' was what he'd been waiting all his life to find out, but then that's what she'd be hoping for. She was playing games with him again — one of the things she did for fun, to get back at him for what he'd done to her all those years ago. Not that he could really blame her. He'd once asked her how she felt when, as a teenager, he'd run away from home.

'I just wanted you back, unconditionally,' she'd replied. Only then did Mariner fully realise how much he must have hurt her. It had taken him weeks before he'd contacted her to tell her he was okay. What kind of hell must he have inflicted on her in the meantime? It was another item on the list of things that they never talked about. Instead she'd found other ways of making him pay. Well, he didn't have time for her games right now, or to comply with her excessive demands, whatever they might be. But at the same time he couldn't help wondering how Shanila Akram would be holding up. Had Yasmin run away for the same reasons he had: because she'd felt stifled by her family?

Instead of his mother, Mariner phoned Anna. 'How's the fundraising going?' he asked, out of politeness.

The irony in his voice didn't wilt her enthusiasm. 'It's great. Everyone's being so generous, though we're still waiting for contributions from certain people.' It was a blatant hint.

'I'm thinking about it,' he stalled.

'Yeah, well don't think too long, eh? Where are you up to with the missing girl?'

109

'Don't count on my company for the weekend, will you?'

'Interestingly enough I never count on much where you're concerned, but that's okay,' Anna said cheerfully. 'Good thing we both know the score, isn't it?'

'Sure.' Mariner's chest tightened.

'I know you're not allowed to say, but how *is* it going?'

'Even if I could say there'd be nothing to tell. It's frustrating, to say the least.'

'Mm, well,' she said slowly, her voice dropping half an octave. 'We can't have you frustrated, can we? There ought to be something I can do about that. What you need is a few soothing words to help you relax.'

'How's Jamie?'

'Jamie's fine. Glued to the TV as we speak. Want to know what I'm wearing?'

Mariner settled back in the armchair. 'Go on then . . .'

'Is that better?' she asked him a little later.

'Much,' he said, although he didn't like to dwell too much on the fact that this was what their relationship had come to.

* * *

The next morning Mariner gathered the team together to review what they'd got so far. It wasn't much. The incident board displayed a blown-up version of Yasmin's photograph, an enlarged section of the street map covering the area where she'd disappeared and a time-line leading nowhere. Colleen's complaint about the absence of a press conference for Ricky seemed unfounded since Yasmin's had yielded precisely nothing in the way of new leads. Only one call received had produced anything of substance to follow up and that had since turned out to be a dud too.

'What are the options?' Since he looked more like his usual lively self this morning, Mariner addressed the question to Tony Knox.

'If we rule out accidents, basically there appear to be three possibilities at this stage, boss,' said Knox. 'First possibility: Yasmin has gone off of her own accord.'

'Why would she do that?'

'She'd had a row with her parents,' said Millie.

'Not her mother. Her mother had given in to her,' Mariner reminded them.

'She'd rowed with her dad though, and he seems to be the one who wields the power.'

'And maybe she's just had enough,' offered Knox. 'From what we've heard, it's not the first time the old man's been down on her.'

'Okay,' said Mariner. 'But if that is the case, would Yasmin let things get this far? She's an intelligent and, so we're told, considerate girl. Surely wherever she was, she'd eventually let her parents know that she's safe. We're three days in now and nothing. And she doesn't appear to have taken any money with her, so how is she living?'

'All right then,' Knox said. 'Second possibility: she's been abducted and is being held against her will.'

'Who by?'

'Peter Cox and his mates?' Millie chipped in.

Mariner was doubtful. 'Now that we've talked to him, I don't quite see it. It's not really Cox's style and if it was one of his followers, I'm not convinced that they'd be well-organised enough. Cox may be clever, but according to DS Jordan most of his honchos are pretty inadequate.'

'Could be just a random pick-up,' suggested Knox. 'Someone offering her a lift home from the station.'

'But we keep being told that she's a bright, sensible kid,' countered Millie. 'She wouldn't have gone off with a complete stranger.'

'And why would she need a lift? It's not that far to her house from there and, like we said, it's a warm sunny evening. What reason would she have to get into a car with just anyone?'

'Might not have been a stranger,' Knox persisted. 'Yasmin would know the Sheron family. We haven't ruled them out yet and Hasan drives a minicab. It would be the most natural thing in the world for him to offer her a lift.'

'It's risky though in broad daylight. Chances are that someone would remember seeing him.'

'Except that it's exactly the kind of commonplace occurrence that most people don't notice,' said Knox, quite accurately. 'The alternative leaves us looking at a total unknown, perhaps connected to the earlier attacks on the university campus, which would stand out even more.'

'And there are no reports of anyone in the area seeing or hearing anything out of the ordinary on Tuesday afternoon,' said Millie. 'Implying that Yasmin did nothing to draw attention to herself. Even though term has ended, there are still quite a few students around.'

In the silence that followed Mariner conducted an internal debate about whether to voice what had been nagging at him now for some time. Eventually he had to come out with it. 'What we haven't yet given any thought to is the possibility that Yasmin could have stayed on the train and got off at a different stop.' No one had even considered it because they didn't want to — Fiske had effectively driven them off that particular scent.

'Jesus,' said Knox. 'If Yasmin stayed on the train she could have gone into the city. That would really open things up.'

'But we saw her on the CCTV,' Millie reminded them. 'We watched her get off the train at the university.'

'Did we, though?'

To humour him they loaded the video and watched again, comparing the two clips. 'See, to me it doesn't look like the same person,' he said. 'The gait is different.'

'How can you tell?' said Millie. 'She's running on the first, walking on the second.'

'I know, but it still doesn't look right to me. The second girl is of a slightly bigger build.'

'There's not much in it,' said Knox, peering at the screen.

'No, that's true.'

'So it could just be camera angle.'

Mariner was getting the distinct impression that he was alone on this. Everyone else wanted, understandably, to believe that Yasmin had, as usual, got off the train at the university. It would make their lives so very much simpler.

'If she went into the city she could have gone anywhere.' Knox put their thoughts into words. It opened up the possibilities of London, Glasgow — anywhere in the country in fact.

'But she had no money and, as far as we know, wasn't planning to meet anyone,' Millie reminded them.

'As far as we know.' But Mariner was increasingly beginning to feel that, where Yasmin Akram was concerned, they'd barely even scratched the surface.

'It still brings us back to the *likelihood* of someone she knows being behind it,' said Knox, making for safer ground.

'Sure, statistically we have to consider the immediate family,' conceded Mariner. 'Mum and Dad have been less than forthcoming all the way along, which makes me wonder what else they haven't told us. But it's a long way off any kind of motive. We need to do some more digging, folks.'

Mariner's phone rang and Millie picked it up. Cupping the handset, she held up a hand. 'Wait. I think we might have something,' she said.

CHAPTER 12

The call nearly hadn't made it past the incident room, due to the perceived reticence of the caller, who'd had a change of heart halfway through. One of the less experienced civilian staff had fielded it and almost logged it as a time-waster. It was only thanks to the intervention of a more experienced girl named Tanya, who'd recognised its importance, that it hadn't been missed completely. She played back the recording of the initial contact.

'Hello, is that the police?' It was the voice of a young woman, timid and hesitant. It didn't sound to Mariner like any of Yasmin's school friends.

'You're through to the incident room, yes.' A pause. 'How can I help? Do you have some information?'

'Yes. No. I don't know.'

'Who's speaking please?'

'I can't tell you that.'

'That's okay. Is it about Yasmin Akram?'

'There's something you should know.' Another long pause, broken only by the uneven rasp of shallow breathing: someone poised on the brink of a decision.

'What is it you want to tell me?' asked Tanya, kindly.

'Nothing. No, sorry. It's nothing—' A click and then the empty line hummed.

Mariner exhaled, suddenly aware that he'd been holding his breath throughout the exchange. 'You said you'd traced it?' he asked Tanya.

'It's a doctor's surgery in Edgbaston.' She gave them the address.

'It's a couple of streets away from the Akrams',' remarked Millie. 'The family GP?'

'I bet the doctor didn't make that call. She was young, less confident.'

Praising Tanya for her vigilance, Mariner called to verify the number and check the surgery's opening hours. He didn't want to scare anyone off so he'd do this alone.

* * *

By ten thirty he was parked outside the converted bungalow and watching the last of the patients leave after morning surgery. When he'd seen no one enter or exit for a full ten minutes, he locked the car and walked up the footpath. Behind the desk, the young receptionist was still hard at work, her faced tense with concentration as she entered data into a computer.

Taking a gamble Mariner walked up to the desk and showed her his warrant card along with what he hoped was a friendly smile. 'Hi,' he said quietly. 'Did you make a telephone call at eight fifty-four this morning?'

Wide brown eyes looked up into his as she considered her options. 'How did you—?' Her voice was just a whisper but Mariner recognised it at once. He heard a door open behind him.

'Is everything all right, Nadine?' Mariner turned to see an older woman, mid-forties perhaps, with dark, penetrating eyes. She barely came up to his shoulder. More Middle East than Asian sub-continent, her short greying hair was swept back off her forehead and she was casually but immaculately dressed in slacks and a sleeveless blouse.

115

'I'm Dr Shah. This is my practice,' she said, regarding him with some curiosity.

'DI Mariner.' He let her see his ID. 'I'm the senior officer investigating the disappearance of Yasmin Akram,' Mariner explained. 'I think Nadine might have contacted our incident room this morning with some information, but unfortunately the call was terminated before she was able to pass it on.'

'Nadine?'

The girl's eyes flicked from one to the other of them, finally resting on her boss as she nervously licked her lips.

'Come into the consulting room,' Dr Shah said to Nadine. 'I'll make some tea.' She turned to Mariner. 'I don't know what's going on here but, if you don't mind, I'd like to talk to Nadine alone first. Yasmin is a patient here, so I should make sure that anything Nadine has to tell you is not likely to be in breach of confidentiality.'

Mariner fought down his frustration. 'If Yasmin is in some kind of danger then patient confidentiality may be an irrelevance,' he said. 'It's important that we have access to any information that will help us to find her.'

'I appreciate that, Inspector, but I would ask you to respect my professional judgement. Yasmin is my patient and needs to know that she can trust me. Any decision about what to tell you is mine and mine alone. I will listen to what Nadine has to say. If I consider that there is anything that will help in your investigation without compromising my relationship with Yasmin then I will allow her to pass it on.'

Mariner had no other option than to wait. While the two women were closeted in the doctor's consulting room, he paced the waiting room outside like an expectant father. Then abruptly the door opened and Dr Shah appeared looking grim-faced. 'Inspector, I think you should join us.'

In the tiny room Mariner pulled up a chair facing the two women.

'It is with reluctance that I tell you this,' said Dr Shah. 'But if it does, as you say, put Yasmin in danger then I would be unable to forgive myself for not passing on this information. I would just ask that you use it judiciously.'

'Of course,' said Mariner.

'I've been the GP for Yasmin and her family for nearly ten years, so I know Yasmin very well. About six weeks ago, Yasmin came to see me because she wanted to begin taking the contraceptive pill.'

'The pill?' Mariner could barely contain his surprise. It flew in the face of everything they'd been told so far about the girl.

'You understand that ordinarily I would not be telling you this.' The doctor was still wrestling with the dilemma.

'You're doing the right thing,' Mariner said.

The doctor seemed less convinced, but she continued. 'At seventeen Yasmin is, of course, technically above the age of consent, but knowing her family's traditional views I also was more than a little surprised by the request. She openly told me that she had not discussed this with either of her parents and had felt unable to do so. But as we talked it over it became clear that Yasmin was already seeing someone and intended to proceed with or without my help.'

'I see,' was all that Mariner could muster. So much for honesty and openness with her parents, he thought.

'She seemed a little apprehensive,' Dr Shah continued. 'But made it clear that she was going ahead with the physical relationship and wanted to have some control over protecting herself. Yasmin is a bright girl and had clearly thought this through. The logical thing for me to do was to at least prevent her from getting into difficulty. I also agreed that I would respect her privacy in this matter.'

'So her parents don't know.'

'That's right.'

'And you're sure that Yasmin is in a relationship?'

'Of course, I can't be absolutely certain, but that's what she told me. I had no reason to disbelieve her.'

'Did she mention a name?'

'That side of it really isn't my business.'

'Well, thank you, Dr Shah. That certainly adds a new dimension to our investigation.'

Dr Shah looked over at Nadine, who had sat silent throughout. 'There is a little more to it,' she went on. 'Contraceptive pills affect women differently and I wanted to ensure that Yasmin would have no side-effects with the one I prescribed, so initially she had only a month's course as a kind of trial. The plan was that if she was happy with it she would come back for a full six months' prescription, which she did, at the beginning of last week.

'On the day Yasmin came in for her repeat prescription our computer system was down so I wasn't issuing any non-urgent prescriptions. I feel that those printed are preferable as there can be no query about the interpretation of handwriting. Yasmin didn't need the pills immediately so we agreed that as soon as it was ready the prescription would be left at reception for her to collect when she could. The following day our computer was working again, so I prepared the prescription and it was put in the envelope marked with Yasmin's name to await collection.' She turned to the receptionist. 'Tell the inspector what happened, Nadine.'

The girl cast Mariner an anxious look. 'Mr Akram has also been receiving ongoing treatment for high blood pressure.' Somehow that didn't come as any surprise to Mariner. 'He came into the surgery to collect a repeat prescription and he must have seen the envelope with Yasmin's name on it. He asked if it was for his daughter. He gave me her address and date of birth, and I checked and found that it was hers, so I gave it to him to pass on to her.'

'Isn't that against the rules?'

Nadine's face told him that it was. 'I'm really sorry.'

'She is new to the job,' Dr Shah said. 'We have talked about this, but clearly I didn't place enough emphasis. I must take full responsibility.'

'So you handed Mr Akram a prescription for his daughter for the contraceptive pill that he had no idea she was taking? Did he look at it?'

'No, he left the surgery. But he must have looked at it when he got outside, because he came back a few minutes later and wanted to know why Yasmin had been to the doctor and what was wrong. When I said I didn't know he started to get angry. He demanded to know what the prescription was for.'

'And you told him.'

'I recognised it and I didn't think. I said I thought it was for a contraceptive pill.' The girl was dying inside and Mariner almost felt sorry for her.

The doctor rushed to her defence. 'To be fair, that is almost irrelevant. Mr Akram could have walked into any pharmacy or accessed any number of internet sites to find that out. The damage had already been done.'

'What was Mr Akram's reaction when you told him what the prescription was?'

'He was furious. He didn't say much but I could see from his face. I told him that the pills could be to help regulate Yasmin's menstrual cycle and help with period pain. I had to do the same thing once . . . but he didn't listen. He wanted to speak to Dr Shah and when I said she was out on her rounds, he stormed out.'

'Did he come back?'

'No.' Dr Shah provided the answer.

'Who did you think he was angry with, Nadine?'

'Me, Dr Shah, Yasmin, maybe? I don't know' Being forced to face the implications of what had happened for the first time, Nadine's voice cracked and again she wiped away a tear. Dr Shah put a protective arm around her.

'Thank you,' Mariner said to the doctor. 'I appreciate you sharing this with me. I understand what a difficult decision it has been.'

When Nadine was calm again, Dr Shah walked him out. 'I may never know if I've done the right thing, but that's something I'll have to live with.'

'I feel sure that you have,' said Mariner. 'If it helps us to find Yasmin—'

'When I saw the news of her disappearance I recognised her of course, but the talk has been of racially motivated abduction, and I thought you would naturally find out about any boyfriend through Yasmin's friends. Nadine didn't even tell me about her mistake because she was afraid she would lose her job.'

'And will she?'

'I think everyone should be allowed to get things wrong at least once, don't you?'

Given the number of times he'd screwed up over the years, Mariner felt he was hardly in a position to argue.

* * *

Back at Granville Lane, Mariner was keen to have Millie's take on this news and asked the key question: 'How do you think Akram would have reacted to this?'

'He'd have gone ballistic,' she said, bluntly.

'Hm, that's what I thought.'

'Several things would have upset him: the fact that Yasmin was in a relationship—'

'The receptionist didn't tell him that. He might have accepted her explanation that Yasmin was taking the pill for other reasons.'

'But he'd be annoyed that Yasmin had gone behind his back to arrange contraception and that the surgery had complied.'

'So, as Nadine said, his anger could have been directed at the doctor's practice?'

'He didn't get back to Dr Shah to complain though, did he? I think he'd have been far more upset by the fact that Yasmin might be seeing someone. If he didn't buy Nadine's explanation for the pill then there's probably little worse that Yasmin can have done to anger him. He's already told us how "innocent" she is and now he's suddenly being told he might be wrong about that. We know that arranged marriage is one aspect of Muslim life that the Akrams subscribe to. If it became public knowledge that Yasmin was sleeping around it would make it harder for her parents to find her a husband of any standing. And that would be important to family like the Akrams. They value their reputation in the community and made a good match for their older daughter. They'd want the same for Yasmin. Previous relationships might limit the possibilities. She would be soiled goods.'

'And this is more information they've chosen not to share with us,' said Mariner.

'It would damage the family's pride and reputation. They wouldn't be keen to share it with anyone. It wouldn't be great publicity for their school either, to have their own daughter flouting fundamental Islamic beliefs. Part of the reason many parents choose Islamic schools is to protect them from exactly this kind of thing: the corruption of the outside world.'

'Hasan Sheron wasn't so very far off the mark after all then. How strongly do you think Akram would react to this knowledge?'

'Well, we already know that Mohammed Akram doesn't take things lying down,' said Millie. 'That would be especially true where his daughter's concerned. And we know that he has a short temper.'

'So now, suddenly, we're presented with a fat, juicy motive. No wonder he's been trying to divert our attention elsewhere. Would it give Akram enough reason to harm Yasmin?'

'You've come across honour killings before?' said Millie.

'Abdullah Yones,' said Mariner in reply. 'Stabbed his sixteen-year-old daughter twenty-eight times, for wearing makeup and having a boyfriend. Someone in the community had called her a prostitute.'

'Exactly,' said Millie. 'Her behaviour was an affront to his honour.'

'But Yones was Kurdish.'

'It happens across lots of cultures though. In Pakistan, Samia Sarwar was shot dead with a gun disguised as her mother's walking stick, right in front of her lawyer.'

'You think Mohammed Akram is capable of it?'

'I'm saying it happens, that's all,' said Millie.

'And perhaps Akram wouldn't have needed to go that far,' said Mariner.

'What do you mean?'

'Well, on that Tuesday afternoon Akram travelled up to the school in Bradford. He's got contacts up there. Maybe it would be enough to get Yasmin away for a time. It may even be that he's planning to spirit her away abroad into an arranged marriage before her reputation becomes public knowledge. Remember it was the school who reported Yasmin missing and when we first went to talk to the Akrams he seemed almost irritated with his wife that she'd raised the alarm? He said: "you should have waited." We took it as being a control thing, but perhaps he had planned to let Mum in on it.'

'So why not just come clean about it now? He knows what we're putting into this investigation.'

'Because the timing's wrong,' suggested Mariner. 'If it hasn't been followed through yet he can't afford to disclose it. And he might not want to tell his wife in case she gives the game away or tries to prevent it. By reporting Yasmin missing and involving us straight away, Shanila could have provided her husband with the perfect smoke screen, but one he'd have to keep in place until the job is done.'

'If Akram knows that Yasmin is safe, he's a hell of an actor,' said Millie. 'Remember how anxious he was during the appeal?'

'He's worried about us. In any other circumstances Akram is a law-abiding man.'

'But what he's doing is the best thing for his daughter and his family. He wouldn't hesitate to bend the rules, but he'd also know that at the very least it's a gross act of deception. He wouldn't be comfortable with that.' Millie seemed to have picked up the logic of what he was saying.

'But family comes first,' he said. 'So Dad plays along with the general view that Yasmin has gone missing until she is married off and it's too late to do anything about it. Forcing Yasmin into a marriage against her will is hardly likely to be what she wants.'

Millie agreed. 'And it's a major human-rights infringement. There are all kinds of pressure groups who'd weigh in if he was exposed. None of which would enhance Akram's image as an enlightened, westernised Muslim.'

'The other alternative is that Akram genuinely doesn't know where Yasmin is because she has run away,' said Mariner. 'From what we're learning about her, Yasmin doesn't sound like the kind of girl who's going to sit around and let herself be coerced into a marriage she doesn't want, however necessary her parents might think it is.'

'Either way we need to get Mohammed Akram's side of the story,' said Millie.

'One other thing we haven't found out yet,' said Mariner.

'What?'

'If Yasmin is on the pill because she's in a relationship — who the hell is it with? Someone's keeping a low profile.'

'The relationship was obviously a secret one. I think we can assume the boyfriend knows the way Akram would react too.'

CHAPTER 13

At Allah T'ala, Mariner's call was put straight through to Mohammed Akram. 'There's news?' His hope was palpable. If he was covering up he was doing a brilliant job.

'No, I'm sorry, Mr Akram,' Mariner said. 'But I do need to speak to you again. I wondered if I could meet you at your home. You may prefer to speak to us without your wife.'

'Why would I want to do that?' He seemed genuinely confused.

'I'd like to talk to you about an incident that occurred at your doctor's surgery last week.'

Silence, then: 'I see. I'll meet you at the house.'

* * *

Akram's Mercedes was already parked on the looped tarmac drive when Mariner pulled in behind it. He was surprised when the door was answered by a pretty young woman in purple and black *salwar kameez*. 'Amira,' she introduced herself. 'I'm Yasmin's older sister. I flew in this morning to give some support to my parents until Yasmin is found.' So the tired eyes in such a young face could have been jet-lag or worry. If this was some kind of scam

Mariner doubted that Amira was in on it. 'My father is in the garden. I'll take you to him.'

Mohammed Akram was sitting on a wooden bench in a shaded patch at the bottom of an expanse of sun-scorched lawn that was crowded on all sides with shrubs. He was tie-less and the sleeves of his dress shirt were rolled up and he leaned forward in his seat, poised for action. A collection of other garden chairs was scattered around him and Mariner took his chance on a flimsy white plastic affair. Amira did the same.

Mariner glanced up at the elder daughter. 'Mr Akram, what we have to talk about may be a little sensitive—' he began, but Akram stopped him.

'I want Amira to hear it. At some point I have to tell my wife, so I would like Amira to know.' He seemed fidgety, exuding nervous energy, but then he already knew that this was going to be a difficult conversation.

'All right then,' said Mariner. 'As I indicated on the phone, I have some questions regarding your visit to Dr Shah's surgery. I understand that you had an appointment there last Friday?'

Akram's eyes narrowed. 'How did you find out about this?'

'We have been in touch with Dr Shah.' There was no need to tell him who initiated the contact.

'She had no right—'

'Mr Akram, how we came by this information at this stage is irrelevant. We would have got to it eventually through routine checks on Yasmin's medical history. For Dr Shah it was a difficult decision to make. Like the rest of us, she is worried about Yasmin's whereabouts, but she only found out today what had happened. Would you like to tell me about it now, in your own words and then you may want to explain why you kept this from me.'

Akram looked suddenly exhausted. 'That one's easy,' he said. 'I didn't tell you because this is our family business. I'm not proud of how I reacted — overreacted

— at the surgery and it really has nothing to do with Yasmin's disappearance. We had discussed the situation and resolved it.'

Just like that, thought Mariner. 'I'd still like you to tell me,' he said.

Akram sighed. 'It's only what I expect you already know. On Friday afternoon I went to Dr Shah's surgery to collect my repeat prescription. I was making a further appointment when I noticed an envelope with Yasmin's name on it. I asked if it was for my daughter. I had no idea that it contained a prescription. Girls, women, they have regular health checks and I thought that perhaps it was some kind of reminder. The receptionist asked my address and Yasmin's date of birth. When the details corresponded with what was inside, she let me have it.'

'And you opened the envelope.'

To his credit, Akram didn't look pleased with himself, but then he'd had ample time to concoct this little charade. 'There was nothing on the envelope to say that it was confidential and I thought if it was an appointment Shanila and I would need to think about how we would get Yasmin to it.'

'And when you saw that it was a prescription?'

'I was surprised. I wasn't aware that there was anything wrong with Yasmin or that she had been to see the doctor. Normally Shanila would tell me about anything like that. I went back into the surgery and asked the receptionist. She said she thought it was for a type of contraceptive pill.'

'And you were surprised?'

'Inspector, I was everything you would expect me to be: shocked, horrified, angry and disappointed. I couldn't understand why Yasmin would need this and I was angry with our GP for having written such a prescription without telling me or my wife. She's just a child.'

'You were certain your wife didn't know?' asked Mariner.

'Shanila and I don't have secrets, especially about our children.'

Yet Shanila allowed Yasmin to go to her friend's against your wishes, thought Mariner. He tried to catch Amira's eye but she was gazing intently towards the house, her face troubled by what she was hearing. Instead he said: 'Doctors have certain rules of confidentiality they must-'

Again the anger flared up. 'Yasmin is only seventeen. She doesn't mix with boys. What would she want with the contraceptive pill? What sort of country is this where professionals can make decisions about a child's life without the knowledge of her parents?'

'So you were angry, Mr Akram.'

'At first, yes.'

'Who were you angry with?'

'The receptionist, the doctor, for writing this prescription without my knowledge and, I felt sure, without my wife's knowledge too.'

'And Yasmin? Were you angry with her?'

'Yes, I suppose I was.'

'You said you were angry "at first?"' said Mariner.

'The girl on reception told me that the pills could have been prescribed to control Yasmin's menstrual cycle, that it could be perfectly innocent.'

'And did you believe that?'

'When I took some time to consider it, thought rationally about the facts, it seemed the only reasonable explanation.'

'So you accepted it.'

'It was obviously something I needed to discuss with Yasmin,' Akram said.

'And when did you do that?' Mariner asked.

'I went to meet her from school. I thought we would be able to talk about it in the car on the way home.'

'And did you?'

'When I arrived outside the school Yasmin came out with Suzanne and some other girls. She wasn't pleased to see me. She didn't want a lift, she wanted to walk with her friends. Yasmin doesn't like to show how much she cares about her family in front of them. I told her I wanted to talk to her about something, but she said we had the whole weekend. Suzanne said something to her. She is an interfering b—' Akram stopped himself. 'She had probably put Yasmin up to it.'

'What makes you think that?' asked Mariner.

'The girl has a reputation for being easy with boys. You only have to look at her clothing: it's indecent. She was encouraging Yasmin to behave the same way.'

'Is that the real reason you wouldn't let Yasmin go to Suzanne's house?' asked Mariner.

'That girl is a bad influence,' Akram said, his mouth set in a hard line.

'Did you give Yasmin a lift?'

'Only from the university station. I went and waited for her there when she got off the train. I drove her home and we talked about it then. It wasn't a conversation I wanted brought into the house.'

'And what did Yasmin tell you?'

'She told me the same thing as the receptionist, that she was on the pill to control her periods. They had been irregular and uncomfortable and the doctor thought the pill would alleviate those symptoms. She hadn't thought it necessary to tell her mother or me.'

'Did you believe her?' Mariner watched him carefully.

'I wanted to. Yasmin is growing up. There are certain ways in which we must respect her privacy.'

'That doesn't answer my question. Mr Akram, what would you say if I told you that Yasmin had given the doctor a different story?'

'What do you mean?' He looked up at Mariner.

'Yasmin told Dr Shah that she *needed* to go on the pill, because she was in a relationship that was already physical.' He was deliberately testing Akram to measure the reaction, but to his credit Akram looked genuinely shocked.

'Yasmin denied that and I believed her,' he said.

'So you wouldn't have given Yasmin the impression that you were angry with her? You didn't, for example, raise your voice to her.'

'I might have,' said Akram. 'I was upset.'

'Is it possible that your behaviour could have prompted Yasmin to run away?'

'Yes, of course it's possible.' Sitting back, Akram pushed a hand through his hair. 'Do you think I haven't already thought of that?'

'If Yasmin was seeing someone, a boy, have you any idea who that might be?' Mariner asked him.

Akram fixed Mariner with his gaze. 'Yasmin denied it and she wouldn't lie to me. As far as I'm concerned she has no contact with any boys.'

Mariner paused a beat, studying him, before saying: 'Thank you, Mr Akram.' It brought the interview to a close.

Amira got to her feet. 'I'll show you out.' She took Mariner back up the garden and round the side of the house to his car. When they were out of earshot of her father she said: 'Inspector, it might be helpful for you to know that I can't be as sure as my father that Yasmin wasn't in a relationship. I know that for some months she had been coming under pressure from her friends to live a little. She couldn't talk to my parents about it, but she often rang me for my advice.'

'And what did you advise her to do?'

'I told her to relax. That virginity isn't as important as our parents seem to think and that if an opportunity came along that she wanted to take, with someone she trusted, then she should take it.'

'And has that opportunity come along?' asked Mariner.

She flashed an apologetic smile. 'That's what I don't know.'

* * *

130

Millie met Mariner as he came back into the building at Granville Lane. 'How did it go?'

'Akram certainly seems upset by it all.'

'Guilt,' concluded Millie.

'Trouble is, what kind of guilt? Is he feeling guilty because he knows what's happened to Yasmin and he's stringing us along, or because maybe he's prompted his daughter to run away?' Mariner fed back what Amira had told him, too.

'It would be interesting to get Suzanne's perspective on that story,' said Millie. 'If Yasmin is seeing someone, she'll be the one to know.'

'We'll talk to her on Monday.'

'Yes, sir.' Millie hesitated, about to say something else.

'And?' prompted Mariner.

'Tony Knox,' Millie said. 'Is he all right?'

'In what way?' asked Mariner regretting the hint of defensiveness that he knew was in his voice. It was enough to put her off.

'It's okay. Nothing, I'm sure.'

'His mother-in-law's ill,' said Mariner. 'He's just worried, that's all.' Mariner hoped it was true. He wasn't oblivious to the fact that Knox and Millie didn't seem to have established much of a working relationship when he wasn't there. He'd never seen Tony Knox as a racist, but then the situation that would highlight it hadn't arisen before.

Millie shrugged. 'Yeah, like I said, it's nothing.'

* * *

Nonetheless Mariner took the next opportunity to quiz Knox. 'How are you getting on with Millie?'

Knox seemed surprised by the question. 'Fine,' he said.

'She's a good officer,' Mariner went on. 'I think she's brought an added dimension to the investigation.'

'Yeah.'

Mariner had successfully backed himself into a corner. The next question should have been: *And do you have a problem with her being Asian?* Instead he took the easy way out. 'How's Theresa's mother?' he asked.

'What?'

'Theresa's mother. I take it she's still up there looking after her?'

'Oh, yeah, she's up and down, you know, but T'resa just wants to be there to make sure she's okay.' Knox stared into space, lost for a moment in his own thoughts, before turning his attention back to the database he was working on.

That was definitely it, Mariner thought. It was Theresa's mother that was the problem. Touching that a bloke could be so concerned about the mother-in-law . . .

* * *

A walk-through was scheduled for late Tuesday afternoon, the one-week anniversary of Yasmin's disappearance, and would provide an opportunity for the press and media to assemble to publicise the event to anyone who may have been in the area on the day that Yasmin vanished. Local newspapers, radio and TV were well represented and now that the case was gathering momentum there would be national coverage too. To maximise the potential for witnesses to come forward, they had to opt for the most likely scenario, based on Yasmin getting off the train at the university station as she would normally have done, and walking home. The length and complexity of the journey turned everything into a major production with three different camera crews on the train and at either end of the walk.

Mariner was pleased with the turn out. Even considering that many of the onlookers were in all probability there to rubberneck, the fact remained that the more people there were in attendance, the greater the chance was that Yasmin would continue to be the topic of everyday conversation. And the more she was talked about the greater the chance that someone, somewhere would recall seeing something of relevance last Tuesday afternoon. Posters of the seventeen-year-old adorned the walls of the railway station and officers distributed more of the flyers among the small crowd that had gathered, though Mariner couldn't imagine anyone who hadn't just jetted in from Mars being unfamiliar with that smiling snapshot.

The group of young girls from a neighbouring school, including the one who was to be Yasmin's double, had been carefully primed and taken several times through each step of the journey as Yasmin would have made it. Miraculously at the appointed time everything was ready and Mariner was able to give the instruction to begin. On cue the girls left the high school and began the walk down towards the railway station. A small crowd followed them, supervised by uniformed constables, but despite the numbers, an unnatural hush had descended, interrupted only by the staccato snapping of camera shutters.

On instruction, the girls waited at the top of the road leading down to the station until the train was seen approaching, so that 'Yasmin' could run for the train in the way that she had done on Tuesday. Today the train was several minutes late causing anxious moments while everyone stood about waiting for it. They'd been able to arrange for the original driver of the train to be back on duty, in the hope that his memory would be jogged, but as there was no routine ticket check on board they were relying on other passengers to have seen Yasmin. This was likely to prove difficult as at this time of the afternoon the trains going into the city were almost deserted, all the passenger traffic going in the opposite direction, out of the city, at the beginning of the rush hour.

An additional carriage had been laid on for press only. Based on the assumption that Yasmin had got on the train and continued her journey home they followed her to the university station from where she would have walked home. The route took them along the walkway through the university grounds and past the meadow where Helen Greenwood had encountered the flasher, confirming that it would have been all too easy for Yasmin to draw attention to an unwelcome approach from a stranger. It seemed more implausible than ever that anyone with a gram of common sense would attempt a random abduction in these surroundings and in broad daylight.

A film crew from the regional TV station was there to film this part of the journey and a clip would be broadcast the following evening on the regular *Crimestoppers* slot.

Before long the story would be national news, too. That would really open the floodgates to the time-wasters.

Mariner watched the beginning of the reconstruction before he and Knox drove across to the university to pick up the end. Despite his reservations, Mariner felt that it was going well and that they would have done enough to stir the memories of anyone who was around that Tuesday afternoon. What they really needed was one good, solid lead.

* * *

Mariner's wish was granted, but not from the expected source. The walk-through successfully concluded, he and Knox were on their way back to Granville Lane when the radio crackled into life.

'The manager at Currys electrical superstore has just phoned. He's got something you might be interested in.'

'Like what?'

'Yasmin Akram's mobile phone.'

* * *

In a move worthy of Starsky and Hutch, Knox made an illegal U turn at the next traffic lights and they drove to the retail park where the store was based. Even at this time on a weekday there was a steady stream of traffic in and out of the park. The garden centre next door was displaying everything to enhance the summer experience and they had to pick their way through barbecues, garden furniture and a display of potted plants.

Mariner walked into the electrical store, showed his warrant card and asked to speak to the manager. Mark Williams was an eager young man, clean cut in a dazzling white shirt with the company logo on the pocket. With a dramatic flourish, he put a plastic bag down on the counter. Mariner opened the bag and removed the only item: a purple mobile phone. 'A Nokia 3100 with a mauve oil and water removable cover,' said Williams, though whether the pride was in the phone itself or his own professional knowledge was hard to tell. 'The bloke who brought it in had found it. He came in to check the registration, so that he could return it.'

'He couldn't get that from the phone?'

Williams shook his head. 'It's pay-as-you-go so we had to track the owner on the system. As long as it's registered, every time one of these is bought it's logged with the company: in this case Nokia. You can check it out with anyone who sells the brand of phone. And this one matches up with Miss Yasmin Akram,' he said. 'As soon as I saw that, I knew whose it was, so I thought we should call you.'

'You thought right,' Mariner said. He looked around at the customers browsing the displays. 'Where's the guy who brought it in?'

'Mr Hewitt? He couldn't wait, but he left his address and his mobile number.'

'You let him go?'

Williams' face fell. 'He had to get back to work. I'm pretty sure he's kosher.'

'Let's hope he is, for your sake.'

Mariner called the mobile number. When it was picked up, after several rings, there was noise and disturbance in the background, animals yelping.

'Mr Hewitt?' Mariner enquired, over the din. 'You handed in Yasmin Akram's phone.'

'Yes, that's right.'

'We need to speak to you urgently. Where are you?'

'The animal rescue centre on Barnes Hill.' It explained the soundtrack.

'We'll be with you right away,' said Mariner. 'Don't go anywhere.'

'I wasn't planning to,' replied Hewitt cheerfully.

Meanwhile Knox had bagged up the phone so that they could drop it in at Granville Lane and have it sent on to forensics without delay. That tiny device could prove invaluable in the search for Yasmin Akram.

* * *

In this heat Birmingham could be navigated blindfold, from the acrid Longbridge paint shop to the sickly-sweet halo surrounding the Cadbury factory. The aroma that lingered over Barnes Hill was not entirely pleasant: antiseptic with a hint of dog crap. The pound was quiet, but for the persistent yapping of some kind of small breed dog. It was getting on Mariner's nerves before they even reached the office, but he guessed the staff working there must be immune to it.

'Be with you in a sec.' Paul Hewitt was processing paperwork in a tiny office just behind the reception desk. A lethargic Labrador wandered in out of the heat and plopped itself down in a basket in a corner of the room.

When Hewitt finally appeared, Mariner had a visual impression of a kind of understated Friar Tuck. Medium height and rotund, his shiny bald scalp circled by a fringe that resembled a tonsure. Large square-framed glasses rested on the bridge of his nose and his cheery smile completed the image. 'We'll use the training room,' he said. 'It'll be cooler in there.'

The room was indeed airier and had a table large enough to spread out the map that Mariner and Knox had brought with them.

'So, where did you find it?' asked Mariner.

'Kingsmead Reservoir,' Hewitt said, scanning the map, 'right here.' He jabbed a finger at a spot right on the edge of the map, just beside the blue blob that symbolised water.

Although he'd heard of it, Mariner's knowledge of Kingsmead Reservoir extended no further than a label on the incident room map; an uninhabited wilderness on the other side of the railway track to the station, between the main Birmingham to Bristol line and Birchill Lane. Once functional, the reservoir had ceased to be used after Birmingham began drawing water from the Elan Valley, storing it in the much larger Bartley Green reservoir. What they were looking at now bore that out. 'But that's in the middle of nowhere,' he said.

'I know,' agreed Hewitt.

'So what were you doing there?' asked Knox, more than a little pointedly.

Hewitt was unruffled. 'We got a call from St Clare's, the old folks' home that backs onto it, just here.' He put an index finger on the map. 'One of the old biddies there had got it into her head that she'd seen a man beating a dog. She thought he might have killed it.'

Something crawled up the back of Mariner's neck. 'When was this?'

'She mentioned it to the staff a few days ago, apparently, but nobody took her seriously. The old girl has her "senior" days, if you know what I mean. But she wouldn't let it drop. I think she must have driven them mad over the weekend with it, so to keep her happy they gave us a call, first thing this morning. I drove over with Sue, my partner, and had a look at the place she described. It took some finding, I can tell you. Even though Lillian — that's Lillian Cooper — showed us from her window where she saw it happen, it was still difficult to find a way in. We had to use the A—Z.'

'I'm not surprised,' said Mariner, looking again at the map. There was no obvious access to the site.

'When we got to it, there was no sign of any dog where the old dear said, but just to make sure we had a good hunt around, as far as we could — most of it's like an untamed jungle — and that was when we found the phone lying in the grass. We brought it back to the office, charged it up then keyed in to find the user identity. But because it's one of those pay-as-you-go phones I had to take it to somewhere so they could look up the name and address of the person who bought it. The Currys store's not far away. We've all seen the news bulletins so once they'd looked it up, it didn't take long to put two and two together.'

'Well, I'm very glad that you did,' said Mariner. 'This could be quite a breakthrough.' Suddenly he sensed that there was more. 'Was there anything else you wanted to tell us?'

Hewitt lowered his voice. 'I wouldn't want to be alarmist, but near where we found it there was brown stuff, sort of staining the grass. I didn't say anything to Sue, but it looked to me like blood.'

'We'll need you to take us to the exact spot, Mr Hewitt.'

Hewitt slapped his thighs, a little nervously Mariner thought. 'Whenever you like.'

CHAPTER 14

They drove the route that Hewitt had taken to get to the reservoir, past the railway station, over the line, past a pub called The Bridge and onto Birchill Lane. Flanked on one side by a public park and on the other by wild woodland, the wilderness was broken only by a tall and rambling building that looked as if it had once been a country house of some kind.

'That's the nursing home,' Hewitt said, just as the sign 'St Clare's' came into view. Just along from the home they passed the entrance road to a small industrial park, which was followed by another half a mile or so of sparse, unhealthy looking woodland, which gave way to a row of four derelict cottages. The houses were fenced in by heavy duty spike-topped railings, with a huge pair of steel framed, chain-link gates padlocked against trespassers. A board in the entrance announced that the land was on the market for development.

To the side, a narrow cinder-track service road curled round the back of the cottages into what might once have been their gardens, with perhaps an orchard, but was now an open piece of rough ground of about a quarter of an acre. And it was here that Hewitt took them, Knox easing the car cautiously over the uneven ground to avoid damaging the suspension. They drew to a halt in a small grassy clearing, pockmarked with litter and the sort of detritus left behind by glue sniffers. Here and there were areas of blackened grass where fires had been lit and an old filthy mattress lay on its side, springs spilling out of it like guts from a dead animal. Even in daylight any vehicle parked here would have been shielded from the view of houses on the opposite side of Birchill Lane by the cottages themselves, the trees and the rampant, overgrown shrubs.

'This was the nearest place I could find to park,' Hewitt said. 'I was hoping to find a way through somehow. I was encouraged by the fact that other people obviously use it.' He was referring to the tyre tracks carved out of the hard earth and the little heaps of dog-ends. 'When I looked around I saw that opening there in the trees.'

He'd done well to spot that, thought Mariner. It was nothing more than a small gap in the undergrowth. 'Lead the way,' he said.

By now it was well after seven, but time had drawn none of the heat or humidity out of the day and even in shirtsleeves they sweltered. Knox and Mariner followed Hewitt through the wasteland, along the only clear path that cut a swathe through the low undergrowth and the straggling birch trees that had provided the adjacent road with its name. The dirt underfoot had been hardened by the long, hot summer, but Mariner stopped at a small patch where water drained across the path's width, throwing up a couple of distinct footprints and a narrow tyre track, possibly belonging to a bike.

They smelt it before they saw it: a thick, peaty methane smell. Then, as the path meandered from one side to another, the trees began to thin to low shrubbery, then long grasses and suddenly the path broke out again into the glare of the evening sun, at the edge of the reservoir — if it could still be called that. Today it was simply an expanse of black mud, shrunken and dried by the drought, with a single broad channel flowing sluggishly across the centre from the far side, maybe five hundred yards away, towards where they were standing now. 'Kingsmead Reservoir,' Hewitt announced.

Mariner marvelled at how such an open expanse could exist on their patch without any of them really knowing about it. The size of three football fields, it was a vast and untamed open space, the water's edge crowded with willows and reeds and shoulder-high grasses. The land was bordered along the far side by the Birmingham to Bristol railway line and beyond that a high bank of distant houses: the 'cottages on the ridge' from which the community of Cotteridge had taken its name. The factory site took up much of the near side, almost as far as the trees they'd walked through, though it finished four hundred yards away behind substantial wood-panelled fencing. The only building that had any kind of direct view of the area was St Clare's.

'How could we not know about this?' Knox said.

'I'd heard about it.' Mariner admitted. 'It's part of the River Rea that runs down from the Lickey Hills right through the city and to Spaghetti Junction at the other end. It's been neglected for years but there has been some conservation group, the Rea Valley Trust I think it's called, working on areas further upstream to try and clear it and create footpaths and cycle tracks, that kind of thing. I've seen posters around advertising for volunteers.'

As they surveyed the scene, a train thundered by on the opposite side of the water; not the local train that Yasmin would have caught, but the Birmingham to Bristol express. They heard rather than saw it, the wooden fence hiding it from view and equally preventing any passengers from seeing anything on the reservoir. Anyone operating down here would know that they had almost complete privacy from prying eyes. The thought made Mariner shiver, despite the heat. Alongside the railway were the long production hangars of a glass manufacturer, separated from the track by a fifteen-foot wall topped with broken glass and razor wire. Anything along that stretch could be discounted as means of access.

They had come to a junction of sorts in the footpath. To the right was the rickety bridge that crossed the out-flow stream at the back of St Clare's, but going round to the left, skirting the edge of the reservoir, there were clear signs that other feet had trodden that path.

'We went this way,' said Hewitt, leading them round to the rotting structure of a bridge. Constructed from wooden planks it was in a state of disrepair, the boards mottled with holes, though sound enough to take their combined weight. On one side the railings were snapped in two. Underneath the structure, the water flowed reluctantly onto a square plate of deeply rusted metal, accumulating at a pair of wooden gates. Though firmly shut, there were enough crevices to allow the pathetic dribble of water to slowly insinuate itself through them to where it flowed limply over a concrete shelf and down into a narrow tunnel.

'So what's all this about?' Knox asked, peering over the edge.

'It looks like some kind of slow-release mechanism to make sure the reservoir doesn't go completely dry or flood,' Mariner said. 'They have them on some canals. As the reservoir fills, the pressure builds on that plate until it eventually gets unlocked by the weight and volume of water. The gates open and the water surges down the spillway into the tunnel.' But he was talking to himself. Knox had already lost interest.

Hewitt crossed the bridge to where the path broadened out slightly on the other side. 'This is where Lily said she saw the action and that was where we found the phone, lying just there,' he said, pointing to an area of longish grass just to the side of what would have been a path. 'And that's what I thought might be blood.' Initially camouflaged by shade, on closer inspection there was no missing the stains, which were as dark as creosote on the yellowing grass. Mariner's first thought was how Sue, Hewitt's partner, could have overlooked them.

'But where's our dog?' he murmured to himself. 'Is there a way down here from the station?' he asked looking up at the chain-link fence that separated them from the platforms and car park two hundred or so yards away.

'I think there used to be,' said Hewitt 'But I wouldn't know where exactly it comes out. I can't imagine that anybody uses it anymore because since the factory was demolished it wouldn't go anywhere. The industrial units block off the other side. If you wanted to get to Birchill Lane it would be much simpler to walk along the road instead.'

But considerably longer, thought Mariner making a visual sweep through 360 degrees. As a walker he was accustomed to scouring overgrown tracts of land for signs of a thoroughfare. Many times he'd come to a so-called public footpath across a field that some uncooperative farmer had planted over in the hope of discouraging ramblers. Only a few weekends ago he'd had to battle his way through a field of maize that had grown taller than him and completely obscured the right of way.

Generally speaking he wasn't alone in his determination and there were others who wouldn't be deterred, which meant that usually, as in this case, a soft line marking out the faintest traces of human disturbance could be seen. Nettles and cow parsley stems that elsewhere were waist-high had been snapped and crushed, the long grass swept over. He struck out along it a little way and was proved right. Though not well-used and with hardly a break in the solid foliage, it was a definite path, recently forged down from the back of the station to where they now stood and frequented perhaps three or four times since the early summer. The logical destination would be the cluster of low-level pre-fabricated units a quarter of a mile away, but the greenery in that direction looked undisturbed. 'What have we got there?' Mariner asked.

'Small businesses, that sort of thing,' Hewitt replied. 'There's a sign up on the road.'

'We should have a closer look,' Mariner told Knox. 'Meanwhile, I don't want everyone tramping around here like a herd of elephants just yet. We need to cordon off the area and get a team down here ASAP to do a thorough search.' He scanned the area. It wasn't going to be easy. The surrounding ground had been left to go wild for years and the grass was dense and impenetrable with some vicious looking brambles and nettles. Added to which they'd need to cover the disused cottages. It was all going to take valuable time and manpower. Meanwhile forensics could verify if the staining was indeed blood, though Mariner, from experience, was pretty sure that it was.

He looked at his watch. Gone eight o'clock. By the time they could get anything organised it would be getting on for nine and even at this time of year, the light would start going. In this hostile terrain it would be a nightmare. Despite the urgency, it would be better to have the light on their side to avoid missing anything. In only a few hours the sun would be coming up again.

'Okay, let's go,' he said to Knox. 'We'll get the area sealed off and do a thorough search first thing tomorrow.' They trekked back along the narrow path to where the car was parked and Knox could call through to Granville Lane to organise securing the site. They were just about to leave when a distant roar greeted their ears and another vehicle appeared in the mouth of the clearing, with a lone driver. Seeing the assembled group he applied his brakes, clearly considering whether to continue or to turn and retreat. Before he could decide, Mariner approached, arm outstretched, holding out his warrant card, Knox at his heels. When he was near enough to be clearly identified, the driver reacted with a resigned movement of the head and put on the hand brake.

'DI Mariner, Mr—?' Mariner bent to look in at the open driver's window.

'Pryce, Shaun Pryce,' the man obliged. 'It's all right. I'll come back another time.' He glanced up into the rear-view mirror as if to go, but Mariner had both hands on the sill of the door.

'Would you mind getting out of the car a minute, Mr Pryce?'

Standing alongside Mariner, Shaun Pryce was considerably shorter, a wiry young man of about thirty, his cropped platinum hair edged with lethal looking ginger sideburns. Testosterone oozed from every pore, his stylishly crumpled combats and faded black tank top displaying his muscular arms and shoulders to their fullest advantage, including a couple of elaborate tattoos. He saw Mariner looking at them.

'My personal *homage* to the Robster,' he said, pronouncing the word with an exaggerated French accent. 'That's where you've seen them before. So what's going on then?' he grinned, exposing perfect, gleaming white teeth, his eyes roving from one to the other of the policemen and Hewitt loitering in the background. Leaning back on the car door and folding his arms, Pryce was a picture of nonchalance, but kept a wary eye on Knox who was prowling around the battered VW Golf. Old and scruffy, the vehicle had bits of electrical equipment lying on the parcel shelf, including several coils of plastic sheathed wire. A flag of St George sticker decorated the rear window.

'What brings you here?' Mariner asked, ignoring the question.

'I saw the car and came to see what's going on,' said Pryce. 'I wanted to make sure it wasn't kids messing about. One day they'll set fire to the trees and the whole lot will go up.'

He was lying. No kids Mariner knew had access to a top-of-the-range Vauxhall Vectra, and it was unlikely that Pryce could have seen it from the road, but he let it go. 'So you've been here before,' he said instead.

Pryce shrugged. 'A couple of times. It's peaceful. Somewhere to come and unwind a bit.' As if to authenticate this pastoral image, an evening blackbird chose that moment to begin its repetitive song. For many people, Mariner included, Pryce's response might have been credible, but he just didn't look the type to derive his relaxation from a patch of scrubby rubbish-strewn grass.

Knox leaned in through the car's passenger window and retrieved something from the back seat. 'Come being the operative word, eh?' The magazine he'd retrieved displayed a full montage of photographs of naked women striking far from modest poses. That was more like it.

Unembarrassed by the find, Pryce smirked. 'You know how it is. I have a high sex drive,' he said, all innocence. 'I'm sure you can be a bit of a wanker sometimes, officer.'

'Where exactly do you do this unwinding?' Mariner asked. 'It must be a bit stuffy in the car this weather.'

'Just around.' Pryce's glance took in the general area, none of which looked the least bit inviting.

'Ever go onto the reservoir itself?' Mariner nodded towards the path they'd found.

Pryce shook his head. 'No.' He said it too quickly.

'Never?' Mariner queried. 'Why not?'

'No point. Why walk half a mile through the jungle when everything I need is here.'

'And when was the last time?'

'I couldn't really say. Like I told you, it's only occasionally. Couple of weeks ago, maybe.'

'Can you be a bit more precise?' Mariner pressed.

'I can't honestly remember.' Pryce glanced at his watch, anxious to go now.

'What time of day was it?' Mariner persisted.

'After work.'

'And what sort of work is it that you do, Mr Pryce?'

'Actually, I'm an actor.' So that was why he was enjoying this so much. Kid thought he was in an episode of *The Bill*. 'I'm resting at the moment, except for a bit of modelling but—'

'Been in anything I'd have seen?' challenged Knox.

'As I said, mostly modelling work, although I've been up for an audition for Jimmy Porter at the Rep.'

'I thought you said you came down here after work,' Mariner reminded him.

'When I'm resting I do electrics. I'm working on an extension.'

'Nearby?'

'Just up the road.'

'Ever seen anyone else down here?'

Pryce laughed. 'That's the whole fucking point. It's *private*.'

'Have you ever owned a dog, Mr Pryce?'

Understandably perhaps, the question took Pryce by surprise. 'No.'

Mariner opened the driver's door for him to get in.

'Aren't you going to tell me what's going on?' he asked.

'No.'

But Knox did take details of where he was working before they allowed him to get into his car and watched him reverse skilfully out of the clearing, and at speed.

'Thinks he's God's gift,' said Knox bitterly. 'And that flag of St George was conspicuous in the back window of his car.'

'He might not have put it there,' said Mariner. 'It's a pretty old car. He seemed more new age than National Front to me.'

'That hair though. Would have made any Aryan proud. Even though it was dyed. What do you think, boss?'

'As he admitted himself, he's a little tosser,' said Mariner. 'He didn't come down to check us out, he was surprised to see us. He braked as he came into the clearing.'

'And he's been here more than a few times,' Knox agreed. 'Not easy to reverse out avoiding those potholes, but he did it like a pro. I wouldn't rule out him going right onto the reservoir either. How else would he know it's half a mile of jungle unless he's been through it?'

'No. Shaun Pryce wasn't telling us anything like the truth,' said Mariner. 'The question is, is it because he knows something or is he hiding something else? Let's see if we've got him on our books.'

'Are we looking for anything special?'

'I don't know, but I think Shaun Pryce might be the kind of cocky little bugger who likes to play games.'

They took a last look around, but there was nothing more to be gained here. 'Okay, let's knock it on the head for tonight and get some sleep while we still can,' said Mariner. 'We'll start the search first thing in the morning.'

* * *

It was nearly ten by the time Mariner was ready to leave Granville Lane. He tried to phone Anna to let her know what was going on, but was wasting his time; all he got was her answering machine. It irritated him disproportionately. Looking up, he saw that Tony Knox was doing nothing more useful than staring into space. 'Do you want a lift home?' he asked. Mariner half-expected him to refuse, but this time Knox took the sensible option.

'Fancy a drink?' Mariner added, when they got to the car.

'All right.'

'Spoken like a man who has nothing better to do,' said Mariner. 'How could I fail to be flattered?'

They stopped off at The Boatman, Mariner's local, where tonight the garden seemed the most comfortable option. Even with a pint in front of him Knox's reticence continued and Mariner half-wished they hadn't bothered. 'We've been married too long,' he said, in an attempt at levity. 'Nothing to say to each other any more.'

Knox grimaced, before draining his glass. 'One more before the bell?'

Mariner had hardly started his. 'Okay,' he said, and gulped it down. What a waste. Minutes later Knox was back with two pints and a whisky chaser for himself. 'It's been a long day,' he said.

Mariner had no room to disagree. 'Cheers,' he said, before the silence set in again. 'So how do you think it got there?' said Knox suddenly.

'What?' Mariner was startled by the unprecedented verbosity.

'Yasmin Akram's phone,' Knox went on. 'It's on the other side of the track from where she would catch the Birmingham train.'

'She must have dropped it,' said Mariner. 'Someone else picked it up and took it there. If we're certain that she got on the train it's the only possibility.'

At last Knox appeared to engage. 'Well, we are certain, aren't we? The CCTV footage at this end is pretty clear. We all saw her getting *on* the train. You can't argue with that.'

'I wouldn't mind looking at that footage again though,' said Mariner.

'What for? We've no reason to think that she didn't board that train. Why the hell would she have been going down to the reservoir? There's nothing there.'

'Bearing in mind what Dr Shah has now told us, there already seems to be plenty we don't know about Yasmin. And what did you think about Paul Hewitt? Is he straight?'

'It was just a chance discovery. He and his partner were led to it and there must be plenty of other people involved who'll be able to corroborate that.'

Mariner was inclined to agree. 'It will be easy enough to check with the nursing home and with his partner, Sue.'

'I think it's much more likely someone else picked up Yasmin's phone and took it to the bridge,' said Knox.

'So how does that fit with what Lillian saw?'

'If she saw anything. Hewitt implied that the old girl might not have all her marbles.'

'The bloodstains are there all right.'

'Except that we don't know for certain that they are blood.'

Knox was right. They'd need forensic confirmation that it was human blood and if it was, the next step would be to get a DNA sample from the Akrams to make a comparison. He didn't relish that prospect one little bit.

'It could just be that whoever picked up Yasmin's phone was the guy who Lillian saw beating the dog,' Knox said, at last beginning to give it some real thought.

'I wouldn't rule out Shaun Pryce's involvement either,' said Mariner 'We know now that Yasmin was probably seeing someone. Do you think he could be our mystery man? She could have arranged to meet him anywhere between here and the station.'

But Knox picked on the obvious flaw. 'How would Pryce have known Yasmin? She's a school kid, he's an out-of-work actor and part-time leckie.'

Mariner sighed. 'And we still don't know for certain that there is a man. Yasmin could have invented him in an effort to appear more sophisticated than she really is. We haven't talked to Suzanne yet and it sounds as if there could be some competition going on between the two of them.'

'I do love a simple, straightforward case,' said Knox wryly.

Mariner scoffed. 'What's one of those?'

The thought was enough to render Knox sullen and morose all over again, and by the time Mariner dropped him off outside his house he was back to his monosyllabic self.

Mariner offered up a silent plea for Theresa to come back soon.

* * *

Mariner himself took the briefing at six the next morning, at the entrance to what had become overnight the official reservoir car park. As much manpower as possible had been mustered to conduct the second search and the area was packed with personnel. Finding Yasmin's phone had generated a new buzz of anticipation, introducing — thank God — a point of focus at last. As Fiske was quick to point out, it didn't negate the possibility of Yasmin getting on the train as usual, but suddenly the options had opened up again. The relevant portion of the map showing the reservoir had been enlarged and circulated, and Mariner split the group into teams of three to ensure that every square inch would be covered. 'We'll start with the more accessible areas; the land around, then if we need to, the water itself.' Though with the mud undisturbed that wasn't looking likely, and he was hoping it wouldn't be necessary.

Protective overalls, scythes and secateurs had been provided to assist with the mammoth task of hacking back the undergrowth, making the search party look like *Ground Force* on the rampage. The sun was already climbing steadily and Mariner had arranged for bottled water to be delivered. He didn't want anyone collapsing with dehydration.

Yasmin's phone was already at the lab where it would be checked for fingerprints and any messages analysed. Fortunately on a case like this it would take priority and could be rushed through in twenty-four hours. Mariner sincerely hoped they wouldn't come across anything more conclusive first.

CHAPTER 15

With the search underway, beneath the supervisory eye of DS Mark 'Jack' Russell, Mariner took Knox and went to the nursing home to talk to Lily, the woman who had witnessed the attack.

St Clare's retirement home had exactly the kind of stale hint-of-urine aroma that Mariner would have expected. Sharing his wavelength, Knox shuddered. 'God, I hate these places,' he said.

'One of our fastest growing industries,' remarked Mariner.

'But what's the point of festering away for years in a place like this? What kind of life is it? We're all living too long.'

His supporting argument was right in front of them. The office they'd been asked to wait in overlooked a kind of sun lounge, where high-backed easy chairs were grouped — most of them accommodating an elderly resident, even at this early hour. It was probably like hospitals, Mariner thought, everyone roused at the crack of dawn whether they liked it or not. Close to the TV two elderly ladies stared fixedly at some kind of morning chat show, although whether either of them was actually watching was impossible to tell. A uniformed nurse came and spoke to one of them. She looked about sixteen, ludicrously young to be carrying out intimate tasks for people who must be old enough to be her grandparents. Mariner wondered how his mother would get on in a place like this, but somehow he couldn't picture it. She'd be the world's worst resident. 'They're all white,' he said, suddenly noticing the fact. 'Mohammed Akram's mother won't end up in a place like this.'

'Mr Mariner? I'm Nora.' The woman who breezed in was the member of staff Lily had confided in. A sensible, solid woman of around fifty, Nora's considerable bulk was contained by the starched blue nurse's uniform worn by all the staff. 'Do you mind if we go outside? I'm gasping for a fag.' Gasping was the word. As they walked, Nora wheezed in rhythm with her stride, leaving Mariner wondering how she coped with such a physically demanding job. They stood outside the front door in the shade of a dripping lime as traffic roared by on Birchill Lane just a few yards away.

'Can you tell us what happened on Tuesday afternoon?' Mariner said.

Nora flicked ash onto the path. 'It was tea time,' she told them. 'Lily was in the dining room along with all the other residents when she said she didn't feel well. She's still fairly independent, so we just suggested that she should go back to her room and have a lie down. When I went up a little later to check on her, she was standing transfixed, in the middle of the room, just staring out of the window. She was in some distress. I thought she'd had a funny turn or something, but when I asked if she was all right she grabbed my arm and said we mustn't, under any circumstances, let Casper out because she'd just seen a wicked man beating a dog to death down by the reservoir. I got her to show me, but of course when we looked out of the window there was nothing to see.

'I didn't think any more of it then because although generally speaking Lily's one of our more lucid clients, she does have her moments. Casper was the cat she left behind when she moved in here two years ago, so she was clearly getting a bit confused. When I reminded her of this she realised her mistake, but I could see that something had upset her. Anyway, I helped her into bed and thought it was over and forgotten. But a few days later, Lily said she hadn't been able to sleep for thinking about the poor dog, so I asked her to show me again where she'd seen it.

'She told exactly the same story and the description of what she saw was absolutely consistent. She swore that she'd seen this man and that the dog could only be dead. As it seemed to be bothering her so much I thought the least I could do was humour her, so I called the RSPCA. I hoped they'd be able to go and have a look and confirm that there was no dead dog. And Lily would be reassured to know that she'd been mistaken. There was nothing to lose.' She looked from one to the other of them. 'The man I spoke to said they found blood.'

'Well, we haven't established what it is just yet,' said Mariner. 'But it would be helpful if we could speak to Lily herself, in case there's anything else she remembers. Would she be up to that?'

'I think so.'

'Would any other of the residents have seen anything?' Knox asked.

'No,' Nora said. 'Everyone else was in the dining room on the ground floor, which looks out over the side garden.'

'You said this happened at tea time.' Mariner checked his notes. 'What time would that have been?'

'About quarter to five.'

Twenty minutes after Yasmin had said goodbye to her friends and disappeared off the face of the earth. Mariner didn't like that timing one little bit.

* * *

154

Inside they trooped up a winding staircase to Lily's room, a twelve-by-twelve box of floral wallpaper and chintzy fabrics. The bed was covered with a peach-coloured candlewick bedspread. On top of the mahogany chest of drawers were assorted remnants of her life: a few photographs and a couple of porcelain figurines alongside a varnished conch shell purporting to be a gift from Bridlington. It didn't seem much to show for eighty-odd years on the planet. Still, as people were so fond of saying: you can't take it with you. The view from the window wasn't much to speak of either, overlooking as it did the jungle of yellowing scrubland that encircled the reservoir. Naturally Lily had her windows open and even up here you could smell the sour, stagnant water. Mariner's heart sank when Lily turned out to be a frail old woman with whiskers sprouting from a face that was as lined and furrowed as the dry ground outside. Her sparse silvery hair had been permed into tight curls, exposing patches of scalp as pink and smooth as a baby's flesh and the cotton frock she wore hung loosely on her withered frame. She was perched on an armchair, her eyes closed, but she opened them as they arrived, huge blue irises staring at them through the full-strength lenses of her glasses.

'Lily, these are the policemen I told you about,' Nora said, in a chivvying tone. 'They just want to ask you some questions.'

'Anything you like,' said Lily, surprisingly gamely, once she'd come round. 'I know what I saw.' Perhaps she would turn out to be a decent witness after all.

'I'll get some chairs,' said Nora, returning moments later with a couple of the moulded plastic variety, which she arranged next to the old lady. Mariner sat, but Knox maintained a disinterested distance, staring out of the window.

'Can you tell us exactly what you did see?' Mariner asked.

'It was tea time, but I didn't feel like eating, especially the rubbish that they give us here: ratty-twee or some such foreign muck.' Mariner waited for Nora to contradict her, but then saw the glint in Lily's eye. Why had he assumed that because she was old, she'd have no sense of mischief? 'Anyway, I came up here, into my room and I could see someone down there on the bridge. I saw him straight away because there's never anyone down there and the movement was . . . well . . . aggressive. He was swinging his arm up and down, up and down, hitting something on the ground.'

'Can you show me where?' Mariner asked.

Using the armrests for support, Lily got shakily to her feet and she and Mariner joined Knox at the window, looking out at where the yellowing grass with its dark kernel was swarming with police officers, moving laboriously through the undergrowth, heads bowed as if performing some ancient religious ritual.

'He was right next to that little wooden bridge,' Lily said, pointing towards it, 'the one with the broken railings, to the left of it where the long grass starts again.' Nothing wrong with her eyesight then.

'Was he standing or kneeling?' Mariner asked.

'He was standing, his legs akimbo but he was stooped over, low.'

'Could you see his face?'

'No, he had his back turned to me. He just kept swinging his arm up and down, up and down.' Her eyes watered. 'That poor little defenceless creature.'

'The dog,' said Mariner.

'Yes.'

'Could you see what colour it was, this dog?' Mariner peered out. It was unlikely that she could have. If what she said was right, the creature would have been hidden by the tall grass.

Lily shook her head. 'Not very well, the grass was too long.'

'But you're sure it was a dog?'

'What else—?'

'Could it have been that he was, say, banging his shoe on the ground to dislodge something that was in it?' Mariner suggested.

Lily gave him a withering look. 'I know what I saw. The way he was hunched over, you could see the hate in him. He sort of stood back to look at what he'd done. The creature was moving. Then it stopped moving.'

'Is there anything else you can tell us about this man? The colour of his hair, say? What he was wearing?'

'I think his hair was brown and he was wearing a suit, like yours.' She looked at Mariner. 'A nice summer suit, except yours is lighter. The one he wore was darker, more of a light brown. I remember thinking that he would spoil it and how warm he must be, too.'

Gazing out of the window Mariner tried to establish whether Lily would have seen the comings and goings of Shaun Pryce.

'You said you never see anyone down there, Lily. Do you mean that? Never?'

'Never.' She was adamant.

'So you've never seen a young girl down there, or a young man, over there on the other side?'

'No.' On that point Lily stood firm.

'Actually, up until about a week ago she wouldn't have been able to see much at all from up here,' put in Nora. That row of cypress trees was so tall it used to completely block the view. It was only then that Mariner noticed the line of tree stumps at the bottom of the garden, their timber inside freshly exposed.

'They were lovely trees,' said Lily. 'I was sad to see them go.'

'Lucky for us that they did,' said Mariner. 'Thank you very much, Mrs Cooper,' he said, absently. 'You've been very helpful.'

He turned to Nora. 'We'll need to come and take a formal statement in the next few days.'

'Of course—'

Suddenly, as they watched, a shout went up and the figures working below began converging on an area a couple of hundred yards away from the bridge where the foliage was at its most dense. Seconds later Knox's mobile rang and Mariner felt a sudden weight in the pit of his stomach. Knox took the call out in the corridor, returning moments later, his face grim. 'We're needed down there, boss.'

* * *

It was only a few hundred yards away as the crow flies, but the drive around to the reservoir was nearly a mile in the car and seemed to take them an adrenaline-fuelled eternity. By the time they got there, the reservoir itself had been cleared of all but the essential personnel. The search parties had retreated to avoid contaminating the area and were now congregated in the car park, awaiting further instructions. As Mariner and Knox bumped over the uneven ground, the mood was sombre, voices low.

Russell greeted them at the edge of the wood. Beneath his tan he was white-faced. 'We didn't find it until we were almost on it, despite the smell,' he said. 'The stink of the reservoir masked it.'

'Is it her?' Mariner asked, but Russell had already set off, eager to get this over with and pass on the find to a more senior officer.

This time they followed the initial path over the bridge, continuing around on the other side of the water. On their last visit this had been uncharted territory, where the searchers before them had been forced to slash away the grass and brambles to create a narrow passage. Even now the thorns clawed at their trousers, their feet catching on loops of tangled grass. It was heavy going, speed impossible and the hike around the edge of the water seemed interminable. The heat beat sickeningly down on Mariner's skull, while his imagination conjured up every possible variation on the horror he was about to see: the psyche's desperate effort to prepare and defend. Even then, it came nowhere close.

As Russell had warned, rounding a clump of burgeoning shrubs it was the smell that hit first, the cloying stench that smelt like nothing else on earth: the unmistakable odour of human decay. After the smell came the noise: the high-pitched, triumphant buzzing of busy insects. Finally the grotesque discovery came into view.

Bile rose in Mariner's throat and behind him he heard the glug of Tony Knox's involuntary retch.

Bizarrely, what first held Mariner's attention were the many different shades and types of grass that had moulded themselves around the body, as if his brain was forcing him to focus on the peripheral detail to avoid the unspeakable. To begin with, the body itself was hard to make sense of, obscured as it was by the dense foliage. An attempt seemed to have been made to bury it under the thick strands of grass.

The soles of the shoes were visible first of all. They were easy, normal looking, like any pair of shoes on any pair of feet. Pulling away the grassy coverage Mariner forced himself to work his way visually up the battered, bloodied and decaying form. And by the time his eyes reached the insect-infested skull he already knew. 'Turn it over,' he instructed Russell. Russell did so. Although the face and side of the head had been half eaten away, it didn't matter. The Nike tracksuit and Manchester United football shirt were unmistakable from the description he'd been given only days earlier. 'It's Ricky Skeet,' he said, dully, while inside he wanted to bellow all the breath from his lungs. Why hadn't he listened to Colleen? Why had he let Fiske bully him into believing that Ricky had just run away? He'd never be able to live with himself over this.

'Call Charlie Glover and get SOCO—'

'They're on their way, sir,' said Russell.

Mariner forced himself to look more closely. SOCO would confirm it, but the state of Ricky's body would indicate that he was the 'dog' Lily had seen being beaten to death.

'We haven't found his bike yet,' said Russell. 'It must be around here somewhere and it might give us a clue about how he got in here in the first place.'

'It might lead us to a witness, as well,' added Mariner.

'There's something else interesting the lads came across too, sir.' Russell walked them back over the bridge, towards where they'd left their cars. This time though he passed the entrance and kept right, skirting under the trees and around what would have been, in wetter weather, the lake's shoreline. The flattened area was perfectly concealed by the high grasses around it, like a small arena. They were standing now on the opposite side of the water to the site where Ricky's body lay and the reason for the location was obvious. Unlike the other side of the reservoir, this area would have been bathed in sunshine for most of the afternoon. 'The guys have found a couple of used condoms too,' Russell said. 'We've bagged them up. But there's no other sign of activity.' Like blood, he might have added.

It was the side nearest to the clearing where they had met Shaun Pryce. Knox stooped to retrieve something from the ground. 'Good place to relax, eh?' He held up a home-rolled dog-end, putting it to his nose. 'Most animals don't shit in their own backyard,' said Knox, grimly. 'Shaun Pryce doesn't come down here on his own and he doesn't settle for the clearing either.'

CHAPTER 16

Even as Mariner saw Charlie Glover approaching from twenty yards away, leading a procession of white boiler-suited SOCOs, he could read the expression on his face. It told Mariner that Glover was racked with the same guilt he was. He waited on the bridge while Charlie went to look at the body.

Five minutes later Glover returned, a handkerchief held over his mouth. 'What in God's name was Ricky Skeet doing down here?' he said, numbly. 'It must be what, three or four miles from his house? And how did he get in?'

Mariner had been giving that some thought. 'The most obvious way in is the one we've all used, but looking around there could be any number of access routes.' He indicated the way up to the station. 'As for what he was doing here, God knows. Good place to hide out though. No one would think to look here for him.'

'Well, we didn't, did we?' said Glover. 'But how would he even know it existed?'

Mariner gazed out over the dark water. 'Ricky's dad used to take him fishing. Maybe there were fish in here once.' They were back on the bridge close to where

Yasmin's phone had been found. 'This whole thing makes no sense. Yasmin's phone here and Ricky's body way over there.'

Glover looked around, saw the brown stains on the grass. 'If it's his blood then Ricky was killed here. He could have somehow come by Yasmin's phone.'

'That's the only plausible explanation. We believe Yasmin was seeing someone, a boy or man. Do you think there's any chance it could have been Ricky?'

Glover thought about that. 'I don't see how. How would they have met? They're at different schools, from different parts of the city. He's two years younger.'

'Unless it was a chance meeting,' said Mariner. 'They could have bumped into each other down here, or at the station.'

'What would have taken Ricky to the station?'

Mariner was equally sceptical. 'All we found was Yasmin's phone. I think a more likely explanation would be that she dropped it and that someone — Ricky perhaps — found it and brought it here.'

'Or he stole it.'

'Ricky doesn't do that. And anyway, when would he have had the opportunity? It's much more likely that Yasmin dropped it. The afternoon she disappeared she had to run for the train. It could have happened then.'

'Haven't you got CCTV on that? It may have recorded the whole scenario . . . it might even show us if Ricky was at the station.'

'Sure,' Mariner said, absently, his mind not really on it. He knew he should be focusing on Yasmin but now all he could think about was Colleen waiting at home in hopeful ignorance. He didn't want to leave all that to Charlie Glover.

Tony Knox was hovering. 'Shall we bring in Pryce?'

'Who's that?' Glover's ears pricked up.

'A guy called Shaun Pryce turned up while we were here yesterday, back in the clearing, but claims that he doesn't come onto the reservoir itself.' Mariner filled Glover in on the main points of the conversation with Pryce.

'But I think he's a more regular visitor there than he let on,' said Knox. 'That flattened area of grass looks tailor-made for him. He wasn't telling us the truth about that and he doesn't come here alone either.'

'Judging everyone by your own standards, Tony?' said Glover.

Mariner winced on Knox's behalf at the reference to his colourful past, but he took it well enough. Would have been something of a double standard not to. 'There were a hell of a lot of fresh dog-ends for one person,' was all he said.

'The weather's been dry for weeks,' said Mariner. 'They could have built up over a period of time. And if he's down here screwing some girl why didn't he just say so? It's no big deal. In fact I'd have thought it was something he'd be only too keen to tell us about.'

'She'll be married, won't she? Didn't you ever see *Confessions of an Electrician*? He'll be having it away with someone else's missus.' There was a bitter edge to Knox's voice. 'Maybe Ricky saw Pryce knocking off some woman and threatened to let it out, so Pryce had to shut him up.'

'How would Ricky know that what he'd seen was illicit?' Glover said. 'For all Ricky knew it could have been Pryce and his wife having a bit of open-air fun.'

'Maybe Pryce didn't like having an audience.'

Mariner shook his head. 'Oh no, Shaun Pryce would love it. He's an actor,' he added, for Glover's benefit.

'He might not be so keen on being watched if things aren't going his way,' Glover said.

'Can't imagine that,' said Knox, sourly.

'Perhaps Ricky was a regular visitor down here, too. Had seen what Pryce was up to and been blackmailing him.'

'Well, Pryce is the only other person we can place down here, so we need to talk to him again.'

'Yes, we do,' agreed Mariner. 'We need to know *exactly* what Pryce has been getting up to down here, when he was around and for how long, going back for the last couple of months. There's no immediate hurry though. I get the feeling that Shaun Pryce will be in a more talkative mood once news leaks about where we've found Yasmin's phone.'

'You're sure he won't disappear?' Knox said.

'Oh no.' Mariner was confident. 'Judging by yesterday's performance, if he is involved, he'll want to be around for his bit of the limelight.'

'I'd better go and tell Ricky's mum,' Glover said to Mariner. 'Do you want to come?'

Mariner ran the scene in his head; Colleen screaming and sobbing as she beat her fists against Glover. 'Not yet,' he said. 'She needs to know that you're in charge. And we've got things to do.' Or was he just a coward, unable to face Colleen after letting her down so badly, afraid of the hysteria that would ensue? Later Charlie told him it hadn't run like that at all. She'd taken the news in a stunned silence. Somehow that had been even worse.

* * *

As they left the site, a low loader bearing a Portakabin was driving towards the scene. The incident room would be set up there to maximise the use of local intelligence and deepen the search. One of the first tasks would be a door-to-door to try and establish when and where Ricky was last seen. The murder investigation unit would support Charlie Glover's OCU investigation and a team would be put onto searching the reservoir area for the murder weapon. The diving team would have to be contracted in from a neighbouring force, since their own divers had gone the way of the mounted division and fallen victim to budget cuts. Trawling the reservoir would make for an

164

interesting task given all that thick black mud. Close behind the truck, Mariner could see a couple more unmarked vehicles.

'The vultures are moving in,' observed Knox. Inevitably the press would have picked up news of this morning's activities from the air waves. 'Want me to get rid of them, boss?'

'Be as unpleasant as you like,' said Mariner.

* * *

What Mariner was less prepared for was the mob of reporters already assembled outside the entrance to Granville Lane. News had travelled fast and they were not a happy throng. Knox and Mariner got out of the car just as Fiske appeared at the main doors to read a prepared statement. 'We will do everything within our power to bring the killer of Ricky Skeet to justice,' he concluded.

'Is that the same kind of everything you did to find him when he went missing?' someone called out.

'We followed all possible lines of enquiry,' said Fiske, defiant. 'I have no doubt that my officers did all they possibly could to prevent this situation from occurring.'

'Mrs Skeet doesn't seem to agree with you on that.'

Fiske was getting hot under the collar. 'Any complaints about the way this enquiry has been handled will be dealt with through the usual channels.'

'Whitewashed, you mean.'

Mariner signalled to Knox and they jogged around the building and in through a side door. Along the corridor they ran into Fiske making his escape. 'Bloody press,' he grumbled.

'Perhaps they've got a point this time,' said Mariner.

'And what the hell's that supposed to mean?'

'We didn't exactly pull out all the stops for Ricky, did we?' Mariner reminded him.

Fiske bridled. 'Given his profile we followed the correct procedures.'

'I'll tell his mum that. I'm sure she'll feel greatly reassured. "Your son's dead, but given his profile, we did everything by the book, Colleen."' Deep down Mariner recognised that he was angrier with himself than he was with Fiske. If he'd made more of a stand against the arrogant bastard instead of caving in at the beginning this might not have happened. 'And now we've got a kid we hardly looked for dead and another we've wasted energy on looking for who might have eloped with her boyfriend,' he said.

'We got it wrong,' said Fiske. 'Sometimes it happens.'

'You don't say.'

Millie was working up in CID. 'You heard?' Mariner asked.

Her face said it all. 'I'm sorry.'

'Yeah. But we have to turn our attention back to Yasmin. There's always the chance that the two cases aren't linked. I know the probability has dropped a couple of notches, but still the only two people we can definitely place down at the reservoir at any time are Shaun Pryce and Ricky Skeet. Yasmin's phone might have been there, but we don't know for sure that she was too. Let's deal with the real possibilities first, before we go off speculating about other things.' The seventeen-year-old had been gone more than a week now and their one breakthrough had come to nothing.

'Let's have a look at the CCTV footage again,' Mariner said. 'I want to be absolutely sure that it's her getting on that train.'

'But we've been over that, boss,' Knox whined.

Quashing his complaints, Mariner played the tape yet again. As on every previous occasion, they watched as Yasmin boarded the train. After about half a minute — during which time another passenger got on — the door closed and as the train began to draw away, Knox switched off the tape.

'That's definitely Yasmin,' said Millie, swivelling in her chair. 'She looks right into the camera.'

'And no sign of her dropping her phone,' said Mariner.

'But she'd started running from the top of the road,' Millie reminded him. 'She could have dropped it anywhere before she comes into view.'

Their disappointment was tangible. 'Well, we may soon find out about that anyway,' Mariner said. He had half an eye on Tony Knox, who had put another DVD in the player and was winding and rewinding, like a hyperactive four-year-old. 'Her phone should be back from—' Mariner was about to snap at him to concentrate, when Knox froze.

'Look at this,' he said.

Mariner glanced back at the screen as Knox back-tracked the footage at speed. 'But we've already seen—'

'No, wait,' said Knox. 'This is the second camera, further up the platform.' It was a different view of the train, this time the front carriage. He pointed at the corner of the screen. 'According to the digital counter, this is the precise moment Yasmin got on the train at the back.' They watched and waited. Nothing happened. Then, just before the doors closed someone passed across the screen. Knox hit freeze.

'It's Yasmin,' said Millie.

'She got off the train again,' said Knox, with a degree of satisfaction.

'Shit,' said Mariner. 'Why didn't we think of that?'

'Think of what?' They were so caught up in their find that Fiske's voice startled them. Creeping up on them was becoming a habit.

'Yasmin Akram had us all fooled,' said Mariner. 'Play it back Tony.'

'What ag—?' Mariner glared at him and dutifully Knox re-ran the recording yet again.

As they watched Mariner provided the running commentary. 'She runs for the train, giving her friends — and us — the impression that she was going home as usual, but gets off again before the train pulls out.' He looked up at Fiske, calculating how far he could go. 'She never even got as far as the university.'

Fiske stared at him. 'Are you trying to make some kind of point, DI Mariner?'

'Only that perhaps we could have saved ourselves considerable time and resources if we'd been a bit less hasty with the search, sir,' said Mariner calmly.

But Fiske wasn't so easily beaten. 'We did the right thing based on the information available at the time,' he replied, icily. 'Not forgetting of course, the sex attacker we've exposed.'

'Oh, nice one, sir,' Knox grinned inanely, before realising, along with everyone else, that the pun was entirely unintentional.

'Given that new information has come to light, I'd have thought your time would be more usefully spent following it up rather than playing games of "I told you so."' And with that Fiske turned and walked out.

'Fucking moron,' muttered Knox.

Mariner should really have reminded him about respect for senior officers, but it made a change to see Tony Knox back on form again. Instead he brought them back to task. 'So why does Yasmin get off the train again?'

'Maybe she realises that she's dropped her phone, goes back to look for it.'

'Which still wouldn't explain how it ends up at the reservoir,' said Mariner. 'Unless in that short space of time someone else has found it and picked it up.'

'Maybe she has other plans,' Millie speculated. 'What we can't see is where she went next.'

'There is a camera positioned at the back of the station though,' Knox remembered. 'It would be worth checking out the tape from that. If she heads towards the footbridge, she could be crossing the line.'

'In more ways than one,' said Millie. 'Yasmin's just full of surprises, isn't she?'

'Let's get the tape.'

* * *

Yasmin did indeed appear on the footage from the back of the station, descending the footbridge and across the screen towards the station car park, but that was as far as the camera covered.

'So where's she off to?'

'Suddenly it's not beyond the realms of possibility that Yasmin dropped her phone at the reservoir.'

But as Knox went to switch off the TV, Mariner spotted something else on the screen. 'Look at that — way behind her, in the background.' Next to the kerb was the offside wing and part of the bonnet of a dark vehicle.

'It's a Merc,' said Knox. 'You can tell from that radiator grille.'

'Is there anyone in it?' asked Millie, as they all squinted at the screen.

'Hard to see. It's not a good angle. Can we home in on that licence plate?'

They could, but it was still too blurred to be of any use.

'Mohammed Akram drives a black Mercedes,' Mariner reminded them.

'Now there's a nice coincidence. Maybe Yasmin got off the train again because she saw someone she knew.' The time on the corner of the screen said 16:29. 'According to Akram he'd been to the printer's and was on his way to Bradford by that time — all the way up the motorway,' said Mariner.

'Is the printer's in the city?' asked Knox.

'I assumed it was in Sparkhill, near the school. TMR, it's called. It was on the prospectus Hasan Sheron showed us.'

Knox reached for the Yellow Pages and flicked through until he found printers.

'Here we are. TMR Reprographics. Two branches, one in the city and another—' He looked up for dramatic effect. 'On Birch Close.'

'Shit,' said Millie.

'Thanks for that valuable contribution,' Knox said. But he did seem to be joking.

'And from there it's just a short drive up to the station where the CCTV picks up Akram's car,' said Mariner, '— if it is his car.'

'And it would be easy enough to get onto the motorway from here,' said Knox. 'There's nothing stopping him from going back out through the city centre and up to Spaghetti Junction, or even up the Wolverhampton Road to the M5 then M6. The fact that Yasmin stayed for art club and left school late would have helped him out. He'd also probably have known that she'd be on her own at the station, so it would have been the perfect place if he didn't want to confront her in front of her friends, or back at home.'

'He could easily have picked her up from the station and taken her with him,' said Mariner.

'What time did he check into his hotel in Bradford?' Millie wanted to know.

'Not until nearly eight. But he says he stopped off at Sandbach services for something to eat on his way and that there were road works on the M62 — which there are.'

'It doesn't rule him out though,' said Knox. 'It's still a bloody big coincidence if he was in this area at all at around that time.'

'An appeal on local news can help to rule out anyone else,' Mariner said.

'When did he say he'd confronted Yasmin?' Millie asked.

'On Friday,' said Mariner. 'He said they'd sorted it out. But perhaps they had unfinished business.'

'What if Akram talked Yasmin into going up to Bradford with him?' Millie suggested.

Mariner was dubious. 'Without telling her mother what was going on?'

'It's probable that neither of them would have wanted her to know about the pill.'

'But that doesn't tie in with Akram forbidding Yasmin to go to Suzanne's,' said Knox. 'He couldn't have known that his wife would give in and let her go.'

'Unless he knows his wife better than she thinks,' said Millie.

'The receipt from the service station only indicates a meal for one.'

Mariner sighed. 'Okay, folks, we're starting to speculate again. Let's get back to the facts.'

'We have Ricky, Yasmin and Akram all in the same area at the same time,' said Knox. 'That's a fact.'

'Only if that is Akram's car on the CCTV.'

'And I still don't get where Ricky comes into this,' Millie said.

'He might not,' said Mariner. 'We could easily still be looking at two entirely unconnected events. Maybe Ricky's only part in this was to find Yasmin's phone at the station and take it with him to the reservoir, where he was attacked and he dropped it — simple as that. Meanwhile, Yasmin, unaware that she's even lost her phone, meets her dad at the station.'

'Are we absolutely certain that Yasmin and Ricky didn't know each other?' Knox asked.

'I just don't see how they would,' said Millie.

'But we don't know for sure that they didn't,' Knox insisted, the tension in the room thickening.

171

'And they don't have to have done,' said Millie suddenly. 'If Ricky was in the wrong place at the wrong time Akram could have just jumped to the wrong conclusion.'

'What are you talking about?' Knox pulled a face.

'Maybe the phone *is* the link,' Millie persevered. 'How about if Ricky finds the phone, as we thought. Yasmin's home number is on it. Ricky phones that number to establish its owner, gets Akram who arranges to meet him and collect it. Akram's going to be at the printer's, Ricky knows the reservoir, so they arrange to meet at a mutually convenient spot. Akram is still wound up about Yasmin being on the pill, jumps to the wrong conclusion about Ricky having her phone and loses it.'

Knox's facial expression fell just short of contempt. 'That's a hell of a conclusion to jump to. A kid finds his daughter's phone so he assumes they're having sex?'

'We don't know what's on that phone.' Millie stood her ground. 'There might be some interesting messages or pictures. Could be that Ricky tried blackmailing Akram, perhaps he demanded money before giving it up. Akram's already pissed off about all the hassle he's been getting. This could've been the final straw.'

Mariner could see Knox's colour rising. 'It's an interesting idea, but knowing what we do about Ricky, it's a bit far-fetched,' he said, calmly.

Millie shrugged. 'He'd run away from home. That wasn't his kind of thing either. And if he wasn't planning on going back he was going to need more money.'

'So why did Paul Hewitt find the phone still lying there?' Knox said. 'Akram would have taken it with him.'

'Ricky was in a bad way, wasn't he? The attack must have been violent, impulsive even. Maybe Akram just lost it and in the heat of the moment he dropped the phone and it got forgotten. He'd have been pretty caught up in what he was doing.'

'Or somebody disturbed him,' Mariner suggested.

'Down there?'

'Okay. He looked up and saw Lily watching him.'

'I doubt that he'd see her from that distance,' said Knox. 'And even so, you're saying this was all about the phone . . . he'd hardly have left it behind, would he?'

'Or go in bloodstained clothing back to the station to meet his daughter,' Millie conceded.

'He was going away overnight though,' Mariner pointed out. 'He would have had a change of clothing in the car.'

'I don't buy it,' said Knox. 'If that *is* what happened, Ricky would have had hardly any time to find the phone, alert Akram and arrange to meet him. I'd say it was virtually impossible.' He glared at Millie, who refused to be intimidated.

'And I think we're getting a bit carried away here, folks,' Mariner intervened. 'We need to look at it from every angle, but this isn't getting us any nearer to knowing where Yasmin's gone.'

'I think we need to check her dad's movements up in Bradford,' Millie insisted. 'If she has simply been spirited away it would explain why he didn't seem so anxious at the start.'

'Look into that, will you?' said Mariner. 'It remains a possibility, but one of several. At the moment all we have is Yasmin's phone, Ricky dead and Yasmin vanished.'

'Like one of those lateral-thinking problems,' said Knox.

Millie pulled a face. 'I was always rubbish at them.'

'I need some fresh air,' said Knox.

When he'd left the room Millie asked the question Mariner had been dreading. 'Are you sure it's not me?'

'Tony just takes the job very seriously,' said Mariner brushing it off.

'Implying that we don't?' She had a point.

Mariner was saved from further awkwardness by the news that Charlie Glover was back from the pathologist's office with the preliminary findings.

CHAPTER 17

When Knox had returned, Glover cut to the chase. 'Everything so far says the blood on the grass is definitely Ricky's. It was a frenzied attack involving repeated blows to the skull with a blunt instrument. It would have been messy.'

'So the clothing the killer was wearing—?' Mariner began.

'—would be pretty well covered in blood.'

'According to Lily it was some kind of brown suit.'

'Yeah, I've spoken to her. Her eyesight seems pretty sharp and what she's told us seems accurate so I think we can go on that. So the brown suit would have needed to go to the cleaner's or even more likely would have been destroyed. Hard to explain to the dry cleaner why your suit is covered in someone else's blood.'

'Have we got a time of death?' Mariner asked.

'Thanks to the weather the body was pretty ripe, as you saw,' said Glover. 'But they're saying sometime late on Tuesday afternoon.' Lining it up nicely with the last time that Yasmin was seen alive. Mariner tried not to deliberate too long on that equation.

'Anything else?'

'Only what Lily's already told you; she's pretty certain that the man she saw had dark hair.' Like Mohammed Akram, thought Mariner. Did he own a brown suit? 'It could, of course, depend on the angle of the sun at that time,' Glover went on. 'If the sun was behind or overhead it could be one detail that she's mistaken on.'

'It's possible,' agreed Mariner. 'What about Colleen's boyfriend, Marsh?'

'We're checking him out, but so far his alibi looks sound. He was still at work.'

'That's a pity,' said Knox.

'Yeah, isn't it?'

'Any thoughts on how it played out?' Mariner asked.

'Well, we have blood on the grass by the wooden bridge, but around that, nothing. And no sign of disturbance. However, working back from where the body was found is a kind of tunnel through the grass leading almost back to the bridge and also smeared with blood. Indications are that Ricky was killed at the bridge, then his killer carried him into the long grass and dumped him, coming back to the path to cover his tracks. It looks as if Ricky could have dragged himself further through the grass creating a kind of tunnel, to the point where we found him.'

'Oh God, so he wasn't dead,' said Millie.

'And crawling even further from the path did his killer a favour by delaying the discovery of his body. We're continuing the search in the direction he was going to see if he was making for anything in particular. But he may just have been trying to get away. And you were right about the reason for Ricky being there,' Glover added. 'I asked Colleen. His dad used to take him fishing on the reservoir, but they hadn't been for years. We still haven't found his bike, but did they tell you about the Anderson?'

'I didn't get time to check in yesterday.'

'Further round still from where Ricky's body was found we came across an old Anderson shelter. From all the empty cans and crisp packets it looked as if Ricky had hidden out there before.'

'He used to go off for the day at weekends,' Mariner said, recalling the conversation with Colleen. 'Is this all going to the press?'

'It might have to. Fiske is desperate to get them off his back. How does a berk like him get to be in charge?'

'One of life's mysteries,' said Mariner. 'Did you ask Colleen about Yasmin?'

'Yeah, and nearly got a black eye for it.' Glover recounted the conversation, conducted under the beady gaze of Steven Marsh. 'He didn't seem to appreciate the timing.'

Mariner grimaced.

'And Colleen just took it as further proof that we were more concerned with Yasmin than with Ricky, but basically the answer was no. She couldn't see how Ricky would have known that "posh little Asian kid" even when I told her about the phone.' Glover paused. 'Question is though: would Colleen have even known?'

* * *

Sometime later Mariner and Knox drove over to *Allah T'ala*. For once Knox was quite chirpy, the rest of the time his jaw working hard on a gobbet of chewing gum, which he'd lately taken to chewing almost constantly. They were shown up to the same office where Mariner and Millie had first gone, and where Mohammed Akram, in shirtsleeves, his tie hanging loose, was studying some architect's drawings. He jumped up as they went in, his face a turmoil of emotions. 'You've found something?'

'Nothing more. I'm sorry,' said Mariner. 'PC Khatoon has kept you up to date?'

'She told us about the boy and that you found Yasmin's phone. Do you think—?'

'We're trying to establish the facts,' said Mariner, 'which is why we need to clarify a couple of things with you.'

'My wife is teaching a class.'

'That's fine,' Mariner said. 'I think you should be able to help us. The printer's you were at in Kingsmead on Tuesday afternoon,' said Mariner. 'It's some distance from your school. Why there?'

'My last supplier closed about a year ago,' said Akram. 'I happened to mention this to one of Yasmin's teachers at parents' evening. Yasmin had been awarded a certificate and I asked where they had been printed. She recommended the place. I decided to try them.'

'And tell me again, what time were you there on that Tuesday afternoon?'

'Around four o'clock,' said Akram. 'I left about twenty or thirty minutes later. The meeting didn't take long. I just needed to look at some proofs. But you know all this — I already told you.'

'Will the printer be able to confirm that timing?'

'I'm sure that he will.'

'And from there you drove up to Bradford?' Mariner confirmed.

'—as I've already told you,' said Akram irritably.

'Did you go anywhere near Kingsmead station?'

'No.' He frowned. 'I had no reason to do that.'

'Yasmin would have just been leaving school at that time.'

'I suppose she was. I didn't really think about it.'

'You weren't tempted to meet her to discuss your recent disagreement?'

'As I said before, that matter had been resolved.'

'Mr Akram, do you own a brown suit?'

A slight pause. Surprised at the question or considering his answer? 'Yes I do. As a matter of fact I have it here. It's due to be dry cleaned.'

That was a piece of luck. 'Could we see it?'

'Er, yes.' Akram left the room and several minutes later returned with the suit, protected in a plastic cover. It was a shade of mid-brown. For a suit that was going to the cleaner's it also seemed spotlessly clean.

'Mr Akram, I'm going to ask you again. Do you have any idea about the whereabouts of your daughter?'

Akram looked Mariner straight in the eye. 'And I will tell you again, Inspector. No, I do not.'

* * *

'That suit looked okay to me,' said Knox, back in the baking heat of the car.

'We didn't ask him if he owns more than one.'

Knox gave him a sidelong look. 'Just because all your suits are exactly the same colour—'

'Two colours actually,' Mariner corrected him.

'All I'm saying is, most of us are a bit more adventurous.'

'Thanks.'

'Any time.'

* * *

'Akram is consistent about the timing though,' conceded Mariner. 'Did the printer verify it?'

'Over the phone, yes.'

Mariner sighed. 'Even with the techies' enhancements on the CCTV footage, I'm not sure that we'll be able to determine the licence plate or the driver of that car.'

'And if he's telling the truth he'd have left the city before that was filmed.'

'Did you believe him, that he didn't realise Yasmin would be at the station at that time?'

'Yeah,' Knox nodded. 'You're not thinking about your kids all day long, especially when they get to that age. You're starting to lead separate lives.'

'Some more than others,' said Mariner. 'It just would be nice to know for sure.'

As it turned out, they soon did. The appeal the night before had brought forward a young woman.

'A Miss Devreaux called in just after you left,' Millie told them, on their return to Granville Lane. 'Her fiancée met her from the station yesterday in his midnight blue Mercedes. He parked exactly where the camera is pointed. They even had a row because she was late.'

'Shit.'

'Does it rule Akram out?' Millie asked.

'It confirms that he wasn't at the station then.' Mariner sighed. 'But Yasmin's phone was found *between* the station and the printer's. 'I want to go and talk to the printer.'

'Nothing like going over old ground,' muttered Knox.

'It's called being thorough,' said Mariner.

'Yes, boss.'

* * *

Printer Tim Randall was pretty certain about the timing of Akram's visit. He told them so in his design office, while a couple of his graphic artists were laying out proofs. 'We were in the middle of a big print run and as he left I remember looking at the clock to see how much time we'd got left to finish up. We were cutting it a bit fine.'

'And what time was it?' asked Mariner.

'A couple of minutes off half past four, give or take. That clock probably isn't a hundred percent accurate.'

So that was that.

'He didn't drive off straight away.' The young man who spoke up was leaning over the drawings, cornrows sprouting from his head.

'Are you sure?' asked Mariner.

'Yeah, I went out for a fag about quarter to five and he was still there, his flashy Mercedes parked down at the end of the loop, by the bins.'

The lad wasn't wearing a watch, Mariner noticed. 'How can you be so sure of the timing?'

He grinned. 'I'm trying to quit, so I'm spacing them out. This week I'm out there at five o'clock, last week it was quarter to.'

'Did you see him drive off?'

'No. He was still out there when I came back in. Doesn't take long to smoke a fag and I'm only allowed the one.'

'Was Mr Akram definitely in his car? Was there anyone with him?' Mariner asked.

He tilted his head doubtfully. 'All I noticed was the car.'

* * *

Outside they looked down towards 'the loop,' the neck of the cul-de-sac, where a row of industrial-sized steel bins backed up against a wooden fence — on the other side of which was the reservoir.

'The kid saw Akram's car parked outside at quarter to five. It doesn't mean that he was in it. He could have easily been down there with Yasmin,' said Knox.

Mariner wasn't so sure. 'When we were on the bridge I remember looking up to this industrial estate,' he said. 'If there was a way through to the reservoir from here, don't you think we'd have noticed it?'

'Not if we weren't looking for it,' said Knox. 'And it may only have been used once or twice. If Akram did have unfinished business with Yasmin, it would have been a much more private place to meet her.'

That was true enough and they found what they were looking for in minutes. Behind the giant bins a panel of fencing had split, creating an opening easily large enough for someone to squeeze through. Standing on the concrete plinth Mariner could look down towards the bridge and the sludge beyond. Running through the long grass was the unmistakable pale line caused by a single passage through it.

'So what now? Back to Mr Akram?' Knox asked.

But Mariner shook his head. 'We need to keep onto everything else, too. I'd like to have a closer look at what you found on Shaun Pryce first.'

* * *

But the database had turned up little of interest. 'Only one minor offence in the past, boss: possession of cannabis.' Knox closed the record sheet. 'I thought this was more interesting.'

He'd bookmarked a site and when he double-clicked it, a whole webpage appeared devoted to Shaun Pryce: actor and model. On it Pryce was described as a 'talented and versatile' character actor who'd played a range of diverse and challenging roles, most notably that of romantic lead, and who was also available for modelling and voice-over work. 'I bet he wrote that himself,' said Knox. 'Shame we can't bring him in for blatant self-promotion.'

'I want to talk to him again though,' said Mariner. 'He frequents the reservoir area and I'd like to know what he really does there. SOCO have found spliffs and condoms. I want to see if there's anything else we can shake out of him. I wonder if Charlie Glover would like to come.'

'Sounds like fun,' was Glover's reaction.

* * *

The daytime contact Shaun Pryce had given them belonged to a property about three quarters of a mile from the reservoir, one of a collection of houses in what estate agents would refer to as a 'much sought-after area.' Consequently most places had been extended in one way or another. The addition that Pryce was working on would practically double the size of the property — plenty of electrical work here to keep him busy. There was no sign of his VW Golf alongside the assorted vehicles parked outside, but when they asked Mrs Paleczcki, the owner of the house she took them through to where Pryce was working alone, in what looked like a newly created ground-floor room. 'Shaun, there's someone to see you,' she said.

Pryce turned from where he was kneeling on the floor fixing a double socket to a freshly plastered wall. Their footsteps echoed on the bare floorboards and the air glistened with dust. Raw wires sprouted from walls elsewhere around the room awaiting his attention. A tinny radio blared some kind of phone-in programme that ricocheted around the emptiness. Elsewhere in the house was the tap-tap, bang-bang-bang of other work progressing.

'Would you like a cup of tea, love?' Today Pryce was in T-shirt and shorts, his tattoos standing out vividly against his bronzed skin and there was no mistaking the look on Mrs Paleczcki's face as she spoke to him. Knox had been close to the mark: it was *Confessions of an Electrician* all over again.

Pryce grinned. 'You know just what to say to a man.'

The hospitality wasn't extended as far as Mariner or Glover. Mrs Paleczcki not encouraging them to hang around any longer than was necessary.

'How can I help?' Pryce asked, his demeanour casual, but the voice guarded. He seemed to have lost some of the confidence he'd had a couple of days ago. But a lot had happened since then and he must know that they'd found Ricky.

'You can stop pissing us around and tell us what you really get up to at the reservoir,' said Mariner, without ceremony.

'Is that where they found that kid?'

'You know that very well. We've found your little retreat, too.'

'Oh.'

'So? What is it you do there?' Mariner repeated.

'I go there to top up my tan,' said Pryce.

Mariner wasn't sure whether to believe that. 'Most people sunbathe in their own gardens or in the park,' he said.

'I live in a first-floor flat,' said Pryce. 'And anyway, some of the modelling work I do, my tan needs to be . . . comprehensive.'

'You sunbathe nude,' said Glover.

'I'm not harming anyone.'

Mrs Paleczcki came back in with the tea. Mariner wondered if she knew about Pryce's all-over tan and decided that she probably did. 'When was the last time you were there?' he asked Pryce, when she had gone. 'And this time we'd like the truth.'

Pryce hesitated, no doubt deciding what to say to avoid incriminating himself. 'The day I met you lot,' he said, eventually.

'Don't be a smart arse, I mean before that.' Mariner's impatience was beginning to show.

'The week before, I suppose.'

'Day and time?'

Pryce considered for a moment. 'Tuesday, about one o'clock.'

'Till when?'

'I don't know. Half one, two.'

'Is there anyone who can verify that?'

'The rest of the crew here can vouch for me.'

Mariner looked around him pointedly. 'And they are?'

'Upstairs right now. We started on the loft conversion this week.'

Mariner could only guess at the motley bunch that comprised Pryce's co-workers. He'd have laid bets that, like Pryce, they'd be mainly casual labourers with more than a couple of criminal records between them, and therefore didn't have much confidence in any of them as a firm alibi. Nonetheless he signalled Glover to go and check it out.

'So what were you doing for nearly an hour? And don't give me any bird-watching bullshit. We all know you wouldn't know a redshank from a shag.'

'I was chilling out,' said Pryce sulkily. 'It may not look like it to you but this is bloody hard work, especially in the heat. Sometimes I have to help with the labouring too.'

'My heart bleeds. Take Mrs Paleczcki with you?'

'She's a married woman,' Pryce said, avoiding the question.

'But you've taken women there before. Either that or you're the only man I know who practises safe sex with himself.'

'You sure they're mine? I'm a good Catholic boy, me.'

'When's the last time you took a woman there?' repeated Mariner.

'Not for a while.'

'Oh? What about your insatiable sexual appetite? Losing your touch?'

'The last one I took there didn't like the long grass. Said it scratched her. Got into all those uncomfortable little places. So I haven't bothered since.'

'When was that?'

'Ages ago. Probably sometime back in May. It's hard to remember.'

'See a lot of women, do you?' said Mariner.

'I can't help it if they find me irresistible.'

'Anything else? How about a smoke?'

Pryce could tell that they'd found the cannabis. No point in denying it. 'I might have smoked a couple of joints.'

'Does your employer know about your habit? It must improve your wiring skills no end.'

'I know what I'm doing. I'm careful.'

'Do you know a boy called Ricky Skeet?' Mariner asked.

Pryce was suddenly wary. 'Is that—?'

'—the boy who we found yesterday afternoon by the reservoir? Yes. He'd been bludgeoned to death. We have the estimated time as sometime on Tuesday afternoon.' Shaun Pryce looked as if he was about to throw up. 'Did you know him?'

Pryce's voice dropped to a whisper. 'No.'

'What do you wear when you're working?' Mariner asked suddenly.

'What?'

'What do you wear? Your clothes?'

Pryce splayed his arms. 'What you see. Jeans, T-shirt, shorts if it's a hot day.'

'Do you own a brown suit?'

Pryce sneered. 'Shit colour, you mean? No thanks.'

'What about overalls?'

'Too restrictive.'

Glover appeared in the doorway and gave the faintest nod.

'Right,' said Mariner. 'That's all for now. Thanks for your time.'

'What do you mean "for now?"' said Pryce, uneasily.

'You've admitted to being close to the scene of a murder at around the time it was committed. We may have some further questions. Don't worry, we'll see ourselves out.'

As they were leaving, Mariner turned back to Pryce. 'Where's the car today?'

'I left it at home. Came on my bike. I do, when I get up early enough. Helps keep me fit.'

'Is that what you did on Tuesday? Were you on your bike then?'

'I might have been,' said Pryce. 'I don't honestly remember.'

* * *

Glover and Mariner got reluctantly back into their sweltering car.

186

'He seems pretty casual,' Glover observed. 'He didn't hesitate about owning up to being at the reservoir on that Tuesday.'

'Which could mean he has nothing to do with this.' Mariner was disappointed, '—or just that he's good at covering up. He's an actor after all. As long as he sticks to the timing there's not much we can do about it. What about his alibi?'

'The other guys are saying that he was back after lunch and then they didn't knock off until nearly six,' Glover told him.

'So we may have to accept that Pryce probably wasn't there when Ricky was killed. If we choose to believe them.'

'The other three have been working on the loft all week while Pryce has been downstairs more or less on his own. Would they even know if he disappeared on his bike for an hour? He could easily get down to the reservoir in that time.'

'I can't shake off the feeling that he knows something, that there's something he's not telling us,' said Mariner.

'Do you believe the nude sunbathing?'

'It fits with the image.'

'But he denied having a brown suit. Are we going to push him on that?'

Mariner turned to face Glover. 'Maybe we've seen his suit already, most of it — a light brown suit? It's this famous all-over tan he keeps bragging about. Wouldn't have to take that to the dry cleaner's, would he?'

CHAPTER 18

When Mariner got home late that night he realised he still hadn't contacted his mother. He tried, but the phone just rang on and she had no answering machine or service to catch it. She'd probably got the TV on too loud to hear. He thought about calling one of her neighbours but didn't want to get anyone out of bed, so he let it go.

By next morning the analysis of Yasmin's phone was waiting for Mariner in CID, along with Mike Finlay, the technician who would be able to clarify anything that didn't make sense. Mariner asked Knox and Millie to sit in on the conversation. Most of the fingerprints on the handset were of the right size to be Yasmin's and matched with those taken from her room at home. A couple of larger smeared prints were as yet unidentified. 'But could belong to the parents,' Finlay said. 'We're checking that.'

A transcript of all her saved messages was attached to Finlay's report. Mariner had never signed up to the text message culture, continuing to use his own mobile like a traditional telephone, and to his unfamiliar eyes the document read like the Enigma code.

'These are all messages?' Mariner asked the technician, feeling ignorant.

'It's been set to a save cycle of about a month,' Finlay told him. 'Automatically saving incoming and outgoing messages.'

'So we've got everything Yasmin sent and received over the last month?'

'Not quite. Some messages have been deliberately deleted. I'm not surprised either given the content of some of the others.'

'Oh?'

'She didn't hold back,' said Finlay, confirming that Yasmin wasn't quite the innocent they'd first thought her to be. 'Where we can we've linked the numbers to Yasmin's phone book, so most of the messages, though not all, can be attributed. Messages to and from her parents and sister were easy to identify, especially as there aren't that many. Some of them also have only an initial or what looks like a nickname to identify them.'

'And the hot ones?' Tony Knox asked.

'They all appear to be to or from someone known as Lee.'

Lee. So Amira was right. Yasmin could have been seeing someone after all. The contraceptive pill wasn't just about trying to be grown up, impressing her friends. She really needed it. But why had none of those girls mentioned Lee?

'The one you'll be most interested in is this one,' said Finlay. 'It's the last message sent, on Tuesday at around lunchtime: *CU @4 things 2 TL U.*'

'What does it mean?' asked Mariner.

'It makes more sense if you read it out loud,' said Finlay. '*See you at four. Things to tell you.*'

Something to tell you . . . where had Mariner heard that before? Suddenly he remembered. 'That's what she told her friend Suzanne, too. I'd assumed that Lee was the 'something'. Maybe she was planning on telling him that she was on the pill, so it was all systems go.'

Finlay nodded sagely. 'It looks as if Yasmin had arranged to meet this Lee at four o'clock on the day she disappeared. I think you need to speak to him.'

'Do you reckon?' Knox was straight-faced.

'There's one other message received after that, in the middle of the afternoon but she's deleted it,' said Finlay.

'How can you tell that?'

'It leaves a trace, a bit like the imaging you get on a computer hard drive. Perhaps she deleted it because it was a bit strong for her parents' eyes.'

'Thanks,' said Knox. 'We'll bear it in mind.'

'Can we be sure from this that Yasmin had her phone right up until Tuesday afternoon?' Mariner asked.

'Somebody did. The prints would indicate that it was probably her, because those are the clearest. The rest is for you to find out.'

'Thanks,' said Mariner. 'That's been helpful. Okay,' he said to the other two, when Finlay had left them. 'At least we now have the boy Yasmin was seeing, and we know it wasn't Ricky.'

'Unless he was using an alias,' Millie suggested.

'Let's not complicate things for the sake of it. We should go and talk to her family about this.'

'I think we'd be better off talking to her friends first, sir,' Millie suggested. 'They're more likely to know who she's been texting, especially given the content of some of these. It's not the kind of stuff she'd want to share with her mum and dad.'

* * *

On returning to the school Mariner took with him photographs of Akram and Pryce. A cluster of girls were gathered outside the school gates. 'Isn't that Suzanne?' said Millie.

'Yes, let's get her on her own. She may be more inclined to talk.'

Millie pulled over to the kerb to let Mariner out of the car.

'Suzanne,' he called across. 'Can I have a word?'

The girl turned and gave her friends a knowing smile before breaking away from them and sashaying over to Mariner, obviously pleased to have been singled out for special attention. 'What can I do for you?' The suggestion in those few words made Mariner's skin crawl.

He kept it strictly professional. 'You've probably heard, we've found Yasmin's phone. There are several text messages on it from someone calling himself Lee. Do you know who that might be?

'I might.' Suzanne shrugged and glanced over at her friends, eliciting a bout of giggling. Another one playing hard to get. Mariner snapped. 'Suzanne, a boy has been murdered. And not far from where we found his body we also found Yasmin's phone. You need to tell us everything you know. Loyalty to friends is commendable but it's not going to help Yasmin. At the very least she may be in serious trouble so we need to find out where she is.'

His tone seemed, at least, to shock her out of her complacency. 'Lee is a boy Yasmin knows,' she pouted. 'And it's not really Lee. That's just his tag.'

'What is his real name?'

'Lewis Everett. He just calls himself Lee.'

'Are you sure about that? Did Yasmin know a boy called Ricky Skeet?'

'Is that the boy who—?' The veneer of confidence was all but gone now.

'Yes. Did Yasmin know him?' Mariner asked.

'I don't think so. I've never heard that name before.'

'How well does Yasmin know this Lee?'

'They sort of went out for a while.'

Finlay had been close to the mark. 'Why didn't you tell us about him before?'

She wrinkled her nose. 'It's history. Yaz hasn't seen him for weeks.'

Except, thought Mariner, that he was still texting her as recently as the day she disappeared. And Yasmin had recently gone to the doctor's to go on the pill.

'He goes to the boys' school up the road,' Suzanne continued. 'We met them on a school trip, to London.' The tickets in Yasmin's treasure box.

'Them?'

'He's mates with my boyfriend, Sam. We were all on the same trip. Yaz and Lee started it really. We all went off to see the London Eye, then we couldn't find our way back to the bus. We got on the wrong underground train. It was wicked. All the teachers were going apeshit because me and Yasmin had gone off with boys. They were worried about what her parents would say.'

'What about your parents?' asked Mariner.

'Mine don't give a toss,' she said. 'It was Yaz's they were worried about. Pretty rich coming from them.'

'What do you mean by that?'

'Darrow and Goodway. You should have seen them; they were all over each other. It was disgusting. Mr Goodway's wife had only left him a couple of weeks before, but she couldn't keep her hands off him.'

Was this a further example of teenage fantasy? 'But surely Mrs Darrow is—'

'Ms actually. She's divorced.'

Mariner needed to get her back on track. 'How did Yasmin's parents react to what happened on the trip?'

'They never found out. In the end Yaz persuaded them not to tell. She promised that she wouldn't see Lee again so she had to meet him in secret after school.'

Mariner was confused. 'But you said she isn't seeing him now.'

'She isn't. It's over.'

'Who finished it?'

'Lee did.'

'Why?'

'Yasmin hadn't got the guts.'

'For what?'

'What do you think? What do any boys want? You're all the same.' She looked Mariner up and down with eyes that were experienced beyond her years. 'Eventually Lee got the message that it wasn't going anywhere.'

'That Yasmin wouldn't sleep with him.'

'Yeah. She was "saving herself" for the right man, the one her parents were going to choose for her. Silly cow.'

'When did all this happen?'

'Ages ago.'

'Was Yasmin upset about the split?'

'Yeah. She wanted me to come out in sympathy and finish with Sam, too.'

'And did you?'

'No. It was totally unreasonable.'

'So you're still seeing Sam?' asked Mariner.

'Yeah.' She smiled. 'He totally rocks.'

'Is that why you and Yasmin haven't been such good friends lately?'

'We don't have so much in common any more. Yasmin can be so immature.'

'Do you think Yasmin could be jealous of you and Sam?' Mariner asked. 'Did she think she was missing out?'

'It was up to her, wasn't it? She'd made her choice between her parents and Lee. She chose her parents.'

He needed to tread carefully here. 'And do you and Sam have a . . . er?'

'Do you mean sex? Of course we do.' Treating the question with the disdain it deserved. 'Sammy's hot. But I'm not stupid. I've been on the pill for months.'

'Did you ever suggest to Yasmin that she should go on the pill?'

'We talked about it, sure, we all know guys don't like skins, but it was too late for that. Yaz blew it.'

'What would you say if I told you that Yasmin was texting Lee as recently as the day she disappeared,' said

Mariner. 'And that she'd asked her GP to prescribe the pill?'

Suzanne's eyes widened. 'I'd say fucking good for you, Yaz. She's finally decided to do it. That must have been what she was going to tell me.'

'That's what we think, too. But why would Yasmin suddenly change her mind about sleeping with Lee? Has anyone been putting her under pressure?'

'Yaz doesn't need anyone else to do that. She's well good at doing it for herself.'

'If Yasmin was going to meet Lee again, where would she have met him?' asked Mariner.

Suzanne thought for a moment. 'When they were going out he sometimes used to meet Yaz from school, or they'd meet down near the station where she gets her train. Lee gets the train home too. He lives in this big posh house in Barnt Green with a pool and everything. There's a pub down by the station called The Bridge. Yaz used to talk about seeing Lee at The Bridge.'

. . . Except that Mariner was pretty sure that Yasmin hadn't meant that bridge. It was beginning to look possible that it was she who had dropped her mobile phone. But was it before or after Ricky had been attacked? And did the two occurrences have anything to do with each other?

Millie had parked the car and caught up with Mariner outside reception. He reported back on the conversation. 'So perhaps that's what it's all about: Yasmin trying to keep up with her friends. The status of being on the contraceptive pill.'

'Better than the status of being landed with a baby at seventeen,' said Millie. 'Like Finlay said; we need to go and talk to Lewis Everett.'

'I'd like to get the official take on what Suzanne told us too. Let's see if *Ms* Darrow is around.'

* * *

The head teacher was in her office and they were shown in just as Mr Goodway was leaving. Mariner couldn't help but look at those two in a new light, though it was hard to tell if what Suzanne had said was true. As Ms Darrow herself had said, teenage girls could be prone to overactive imaginations.

'Can you tell us anything about the Year 12 trip to London in the spring?' Mariner asked, when they were seated.

'Oh. That was months ago,' said Ms Darrow. 'Some of the girls went on an art trip to the Tate Modern with some pupils from the boys' school. Mr Goodway and I took them, along with a teacher from the boys'. We run quite a few joint trips. It cuts down on the expense and also allows the youngsters to mix, which is an important part of their social development.'

'From what I understand, the trip certainly enhanced Yasmin's social development,' said Mariner.

'Ah,' said Ms Darrow. 'You know about the incident then.'

'We've heard one version but would be interested in your account of events.'

'It's very simple,' she said, making light of it. 'When the time came to leave, all the children were accounted for except Yasmin and Suzanne, and two of the boys. They eventually turned up at the coach almost two hours late. People were beginning to get worried.'

'Where had they been?'

'Sightseeing.' She shrugged. 'It was all perfectly innocent. They simply got lost and had to get the tube back to the meeting place. London's a big place, Inspector. I wouldn't be taken in by any embroidery that might have been added.'

'Did you tell Yasmin's parents about what happened?'

The smile went and the defences came down. 'We didn't think it necessary.'

'Because you knew how they would react.'

'We didn't want to jeopardise Yasmin's education because of one foolish episode.'

'Or jeopardise the generous donations Yasmin's father was making to the school.'

'That's a very cynical view, Inspector. The truth is that it was just one of these little crushes girls have: completely normal and harmless, and over before it had begun. It had run its course so there seemed no need to rock the boat.'

'It wasn't quite over though, was it?' said Mariner.

'What do you mean?'

'Yasmin was still in contact with the boy in question, Lee, up until last Tuesday. And she had begun taking the contraceptive pill. Her father found all this out shortly before Yasmin disappeared. I wonder how he would feel if he knew that you are responsible for introducing Yasmin to her lover and then allowing things to "run their course?"'

Under her makeup Ms Darrow seemed to lose some of her colour.

'Thank you, that's been helpful,' said Mariner. 'We will naturally have to discuss this with Yasmin's parents. You may want to prepare for the fallout.'

Subdued by these revelations, Ms Darrow showed them out into reception again, where Mariner's attention was caught anew by the body art sketches. This time though they triggered a recent memory. He'd seen some of those designs somewhere else, only yesterday afternoon.

Digging it from his inside pocket he thrust the picture of Shaun Pryce in front of Ms Darrow. 'Has this young man been here, to the school?'

'Sorry?' She was still distracted. 'Oh, yes, he's an actor, or so he says. He came and did some modelling for us about a year ago. We try and include life portraits in the art syllabus where we can. It was a mistake though, really.'

'Why?' Millie was surprised. 'The pictures are very good.'

'The young man in question liked to flirt with the girls. He seemed to get them rather excited.'

'I'll bet he did,' murmured Mariner. 'Did he model for Yasmin's class?'

'He might have.'

'Think,' barked Mariner, getting tired of the prevarication. 'Did he?'

'Yes. I think so.'

* * *

'So Shaun Pryce has a link with the girls' school and may have known Yasmin' said Mariner as he and Millie walked back to the car. 'Now why didn't he tell us that?'

'Do you want to go and talk to him again?' asked Millie, fishing for her keys.

'Not yet. Let's get Lee out of the way first.'

* * *

Built during the same era, the boys' school was structurally a mirror image of the girls', but there the similarity ended. Less well-cared-for, soft greenery gave way to showcases full of competition trophies and raw testosterone hung in the air. Mariner identified himself to the matronly receptionist. 'We need to speak to one of your students: Lewis Everett,' he said.

'I'll just need to check with Mr Blyth. One moment, please.'

Head teacher Gordon Blyth, a small man with thinning black hair and a voice from the valleys of south Wales, came out to speak to them in person. 'I'm afraid Lewis isn't here at the moment,' he said. 'He's doing work experience.'

'Where?'

Blyth had to go away and consult with the person responsible for organising these things. He was back moments later. 'At a place that makes kitchen units, on Birch Close. It's—'

'Yes, I know where it is,' said Mariner. He looked at Millie. 'Now we are going round in bloody circles.'

CHAPTER 19

Within a few minutes they were back on the small industrial estate, four units down from TMR Reprographics. Imran Shaikh, the manager of Dunhill's Kitchen Design was not a happy man.

'Work experience, is that what they call it? Little bugger hasn't turned in for work again today. He cleared off last Tuesday afternoon and I haven't seen him since.'

'What time on Tuesday afternoon?' Mariner exchanged a look with Millie.

'About half one. The kid's a waste of space. He's hardly put in a full day since he started here. I ask you. What kind of a worker is he going to make?'

'Have you rung the school to find out where he is?' asked Mariner.

'I haven't got time to go chasing round after him. I've got a business to run,' said Shaikh. 'It'll just go on his report at the end of the week. He wasn't much use anyway. He's a spoilt little rich kid who doesn't like getting his hands dirty.'

* * *

Outside, just a few metres away, were the refuse bins which concealed the gap in the fence. Mariner put through a call on his mobile to the head of the boys' school. 'We're at the kitchen workshop, but Lewis isn't. In fact he hasn't been here since last Tuesday. I trust you didn't know that.' The pause at the other end of the line confirmed it. 'I'd like Lewis's home address please.'

Lewis Everett's daily train journey home terminated at the exclusive hamlet of Barnt Green that nestled complacently at the foot of the Lickey Hills, just outside the city. The Everetts' house was 'big and posh,' as Suzanne had described it, hemmed in on all sides by woodland on a private road that wasn't even graced with a name. The house itself was called Hawthorns — and Mariner suspected that moniker had rather more to do with the shrub than with the home of West Bromwich Albion. Mariner tried to picture the Akram family living round here. He couldn't. Number four, Hawthorns consisted of five room-widths of 1950s mock-Georgian with a broad double garage, behind impressive wrought iron gates and a York stone drive. Burgeoning ten-foot leylandii divided the property from its neighbours. A side gate was unlocked and they pushed through and approached the building. Mariner stepped over a dark stain that marked the otherwise flawless drive, but closer inspection revealed only engine oil. Pushing the button on the studded oak front door prompted nothing more than the jangle of a bell deep inside the house. Millie peered in through the window to see a neat and tidy house, plush carpeting, gleaming antique reproduction furniture — everything in its place.

'At work I suppose,' Millie said. 'We'll have to come back later.'

'On holiday,' called a disembodied voice from behind the hedge. The rhythmic chopping that had been a barely noticeable background noise, abruptly ceased. Mariner followed Millie back out through the gates and round to the adjacent property, an equally imposing edifice with tall windows and curving bays, in the style of Rennie

Mackintosh. A man, tall and white-haired, with a weathered face and sinewy arms, stood mid-way up an aluminium stepladder brandishing a pair of garden shears. 'I do their garden, too,' he said. 'And they've gone away. Mr and Mrs have anyway. Three weeks in the Bahamas. They do it every year at about this time. Due back early hours of Friday morning.'

'It wasn't Mr or Mrs we were looking for,' Mariner said. 'It was Lee. Lewis.'

The man thought for a minute before slowly shaking his head. 'Haven't seen him for a few days either.'

'You're here every day?' asked Millie.

'Look at the size of these gardens. This street is a full-time job for me. This time of year I get here at seven in the morning and don't go home until at least six, sometimes later if I've a job to finish. And by the time I get to the end I have to start all over again.'

'So when was the last time you saw Lee Everett?' Mariner asked.

The man paused to think. 'Monday. He was around then, driving that car of his too fast up and down the road. Only a matter of time before he kills someone.'

Mariner and Millie exchanged a look. 'You didn't see him on Tuesday?'

'Let me think. Tuesday I was doing the back lawn at number eight. I'd have been round there for most of the day. They've got more grass there than at Wentworth.'

'And you definitely haven't seen him since?'

'No, but you might want to check with Margaret.'

'Margaret?'

'Yes, Margaret Ashworth. Their daily help.'

'Do you have her phone number?'

'I don't.' He shook his head, before nodding an acknowledgement towards a green Land Rover Discovery that was pulling into the driveway opposite. 'But Mrs Goldman would.'

Hurrying across the road, Mariner and Millie sneaked into the property before the electric gates could close. Mrs Goldman was stepping down from her Land Rover Discovery, stretching out long legs clad in gleaming white cotton jeans, her equally dazzling blouse contrasting with the deep tanning on her arms. On seeing Mariner's warrant card, the friendly smile dissolved to a troubled frown. 'Not another burglary,' she said, opening up the boot of the vehicle to retrieve Waitrose carrier bags. 'Who is it this time?'

'It's nothing like that,' Mariner reassured her. 'We need to get in touch with your cleaner, Margaret Ashworth.'

'Margaret? Why? What's happened?'

'We're trying to track down Lewis Everett.'

'Oh. Do you have to?' she said with feeling, slamming shut the tailgate. 'It's been so peaceful these last few days.'

Mariner offered to carry a couple of bags.

'Thanks.'

They followed her round to the side of the house where she let them into a kitchen the size of Mariner's entire ground floor. It was sparse and modern, with wall-to-wall limed oak cupboards, topped with granite, and a wide central station that held a butcher's block. Another wall was dominated by a huge green-enamelled Aga. Otherwise the appliances were in clinical stainless steel, everything as spotless as Mrs Goldman herself. Margaret was obviously a treasure.

'Can I offer you something to drink, something cold perhaps?'

Mariner placed the bag alongside the others she'd deposited on the counter top. 'That would be very welcome. Thank you.'

Opening a fridge the size of a wardrobe she dropped chunks from an ice dispenser into beautifully crafted crystal tumblers, topping them up with exotic fruit juice.

'You remarked on how quiet things have been over the last few days,' said Mariner, 'implying that it's not always the case.'

'Lewis takes full advantage of his parents being away,' she said. 'We get treated to the latest rock bands at full volume most evenings. The warm weather encourages him to open all the windows too, of course, which makes it worse.'

'No one complains?'

'Oh, one or two of the neighbours have tried talking to him. It's a question of getting through though. Lewis is a very intense young man. The sulky and broody type, a regular Liam Gallagher — or is it Noel? You never quite know what's going on inside his head. To be truthful, I think his parents may be a bit afraid of him and they're lovely people so nobody really wants to upset them. We all just put up with it. When you live in a little community like this one it's important to get along. And to be fair Lewis isn't that much trouble when his parents are around.'

'When was the last time you saw him?'

'Hmm, I haven't seen him — or heard him — for about a week. Last Monday or Tuesday, I think.'

'If we could just have Margaret Ashworth's number—' Mariner said, finishing his drink.

'Yes, of course. I'll get it for you.' Mrs Goldman was also good enough to let Mariner use her phone, but Margaret Ashworth was out shopping. Her daughter was expecting her back in a couple of hours.

'We may as well go back to the station,' Mariner said to Millie. 'Thanks for the drink, Mrs Goldman.'

'Not at all. Good luck with Lewis.'

* * *

The route to Granville Lane took them back past the girls' school. It was the end of the afternoon and they happened to see Suzanne Perry arguing with a man beside a big flashy car, as girls swarmed out past them.

'Look at that,' said Millie. 'What do you think's going on there?'

Mariner put a call through to Knox back at OCU 4. 'Could you run a vehicle check on a Volvo estate, personalised plate SDP 2?'

Moments later Knox came back. 'The car is registered to a Mr Stephen Perry, 39 Oakwood Rd, Kingsmead.'

'She was just being shown up in front of her friends by an over-protective father,' Millie concluded. 'Now who's being paranoid?'

* * *

Charlie Glover was also checking in at Granville Lane, where they found him brooding over the incident room map.

'How's it going?' Mariner truly wanted to know.

'Slowly,' Charlie said. 'There's still nothing to indicate that Ricky would have known Yasmin. It's looking more and more like sheer coincidence that they were around there at the same time.'

'Anything else new?'

Glover shook his head. 'We're still looking for a murder weapon. How about you?'

For the benefit of Knox, too, Mariner filled Glover in on the afternoon's developments. 'So now we have Yasmin and the boyfriend missing. The boyfriend works at the industrial units and Yasmin's phone is found between the station and there. It gives us a whole new scenario.'

'If Yasmin was trying to prove to Suzanne that she could cut it in the romance stakes and if she wanted to get away from her parents, what better way to do both than to elope with her boyfriend?' said Glover. 'She could have planned the whole thing, including the sleepover at Suzanne's, which she never had any intention of following through on.'

'But Suzanne seems certain that the relationship is finished,' Millie reminded him.

'That's what Yasmin told her,' said Mariner. 'That way, the bigger the surprise when her friend finds out what she's done. Suzanne also said that Yasmin was excited, had something to tell her. It might have been rather more than we thought.'

'If Yasmin has eloped, she hasn't taken much with her,' Millie said.

'She wouldn't need to, would she? Boyfriend Lee isn't short of a bob or two.'

'Where does that leave us with Pryce?' asked Glover. 'Potentially we now have four people on or around the reservoir that afternoon, three of whom know each other; Akram knows Yasmin, Yasmin knows Lee.'

'—and as we found out this afternoon, Shaun Pryce is at least acquainted with Yasmin.' Mariner explained to Charlie.

'But Pryce insists he was there much earlier,' Knox reminded him. 'Surely we can rule him out now.'

'If we believe him,' Mariner was sceptical. 'I'm sure there's something going on with him. And Akram's still a possibility, but no more than that.'

'Which leaves us with Yasmin, Lee and Ricky at the scene,' said Knox. 'As far as we know Ricky doesn't know Lee or Yasmin, but perhaps he saw something, tried to stop it and Lee turned on him.'

'Perhaps eloping wasn't on the agenda,' Millie put in. 'We know for sure that Yasmin had just gone on the pill and that she was ready to lose her virginity. Maybe that's what they were meeting for. Shaun Pryce could have even suggested the location. We don't know how he gets his kicks. Perhaps he was planning to watch. So Yasmin gets there. Lee turns up with high expectations, but Yasmin then gets cold feet and won't play. Lee gets rough with her and Ricky, there by sheer coincidence, intervenes to help her—'

'And Lee turns on him.'

'Mrs Goldman said he's a bit of a sullen bastard,' said Mariner.

'And Imran Shaikh called him a spoilt kid,' Millie added. 'Implying that he's used to getting what he wants.'

'Then Lee and Yasmin panic about what's happened and disappear together.'

'Or Lee panics and forces Yasmin to go with him?' Mariner concluded.

'And Pryce?'

'Pryce witnessed the whole thing, which is why he's playing silly buggers with us.'

'So why doesn't he just tell us?'

'Because he could be implicated on some level — especially if he just stood back and watched it all happen.'

'Or more than that, it turned him on.'

Mariner sighed. He couldn't ever remember standing on such fast shifting sand. The phone rang.

'Margaret Ashworth,' said Millie. 'She'll meet us at the Everetts' house.'

CHAPTER 20

'Have you got a warrant?' were Margaret Ashworth's first words to Mariner and Knox, when they arrived. Fortunately Mariner was able to persuade her that it wasn't necessary since she was merely co-operating with the police enquiry. 'We don't want to search the premises,' he said, 'only see for ourselves that the place has been uninhabited for a few days.' They had to wait while she disarmed a complex security alarm and then carefully removed her shoes in favour of fluffy pink mules — waiting just in front of the door — glancing disapprovingly at the men's own heavy footwear.

'You wouldn't want me to take them off, love, believe me,' said Knox.

Margaret took them up a sweeping staircase to Lee's room off the first landing at the back of the house. The curtains were drawn rendering it almost pitch-black inside.

'He likes them kept closed at all times,' Margaret told them. Switching on the ceiling spotlights revealed a room that was a far cry from the single bed, nightstand and wardrobe that had furnished Mariner's room at the same age. There was a double bed, a bank of technology including PC, games console, stereo, TV and DVD player, even a kettle, fridge and microwave. It was virtually a self-contained flat with everything a young man could want. 'Jeez, if I had a place like this and the folks were away I wouldn't do a disappearing act,' was Knox's comment.

Spaces on the purple-painted walls were covered with posters of surfers riding massive waves, along with some of Lee's own gruesome drawings. A battered skateboard leaned against the wardrobe. Mariner picked over the untidy desk, a jumble of papers, books, CDs and lad magazines. He was itching to rifle through the drawers too, but Margaret was keeping a beady eye on them from the doorway.

'How about a cup of tea, love?' Knox asked, summoning the best of his scouse charm. 'I'm parched.' But Margaret wasn't having any of it and her arms remained resolutely folded.

'You're losing your touch, mate,' murmured Mariner.

'Tell me about it,' Knox retorted, with surprising acrimony. The rubbish bin had been emptied so there were no clues there, but tucked behind it Knox found a small silver tin of the kind that normally holds travel sweets. This one didn't. Knox sniffed the dried green substance. 'He's got something in common with Shaun Pryce then.'

Mariner wasn't entirely surprised. He walked over to inspect the switched-off computer and his eye was caught by a glossy scrap of paper that had slid underneath the processor. He edged it out with a fingernail. Dusty and slightly bent at one corner, it was a strip of photographs of the kind taken in an instant photo booth. 'Tony.' He held it up to show Knox. Lewis Everett and Yasmin Akram grinning broadly, their faces squashed together to fit into the shot. 'At least it confirms that they've been an item.'

'Not much care taken to preserve it,' said Knox. 'Looks like a bit of a one-sided relationship, doesn't it?'

'It does,' said Mariner. Another one, he thought, suddenly. Downstairs, a kitchen memo board bore postcards from various locations around the world, along with a number of business cards for local tradesmen and a couple of dental appointment cards. The answering machine might have been a source of additional information, but until they had permission, it was off-limits.

'Have you any idea where Lewis might have gone?' Mariner asked Margaret, who was hovering, ever vigilant, watching over them. 'Did he say anything to you about his plans?'

She snorted. 'He doesn't even tell his parents what he's up to. He's a law unto himself.'

They did however get from Margaret a good description of Lewis's car and its registration and she even, if a little reluctantly, allowed them to borrow a more naturally posed recent photograph of the man himself from a display in the lounge. He was as Mrs Goldman had described him, scruffy and staring defiantly into the camera.

'It'll help us to eliminate him from our enquiries,' Mariner said, as a sop, though in reality Lewis was inching nearer by the minute to the main frame. It would have been good to be able to delve a little deeper, but until Mr and Mrs Everett returned their hands were tied. Mr Everett was apparently a director of several small companies, so would certainly have some legal connections. He wouldn't be too pleased about coming home to find his house had been ransacked when there was no concrete evidence for doing so. They had little choice but to wait a day or so and hopefully do it with the Everetts' blessing.

What they could do instead was issue a nationwide description of Lewis and his car, highlighting to colleagues in other forces the possible link with Yasmin. Mariner would go with Millie to talk to the Akrams as well. Their reaction to all this information would be educational.

* * *

Mariner wanted both parents together, so they went back to the house in the early evening. Amira was present too, giving her mother some much needed support. Shanila Akram was displaying increasing signs of strain. Her eyes seemed sunken in her pale face and Mariner guessed that food and sleep had become irrelevancies. Mohammed Akram was wearing better — was that because he knew that his daughter was safe, or was he just better at putting on a show for them?

'We're fairly certain now that Yasmin may have been seeing a boy called Lee or Lewis,' Mariner told them, when they were gathered in the garden. 'Has she ever mentioned him to you?'

'Yasmin doesn't know any boys, only her cousins.' Mohammed Akram was calm but firm.

Mariner had no choice but to hand over the photo-booth snaps and watch shock and bewilderment creep over their faces once again. 'As you can see, there's no doubt that Yasmin knows this particular boy. She met him on a school trip when they spent some time together. We've also confirmed this with the school. He has also disappeared, which means that we have to consider the possibility that Yasmin could be with him now.'

In an unprecedented outburst Shanila Akram turned on her husband. 'Do you see what we've done? We've pushed her into the arms of a boy. If we had let her do this out in the open and if you hadn't—!' She stopped herself and for a moment the air was thick with what she left unspoken.

'Hadn't what, Mrs Akram?' Mariner prompted.

'I was going to say "argued with her,"' Shanila Akram replied, weakly. Mariner didn't believe her, but the moment had passed and she was no longer prepared to say what she'd intended.

'It's my fault,' said Amira, shakily. 'I encouraged her.'

Her mother stared. 'But why? Yasmin is so young. She should remain pure for her future husband.'

'Mum, that's ridiculous antiquated nonsense,' said Amira, her voice strengthening. 'I had been with several men before Ravi and I married.'

'Amira!'

'It's true. But Ravi doesn't mind. In fact he liked that I had some experience and knew what to do. Yasmin is the same. She needs some experience. She should get to know some boys.'

'So you told her to make a whore of herself?' Mohammed Akram was beside himself.

'Of course not,' Amira replied, evenly. 'I just told her that if a chance presented itself she should take it. Virginity is overrated. And I know that Yasmin was under pressure from her friends. She felt excluded.'

'It takes a special kind of courage to stand by your principles,' said Akram coldly. 'And this is the price we pay for giving in to temptation.' He turned to Mariner. 'We would like to be left alone now, Inspector.'

* * *

'Whatever other skills she has, Yasmin's pretty adept at keeping all the different facets of her life separate from one another,' said Millie as they drove away.

'It's something we all learn to do, some more efficiently than others,' said Mariner, thinking that he'd managed to get it down to a fine art, his work, mother and Anna all running on separate, parallel tracks.

* * *

Kings Rise was holding a memorial service for Ricky the next morning at a local church to help pupils through the grieving process, though how many of them would genuinely be mourning the boy was open to debate. It was another unrelentingly hot and dry day and it seemed obscene to Mariner that the sun could shine so cheerfully over such an event. Fiske had insisted on accompanying him and Charlie Glover, keeping the police presence to a minimum. The three of them slipped into the back of the church and the place was so packed with family and school friends that they had to stand in the unbearable heat. Half the church seemed to be filled with spotty adolescent kids. If this lot was anything to go by, Ricky had more mates than his mother knew.

One of Ricky's uncles spoke nervously and with hesitancy about what a 'grand lad' Ricky had been, while Colleen's sobbing seemed to echo around the whole chapel throughout. Mariner detested the indignity of these manufactured occasions and, as the congregation rose falteringly to its feet and began an uneasy rendition of the final hymn, he noticed one or two of the kids stifling giggles. When Fiske's pager went off he wanted to punch his superior officer in the face.

Afterwards they joined the long line that filed past the family to pay their respects. 'What the hell is he doing here?' demanded Colleen emotionally as Fiske appeared in front of her. 'You did nothing. Nothing!' Suddenly she lunged for him. Mariner heard camera shutters clunk behind them and knew that this would not be Fiske's finest hour. Turning his back on the debacle, Mariner walked over to where Charlie Glover stood lighting up a cigarette. At least Colleen would appreciate that particular brand of camaraderie.

* * *

They drove in an uncomfortable silence back to Granville Lane where Tony Knox had mixed news. 'Lewis Everett's parents are home. They flew in from the Bahamas early hours of this morning, boss. But they don't know where he is either. As far as they were concerned their precious son was looking after the house and doing his work experience. They admit that he can be a bit wild but they don't see him eloping with anyone. Too selfish for that so they say.'

* * *

212

The neat and tidy vestibule they'd entered the previous day was this afternoon clogged up with matching Louis Vuitton and a bulging sack of golf clubs. Mr and Mrs Everett were nicely tanned, but they didn't look very relaxed.

'Thank you for seeing us so promptly,' Mariner said. 'I realise you must be tired and jet-lagged and have things to do.'

'This is not the kind of reception you expect or want on returning from a peaceful holiday,' admitted Mr Everett, with a sigh of irritation. 'But we'd like to sort all of this out as soon as we can.'

'You'll be aware by now that a young girl has gone missing in the area. We have reason to believe that she was in a relationship with your son.' Mariner produced the photo. 'This is Yasmin Akram. Did you know that Lewis was seeing her?'

Everett gave the picture a perfunctory glance before passing it to his wife. 'Lewis has had a number of girlfriends. We don't always meet them.'

'And Yasmin?'

'I don't recall her, do you, darling?'

Mrs Everett was studying the snapshot more carefully. 'No.'

'And have you any idea where Lewis may have gone? We need to find him. He may be the last person to have seen Yasmin before she disappeared.'

'I've had a look round,' Everett said. 'Some of his camping gear has gone from the garage, but as to where he's gone I wouldn't know.'

'We'd like to do a more thorough search of his room if that's all right.'

Everett stifled a yawn. 'If you must.'

'Do you know if Lewis kept any kind of diary?' Mariner asked Mrs Everett.

'I don't think so.'

'Perhaps we could have a look on his computer.'

Even on the more thorough search, the only paperwork they could find was a school planner, but it contained nothing personal. On Lewis's PC they looked for traces of records on Outlook but there was nothing.

'What would Lewis do for money while he's away?' Mariner asked.

'He has an allowance paid into his bank account and a debit card that he can use to withdraw cash from ATMs. He has a credit card too,' Everett told them.

'We'll need the details. The credit card company may be able to help us track his movements.'

Lewis's credit card records provided the break they needed. A phone call to his credit card company revealed that since the day of his disappearance, Lewis had been spending heavily at petrol stations, restaurants and surfing shops in the area around Newquay in Cornwall. Knox contacted local police with the description of Lewis and his car, with a request to publicise it widely, especially around campsites in the area.

'That could take some time,' he was told 'There's dozens of them and in this weather they're pretty full, too.'

'Do what you can, will you?' Then it was back to the waiting game.

* * *

When Mariner got home that evening he saw his answering machine had been working overtime again. An unexpected message from Anna told him that she had the chance of a night's respite from Jamie if he felt like calling round. It happened occasionally when the facility had an overnight vacancy. Mariner looked at his watch, it was ten fifteen. It didn't take long to make up his mind.

The house was dark: Anna making the most of the opportunity for an early night. Her sleep was so often disturbed by Jamie's nocturnal wanderings that she took a full night whenever she could. Mariner let himself in and after a long, cleansing shower eventually slipped into bed beside Anna.

'Hello, you,' she murmured, sleepily.

'Hi.' In the heat of the night she'd thrown off the duvet and he could make out the luscious curves of her body. He slid a hand round over her stomach and up towards her breast, feeling his own body starting to respond.

But Anna wriggled away. 'Mm, I'm really tired.'

Pity. Sighing heavily, Mariner had to content himself with moulding his body to hers and breathing her scent. He lay there for a while trying to drift off, but he was too turned on and sleep just wouldn't come. Eventually he got up and prowled the rooms, coming to rest at the bedroom window where he stared out at the eerie orange glow cast over the street by the sodium light until it was overtaken by the dawn. The next morning he felt like death warmed up while Anna looked as fresh as a daisy. 'I've got a meeting with Simon about the festival this evening,' she bubbled. 'Any chance you could sit with Jamie for me?' Suddenly Mariner began to question the motives for that late-night phone call.

'Sure,' he said, indifferently.

She picked up the undertone. 'Is that going to be a problem?'

'Of course not,' he said, but he wasn't convincing.

She was still watching him carefully when the phone rang. 'It's the wife,' she said, handing it over.

* * *

In fact it was Tony Knox. 'Cornwall police have come back to us. They've found Lewis Everett. But he's not there with Yasmin. He's there with his mate Daniel who's also skiving off work experience.'

'Really gives you confidence in the future generation, doesn't it?' said Mariner. 'Are they on their way?'

'They're being escorted back this afternoon.'

'We'll talk to Lewis as soon as he gets here.' Which, he realised, might mean interviewing him through the evening. He gave Anna an apologetic look. 'I'm sorry, I won't be able to make it tonight after all, something's come up.'

She studied him for a moment. 'That's OK, I can take Jamie with me. Simon won't mind.'

Mariner picked up his jacket. 'I'll see you later then.'

'Sure, have a good day.' No hint of disappointment, not even the demand for further explanation, so why, as he walked out to his car, did Mariner feel so piqued? Because Simon *wouldn't mind*. He wouldn't, would he? Bastard. In all honesty, what Mariner had really wanted her to say was that she would cancel the appointment. Knowing that he was being unreasonable, he recognised the growing feeling inside him for what it was. He was jealous — of Simon Meadows, with whom Anna seemed to be spending ever increasing amounts of time.

It was essential to her autistic brother's well-being that Anna and Meadows should get on, so it came as a bit of a shock to Mariner that he should begin to resent their relationship. But it was becoming something he couldn't deny, even to himself. After all these years of bearing witness to the devastating impact of human jealousy, a tiny part of him was beginning to appreciate its power.

CHAPTER 21

Lewis Everett arrived back in the city in the early afternoon and had legal representation right from the start. His father made sure of that and insisted on being present, too. Approaching six-foot tall, Everett was lean and lanky in that gangling post-adolescent way, his hair fashionably mussed and with a few days' fuzzy growth on his chin. The first thing to draw Mariner's attention, as they faced each other across the interview room table, was the tattoo on his left forearm. Mariner wondered if he'd got it at the same parlour as Shaun Pryce. 'I understand you're seeing Yasmin Akram,' Mariner began.

'*Was* seeing,' said Lewis, sleepily. 'Past tense. It was months ago.'

'How did it start?'

'We met on a school trip.'

'Oh yes, the trip to the Tate,' said Mariner. The two of you were late back to the bus.'

'We went sightseeing. Got carried away.'

'And lost. You continued seeing Yasmin after that?'

'Not for long.'

'Who broke it off?' Mariner asked.

'I did. She was a prick-tease.'

'Lewis!'

'Thanks, Mr Everett,' said Mariner calmly. 'What do you mean by that Lewis?'

'She used to wind me up. Hands all over me, going everywhere, then suddenly the parents and their religious beliefs would come into her head and she'd want to stop. She'd say she couldn't go any further. I got fed up with it.'

'But you saw her again recently.'

'Can't help it,' said Lewis sullenly. 'Sometimes she's across on the other platform when I get my train. Then, a couple of weeks ago she sends me a text. Says she wants to meet me again, she's got something important to say. She said I should meet her from school.'

'And?'

'I wasn't going to be at school that week. It was when I started my work experience up at the factory centre.'

'Huh.' Lewis's father couldn't stop himself. Mariner silenced him with a glare.

'I told her to come over to the centre on Monday after school.' Lewis was getting warmed up now. 'She'd be finished before me.'

'And did she come?' asked Mariner.

'Eventually. She was late. She'd walked all the way round on the road. It's miles.'

'She didn't know about the short cut over the reservoir?'

'No, but I told her so she'd know next time. Anyway,' Lewis said. 'By the time she got to Dung Heap's it was nearly time for her to catch her train home.'

'And did she tell you?' prompted Mariner.

'What?'

'The "something important" she wanted to say.'

Lewis snorted. 'She said she really missed me and that she'd changed her mind.'

'About what?'

'About doing it — sleeping with me.'

'What had brought this on?'

Everett lifted his bony shoulders. 'Who knows? Her mate Suzanne had been giving her a hard time. And there was something about her sister too.'

'So she was planning to go through with it this time?' Mariner confirmed.

'So she said.' He sounded sceptical. 'I said great, but what was she going to do about protection. I said it would be easier if she just went on the pill.'

'Very noble of you.' Until then, Knox had sat quietly.

'If you must know, I thought when I said that she'd back down again,' Lewis gave Knox a pointed stare.

'But she didn't,' said Mariner, keen to keep things moving.

'No. She'd already sorted it. I was pretty stunned. Her dad had even found out, but she'd fixed him too.'

'She told him she was on the pill for medical reasons.'

'Whatever.'

'So what did you do?'

'I said I'd meet her again on the Tuesday afternoon, after school. I was going to get off work early and we'd go back to my place. She was going to tell her parents she was staying at her mate's house for the night.'

'So what happened?'

'Monday night, Dan called with this big plan about going down to Cornwall. But it was cool. I could meet Yasmin as planned then we'd go down afterwards, drop her off at the station or something on the way.'

'Have your cake and eat it,' Mariner observed.

'Then Tuesday morning Dan called to say we'd have to set off early, or we wouldn't get a pitch at the campsite. I texted Yasmin, to let her know I wouldn't make it and that I'd see her when I got back.'

'Just like that.'

Lewis shrugged again. 'I felt bad letting her down. She'd gone out on a limb for me but, well, you know—'

'Girls in Cornwall more of a certainty?'

Lewis folded his arms. 'Less complicated,' he said. 'Yasmin had messed me around before. How did I know she wouldn't just do it again?'

'What time did you send the text?'

'Dunno. Some time that morning.'

'What exactly did your message say?'

'"I'm going to Cornwall with Dan, don't bother turning up at the reservoir." To be honest, I didn't think she'd come anyway. I thought she'd bottle it at the last minute like before.'

'Is there any way Yasmin could have misunderstood?' Mariner asked, though it sounded pretty clear. The shrugged responses were beginning to get on his nerves. 'And what time did you leave to go to Cornwall?'

'I left the workshop at lunch time, about one fifteen. I told them I didn't feel well—'

'Christ, Lewis!' Everett senior could hardly contain himself. 'When are you ever going to do a decent day's work?'

'Mr Everett, please.' Mariner turned back to Lewis. 'Then what did you do?'

'I went home and packed my stuff, and waited for Dan. But his car was leaking oil—'

'All over my drive I notice,' Lewis's father interrupted.

Mariner's patience was at an end. 'Mr Everett, if you can't remain silent, I'll have to ask you to leave. Go on, Lewis.'

'We didn't fix it till nearly four.'

'And you went on the motorway?'

'Straight down the M5.' Lewis sliced through the air with the edge of his hand.

'Does Yasmin talk to you much about her parents?'

Lewis scoffed. 'She's always moaning about how strict they are.'

'She ever talk about running away?'

'Not for real.'

'But she has mentioned it?' said Mariner. 'Did she say where she would go if she did?'

'No.'

'Did you think about taking her to Cornwall with you?'

'No.'

'Will anyone be able to corroborate the time you left?'

A shrug. 'Dan?'

'Your best pal? Not much of a backup,' said Knox.

'The traffic cameras might pick up the car.' Lewis was hopeful.

But Mariner kept pushing. 'I still don't understand why you turned down a perfectly good opportunity on your doorstep to drive all the way down to Cornwall. Especially given that Yasmin had started contraception for your benefit. What was it; was she too tame for you?'

Lewis's face screwed up in a flash of irritation. 'She was using me too, man. All of a sudden she had this thing about losing her virginity. That's all she wanted me for. Listen, I really like Yasmin, but like I said, she's complicated. When we were going out she didn't really know what she wanted. I didn't like the sound of her dad much either: seriously scary. Cornwall was just fun, a chance to get away from all that.'

'Without the responsibility,' put in Mr Everett.

His son stared back insolently. 'Yeah, that's right.'

'Ever heard of a boy called Ricky Skeet?' Mariner slid the photograph across the table. 'This is him.'

Lewis looked at the picture, at ease with the question. 'No.'

Knox produced the tin of weed and placed it on the table. 'We found this in your room.'

'It's for personal use,' said Lewis instantly. 'To be honest it's been there ages. I'd forgotten all about it.'

'Where did you get it?' Knox asked.

'A friend got it for me.'

'What's his name?'

'John Smith.'

'You sure it wasn't Shaun Pryce?'

Again, the smooth response. 'No.'

Mariner put the second photograph on the table. 'This is him.' Lewis frowned.

'What?' said Mariner.

'It's just . . . weird. I'm pretty sure I don't know that guy, but it's like I've seen that picture before.'

'This picture? Or one like it?'

'Could be one like it.'

'Have you ever been into the girls' school?'

'No.'

'That is weird then.'

* * *

They let Lewis go home with his father in the late afternoon. His car was impounded for fingerprinting but Mariner felt it was a waste of time.

'Young lad like him, you'd have thought that he'd jump at the chance of a girl offered to him on a plate,' Mariner said to Knox afterwards. 'Would he really forgo that opportunity?'

'He was hedging his bets. Yasmin wasn't exactly consistent, was she? The girls in Cornwall must have seemed a safer bet.'

'He seems relaxed enough talking about Yasmin. On balance I think he's telling the truth. And it will be easy enough to check out his story with this Dan.'

'Yes,' said Knox. 'After all, they've had the whole drive back here to get their stories straight.'

* * *

Knox followed up by talking to Dan, who confirmed Lewis's version of events in every detail. And though the occupants were a blur, Dan's battered and dusty Grand Vitara could be picked out on motorway CCTV passing Bromsgrove at 4:09 p.m. on that Tuesday afternoon. In all probability they'd drawn another blank and Mariner could reasonably have taken the rest of the evening off to help out Anna. But he chose not to.

Instead he went back to Finlay. 'Is there any way of knowing the content of Lewis's last message, even if Yasmin deleted it afterwards?' he asked.

'There is one deleted message: the last one received, which would have been it,' said Finlay. 'As I said before, the ghosting is there. But there's no way of knowing what that message said.'

* * *

'So, we only have Lewis's word that the text was calling off the meeting,' Mariner told Knox and Millie a little later.

'But if she got the cancellation message, why would she still go there?' Knox wanted to know.

'We still don't know for certain that she did,' said Mariner. 'Only that she got off the train again.'

'But somehow her phone found its way to the bridge,' said Millie.

'All right. Supposing she did go to the bridge,' Mariner said. 'Say she misunderstood what Lewis had said. What would she do when he didn't turn up?'

'I'd expect her to wait around a bit, then once it was clear he wasn't coming, go back to the train station,' said Millie.

'On the other hand, it could have been the opportunity she was waiting for,' Mariner suggested. 'She's getting grief at home and with her friends. Suddenly she's in a position where she's accountable to no one. Her mum thinks she's with Suzanne. Her dad's far enough away not to be giving her much thought. A window opens up of a few hours when no one's going to miss her, a chance to get away.'

'On a West Midlands travel card?' Knox was doubtful.

'Don't forget that this is all at about the same time Ricky is killed on that very spot. We've thought about Ricky witnessing something and being killed for it, but what about if Yasmin saw what happened to Ricky and it frightened her into running away.'

'Which brings us right back to where we came in last Wednesday,' said Millie. 'Where has she gone?'

Mariner got up from where he'd been sitting, massaging his temples to ease the headache he was developing. 'Potentially we've got several people at the reservoir at that time and now we have photographs to go with them. Let's go and talk to Lily again, see if we can prompt her into remembering anything new.'

* * *

The air was closing in on them as Knox drove them back to St Clare's, armed now with photographs of Yasmin, Lee, Mohammed Akram and Shaun Pryce. Dusk was a couple of hours away but the sky had dulled to a misty grey and when they got out of the car their shirts were speckled with tiny storm flies. Mariner was hoping that Lillian would recognise at least one of the photographs, but she simply shook her head at each of them.

'Are you saying you can't be sure?' Mariner asked.

'No. I'm saying none of those are him.'

'You're sure?'

'Absolutely.'

'Well, thank you for looking.' It was hard to conceal his disappointment.

'Not at all,' smiled Lily, regardless. 'You were lucky to catch me again, Inspector. I shan't be here for much longer.'

'Oh?'

She beamed with pride. 'I've won a competition. Twenty-five thousand pounds.'

Mariner was impressed. 'That's wonderful. What competition was that?' Shuffling over to the little table she picked up a letter and passed it to him. It was the sort of 'Congratulations! You have been selected to receive one of our stunning prizes' variety of junk mail that every household receives on a weekly, if not daily, basis. All it required in return was that the recipient sign up to a monthly magazine to be entered into a prize draw.

'Lily, this isn't—' Mariner began gently, but Nora caught his eye and gave a tiny warning shake of the head.

'I'm going to buy a nice little house.' Lily went on, enthusiastically. 'And I'm going to have a party for all my family and friends too. You must come, Inspector.'

'I'd love to,' said Mariner, with a sudden sinking feeling.

Nora showed them out of the building. 'I know what you're thinking and yes, it's true, she does have days when she's confused, but they're rare. She still saw what she saw.'

'I know.' But now Mariner was beginning to question exactly what that was.

* * *

On the way home the pain that had been moving round his skull for most of the day began to tighten like a vice, as thoughts darted around his head, seeking out connections. Should he go to Anna's? He considered it again, but something stopped him. What he needed was time on his own to think. Back at the cottage he washed back a couple of painkillers, collapsed in the armchair and closed his eyes.

* * *

Mariner was woken around midnight by what he thought must be fireworks. These days waking all the neighbours seemed to have become the universal way to celebrate any special event, especially in summer. But the air had grown stickier still and the next rumble he heard was preceded by the unmistakable flicker of lightning. The storm crept slowly towards the city like a slothful beast, grumbling and complaining, building in strength until the thunder rattled the windows and lightning flashed with dazzling intensity. Then came the rain, pounding on the water and trees like no rain Mariner had heard before. He pushed open a window and leaned on the sill to breathe in the cool freshness, after weeks of intolerable heat. Then, taking his keys from the shelf and stepping outside into a puddle that covered his shoes, he just started walking. Shining under the streetlights, the gutters had become rivers, gardens vast ornamental ponds, as the water sought a way through the hard, dry earth.

Within seconds Mariner's clothes were soaked through and his hair plastered to his head, but the heavy drops beating down on his head and shoulders as he walked the deserted streets had a strangely soothing effect. All the while the storm raged overhead, finally admitting defeat before moving off to terrorise other neighbourhoods elsewhere. As the rain weakened to a light drizzle, Mariner let himself back into the house. He stripped off his wet clothes in the hall and collapsed into a restless, dream-ridden sleep as dawn was beginning to prise open the sky.

* * *

He was woken from a deep, heavy sleep by the phone. It was Fiske. 'Yasmin Akram,' he said. 'There's been a development.'

CHAPTER 22

Not 'breakthrough,' Mariner noted, but 'development.' It didn't sound good. Fiske, playing the drama queen again, couldn't just come out and tell him. But it was serious, judging from the number of people who had been contacted and brought in on this Sunday morning. With everyone crammed into the small and stifling briefing room, Fiske broke it to them. 'The body of a young Asian girl has been found in the river that runs through Kingsmead Park,' he said. 'We think it's Yasmin Akram. It looks as if she has been strangled.'

From missing person to murder victim in three simple sentences. Murmurs of disgust rippled round the room, as everyone struggled to accept the sickening news. 'She was discovered early this morning by a park ranger.'

'How close is that to where her phone was found?' someone asked.

'It's about a mile away, down from the station but on the other side of Birchill Lane. We'll be setting up an incident room as soon as the identity is confirmed.' He turned to Mariner. 'DI Mariner who has been investigating her disappearance will continue to lead on the ground.'

* * *

The flash storms had caused chaos across the whole of the Midlands. Many towns along the River Severn — Bewdley and Bridgnorth, places that had seemed to be almost permanently under water during the autumn and spring — had fallen victim yet again. And in Birmingham itself they drove through streets that were still submerged by several inches. And the freshness was short-lived. It continued to be a sticky and stormy day, the sun a white smear against the grey-yellow sky, the peculiar half-light threatening more rain.

It was a slow drive down past the railway station and to the park, in a convoy of cars that inched its way through patches of deep flooding. In the car park a small group had already gathered and uniform were having a nightmare task keeping kids away from what had become an instant water park. 'Who found the body?' Mariner asked the nearest officer.

'Andy Pritchard.' He pointed over to a young lad in khaki shirt, trousers and high waders standing isolated from the pack. 'Park ranger. There's a couple of them cycle around all the local parks dealing with vandalism, that kind of stuff. Today he's on his own.'

'The lone ranger,' observed Knox.

Andy Pritchard had one of the worst cases of acne Mariner had ever seen. He was virtually hiding behind the peak of his ranger's cap. Nearby two more officers were transferring soggy books and papers into evidence bags. A saturated backpack lay at their feet. Mariner recognised it from the description of Yasmin's. Putting on waders, Knox and Mariner went with Pritchard to where he'd found the body, in an obscure corner of the park.

'I saw the books first of all,' he told them as they sloshed through water eight inches deep, 'floating along on the water. I couldn't work out where they would have come from. Then I saw the bag. So I went upstream to see if there was anything else and that's when I noticed what I thought were clothes caught on the tree roots on the other bank. When I had a closer look,' he lifted the binoculars, 'I could see that it was something more.' They had come to the main channel of the river although there was no distinguishing it from the pond they'd just waded through. Pritchard pointed across to the opposite bank a couple of metres away, where they could now see a dark sodden bundle of clothing, long black hair fanning out behind. 'Then I saw her face.'

As if to confirm Pritchard's story, the water suddenly swelled, turning the body and for a split second they looked into what was unmistakably the pale lifeless face of Yasmin Akram.

'What time was this?' asked Mariner.

'About seven o'clock. We work dawn till dusk in the summer months.'

'But you didn't call it in until nearly eight,' said Knox. 'Why was that?'

Pritchard flushed. 'I wasn't sure what to do. I thought about trying to get across to her but the water was too deep and too fast flowing. I thought I might lose my footing. It's gone down a bit since then. I thought the best thing was to call you.'

'It was the best thing,' said Mariner, though preserving this scene was going to be a joke. 'Is there a way round on the other side?' He looked up at the steep embankment, knowing the answer already.

Pritchard shook his head. 'This is the closest we can get. You'd have to wade across.'

Here the main course of the stream was six or seven feet wide. From where they stood, the level had risen over Mariner's knees, and now and again he had to brace himself against the powerful current.

'Okay, thanks Andy, we'll take it from here,' said Mariner. 'If you go back up to the road someone will take a full statement from you.'

Pritchard on his way, Mariner turned to Knox. 'Want to try and get a bit nearer?'

'After you, boss,' said Knox.

They edged out towards the middle of the fast-flowing brown water, dodging the debris that rushed by, until the level was up to their thighs. The floor of the stream was soft and yielding, and a sudden surge caught them unawares. Knox staggered, almost falling, but found his footing again. 'The flow is uneven,' said Mariner, bracing himself. 'We just need to get the timing right to get across the deepest section . . .' He watched and waited. 'Okay — now!'

Taking advantage of the next lull, they pushed across the mid-stream, landing in the shallower water on the opposite bank, grabbing at sodden vegetation to steady themselves. Now they were standing directly over the deceptively animated body as it danced and swayed on the water, the clothing grasped firmly by the exposed roots of an overhanging willow. Despite the bloating effects of the water, there was no doubt as to the identity. Several dark blemishes on Yasmin's face threw up the possibility that her death had been accompanied by violence. For Shanila and Mohammed Akram the agonising wait was over, but about to be replaced by something infinitely worse. Millie had that job to do. She was probably there right now. Mariner forced himself not to think about it.

Straining to keep his balance in the surging water Mariner looked around him. It was unlikely, as far as he could see, that Yasmin would have been hidden here. He voiced the thought to Knox. 'To get to this point she'd have to have been carried the way we came through the park, which, in the sort of weather we've been having, would have been busy into the late evening and far too public. The only time to have done it would have been under cover of night.'

'Even then it would have been risky,' said Knox. 'People walk through this park to get from the main Pershore Road through to Birchill Lane.'

'We need to look further up.'

They were hailed by a shout from the other side of the stream. SOCO had arrived in overalls and waders.

'It's definitely her?' asked DC Chris Sharp.

'No question,' said Mariner, raising his voice to carry across the river.

Sharp shook his head sadly. 'Trouble is now, that after last night's rain, all your physical evidence will have been washed away.'

'Thanks,' said Mariner, not without irony. 'Just do what you can, eh?'

Mariner and Knox left SOCO to do their work. Battling against the rushing torrent and clutching at the overhanging bushes, they staggered upstream as far as they could get, to where the stream emerged from a tunnel beneath the road.

Knox looked up towards the parapet, a brick wall topped with waist-high railings. 'She could have gone in here,' he said. 'It would only take a couple of minutes. Stop the car, open the boot and tip her over the edge, she then gets carried downstream.'

'It's a busy road,' said Mariner. 'Late at night would be easier, but you'd still run the risk of someone driving past and seeing.' Looking up on the other side of the road, he noticed they'd come out opposite St Clare's retirement home.

'This stream must connect to the reservoir,' he said.

Knox foraged in his pocket and produced the rather crumpled map. 'You're right, boss. It looks as if we're just further down from the bridge on the other side of St Clare's.' Where Ricky Skeet was killed and where Yasmin had arranged to meet Lewis Everett.

'How does the river progress down to here?'

Knox traced a finger down the map and Mariner was surprised to see how chewed his fingernail was. 'It looks as if it must be under the ground, through some kind of tunnel,' Knox said.

'And above the ground it's all green, so more of what we can see: rough woodland — and pretty impenetrable at that. And the river doesn't surface at all?'

They both studied the map. 'Doesn't look like it, boss. The next place it appears on the map is at the spillway next to the reservoir.' Knox looked up. 'You think she could have been put in there?'

'It's where we found her phone.'

'She travelled all this way underground?' Knox was doubtful.

'Let's go and have a look. And get hold of someone who knows more about the river.'

* * *

Millie had been adamant at the time. She could handle this on her own. The Akrams had got to know her and Shanila, in particular she felt, trusted her. But now she was here, it was different. She'd spent the drive over going through all the different possible strategies for breaking the news; set pieces she'd previously rehearsed only during training. Prepare the way but don't prolong the agony, use their names and make it personal. She needed none of it. Taking one look at Millie's face, Shanila knew why she'd come. 'You've found her, haven't you? Oh God, you've found her!' Before a horrible gut-wrenching wail, that went on as long and as hard as her lungs would allow.

* * *

The reservoir had undergone subtle changes since their last visit. Foliage had been beaten flat in places, the tide mark was higher and the rank, sulphurous smell had been replaced by the fresher scent of damp plant-life. Looking more closely they could see that the channel down the middle was moving and a torrent of water gushed noisily down the spillway. On the bridge the damage was clearer. The wooden gates, there to control the flow of water had been cast aside and lay in a jumbled heap at the base of the concrete shelf along with bricks that had broken loose from the mouth of the tunnel.

'It's flowing pretty fast now,' said Knox. 'Fast enough to take a pretty big object with it.'

'But you saw how it was on the day Hewitt brought us here,' Mariner reminded him. 'It was barely a trickle because we'd had no rain. It would hardly have carried a feather down with it.'

'But Hewitt also said something about the water collecting and releasing every so often. Maybe the day Yasmin was killed was one of those days. We need to find out more about this.'

'Mister Mariner?' The elderly gentleman approaching them looked as if he should have been residing with Lily in St Clare's. He came unsteadily along the path using a stick for support. Once he'd almost reached where they were standing, he proffered a hand. 'Eric Dwyer,' he said. 'One of your colleagues asked me to meet you here. I'm the chairman of the local river conservation group.' His cheeks were weathered a rosy pink, but much of the rest of his face was obscured by glasses and a pair of extravagant mutton-chop whiskers.

'So you know all about this reservoir,' said Mariner, shaking the bony hand.

'I dare say I know as much as anyone.' Eric looked out over the water. 'It was built at the turn of the century to top up the canal system in times of drought. It's what's known as a feeder lake, the water diverting away from and back into the canal.' He peered over the bridge. 'My, my, that's taken a battering.'

'I understand that these gates were meant to open under pressure.'

'That's right.' He went on to describe what Mariner had already surmised.

'How big a release is it when it goes?' asked Mariner. 'Enough to carry something big with it, say seven or eight stone in weight?' He wondered if Dwyer would have any idea what kind of object they were talking about.

'Given the gradient of the incline I'd say easily,' said Dwyer. 'I've never seen this one in full spate, but I've seen other similar mechanisms and they usually flow at about ten cubic feet per second. That's quite a force.'

'How often would this release occur?'

'At this time of year, as you'd expect, not very often. The drier the weather the longer it takes for the pressure to build. It'd be once a day if you're lucky.'

'And would there be any way of telling what time of day this has been occurring recently?' Mariner wanted to know.

'Unfortunately not.' Dwyer scratched his whiskers. 'It would depend on the flow into the reservoir, you see.'

'And after heavy rain, such as we had the other night?'

'After heavy rain the water would go straight through, much as it's doing now. The gates would be permanently open, almost as if the reservoir were just part of the river. The river flows to here from its source in the Waseley Hills right through to Spaghetti Junction. After last night's storms, by the time it got to this point it would have been torrential, hence the damage. That will take some sorting out.'

'So what's down there?' Mariner pointed into the tunnel.

'At this end, a series of valves and valve vaults to control the flow.'

'Would they hinder anything passing through?'

'To a degree. The mechanisms are old, have been there for years and under no particular pressure, but the sudden influx of last night's rain was clearly enough to break the sluice gates and could have equally damaged or destroyed the valves too.'

'But we've had rain like this before. Why would this happen now?'

'Probably because of the work we've been doing up stream, clearing all the rubbish and dredging out where the river has got clogged up.' He shook his head regretfully. 'We obviously did too good a job.' He looked back over the pool itself. 'The water hasn't had such a clear run for years.'

'Sounds like hard work,' said Mariner.

'It's not always. We're quite a sociable group, too.'

'Ever had a guy called Shaun Pryce join you?'

'Shaun Pryce? I don't remember the name.' Mariner described Pryce to Dwyer.

'He doesn't fit our profile. We're mainly middle-aged, retired folk with too much time on our hands and a concern for the preservation of our city. But that said, people come and go. Occasionally we get more ecologically aware students who come and join us.'

'I wonder if you could let me have a list of your members some time.'

'Consider it done.' He leaned with both hands on his stick.

Mariner scanned the wasteland of the reservoir. 'So your work hadn't brought you as far as this then?' Mariner asked.

'Not yet. We're running a bit behind schedule, dependent as we are on volunteers. But we did all the prep work some time ago.'

'What does that involve?'

'Myself and another member coming down here with someone from the rivers authority to look at what there is and what needs doing,' said Dwyer. 'That's how I know about the tunnel.'

'When did you come here?'

'It would have been in about March, I suppose. We were being somewhat optimistic as it turns out.'

'And who came with you?'

'Sheila Carr was the other member. It's interesting because I'm sure that the railings weren't broken at that time. It's not something we added to our work list.'

'Well, thanks for coming down here, Mr Dwyer,' said Mariner. 'You've been very helpful.' And he shook the man's hand. Watching Eric Dwyer go, Mariner took another look around, noticing anew the break in the timber railings. 'Lily mentioned that,' he recalled.

'It's not recent,' Knox was examining them. 'The wood on the inside of the break is weathered too.'

'I think we have to consider the probability that Yasmin was put in the water here,' Mariner said.

Knox nodded agreement. 'But is this where she was killed?'

CHAPTER 23

Arriving at the Newton Street mortuary later that afternoon, Mariner's stomach began to bubble gently. Outside the temperature had soared again, a signal that the storms had been just a blip on the meteorological radar.

'Lucky for us that they happened at all,' remarked pathologist Stuart Croghan. 'Or Yasmin's body might have remained hidden.'

This wasn't the first child murder Mariner had worked on, but contrary to popular belief, the average detective rarely deals with murder cases, whatever the age of the victim. The experience was guaranteed to be traumatic. Croghan had been working non-stop since the body had been brought in a couple of hours ago and already the file on Yasmin Akram was building up with detailed notes. Much of this information would be saved for the inquest, so Croghan confined himself to the salient points, knowing exactly what would be of practical use to Mariner now.

'Death was by asphyxiation,' Croghan told him. 'She was strangled with some kind of ligature, probably wire. There's no apparent discolouration or abrasion in the ligature wound so it was a clean or treated wire.' He indicated where the thin, red groove could be seen.

'Plastic coated?' asked Mariner.

'Could be. It was quite soft, around a twenty-eight gauge — about 3mm thick. You can tell that from the shape and depth of the groove.'

'Some kind of electrical wire perhaps?' Mariner was hopeful.

'It's possible but I couldn't be certain.'

'But not an accident then.'

'Definitely not,' Croghan confirmed. 'She was already dead when she went into the water. There are diatoms in the throat area but not in the bloodstream, heart or lungs.' Meaning she hadn't inhaled water. The microscopic algae were always a giveaway.

'Decomposition is patchy though, which is unusual, not in keeping with being totally submerged throughout. Different parts of the body seem to have decomposed at different rates.' Croghan pointed out a couple of areas.

'Consistent with spending a few days in a drainage tunnel with an irregular through-flow?' Mariner speculated.

'That would probably do it, yes.'

'How long had she been exposed to the water?' he asked.

'I'd say several days. The decomposition pattern is going to make it hard to pinpoint the time of death very accurately. We'll analyse stomach contents but there's a limit to what that can tell us, too.'

'But we're looking at her being killed roughly when?'

'It's more than a week ago.'

Mariner gave Croghan a look that said 'Thanks for nothing.'

'I did warn you,' the pathologist said.

'Anything else that would help?' asked Knox.

'Quite a bit of post-mortem bruising that would imply that she had a rough journey after she was put in the water.' Yasmin progressing through that underground tunnel.

'Any sign of a sexual assault?' asked Mariner.

'No physical signs as far as I can see. And from the internal I'd have said that she wasn't sexually active. However she wasn't wearing any underwear. Curious.'

Croghan was right, that was curious.

* * *

'So Lewis's message could have been confirming their meeting,' said Millie. She looked shattered after her visit to the Akrams, but had insisted on being present for the debrief. They'd gathered again in Mariner's office — it was becoming a regular club meeting. 'Yasmin disappeared at around the time Lewis left. He could have done it before he went. Perhaps he wanted her to go with him and she refused.'

'And the missing underwear would mean some kind of sexual activity, or the start of it,' Knox added.

'But as Croghan said, this doesn't look like a spur of the moment thing. It smacks of premeditation. I can't imagine that Lewis would set out to kill Yasmin.'

'No. It would have to be someone who just happened to have about their person a piece of electrical wire,' put in Knox. 'Like Shaun Pryce.'

'Maybe that's what Ricky saw,' said Millie. 'Someone assaulting and killing Yasmin.'

'So why didn't the killer tip him over the bridge too?'

There were still so many questions. 'I should go and talk to Yasmin's parents,' said Mariner. 'They'll want to know what comes next.'

'I'll come with you, sir.'

* * *

The smiling face of Yasmin Akram beamed at Mariner from where the photo sat at the centre of the shrine for family and friends to pay their respects in the sitting room where Millie and Mariner had been shunted to wait. Bypassing the huddle of people on the pavement outside, they'd been shown directly into the cool, formal room. It was lavishly furnished, spotlessly clean and, Mariner guessed, rarely used.

The house was busy, yet in here an eerie silence reigned. If the body were not still being held at the mortuary, they would, Millie told him, be looking into an open coffin. A knock on the door preceded Amira, her dark mourning clothes emphasising the paleness of her skin. Millie got up and gave her a hug. 'How's your mum bearing up?'

'She's okay. Dad's taking care of her.' Her face crumpled. 'All this is my fault,' Amira said. 'If I hadn't encouraged her—'

'That's not true, Amira,' said Millie firmly. 'Someone else did this. They are responsible. You just wanted what was best for Yasmin.'

'I've let them all down.' With a shudder Amira burst into tears and while Millie attempted to console her Mariner was suddenly struck by the inappropriateness of his presence here. Their intrusion on the family's grief, bringing the constant reminder of unnatural death was the most repulsive aspect of the job. He got up suddenly. 'I'll come back another time,' he said.

* * *

Millie chose to stay and when Mariner drove away he found himself close to Anna's house. Suddenly he was aware that he'd been letting down a number of people too. The Akrams he could do little about for now, but he could make amends with Anna. He took a chance and stopped by, but was disconcerted to see an unfamiliar car on the drive. Draped across the parcel shelf was a green sweat shirt bearing the embroidered Manor Park logo. Parking up he walked round to the side of the house from where he could smell the charcoal fumes from a barbecue and hear the sound of music and laughing, as if a party was in full swing. The voices sounded predominantly male.

The first person Mariner saw, when he opened the side gate, was Jamie, typically detached from the group pacing the edge of the lawn, head down, muttering to himself and wringing the hem of his polo shirt in his hands. He was wearing shorts; something that a few months ago he wouldn't even have countenanced. Good old Manor Park. At the far end of the patio, nearest the kitchen door, Anna stood leaning against the picnic table, wine glass in hand and deep in conversation with a man who lounged on a garden chair directly in front of her, his back to Mariner. Anna wore a scrap of a vest and a denim skirt short enough to offer strong competition to the Kingsmead girls. Her face was open and smiling and her attention focused one hundred percent on her guest, whose gaze would have been at about the level of her smooth lightly-tanned thighs. No prizes for guessing where his mind would be.

'Any more drinks out there?' called another man's voice from the kitchen, someone else clearly at home.

Sickened, Mariner turned to go, but he was too late. Without even seeming to glance in his direction, Jamie had seen him.

'Spectre man,' he said loudly.

In those early days when Anna had addressed him as 'Inspector Mariner' Jamie had found it impossible to get his mouth around it and *spectre man* was the closest he could get. Highly appropriate today when Mariner felt just that: the spectre appearing at the feast.

'Hi, Jamie,' he said.

Anna immediately looked up and Mariner tried to read her face. Surprise certainly, but anything else? Hard to tell. She left her guest and came over. Big smile but no kiss — maybe he was giving off the wrong signals, or maybe not. 'Hi. We weren't expecting you. Coming in?'

We? 'You've got visitors.'

'That's okay. Come and join us. You can meet Simon and—'

'I'm not much in a party mood,' said Mariner. 'We found Yasmin Akram.'

'Yes, I heard about it on the news. I'm sorry.' She touched his arm. 'Why don't you stay anyway and have a drink?'

He did consider it, but only for a split second. 'No. It's fine. There's a lot to do.'

'All right.'

It was one of those occasions when she disappointed him. It had been a difficult day and Mariner wanted to share it with someone. For once his own company wasn't enough, so for want of anything better to do he went back to Granville Lane. After a while Millie returned from the Akrams', looking drained, and by nine thirty only the two of them remained in the incident room.

'Come on,' Mariner said. 'I'll buy you a curry.' Then he realised what he'd said.

Millie just laughed. 'I know a place where you can get the best,' she said.

* * *

The place turned out to be her flat, on the ground floor of a Victorian town house in Acocks Green.

'This is fantastic,' said Mariner as he scooped up rogan josh with a spicy naan that was as light as a feather. He hadn't eaten all day, or realised how hungry he was.

'Don't get too excited,' said Millie. 'I didn't cook it myself. My mum sends it over now and again. I think it helps to ease her conscience now the rest of the family won't have anything to do with me. Dad doesn't know she does it.'

'Oh?'

'Long story,' Millie said.

'I've got time,' said Mariner, sitting back. 'But only if you want to.'

'Why not?' She dropped her chunk of bread into her dish and sighed. 'My parents aren't quite so enlightened as Yasmin's. They always expected that I'd be a traditional Pakistani wife. I had to learn to cook and sew — all the usual. But when I got to about Yasmin's age I started to realise that there could be more to life than that. I was doing pretty well at school and decided I wanted to go to university. I fancied being a forensic scientist, actually. But my dad has rather more rigid views than the Akrams. Within our community a woman's sole purpose is to look after her husband. So, I had to do it the hard way. Over a number of years, I saved enough money to start paying my way through college, but a few weeks before I was due to go, Dad got hold of my building society book, confiscated my savings and that was the end of it.'

'God Millie, I had no idea.' Mariner was horrified.

'Naturally I had a massive row with my dad, called him a lot of things that I shouldn't have and effectively managed to cut myself off from the family and the rest of the community. I left home and came to live with a sympathetic auntie in Alum Rock, and this job was the nearest I could get to what I really want to be.' Mariner could sense her struggling to keep the story light. In an attempt to conceal her emotion, she got up and carried her plate through to the kitchen.

Picking up his own empty dish, Mariner followed her through. 'Do you still have ambitions of getting into forensics?' he asked as they loaded the dishwasher.

'I don't know,' said Millie. 'I like what I do now.'

'You're bloody good at it,' he said.

'Thanks.'

'I mean it. You've built a great relationship with the Akrams.'

'Today was horrible, having to tell them.'

'It was always going to be. I'm afraid it's one of the bits of the job that won't get any easier.'

'I keep trying to imagine what they must be going through.' Folding her arms, Millie leaned back on the counter. 'Their own child. It must be—' her eyes watered and she wiped at them crossly.

Mariner put a hand on her shoulder. 'You made it as easy for them as you could,' he said. 'You supported them. It's all you can do. You can't bring her back.'

'No, but I still wish I could.'

Afterwards Mariner couldn't really be sure how it happened. One minute he had his arm around Millie comforting her, the next her lips were fused to his, her tongue, sweet and spicy, probing his mouth. Maybe the curry had aphrodisiac properties, or perhaps seeing Anna like that had left him gagging for it. Whatever it was, it seemed like the most natural thing in the world that he should kiss her back, his hands roaming her shapely body. And by the time her hand slid down to unzip him he was already hard.

They made love urgently, only making it as far as the sofa, Mariner's trousers shoved down to his thighs. For him it was over in minutes, too soon for Millie, who continued her frenzied pumping on his softening member for what seemed like an eternity, until spasms rocked her and she finally allowed him to withdraw, deflated and sore.

'Sorry,' Mariner said, stifling a belch. 'That wasn't up to much.'

'No,' she seemed not to mind. 'But probably about what you'd expect from a couple of drunks. I'll call a taxi for you.'

Thankfully Mariner made it inside his own front door before his bowels decided to gurgle and erupt. He awoke the next morning, still half-clothed, mind and body feeling lousy in equal measures. His system clearly wasn't accustomed to industrial strength curry and Millie's mother's, delicious though it was at the time, had consigned him to the bathroom for much of the night. He'd a thumping hangover and his dick hurt about as much as his ego. He didn't think Millie was the type to broadcast details of their pathetic encounter around the station, but you could never really tell with anyone.

* * *

When the phone rang he really hoped it wasn't Anna. It wasn't. It was Mark Russell. 'I thought you'd want to know, sir, we've got another body.'

Somehow Mariner dragged himself under the shower. Every time he moved his head pain jangled round it like vibrations in a bell. Forcing down coffee and a couple of strong painkillers, he put on his sunglasses against the glare of daylight and got a taxi to Granville Lane where he saw that his own car had materialised in the station car park. The movement of the journey had made him feel queasy again, but somehow he managed to roll down the blinds in his office and make it to his desk where Russell came to update him on the latest discovery. 'She was found a little way downstream from where Yasmin was discovered.' Russell was saying, but Mariner was momentarily distracted by Millie walking into the bull pen. She smiled a brief good morning to them both through the glass partition, but her face gave nothing away.

'Sir?' Russell said, looking up from his notebook.

'I'm listening.'

'She was found by Ben, a liver and white springer spaniel who's apparently a keen swimmer. His owner, a Mr Lovell, took him to the park this morning as usual, and Ben had what I s'pose you'd call a "swamp day." Mr Lovell had to go looking for him and that was when he saw the woman's body, caught on an old bit of fencing that runs alongside the stream. Yesterday that part of the park would have been completely under water but the flooding has subsided overnight.'

'And what do we know about her?' Mariner forced himself to concentrate.

'Not much yet. She's an older woman: late forties or fifties. The pathologist at the scene said she's been in the water a lot longer than Yasmin — could be weeks or even months. She's got similar kinds of bruising though.'

'So she could have been released at the same time, when the mechanism disintegrated,' said Mariner, thinking aloud.

'Maybe,' Russell agreed. 'They think there won't be much in the way of forensics, thanks to decomposition, but we've got a pair of earrings that may help with identification and there was a large splinter of wood caught in her cardigan.'

'From the bridge?' Mariner thought of the railings.

'SOCO are down there now.'

'Do we know how she died?'

'There's a head injury, but we can't be sure that that's what killed her. Croghan seemed to think that may have happened when she fell into the water.'

Mariner fought down a wave of nausea. 'Any ID?'

'Not yet. Tony Knox is going through the missing persons.'

'Okay, let me know when you find anything.'

CHAPTER 24

The best solution to avoid throwing up, Mariner found, was to remain as inactive as possible. He got Russell to bring him some water on his way out then began sifting through the messages that had accumulated on his desk. He didn't trust himself to return any of the three calls from Anna and consigned those yellow slips to the bin. The next was from a Sahira Masud. Mariner couldn't place the name, not even in connection with Yasmin Akram, and in the end he had to pick up the telephone to find out who it belonged to.

'I live next door but one to your mother,' Mrs Masud reminded him. 'I wasn't sure that anyone would have let you know — I'm afraid she's had a slight stroke.'

The words had more of an impact than Mariner could ever have imagined, his own fragility instantly forgotten. He'd known this day might come of course. But, thanks to the ever-dwindling contact between his mother and him, Mariner had always expected to feel numb to any such news. He'd been wrong. Now he felt bad that he hadn't returned her calls. Was that what she was ringing about, to tell him she wasn't well? 'Is she all right?' he asked, his voice thin with anxiety.

'She's fine,' Mrs Masud was instantly reassuring. 'But they've taken her into Warwick hospital to keep an eye on her overnight. You might want to—'

'Yes,' said Mariner. 'Thank you for letting me know.' Visiting the hospital was a decision that Mariner would make himself, after weighing up whether it was likely to make her worse or better.

'She's on ward eight.'

'Thanks.' Mariner looked up to see Millie standing in the doorway, dangling his car keys from a finger. She came and laid them on his desk, all the time studying his face, which Mariner guessed was probably an interesting shade of grey.

'Everything okay, sir?' she asked.

Mariner nodded and instantly regretted it. 'Look, about last night,' he said. 'I was pretty pissed.'

She returned a wan smile. 'You and me both, sir. To be honest I can't remember much about it. Probably best forgotten.'

'Yes, I'm sure you're right.' Mariner was weak with relief.

'In my job I move around a lot,' she went on. 'I try to bag an inspector at every OCU I'm assigned to. You did enough.' Mariner stared. 'Joke,' she said, deadpan, before walking away.

* * *

Tony Knox was next in line. The bacon sandwich in his fist nearly had Mariner reaching for the bin, but Knox remained oblivious to Mariner's state. Then again, he didn't look all that hot himself. His shirt was creased and slightly grimy, and he didn't appear to have had time for a shave today.

'We've got a possible match on the body, boss,' he said. 'Barbara Kincaid. IC1 female, aged forty-four, reported missing back in March from an address on Banbury Road.'

'That's what?' said Mariner, forcing his thoughts back to the investigation. 'About half a mile from the reservoir?'

'The other side of the station.' Knox nodded. 'According to the husband's statement at the time she'd been suffering mental health problems, depression. She left the house late one evening and didn't come back. The description of what she was wearing matches the clothing on the body and we've asked him to come in and identify some jewellery she was wearing.'

'Russell said something about a splinter of wood?' Mariner said.

'Yeah. It's a possible match with the wooden railings of the reservoir bridge.'

'So she went in at the same place Yasmin did.'

'It looks like it. She could have been the one who leaned on them and broke them.'

'It wouldn't have taken much. They were pretty well rotten through. What do you think?'

'Either that or she threw herself in, got tangled up in the drainage mechanism,' said Knox. 'It's a bit desperate though.'

'Desperate feelings lead you to do desperate things,' said Mariner, trying not to think of last night. 'Let me know when identity's confirmed.'

* * *

The final straw was Fiske, who hovered in the doorway at first, distinctly reticent, and Mariner was soon to find out why. 'The Skeet family have made a complaint,' he said, eventually.

'About what?' said Mariner, though he could fairly easily guess the answer.

'They don't think their son's disappearance was made enough of a priority. How far do you think they'll take it?'

'What do you mean?'

'Is Colleen Skeet the vindictive type?'

If it hadn't required the effort of standing up, Mariner would have been tempted to walk over and punch his smarmy face. 'Colleen Skeet isn't any "type," sir. As I seem to remember, it was thinking of her family as a "type" that got us into trouble. Right now she's a woman grieving for her son. I couldn't begin to understand what's going on in her head.'

'I thought you said you knew her.'

'I know Colleen, sir. I know very little about those who might have any influence over her, especially at a time like this.'

'Will you talk to her?'

'I'm not sure that that's a very good idea,' Mariner said truthfully.

'I do hope that as a fellow officer I will be able to count on your support, Inspector.' Not a request, just a statement. But it would be a difficult one to adhere to. Mariner felt not a shred of fellowship for the man.

* * *

Nonetheless, his brush with Fiske gave Mariner the nudge he needed and by mid-afternoon — having exhausted all the paperwork he could reasonably do at this point in the case and starting to feel halfway human again — he ran out of options. He hadn't had the guts to face Colleen since Ricky's death. Now was as good a time as any and from there he could go over to see his mother. Moving very carefully, Mariner picked up his jacket and keys and walked out to his car.

He went to pass through the exit at the same moment as a man being shown out of the building by Mark Russell.

'I'm sorry.' To avoid a collision the other man stepped back at the same time as Mariner did.

'No, after you,' Mariner found himself looking into a vaguely familiar face, but there was no reciprocal recognition and he dismissed it. It happened all the time in this job, a consequence of meeting so many people. Then, crossing the car park, it came to him. He went back into reception.

'That man who just left. What was he doing here with Russell?' he asked Ella.

'I think he's the guy who came in to identify his wife's jewellery. The latest body that was found. Poor bloke.'

'Can I use your phone?' Mariner called up to Russell. 'The body found today, she was Mrs Kincaid.'

'Ms,' said Russell. 'She kept her maiden name when she got married.'

Poor bloke indeed, thought Mariner.

* * *

He found Colleen sitting smoking on the front step in the yellow late afternoon sunshine, a grotesque pastiche of contentment. 'You've got a bloody nerve,' was all she said as he walked up the path.

'I'm sorry, Colleen, really sorry.' Was there ever a way of instilling those words with enough sincerity? Mariner doubted it.

'I bet you are,' she said. 'Sorry that you're all in the shit.'

She was wrong about that, but there was no point in arguing. 'Are you really going through with it, the complaint?'

'Yes, she fucking is,' snarled a voice from behind her. It belonged to a giant of a man with thick muscles and apparently no neck. Steve, Mariner guessed. 'So why don't you piss off out of here and stop harassing her?'

Yeah, why didn't he? 'I'm sorry, Colleen,' Mariner said again and turned and walked back to his car.

'Tom?' she called after him, her voice smaller than before. He turned. 'I know it wasn't your fault.'

Mariner nodded briefly and walked on.

* * *

251

Back in the car Mariner thought again about what he'd just learned from Russell. The reservoir, Yasmin Akram, Barbara Kincaid and, through her husband, the link between them all: Shaun Pryce, with his apparent predilection for middle-aged housewives. Mariner wondered if there was any way Barbara Kincaid could have known Shaun Pryce too. Pryce must have come across her husband. On his way out to Leamington to visit his mother Mariner would have to drive along Banbury Road. That was fortuitous.

* * *

There was a considerably delayed response when he rang the doorbell of the three-floor terrace, but eventually the door opened on Brian Goodway. His shoulders were hunched and even on this warm afternoon he wore a thick cardigan over his open collared shirt, his body temperature thrown off-balance by shock. He was apologetic. 'I was upstairs. The kids are at home but they never answer the door, even though it's usually for them. Teenagers, eh?' He shook his head despairingly but his heart wasn't in it, he hadn't got the energy.

Mariner felt another surge of sympathy for the man. 'Mr Goodway, I know this is a difficult time for you, but I understand you identified your wife's jewellery this afternoon.'

'That's right.'

'As you know, I'm investigating Yasmin Akram's death. This may be important. I wonder if you could spare a few minutes.'

'Um, yes, of course.' He seemed disorientated and vague and Mariner almost changed his mind. But he was here now and followed Goodway past bikes propped in the hallway into an untidy lounge with a high ceiling and a wide bay with sash windows. Like the Akram's sitting room it felt cool and unlived in, probably because most of the space was taken up by a polished walnut baby grand piano.

'Barbara's,' Goodway said, although Mariner hadn't asked. 'She used to teach part-time. The number of pupils had dwindled over the years but she liked to do it. It was something for herself.' Already used to speaking about his wife in the past tense, but then she'd been missing from his life for months.

'Is that why she kept her maiden name?'

'Yes, it was like a stage name really. Barbara was a performer: music, amateur theatre, that kind of thing.'

For the first time Mariner saw a black-and-white portrait photograph. The subject was strikingly pretty and not at all the kind of woman Mariner would have thought of as a natural partner for Goodway. 'Is that her?' he asked.

'Yes, taken a few years ago now. At the time we married she had quite a reputation locally, so understandably didn't want to lose that. Inevitably though once the children came along family became more of a priority and she had to put her other ambitions on hold.'

'That can't have been easy,' said Mariner.

'No. I know she found it frustrating at times. She was very artistic. But she continued to provide accompaniment for a local drama group from time to time. Please sit down, Inspector. Can I get you anything? A cup of tea?'

'That would be good, thank you.' It was the last thing Mariner wanted, but it would give Brian Goodway something else to focus on while they talked. He sat down on a lumpy sofa, draped with an Indian print throw. Somewhere in the house a low bass throbbed a steady beat. Looking around it was clear that this room wasn't a priority for decoration, being papered with ivory coloured anaglypta that had gone out of fashion ten years ago. A vertical strip from the light switch to the ceiling had been torn away and fresh pink plasterwork inserted. It was precisely what Mariner had been hoping for.

Goodway returned with two mugs, handing one awkwardly to Mariner, before perching on the piano stool opposite. 'They said they found her downstream from the reservoir,' he said, talking into his tea mug. 'Near to where Yasmin was found.'

'So I gather,' said Mariner.

'Oh God.' Dropping his gaze, Goodway fumbled in his pockets, coming out with an old-fashioned cotton handkerchief, which he used to noisily blow his nose. 'I'm sorry.'

'Not at all, Mr Goodway. I realise how hard this must be for you. But I won't keep you any longer than necessary.' To give Goodway time to compose himself, Mariner turned his attention to his tea. The green mug had seen better days and Mariner could barely pick out what was left of the design, a row of cartoonish trees that had succumbed to the regular abrasion of a dishwasher. He took a scalding mouthful.

Goodway sighed. 'It wasn't a huge surprise when Barbara went missing, you know,' he said. 'She'd been depressed on and off for years, and since last Christmas it had got much worse. We've got three children, all in their teens and for the last five years we've been looking after my mother, too. Sometimes things got on top of her. It was exhausting. Barbara said more than once that she could fully understand these women who just walked away from it all and never came back. I just never thought she'd actually—'

'Did your wife often walk near the reservoir?' asked Mariner.

Goodway shook his head. 'I don't know. I didn't even know there was a reservoir there until the body of that boy was discovered there and I saw it on the news.'

Just like the rest of us, thought Mariner.

'Barbara did go out a lot, just walking, particularly in the evenings. She needed to, to get a break from everything. But I didn't really know where she went. There are parks around and I suppose I just thought that she walked the streets.'

'Did your wife ever talk about meeting anyone?'

'No,' said Goodway instantly, then he seemed to reconsider. 'Although it did cross my mind once or twice. She was a very attractive woman, but I'm sure—'

'I'm sorry,' said Mariner. 'I'm just exploring the possibilities.'

Goodway frowned into his mug. 'The thing I don't understand is that the reservoir is quite a long way from here.'

'There's a quicker way down to it from behind the station,' said Mariner. 'Your wife must have known about that.'

'She lived in this area all her life,' said Goodway, as if that explained it. He looked up at Mariner hopefully. 'I keep wondering if perhaps it could have been an accident,' he said. 'The children . . . it would be so much easier . . .'

Mariner thought of the broken railings but he didn't want to give the man false hope. 'There will be an inquest, of course, but it's possible. The coroner will consider all the evidence.'

'Barbara was taking anti-depressants at the time. She wasn't always thinking clearly.'

'I understand,' said Mariner. 'Thanks for your time, Mr Goodway.' He got up to go, pausing by the strip of fresh plasterwork. 'You've had some electrical work done recently?'

'Actually it was months ago,' said Goodway. 'I'm not very practical around the house and rewiring was long overdue. I haven't quite got round to decorating again.'

'In a house this size it must have been quite a job. Did you do it yourself?'

'Heavens, no. I'm hopeless I'm afraid. We had a proper electrician come in to do it.'

'Shaun Pryce?'

For a moment Goodway looked startled. 'Yes, it was. How——?'

'He modelled for students at your school,' said Mariner.

Then Goodway remembered. 'Ah, of course, you saw the art work on the walls.' He hesitated. 'It was Barbara who discovered him, you know, at one of her drama productions. I got home from school one day and here he was. We got talking and he said that really he was an actor. I thought he was so striking that I asked him to come and model for the girls at school.'

'Did Shaun Pryce model for Yasmin's class?' Mariner asked.

'Not her class, but I think he sat for the art club on one occasion.'

'Your head said he was quite friendly with the girls.'

'Yes. In fact it became a bit of a problem. He was a bit too friendly.'

And what about your wife? Mariner wanted to ask. *How friendly was Shaun Pryce with her?* But now was not the time. The man had more than enough to contend with.

CHAPTER 25

Mariner would have liked to report this latest news back to the team and get onto Shaun Pryce straight away, but he had put off seeing his mother for long enough. He opted to drive over taking the M42. Even though the rush hour was officially over, the road was still heaving with traffic. Hard to believe that just a few years ago this was the open, green countryside of the North Worcestershire way. On one of his frequent Sunday walks, he'd had the dubious pleasure of peeing on the foundations, right where the services were now.

His mother had rarely been ill. Not enough to be hospitalised, anyway. She would not make a good patient. But this episode might make her consider her own mortality and think about tying up any loose ends. His gut tingled with an edge of anticipation. Maybe now she would finally give in and tell him . . .

He'd been about seven years old when he'd first confronted his mother with the question that had been increasingly bothering him, and that he was being asked by some of his school friends. 'How come everyone else has got a mum and a dad, but I've only got a mum?' In time, of course, he'd come to realise that somewhere on the planet he did have a dad like everyone else, it was just that for some reason unknown to him, this man had failed to take any active part in his son's life and was never mentioned. When he was a kid it had opened the way for all kinds of romantic notions, but with adulthood came the realisation that the truth was likely to be far more mundane: his father had simply been married to another woman.

It had crossed his mind on occasion that his mother, Rose, could have been bluffing all these years; that she didn't really have any idea who his father was. He'd been conceived at a time when women were experiencing the new kind of freedom that the contraceptive pill had brought with it — so in many ways, a chance encounter with a stranger would have made sense. But in the midst of all her vagueness, his mother had always kept her story consistent. And once, when Rose had thought he was too young to notice, he remembered overhearing her say to a friend how much like his father he looked.

* * *

It took him a little over half an hour to get to Warwick. The hospital was some way out of the town, sandwiched between residential areas and business parks, the hybrid collection of buildings a reflection of the town itself. He could have been driving into a supermarket car park, with its brash Pizza Hut-style building squatting beside its older, Victorian forerunners. Ward eight, coronary care, was on the second floor of the old hospital and he arrived, along with a collection of other patients' friends and relatives, just at the start of visiting hours. He spotted his mother right away. A nurse was at her bedside checking her blood pressure.

'This is a turn up,' Rose said, when she saw him approaching. 'West Midlands police having a quiet patch, are they?' The whiplash sarcasm reminded Mariner of where he'd developed a taste for it.

'Hello, son, how nice to see you,' he countered.

She was unyielding. 'I don't have to spell it out, do I?'

'If you did I'd really think something was wrong.'

'This is my son,' she told the nurse. 'He's a policeman.' It was said with savoured distaste. Mariner could recall with great clarity the look on her face the first time he'd turned up unannounced at her house, in uniform. It had been his intention to shock her of course, and he'd succeeded. 'You've done this to spite me, haven't you?' she'd said.

'Don't flatter yourself,' was his reply. 'Why does everything have to be about you? Perhaps I've done this because it's actually what I want.' Impossible to explain that, after the unlimited freedom of his unruly childhood, he craved discipline, order and routine. Only once he'd gained that grounding was he ready to flex his individuality again, when CID had offered him the chance.

'So how are you?' he asked now. 'What happened?'

'I went a bit dizzy and my arm went numb, that's all. But now it's passed and I'm ready to go home. Except, of course, they won't let me until the man from Del Monte says yes. So I'm stuck here until the morning.' Any speculation as to the origin of his own belligerent nature was always instantly dispelled by a conversation with his mother.

'What were you doing?' he asked.

'I was up a stepladder decorating the hall.' Said so casually, it was easy to forget that she was fast approaching seventy. Once she'd got used to the fact that he'd left home she'd reverted to her youthful independence.

'Was that what you were ringing me about?' Mariner asked.

'Oh, so you did get my messages then. Like I said, there was something I wanted to tell you.'

'What's that?'

'Well, obviously it's nothing important enough for you to call me back. So it'll keep.' Leaning back on the pillows she folded her arms and Mariner noticed for the first time how bony she'd become.

All this probably meant it was nothing at all. She was simply punishing him for the time it had taken him to respond. Mariner was tired of his mother's games and he could be as stubborn as she was. He wasn't about to give her the satisfaction of begging for it. She seemed about to tell him anyway but changed her mind. Sod it. She'd do it when she was ready. 'I have been busy,' he said.

'I know. I saw you on the local news. But even a phone call would have been nice.'

'Yes.'

'Anyway, now you're here you may as well make yourself useful.' She leaned over and opened the cabinet by the bed. 'Mrs Masud has brought me all these things that I don't really need. It was kind of her but will you take some of it back to the house?'

'Of course.'

She sorted out a plastic carrier bag of things that were surplus to requirement.

'I'll come and see you tomorrow.'

'Twice in two days, eh?' she said. 'My cup runneth over.'

* * *

Outwardly the tiny, neat cul-de-sac in Leamington where Rose still lived had barely changed since Mariner was resident there too. The two of them had moved quite suddenly from their London home when he was small and it was the only place he could remember living as a child. Built between the wars, the house belonged to his grandparents first and the four of them had shared it right up until Granny and Grandpa had retired to a bungalow in Pembrokeshire, where he'd then spent some summer holidays. Tonight he could hardly get down the narrow road, which like so many, had not been designed for multiple-car families. Even with all the vehicles parked half on the pavement, a practice of which Mariner strongly disapproved, there was barely enough room for another to pass.

The street resounded with the shouts of the usual motley gang of neighbourhood kids playing and getting along or not, regardless of shape, size or skin colour. One or two adults were out too, tending their gardens as dusk fell on the balmy summer evening. Mariner pushed open the iron gate, which sported a recent coat of paint, as did the glossy white windowsills of his mother's house. Guilt nipped at him again. Rose must have given up waiting for him and got on with it herself, and all that effort had probably put her where she was today. It surprised him that she'd gone to the trouble. His mother had always eschewed the trappings of constant acquisition and modernisation, so it was unusual for her to have been decorating at all.

Walking up the path he saw Mrs Masud and called across to thank her for ringing him.

'You're welcome,' she said. 'I wasn't sure if anyone else would have contacted you.'

Mariner wondered what she meant by 'anyone else.' Who else *was* there?

His mother was one of the few remaining white residents in the street. During the late sixties and early seventies Asian families had begun moving in, prompting a mass exodus of whites and leaving his mother in the minority. But she'd always refused to make compromises based on the colour of her neighbours' skin and, to her credit, barely even seemed to notice. He let himself in the front door. The house smelled overwhelmingly of emulsion and white spirit, and it took him a couple of minutes to work out what it was that looked different. The hall stairs and landing were coated in fresh paint, but then he'd known about that already. Then he realised: it was the tidiness.

Following his grandparents' departure, the house that he'd grown up in had always been awash with clutter. Treasures collected along the way from every conceivable source, saved for a rainy day, or in case they ever came in useful: mementoes and keepsakes, all randomly piled on shelves and furniture, with barely a space between them. The genes responsible for orderliness were something he must have inherited from his father. Now though, many of the shelves and surfaces were bare in preparation for more decorating. He walked through the downstairs rooms noting that each one was the same. Rose was blitzing the place, and not before time. It hadn't been touched in years, but even so he couldn't help wondering what had prompted this sudden burst of activity. It crossed his mind that there could be more to her hospital admission than he'd thought, but he rejected the idea almost immediately. Everything had been too relaxed.

Upstairs in Rose's bedroom was a more familiar scene, the dressing table crowded with trinkets. He put away the things that he'd brought home for her and out of habit checked each of the other rooms. In the spare room he found a stack of black bin liners stuffed full to bursting, with some of the stuff that had once taken up shelf space downstairs. There were old clothes and bric-a-brac; artefacts that stirred memories of Mariner's childhood. Some of it was from the second large bedroom, the one that nobody had used since he left home. It too had been decorated. It was still a far cry from Lewis Everett's room. Mariner got a sense that his mother was putting things in order for something, but right now he had little capacity for pondering another mystery. He returned the rest of the items he'd brought with him to what he deemed their most appropriate places and left.

* * *

On the way home he had to drive very close to Tony Knox's house. After the visit to Brian Goodway he wanted to sound him out. There were lights on so that was encouraging, but the look on Knox's face when he came to the door was not. The fumes nearly knocked Mariner off his feet.

'All right, boss?' Knox was surly and suspicious to an equal degree.

'I wanted to talk to you about something. Can I come in?'

With great reluctance Knox stepped aside to let Mariner pass. Mariner almost wished he hadn't bothered. In the living room, Knox repositioned himself facing the TV, in what looked like a permanent dent in the sofa, the result of many hours of sitting. Around him was a sea of detritus that could only have accrued over considerable time: a handful of mugs, several squat, green beer bottles, a plate bearing the remains of an unappetising looking sandwich . . . some fresh air would have been welcome too. Even Knox himself looked neglected and unkempt, wearing a grubby T-shirt over faded jeans that hadn't seen the inside of a washing machine for a while. And for the first time Mariner noticed that Knox's trademark buzz-cut was beginning to grow into a crew.

'Theresa not back yet?' he asked, unnecessarily.

Knox grunted. 'She's not coming back.'

'Her mum's taken a turn for the worse?' Mariner asked, struck by what a strange coincidence that was.

But Knox blew that one out of the water. 'It's our marriage that's taken a turn for the worse,' he said. 'Theresa's left me.'

'What? Are you sure?'

Knox gave him the withering look the question deserved.

'I mean, are you sure this isn't just a . . . temporary thing?' said Mariner.

'I'm sure,' said Knox. 'It hasn't happened overnight.'

'So what have you been up to this time?' Mariner had already witnessed Knox's extra-marital activities, first-hand, more than a year ago when Knox had hooked up with a student called Jenny. When Theresa found out and had kicked him out of the house, the couple had ended up staying at Mariner's place. At the time, the consequences had seemed catastrophic, but happily it was only a matter of weeks until Knox saw sense and Theresa found it in herself to forgive him.

Mariner wasn't aware that Knox had been dipping his wick again but it didn't mean that he hadn't. He'd never really understood what made Tony Knox tick. But surely even he was bright enough to grasp the obvious truth: that a woman will only put up with so much. 'I thought you were meant to have stopped all that,' he said.

'Not guilty, boss.' Knox held up his hands in defence. 'I haven't played away from home since Jenny. Then just as the halo was polishing up to a nice shine, Theresa told me she was going.'

'Maybe she just needs some space,' Mariner said, cringing inwardly at how glib that sounded.

'She's moved in with another bloke. Does that sound to you like she needs space?'

'Bloody hell,' was the best response Mariner could come up with. 'Why didn't you say?'

'It's embarrassing,' said Knox. 'She met him over the internet. It makes it worse somehow. It's so bloody tacky.'

'—only because of what you and I know. I'm sure there are plenty of responsible people who use the internet as a legitimate means of communication.'

'Is this what you'd call legitimate? They've been at it for months, years for all I know. All the while I thought she was going back up to Liverpool to visit her sick mum she was really busy rekindling an old flame. Romantic, isn't it? All she was waiting for was for our Gary to leave home before she followed suit. She doesn't need me anymore. She said that her job with the kids was done so there was no other reason to stick around.' He faltered. 'When I asked her what about us, she said, "what us?"'

The word for all this was 'ironic' but all Mariner could muster was: 'Fuck. I mean, *fuck.*'

Knox grimaced. 'That the best you can do? No lecture about poetic justice?'

'You know me better than that,' said Mariner. 'And I'm not about to feed the gossip mill either.'

'Doesn't matter, does it? It won't be long before it's all round the canteen. There'll be a few sides splitting over this. The sad old fart's got what he deserved.'

'I'm sorry, mate.'

'Not half as fuckin' sorry as I am,' Knox retorted, bitterly. 'It's like, this whole other little parallel world was going on that I never even knew existed, but suddenly hindsight opened the door and there it was. Suddenly I can see what a total shit I've been. I thought I had it all under control and meanwhile Theresa's been the one pulling the strings, letting me self-destruct. And do you know what the biggest fuckin' irony of all is? Now that I'm free to go out with any woman I like, I'm just not interested.'

'Do you know who this other man is?' asked Mariner carefully.

'Oh yes.'

'She told you?'

'She didn't have to. Come and look at this.'

Mariner followed Knox up the stairs to a small back bedroom where a PC sat on a desk. Knox logged onto the internet and typed in a web address. 'Old Friends' said the banner that unfurled before them.

'What's this?' asked Mariner.

'It's one of these school reunion websites. Watch.'

Mariner looked over his shoulder as Knox typed in the name of a school and a date and a list of names appeared on the screen. Theresa Fitzpatrick (Knox) was among them. But Knox ignored it, instead clicking on Stephen Lamb. Up came the details: a brief paragraph revealing that Lamb, now forty-nine had built up a successful construction business and after a recent divorce

265

was single again. The end of the message asked if anyone knew the whereabouts of Theresa Fitzpatrick. It was followed by an email address and a crystal clear invitation.

'Do you think somebody told her?' Mariner surmised.

'She was well capable of finding it herself,' said Knox. 'She's been emailing him for months. And all that time, not a hint of what was going on.'

'When did you find out?'

'Thirteen days ago. She went up to her mother's, so I thought. But then she sent me the letter saying that she's decided not to come back.'

'Jesus.' The silence that followed seemed to stretch for hours.

Mariner turned his attention back to the monitor. 'So is it weird looking back at your old school?'

'Oh yeah — and the entries go back for years. There are people who were there in 1943. Can you believe that?'

'Are you on there?'

'No thanks. I wouldn't want to own up to my career choice. There's a few people I recognise though, kids and teachers. Some of the stuff about the teachers must be borderline libellous. True, but libellous just the same. You should have a go. Look up your old school.'

'No thanks.' Mariner could think of nothing worse. There wasn't a single person he was at school with that he would have the slightest desire to make contact with again.

'Want a drink?' Knox asked. He'd clearly already had more than enough, but now wasn't the time to point that out.

'All right,' said Mariner and they went back down stairs.

Knox poured two generous measures of Scotch and the silence resumed. 'How long have you and Theresa been together?' asked Mariner eventually.

'Since we were fifteen,' said Knox. 'We met at the Coconut Grove in 1979. There she was, dancing round the handbags with her mates. She was the most gorgeous thing

I'd ever seen. But she was a good Catholic girl. She made me wait.'

'What, until you got married?'

'Till she knew I was serious. Jesus, the number of nights I went home with my nuts on fire.'

'How many times have you been unfaithful?'

Knox visibly flinched. 'You mean the number of other women? Four in total. The first one was the hardest. I felt really bad about it. But after I'd done it that once it got easier to convince myself that I wasn't doing any harm. Theresa was busy with the kids. She was shattered all the time. I told myself I was doing her a favour, taking the pressure off.'

'Did you ever do it out of spite?'

'No. Why?' He looked up at Mariner. 'You haven't—'

Mariner's silence said it all.

Knox raised an eyebrow. 'You've cheated on Anna? What would you want to do that for? I thought she was hot.'

'She is . . .' said Mariner. 'When she's available.'

'You knew about Jamie before you started it.'

'That's the thing. It's not Jamie. His respite hours are increasing all the time. And anyway, just because he's there doesn't mean I can't see her. Jamie's okay with me. He always has been. It's all the other stuff.'

'Like . . .?'

'Well, right now we're organising a fundraising stall for the Bournville festival.'

'The what?'

'You haven't seen it? It's like a country fair but in the city; all home-grown leeks and maypole dancing.'

'Nothing wrong with a bit of pole dancing,' mused Knox.

'Except this is little girls skipping around waving bits of ribbon.'

'I'll bet they attract the same kind of audience,' said Knox, cynically. 'And this fair is what you're jealous of?

Sounds to me like you're getting serious about our Anna,' said Knox.

'Not really.'

'But you don't like it when she plays hard to get.'

'I don't know if she really is. It's just as if what we've got doesn't matter much. It's just one small aspect of her life.'

'Does she know how important it is to you?' Knox asked.

'What do you mean?'

'I mean, have you told her?'

Mariner made a show of thinking. 'Not in so many words.'

Knox laughed. 'You really don't get it, do you? You pathetic loser. I can tell you've never read a women's magazine.'

'My dentist gets the *Great Outdoors.*'

'You've got to talk to Anna. Tell her what you've told me. How else is she supposed to know that you want more of a commitment?'

'I'm not sure that I do.'

'Oh, believe me, you do.'

'What is this? Your new career as Mary Knox: Agony Aunt?'

'Oh yeah. I'm a real expert, me. I bet you've never told her that you love her either.'

Mariner couldn't answer him.

Knox shook his head in disbelief. 'My God, what does she see in you?'

'I'm dynamite between the sheets,' said Mariner, looking on sheepishly as finally, combined with the whisky, he reduced Knox to uncontrollable mirth.

'So who was it?' asked Knox, when he'd wiped his eyes.

'What does it matter?'

'Who?' Knox insisted.

'Millie.'

'With respect, sir, you're a fucking moron.'

'Millie's a lovely—'

'I didn't mean that.'

'No.'

When they'd followed up the whisky with strong coffee and Knox seemed almost human again Mariner expounded his theory. 'It all just keeps coming back to Shaun Pryce,' he said. 'Do you think it was just electrical work that he did, or was he offering Barbara Kincaid another kind of service?'

'He really fancies himself. I wouldn't be surprised,' Knox agreed. 'He was very keen to tell us about his high sex drive and, from what we've seen, he doesn't have a steady girlfriend, so how else does he get by?'

'Do you think Yasmin would have gone for a bloke like Shaun Pryce?'

'Yasmin?'

'I was just thinking, Pryce might have been useful to her,' said Mariner. 'If Yasmin was still in love with Lewis, Shaun could have come in useful for winding him up. She knew Lewis was working at the industrial units and they used to meet on the bridge. Perhaps she arranged to meet Lewis to show him what she was getting up to with Shaun. Maybe she wasn't going on the pill for Lewis at all, but for Shaun Pryce.'

'Except that Lewis is telling us that he didn't show that afternoon,' Knox said. 'I don't really buy that.'

'Okay,' Mariner conceded. 'So what if it was pure coincidence. Maybe Lewis confirmed their date but decided to stand Yasmin up after all. He told us he thought she was leading him on, so perhaps that's the payback; Yasmin turns up at the bridge to find no Lewis. But then the guy who is there, lurking in the grass getting his rocks off, is Shaun Pryce. Pryce recognises Yasmin from the school art classes and he's horny anyway, so he decides to try it on. But Yasmin isn't interested, so Pryce loses it. The river's in full spate so he dumps her over the edge.'

'Lucky with the timing,' said Knox.

'Pryce could have known about the water release, though. He could have easily concealed her in the short term before coming back at the right time to dispose of her properly.'

'But Pryce wasn't there that late in the afternoon.'

'So he says. That day we met him in the clearing he was saying he went there after work. Then suddenly it's one o'clock? You saw him at the reservoir. He was loving it. And at that time he must have thought he was safe. Yasmin's body was well concealed. Barbara Kincaid had been there for months undiscovered, and now there was Lewis Everett in the background to deflect our attention too. Yasmin could have told him that she was meant to be meeting Lewis.'

'The MO for Yasmin indicates a degree of premeditation,' Knox pointed out.

'Not if Pryce just happened to have a length of wire in his pocket,' said Mariner. 'Whichever way you look at this, Shaun Pryce is in this up to his ears. He's the one who connects Yasmin to Barbara Kincaid and we know he frequents the reservoir. I think we should bring him in.'

'You might have to see what Fiske says about that.'

* * *

CHAPTER 26

Fortunately, DCI Fiske had other things to occupy him. In response to the formal complaint from the Skeet family, the IPCC team had arrived to begin their investigation and for once the DCI was happy to let Mariner take the initiative and get on with his job. Thus when Shaun Pryce arrived at Mrs Paleczcki's the next morning he found a two-man welcoming committee waiting for him. Half an hour later Pryce was installed in an interview room while a search warrant was organised, to authorise turning his flat and car upside down. Being in a police station can do it, but Mariner thought Pryce looked even more jittery than the last time they'd met. The actor's mask was beginning to slip. 'I want you to tell me again when exactly on Tuesday, 3 July you were at the reservoir and exactly what it is you were doing there,' Mariner said.

To settle his nerves Pryce made a show of sighing heavily. 'Aren't you lot getting bored with this, too? I went there at about one o'clock. I stayed half an hour. I sunbathed, I smoked a bit of weed. What's the big deal?'

'And you say you were on your own,' said Mariner.

'Yes.' Exasperation was creeping into his voice.

'You're not always alone though, are you?' Pryce shifted in his chair and for a split second Mariner thought

271

they might have him. 'When was the last time you had a woman down there?'

'I've told you. Weeks ago. They don't like the grass.'

'And who was it, Shaun? Was it Barbara Kincaid?'

'What?' He hadn't seen that coming.

Knox went in for the kill, unleashing the vitriol that should have been directed elsewhere. 'We know, you see, Shaun. We know that you're a randy little bastard who can't keep his dick in his trousers. You have very eclectic taste, I'll say that for you. Middle-aged housewives to seventeen-year-old schoolgirls. Very inclusive. Were they both threatening to abandon you? Is that what made you mad? Mad enough to kill them? Or is that just part of the turn on for you?'

Pryce was starting to look panicked now, blinking rapidly to shut out the words. 'That's rubbish,' he insisted. 'I don't know what you're talking about.' But the outburst had unsettled him.

Knox leaned forward threateningly. 'Are you denying that you knew Barbara Kincaid?'

Pryce hesitated. 'No,' he said, petulantly.

'All right then,' said Mariner. 'Tell us about her. How did you two meet?'

'I thought she killed herself,' Pryce whined. Mariner shrugged non-committally. 'So why are you asking these questions?'

'To find out exactly what happened. Just give us an answer.'

'I used to do this amateur dramatics thing,' said Pryce. 'Barbs played the piano for rehearsals. There was a problem with the electrics one night and I fixed it. Afterwards in the bar she came up to me and said their house hadn't ever been rewired and she thought it might be dangerous. She asked me to go and have a look at it. After the run was finished I was resting again so I said I would.'

'When was this?' Mariner asked.

272

'About March time I suppose.' Which would have been around the time that Barbara Kincaid began threatening suicide.

'Was that the only reason she asked you to go to her house?' asked Knox.

'What do you mean?'

'Did she fancy you?'

'A lot of women do.'

'That must be such a burden,' said Knox sarcastically.

'So you went to the house,' said Mariner. 'Was her husband around?'

'No. It was in the day. He's a teacher. He was at work.'

'That's handy. So what happened?'

'I did the rewiring.' Pryce sat back in his seat. 'What?'

'That's all?'

'If you must know, she nearly fucking killed me. I was up a stepladder connecting up a ceiling rose and she came up behind me, giving me all the usual crap about her old man being useless in bed. Then she—'

'What?'

'Touched me up.'

'Very delicately put.'

'I nearly fell off the bloody ladder and took the light fitting with me.'

'But did you respond? Barbara Kincaid was an attractive woman. And we all know about your famously high sex drive.' Pryce didn't know what to say. 'Or was she too old for you?' said Knox.

'Luckily for me her old man turned up.'

'So then you met Brian Goodway, too. Did you tell him you were a model, or had Barbara already done that?'

'It just came up in conversation, you know.'

'And whose idea was it that you should go and model at the school?' asked Mariner.

'I can't remember. His, I think.'

'I bet you jumped at it. All those young girls.'

'It was a modelling job. It's what I do.'

'Did you get paid for it?'

'Why else would I have done it?'

'Mm. Why else would you have chosen to spend your time surrounded by attractive adolescent girls?' Mariner deliberately turned to Knox. 'I can't think. I heard you got pretty friendly with some of them.'

'I like kids,' said Pryce, weakly.

'Particularly teenage girls. Was Yasmin Akram one of them?'

'I don't know, there were a lot of them.'

'You offered to take your clothes off, didn't you?'

'It was one of the kids suggested that. "Show us what's underneath," she said.'

'Who said?'

'Tall, skinny kid: Susan.' Suzanne. 'It was just a laugh.'

'A laugh? These girls were seventeen, a very impressionable age.'

'It was a joke.'

'Ha, ha,' said Knox.

* * *

They took a break. Results from the search of Pryce's house sounded promising so far and were building a good circumstantial case. Not surprisingly, items included electrical wires of every gauge imaginable. His car had also yielded a grass-speckled blanket and samples from it could be tested with soil and grass from the flattened area at the reservoir. Condoms found were of the same brand as the used ones that had been picked up at the scene.

* * *

During the afternoon, Delrose phoned up to tell Mariner that he had a visitor: a woman. He was expecting Colleen and dreading having to face her. Instead he found Anna waiting for him in reception. Nearly as bad.

'Hi,' she said, cheerfully. 'I wondered when I'd see you again.' She studied him. 'You look rough.'

'Had a curry that didn't agree with me.' It didn't explain why he couldn't look her in the eye, but she didn't allude to that. 'What are you doing here?' he asked.

'I tried phoning, but you're a hard man to get hold of. I was nearby, so I thought I might stand a better chance of talking to you if I came in person. I've missed you.'

'I've been busy.' Mariner rubbed the back of his neck. 'We're in the middle of something—'

'I know,' she said. 'But I think we need to talk. Can you spare a few minutes?'

'All right.'

Outside, they crossed the road and walked into the park opposite, where they began a circuit of the boating pond. A couple of little kids with their grandparents were trying in vain to encourage their toy yachts to sail on the smooth expanse of water. Mariner knew how they felt. For days now it had seemed as if the wind had gone out of the sails of their investigation, leaving it stale and stagnant like the water around them. Then, today, the first hint of a breeze. He hardly dared hope.

'I just wondered what's going on,' Anna said, interrupting his thoughts. 'The other evening you wouldn't stay and now I'm beginning to get the idea that you're avoiding me.'

'It's not that—' Mariner began, too tired for this now.

She moved towards him and made as if to take his arm, but a reflex made him move away, putting some distance between them. As they exchanged a look he saw the flash of understanding cross her features.

'Just so that you know,' she said, using that phrase of hers that always preceded any straight talking, 'I'd be really hurt to find out that you're shagging someone else.'

'I know,' he said helplessly, staring ahead.

She was astute enough to take this as confirmation. She stared straight ahead. 'So you are sleeping with someone else.'

'Not exactly.'

'What the hell does that mean?'

'It means past tense. I slept with someone else, a couple of nights ago.'

'Well, thanks for telling me.' She hadn't been lying. He could hear the pain in her voice. It sliced right through him.

'It's not what you think,' he said.

She stopped and turned to face him, her eyes gleaming with the same fury he'd witnessed the first time they'd met. 'So what is it then?'

'The other night when you were . . . busy. I worked late instead and afterwards, Millie Khatoon, she's our—'

'I know who she is.'

'Right, well, Millie asked me back to her place for a curry and we ended up getting drunk and having sex. It was terrible sex. Millie would tell you the same thing. We didn't go to bed, we didn't even take our clothes off and it was over in ten minutes. It will never happen again.'

An elderly couple walking by gazed their way.

'Well, that's all right then,' Anna said, tightly.

Righteous anger rose in Mariner's chest. 'Oh, and I suppose you and Simon are above all that.'

'Simon?'

'You can't seem to stay away from him. Not that I blame you. He's young, not bad-looking from what I could see—'

'—and apart from me, the most important person in Jamie's life.' Anna rounded on him. 'We're talking about Jamie here, who can't communicate, and for whom consistency is a lifeline. That could explain why I spend so much time with Simon.'

'Even on a Friday night, when you're meant to be having a break from Jamie?'

'Sure, that was more of a social call, but if you hadn't walked away you would have found out what it was all about.'

'I wasn't invited.'

'What, you need a written invitation now?' She was incredulous.

Mariner looked out across the pond. 'So what was it about?' Why was it that her questions sounded entirely reasonable and calm, but he just sounded like a petulant schoolboy?

'Simon has asked me to help with the stall on the day of the festival, so he and Martin had come round to discuss—'

'Martin too? That was a cosy threesome.'

'Actually it was fun,' she responded, evenly. 'Martin and Simon make a great couple.' She paused to allow that to sink in. 'Simon is gay, Martin is his partner. And if I'd thought that it was in the least bit relevant, I would have told you.'

But even then, when she'd handed it to him on a plate, he couldn't let it go. 'That's convenient, isn't it,' he said.

'Oh, fuck off, Tom.' And she turned and walked away from him.

Even if he'd had the energy, going after her would be pointless, he could see that. He would only make things worse. So, after watching her go for a moment, he went back to the nick and Shaun Pryce.

* * *

They spent the rest of the afternoon on Pryce, covering the same ground but making no progress. Mariner was distracted and if anything Pryce seemed to be gaining control. He was certainly more relaxed than he had been a few hours earlier. In the end they had to let him go. As he stalked up to the office again Mariner felt ready to kill someone. Unfortunately the first person he ran into was Millie. 'Has the search team come back yet?' he demanded.

'Not yet,' she said glancing up briefly before returning to the report.

Mariner banged his hand down hard on her desk, making everyone in the office turn round. 'So why the hell aren't you out there, chasing them up!' And he strode into his office and slammed the door, leaving Millie staring after him. After a few moments she tentatively opened the door.

Mariner was standing looking out of the window. 'Sorry,' he said, running a hand over his cropped hair. 'It's been a long day.'

'Don't let Pryce get to you, sir,' said Millie. 'If it is him we'll find out in the end.'

He swung round to face her. 'Anna found out about what happened with us.'

'Oh God. How? You don't think I—?'

'I told her.'

'Oh. Good move.'

'I had to. I couldn't stand it.'

'My, you have got it bad, haven't you?'

And that was the problem. He had. For the first time in his life Mariner had found a woman he could envisage growing old with. Someone he couldn't imagine being without. But the deal with Anna had always been no commitment. And now he was in danger of blowing the whole thing sky high.

Mariner's conscience told him that he should go over to see his mother again tonight, but after the sort of day he'd had he couldn't face her. In any case, it was late and by the time he got there visiting hours would be over. Instead he phoned and spoke to the duty nurse.

'She's fine,' the girl reassured him. 'Though I expect she'll be disappointed not to see you.' *I wouldn't count on it,* thought Mariner.

Knox had already left and in any case Mariner didn't feel much like company, so he went home. The evening was warm and sticky again, the air heavy with unresolved tension. Opening up a bottle of home brew, he went to sit on the bench outside his front door, overlooking the canal. Towards dusk the sky darkened ominously and thunder rumbled in the distance. A few spots of rain followed, temporarily making the air smell a little fresher, but this time the storm never quite broke.

* * *

The next morning Mariner was in the shower, considering their next move with Shaun Pryce when away in the distance he heard the phone ringing. When he got out there was a message from the hospital on the answering machine asking him to call back as soon as possible. He hoped it wasn't to let him know that they were letting his mother go home early. That was a diversion he could do without today.

'Mr Mariner, I'm afraid your mother has suffered a slight heart attack. You may want to come in.' The female voice was calm and unruffled, implying nothing more than a setback, though this would inevitably delay her discharge from the hospital. On the drive over Mariner could visualise his mother's frustration as she was wired up to monitors and drips that would further restrict her independence. This had obvious implications for her after-care, too. He'd need to play a more active role, a prospect he didn't relish, but it might mean getting to know each other again, which could in turn present new opportunities. The nursing sister met him on reception and took him into a side room to explain what was happening. 'I'm sorry, Mr Mariner, we weren't able to resuscitate her.'

For a second or two her words didn't make any sense. Then, one by one, their meaning struck him like a forty-foot wave, almost physically knocking him off-balance.

'She died at just after nine o'clock,' the nurse went on, gently. 'It was very sudden, so it's unlikely that she knew anything about it. She wouldn't have been in any pain.' Her carefully chosen words were designed to offer comfort and consolation. They were words of the kind that Mariner had spouted a hundred times before, when he'd broken the news of sudden, unexpected death to the relatives of crime victims. In all that time it had never occurred to him that one day he might be on the receiving end. So this was what it was like. A feeling of complete disorientation, as if time had suddenly slowed to nothing.

'Would you like to see her?' the nurse repeated when he failed to respond the first time.

He had to wait a few minutes, while they made her presentable presumably. But it made no difference. When he went in he didn't see Rose. The life in her was gone, leaving behind an empty shell. In the past he'd watched families say their last goodbyes, kiss the cold cheek of their loved one, but Mariner couldn't bring himself to do that. His mother wasn't there anymore, and all that lingered was a burning pain in his chest. Why did it hurt so much? It wasn't as though he would miss her daily presence. They'd hardly seen each other in recent years. And it wasn't as though the idea of death was new to him; he faced the reminders of his own mortality on an almost daily basis at work. Perhaps it was because now he'd have to accept the possibility that he might never know.

He realised all of a sudden how much he'd taken Rose for granted, expecting her to never not be there. He'd always assumed that she'd be one of those women who lived well into her nineties. An afterthought struck him: she'd never meet Anna now.

They were still holding his mother's personal effects at the nursing station on the ward. 'I'd meant to give them to your dad,' the nurse told him, when she handed them over. 'But he left before I could.'

Mariner gawped. 'My what?'

Had he been thinking rationally and stopped to consider Mariner would have recognised her mistake, but other things began to fall into place. His mother's 'something to tell him,' that his father had reappeared on the scene. It might explain why she was doing up the house, too.

He drove at speed back to his mother's house, where he found an old-style pushbike leaning against the wall. That hadn't been there two days ago. He let himself in with the key. 'Hello?'

'Hello. You must be Tom.' Ted emerged from the under stairs cupboard, and turned out to be a softly-spoken widower who had worked for years as an engineer at Potterton's boilers in Coventry and lost his wife shortly after his retirement.

'How long have you known Rose?' Mariner asked.

'About a year,' said Ted. He'd made tea and they sat companionably at the kitchen table. 'I was planning to move in with her.'

'Were you?' Mariner's surprise was genuine. He was struggling to get his head round the idea that his mother had met another man after all this time. If there had been liaisons over the years Mariner had never been aware of them. As far as he knew there had been nobody since his father, who hadn't even stuck around long enough to see his son born. Just like the Akrams with Yasmin, this was the part where he was finding out how little he knew about his mother.

Ted was flustered now. 'No, it wasn't like that,' he said. 'We were just friends, but I was coming to live here with her. She'd offered me a room.'

'A room?'

'I'm living in rented accommodation at present but the lease expires at the end of the month and the landlord wants me out, so your mother had said I could have her spare room. It was all above board. We had agreed rent.'

'I see.' Typical of his mother to be adopting waifs and strays even at her age. As he spoke Mariner recognised that Ted and his mother had espoused the kind of pragmatic approach to life that is the privilege of the older generation. They'd reached the point where, having taken their share of knocks, they'd realised that they had too little time left to waste it arguing about the minutiae of life. Ted was about to lose his home. Rose had a spare room. The two things fitted logically together, end of story.

'I'm not a con man,' said Ted quickly, answering the very question that Mariner had dismissed inside his head moments before.

'No.' *And you're not my father.*

Ted 'liked to keep busy' as he put it, hence the fresh coat of paint on the house. Mariner's mother had been helping him, but mainly by providing cups of tea, from the sound of it. 'I didn't want her to be up ladders. I don't know why she was.' Ted had come to collect his overalls and brushes. 'No time like the present. I expect you'll want to sell the house and I wouldn't want them to be in the way.'

* * *

When Ted had gone Mariner called the office from his mother's old Bakelite phone and spoke to Fiske.

'I'm very sorry, Tom,' he said, formally. 'Is there anything we can do?'

'No thanks, sir.'

'Complaints are still here.' Fiske couldn't resist mentioning it, even though his timing was so utterly inappropriate. 'They're going through all the paperwork with a fine-tooth comb.'

'That's what they do, sir.'

'Yes.' A pause. 'They'll want to talk to you, too. Tom, I hope—'

'Not really the right moment, sir.'

282

'No.., no, you're right. Well, take as much time as you need.'

'Thank you, sir.' I won't be hurrying back on your account. He'd let Fiske squirm. Even if the DCI were vindicated, the fact that there had been an investigation in the first place could be enough to blight his career. With any luck the mud would stick.

Mariner was still uneasy about his own part in the debacle. He could have been more assertive about keeping Ricky's case and more proactive, both with Ricky and with his mother. Now he'd paid the price for both.

The following day he went to the registry office to record his mother's death. Technically it had been a sudden death, so there would have to be a post-mortem, but it would be routine. The people around her when she died had all been fighting to save her life. Nothing suspicious about that. Sitting on a plastic seat awaiting his turn, it occurred to Mariner that to all intents and purposes he was now an orphan, with very little family to speak of. His mother had a couple of cousins as far as he remembered, but there'd been no family gatherings when he was a kid. It gave him something else in common with Anna. She'd lost her parents several years ago — except of course Mariner couldn't know for a fact that *both* his parents were gone . . . and perhaps now never would.

Ironically if he'd been adopted it would have been simple. These days there were routes to follow. But not for him. He thought about the bond between a father and the mother of his child. Ronnie Skeet was a nasty piece of work but it still didn't stop Colleen from letting him back into the house time after time. *He's the father of my kids*, she'd said.

Mariner's mother had never given him any firm reason to doubt that she knew the identity of his father. Was there an unbreakable bond there, too, however tenuous? However effectively she'd managed to keep this man a secret, would there still be some fine strand connecting them? If there was then there must be some trace of it at her house. It was the only place to start, his only chance of solving the puzzle . . .

For the sake of being thorough he began with all the obvious places, but knowing beforehand that there would be nothing in the bureau in the dining room or in her drawer in the bedroom. Those were too accessible. He found all her current paperwork, bank and building society accounts, letters from the last few years. Most of the entries in her address book were local, friends and contacts made when she moved back up to Leamington. There was nothing from before that time.

Among the documents was his birth certificate, but he'd seen that years ago and it gave nothing away. He was officially a bastard. That would amuse some of the crooks he'd put away in the past. Rose had kept all his old school reports too, most of them variations on a 'could try harder' theme. But it was futile. She'd kept the secret for this long. She'd never leave anything lying around down here that would give it away. Mariner knew where the important stuff was. The past had literally been hanging over his head all the time he'd lived in this house.

When they'd moved in with his grandparents, space was at a premium and consequently many of their belongings had vanished up into the loft, never, to his knowledge, to come down again. Rose had always vehemently discouraged him from going up there on the grounds that he might clumsily put a foot through the fragile floor and into the ceiling of the rooms below, but Mariner suspected the real reason lay deeper than that.

No one had been up there for years, mainly because it was such a hassle getting up there, involving balancing precariously at the very top of the stepladder before launching off into the narrow aperture. But now that Mariner had height on his side, the manoeuvre was relatively easy. The loft space was stifling and dirty, with everything coated in a layer of black dust. A bare bulb, the cable draped over one of the rough timbers provided the minimum amount of light and in the gloom Mariner could see the enormity of the task: boxes and trunks, rolls of faded wallpaper, a collection of old camping equipment that could have belonged to Edmund Hillary, complete with rusting tartan vacuum flasks and heavy canvas groundsheets.

Opening a cardboard carton he found old crockery and cutlery, including a child's porcelain Peter Rabbit dish that had probably been his. In another, a whole willow-patterned bone-china dinner service. One suitcase was stuffed full of dusty dun-coloured blankets. Finally he found what he was looking for in a brown cardboard suitcase whose catches were almost rusted solid. With effort he slid them across and the lid flipped open to reveal yellowing paper: letters, cards, newspaper cuttings and photographs. The dull grimy address label stuck to the inside of the lid had written on it *Rosemary Ellen Mariner* in neat italic ink-penned script. This was his mother's life in London.

She'd been twenty-four when he was born in the middle of another long hot summer, which left him looking for anything dated from around that time. Her twenty-first birthday cards were bundled together, as were letters from his grandmother, even a handful of birth congratulations cards, most from women or couples. There were black-and-white photographs of him as a baby, wrapped in a woollen shawl. Along with these were mementoes from special occasions: tickets from London Zoo, a programme from the Henry Wood promenade concert the previous year, an evening of Sibelius, conducted by Malcolm Sargent.

The only things that might reveal any clues, he decided, were the letters. He sat on an old crate and strained his eyes to read. The letters were addressed to several different places in London, where his mother had lived an apparently nomadic existence. Mostly his grandmother described trivial events in Leamington, though occasionally she made reference to things that Rose must have mentioned in her letters home. It was these brief glimpses that Mariner clung to. In the dim light, the curling italic handwriting wasn't easy to decipher and he took his time, anxious not to miss anything.

But he realised as he came to the last, with overwhelming disappointment, that there was nothing to miss. His neck ached and his eyes stung with the dust and the effort. It had gone cooler. When he emerged back onto the ladder he found out why. It was dark: almost eleven at night. Turning on the landing light he left a black fingerprint on the switch. He looked as if he'd been up a chimney. He was filthy.

His mother had never gone in for showers so he ran a hot bath and lay in it soaking. He had a decision to make. He could waste limitless amounts of time and energy trying to discover something that was probably unattainable, or he could get back to his life. Later he crawled into bed in the spare room to sleep on it.

CHAPTER 27

The morning brought with it a firm decision. Mariner locked his mother's house, having made up his mind that he'd get onto the estate agent in the next few days and arrange a skip and some visits to a local charity shop. At home he found a message on the answer phone from Anna. It wasn't exactly an olive branch, but carefully handled it might have the potential to become one. He called her back straight away, half expecting her recorded message. To his surprise she was there, but the conversation didn't go according to plan. 'Where have you been?' Anna asked. 'I've been trying to contact you.'

'My mother's dead.'

'Oh God, Tom, I'm so sorry. What happened?'

'A heart attack, Thursday morning.'

'But that's two days ago. Why didn't you call me? Are you all right?'

'I'm okay.'

'Do you want me to come over? I can see if Simon could—'

'No!' he snapped. 'It's all right, I'm fine, really.'

'Okay then.' She backed off.

So the experience hadn't changed him. In an emotional crisis he still couldn't manage to tell her how he was feeling. It was so long since he'd done it that he'd forgotten how.

* * *

It wasn't any less depressing back in the office, where in his absence, nothing much had changed. Fiske was still technically overseeing things but his mind was, understandably, preoccupied. The team itself seemed to have lost all coherence, too. Mariner recognised that he was still in a state of shock. Tony Knox seemed lower than ever, and recent events seemed to have generated an awkwardness between himself and Millie — all of which was nicely exacerbated by the fact that, beyond the initial expression of condolences, suddenly no one quite knew what to say to him.

There had been no progress, either forensic or otherwise, to pin down Shaun Pryce. The grass and soil traces on the blanket in his car were a match with the reservoir, but then Pryce had never denied that he went there. There was a feeling all round that both investigations were beginning to lose momentum as demands on resources continued to be made from elsewhere, and there were mutterings about calling in the murder review team. That and the ominous presence of the IPCC was doing little to inspire confidence.

* * *

Partly to get out of the building Mariner went to visit the Akrams, who unusually were both at home. 'You've closed the school?'

'We had to,' Mohammed Akram told him. 'It was impossible to keep going. We hope to reopen in a few days, but we're in limbo. Until we know who did this to Yasmin we can't get on with our lives. It's like unfinished business.'

'I'm sorry,' Mariner said. 'There's no news yet, but we're still doing everything we can.'

'Thank you.'

* * *

Another uncompromisingly sunny day dawned for Mariner's mother's funeral. He put on one of his lighter suits and perused his collection of dreary ties. Had he been Fiske, he'd have had a whole range of jolly cartoon characters at his disposal, but he wasn't, so in the end he chose a sky and navy stripe.

'Well look at you.' Anna was standing in the hallway. She'd let herself in and was waiting by the front door, wearing a simple floral dress and a wide brimmed hat. 'I thought you could use some support,' she said. 'After all, I've had some experience at this.' Over the last few years death had been a loyal companion as she'd seen both her parents and her older brother killed. It was Eddie's murder that had brought them together in the first place.

'Thanks, I appreciate it,' said Mariner, truthfully.

She saw him appraising her outfit. 'Would she have approved?'

'She'd have approved, whatever you were wearing.'

They spoke little on the drive over to Leamington and Mariner was grateful for that, too. His nerves jangled in anticipation. Not because of the funeral; that he could cope with. But ahead of today he had placed announcements in both the local and national press. At the very least he was hoping to meet someone who could tell him who his father was. And then there was the possibility he hardly dared consider: that his father might turn up in person.

In her will his mother had planned out the ceremony to the last detail; a simple cremation with a couple of pieces of music: 'Ave Maria' and the 'Intermezzo' from Sibelius's *Karelia Suite*. It had been on the programme of the Promenade concert he'd found in the loft and hearing it now, he couldn't help wondering if the piece had had a deeper significance for her. It was all she wanted. Mariner introduced Anna to Ted, who sat beside them at the front of the church along with Mrs Masud. Turning to look Mariner saw that the chapel was a respectable two thirds full, a congregation disproportionately made up of women, attributable possibly to his mother's lifelong commitment to the feminist cause. He could tell those who'd known her well; they were the ones dressed for a picnic in the park.

'Anyone else you recognise?' Anna asked him.

'Not a soul.'

There was to be no wake back at the house. His mother had made no stipulation about it in her will, and to Mariner it seemed pointless to invite a group of total strangers to join him in mourning a woman he hardly knew. But he did formally greet people as they left the chapel.

Most of the mourners turned out to be friends of his mother's from Leamington, but then came the encounter that he'd been praying for: a large woman dressed in flowing pink and turquoise, her grey unruly hair loosely pinned back. She smiled. 'You've changed a bit since we last met,' she said. 'I'm Maggie Devlin. I used to sit for you when you were a baby.'

Mariner's heart thumped against his rib-cage. 'We're going for a drink,' he said, with astonishing calm. 'Would you like to join us?'

She agreed to come, but Mariner was in for a disappointment. Maggie had indeed known his mother from her London days, but was as mystified as he was about who his father might be. 'Rose kept that one close to her chest,' she told him over a G&T in the garden of a nearby pub. 'She was a popular girl. She never wanted for male attention.'

'But she didn't give any clue about who it might be?'

'None, I'm sorry. She was good at secrets, your mother. There was just the one day—'

'What?'

'It might be nothing at all,' Maggie warned him.

'Please.'

'When you were born Rose was living in a flat in Holborn. I came to see you when you were just a couple of days old, and as I arrived there was a black car pulling away from the kerb. It caught my attention because it was a big car, especially for round there, what you'd call a limousine, I suppose. It was only afterwards though that I began to wonder if it had anything to do with—'

'Did you get the licence plate?' asked Mariner automatically, before laughing with Maggie at his own stupidity. 'Of course not. Why would you?'

'And I doubt that it would be much help after all these years.'

'No.'

'I'm truly sorry that I can't tell you more. But if I should learn of anything that might help—'

'Thanks.' Clinging to that slim hope, Mariner gave her his card.

* * *

The sun blasting in through the window roused Tony Knox from a deep sleep. He had a throbbing headache and a raging thirst again, even though he thought he'd been pretty moderate with the booze last night. He glanced over at the clock. Bugger! Twenty past ten. He should have been at work hours ago. For a moment he debated whether to pull a sickie, but remembered where Mariner had gone today. It would be good to have something for the boss when he got back. So Knox made himself get out of bed and into the shower.

Everyone at Granville Lane was either out or preoccupied so no one noticed his late arrival and now he was here he couldn't think of anything purposeful to do. While he considered that, unable to resist the urge, he tucked himself away in a corner of the office and logged on again to the Old Friends website. But before clicking onto Stephen Lamb's name Knox checked himself. He'd spent hours staring at that message and all it had done was fuel his anger. Lamb presenting himself as God's gift . . . as he went to exit the website, Knox thought suddenly about Shaun Pryce. Was this the kind of site he'd go in for too? Of course he would, the self-serving little git. If Pryce was keen to publicise himself, one group he'd really want to tap into would be his old school chums, particularly as he'd enjoyed some modest success. He was bound to want to capitalise on that. And in showing off to them, what else might he give away? His exploits with middle-aged housewives? There might be something to learn from the reactions of Pryce's former classmates too. He'd not a clue which schools Pryce had attended, of course, but it couldn't be that difficult to work out. His webpage had indicated that he was a local lad.

All Knox had to do was systematically work through the secondary schools in the area. Right now he couldn't think of a better way to keep himself occupied and Fiske off his back for the day. He'd start with Kingsmead and work his way out. Pryce would have left the school about fifteen years ago, so he'd take it from there. For a moment Knox was tempted to pick up the phone and make his life easier by asking Shaun Pryce the direct question. Pryce wouldn't need to know what it was about. But then he caught sight of the Complaints officer in the far side of the office poring over Ricky Skeet's file and decided they couldn't risk any more aggro. With a weary sigh he began opening up the message envelopes beside each of the names. The computer was on a go-slow so it took forever.

A pattern among the messages quickly emerged. The people who bothered to leave them all had one thing in common: like Stephen Lamb they all had shiny, successful lives. Invariably the message started off with career details: *working as a stockbroker/lawyer/managing director for* . . . There was a distinct dearth of window cleaners, bin men and the unemployed. This was always followed by a description of family life: *married with four children/wife Cordelia, children Dominic (10) and Pandora (8)*, etc. Occasionally someone was bold enough to admit to a second marriage, but even that came across as twice the achievement. Generally speaking, life's failures didn't draw attention to themselves. It was all sickeningly up-beat and did nothing to lift Knox's own blackening mood.

For a little light relief Knox switched to reading the notice board pages where former pupils could post their opinions on anything from their former school days. Usually it was the teachers who'd become the subject of perceived injustices and occasional downright victimisation, prompting outpourings of resentment and angst. This was more like it, Knox thought: bitterness to match his own. He was busy marvelling at the human capacity for blame when he almost overlooked a name he'd seen before, more than once in recent days. Bucking the trend, the attached messages indicated relative popularity. One described in great detail an elaborate April fool's joke taken with good humour. But it was followed by a more cryptic note, posted by someone calling himself 'Stewey': *Goody Goodway: did he jump or was he pushed?* There was one response from a Derrick Farmer: *One of life's eternal mysteries. Gone but sadly missed.*

Knox stared at the screen trying to work out what, if anything, it could mean. The school was another local comprehensive where Goodway must have worked prior to teaching at Kingsmead. Running a search he found Stewart 'Stewey' Blake on the list of leavers from ten years ago.

For the sake of having achieved something this afternoon Knox emailed him leaving his mobile number, and hoping that 'Stewey' was in the habit of checking his inbox regularly. He waited a few minutes in case there was an instant reply, but then, unlike Knox, Blake would have better things to do on a sunny Saturday afternoon than spend it hunched over his computer. And it would probably turn out to be nothing. Sensationalism knitted out of a few shreds of circumstantial information — perfect internet fodder. He looked around the office. Millie was at the Akrams', and Charlie Glover out on a call, so there was no one to enjoy a round of speculation with. He needed a drink. There was also no one to see him leave early, so he picked up his jacket and went.

On the way home, of its own volition, Knox's brain began composing his own message for the reunion website: 'Wife has left me because of my womanising, I'm an embarrassment to my kids. Could have made DS or even DI, if I hadn't shagged a senior officer's wife.' What an epitaph.

Slamming shut his front door the noise reverberated around the empty house for seconds afterwards. Knox tried to imagine hearing that same sound every day for the next thirty years, destined to spend the rest of his life alone. He hurled his keys onto the hall table in frustration. What was the point? What was the fucking point?

* * *

After a couple of hours the handful of people who'd come to the pub with them had drifted away, leaving Mariner and Anna alone at their table in the Coach and Horses. The guest beer was a very pleasing Adnams and the garden was bathed in early evening sunshine, but Mariner couldn't shake off the gloom that had descended.

'Maybe you just have to accept this as one mystery you can't solve,' said Anna, ever the pragmatist.

Mariner flashed a wry smile. 'I'll add it to all the others waiting for me back at the station.'

'It's not your fault,' Anna said.

'I know, but I just can't believe that I'll never know.'

'Does it matter?'

'Right now it feels like the only important thing, but I suppose that will pass.'

'It has before,' she reminded him. 'And who knows, when you clear the house you may come across something that you've overlooked.'

Mariner shook his head. 'She was too careful.'

'Why do you think she kept it from you?' asked Anna.

'Who knows?' Mariner gazed over the garden around them. 'To begin with I thought it was because of who he was. She liked to give the impression he was somebody important; someone whose reputation would suffer if it was known that he'd fathered an illegitimate child. Back then a child born out of wedlock was still a big deal. But later I used to think that maybe she played on that because she thought it would make me feel better to know that he was someone special.'

'So it could have just been a bloke down the street?'

'It might explain why we moved away from London in such a hurry.'

'And there's no one else you can think of who would know?'

'As Maggie said, Rose deliberately severed links with a lot of her friends when we moved from London. There may be somebody somewhere, but I wouldn't begin to know how to find out.'

'So maybe it's time to start looking forward instead of back,' she said, brightly.

Mariner studied his pint for a moment. He had something to say. He just wasn't sure if now was the right time to say it. 'I regret what happened with Millie,' he said at last. 'Really regret it.'

She placed a hand over his. 'I know. And I'm not sure what gave me the right to be so annoyed about it. We've never had that kind of relationship.'

Mariner could almost feel Tony Knox sitting on his shoulder, urging him on. 'I wish we did,' he blurted out.

She wrinkled her nose, as if trying to make sense of her own feelings. 'Yeah, me too.'

A hoard of small children raced by behind them, shrieking with ear-piercing intensity. Mariner swallowed the rest of his pint. 'Let's go home.'

'Your place or mine?'

'Yours. If I turn off my phone nobody can reach me there.'

Back at Mariner's house the land line rang on unanswered.

CHAPTER 28

When Mariner woke the next morning Anna was already up. He could hear her moving around and eventually she walked past the bedroom door, already dressed and her arms full of boxes and bags headed for the tombola. It was ten past eight. Mariner propped himself on an elbow and picked up the mug of tea she'd left for him. Anna saw him. 'You all right?' she asked.

'Fine. You?' When she nodded he said: 'Come back to bed.'

She hesitated.

'Ten minutes, that's all.'

'And then you'll help me?'

'Yes.'

'It's a deal.'

Standing in the shower rather more than ten minutes later, Mariner had a strange feeling. It puzzled him until suddenly he recognised it as a kind of contentment. 'Shall I come with you?' he asked when they'd loaded up her car.

'It's up to you. I'll have to man the stall for a couple of hours,' she warned him. 'I can't do anything about that.'

'I wouldn't want you to.'

* * *

Bournville festival was an anachronistic affair dating back to 1902, at a time long before the model village created by the factory owners had been greedily swallowed up by the suburbs of the spreading city. Although the surrounding area had changed, the event retained its rural village charm, held on the vast green playing fields fronting the chocolate factory that were for the rest of the year given over to cricket, football or bowls, depending on the season. Alongside the fun-fair, exhibition tents, stalls and games had been erected alongside a small arena, the centre of which was dominated by a traditional maypole wrapped in bright red and yellow ribbons. At the far end of the grounds an area had been cordoned off for the pyrotechnic display that would end the celebrations late in the evening.

It took several journeys to transfer everything from Anna's car to where the stall was being set up, and here, inevitably, Mariner came face to face with Simon. If he'd expected to be let off lightly with a caricature of a mincing queen, Mariner realised he was out of luck. Simon was bronzed, muscular and macho, and Mariner found it hard to believe that what Anna had said was true. He could see her watching him.

'It's not always the ones you expect,' she said.

'No.' Progress: he could smile about it.

Anna was going to be busy arranging prizes until the festival opened and there were already enough volunteers on hand who seemed to know what they were doing. Mariner felt like a spare part, so he wandered off to see what else was on offer. There were stalls affiliated with every local organisation imaginable. Even the conservation group was represented, he noticed, seeing Eric Dwyer lurking behind a table of soft toys, wooden carved artefacts and the ubiquitous mugs, trying to encourage new recruits to the project.

Though the festival wouldn't be officially open for another half hour, people were pouring in through the gates. At one end of the field was the West Midlands police trailer. Recognising Jim Watson, a sergeant from the OCU, Mariner made for the home security van. Alongside the advice posters on securing doors and windows was a display with photographs of Ricky and Yasmin, appealing again for any information anyone might have. Now that the heat was going out of the investigations it was essential to take any opportunity to maintain the profile of each case and keep the publicity going, but at the same time it felt gruesome and out of keeping with the atmosphere of the event — even to Mariner. Unsurprisingly, few people were giving the display much attention. Mariner spent several minutes chatting to Watson before heading towards the exhibitions tent.

Inside the marquee it was bright and oppressive, with a smell of warm canvas on grass that took Mariner back to childhood camping expeditions. Long trestle tables were covered with pristine white cloths and a series of displays that reflected every creative pastime open to man: from homemade cakes, flower arrangements and jam, to prize-winning pumpkins and marrows. There were art competitions for children and adults for which certificates would be awarded later that afternoon for different categories and age groups. The adults' theme was 'reflections of Birmingham' and the one that most appealed to Mariner's taste was literally that: an impressive pen and ink sketch of a bank of trees at sunset, mirrored onto what Mariner guessed was somewhere on one of the city's canals. The view was familiar, not dissimilar to the one from his back door.

'Inspector, I didn't know you lived locally.' It was the artist himself who approached Mariner.

'My partner does,' said Mariner, thinking that it was the first time he'd ever referred to Anna that way. 'And I had no idea that you were so gifted. Congratulations, Mr Goodway, it's a superb drawing.'

'Thank you. I'm a bit rusty these days, but suddenly I find myself with some empty evenings to fill. And it can be very therapeutic. Helps to take my mind off things.'

'Of course.' An unwelcome reminder to Mariner that there was still unfinished business. 'Good luck with the competition.'

'Thank you.'

An announcement over the PA system heralded the opening ceremony and Mariner moved outside again in time for the arrival of the festival queen, attended by her flower girls, all of whom were selected from children born on the Cadbury estate. Mariner was swept along with the crowds towards the main arena where the maypole dancing would begin. Judging by the number of video cameras trained on the dancing, each child had a minimum of two sets of proud parents and grandparents there. Scanning the crowd, Mariner spotted another familiar face. It took him a moment or two to place Andy Pritchard, especially as today his ranger's uniform had been replaced by jeans and T-shirt.

He was reaching up to position a digital camera and Mariner wondered if he had a daughter among the dancers, though he seemed to remember Pritchard as a single man. Perhaps a niece then, or goddaughter. At that moment Pritchard glanced up and saw Mariner watching him. Mariner smiled and nodded, but Pritchard didn't reciprocate. Instead, lowering the camera, he turned and began walking away from Mariner into the crowd. Purely out of curiosity Mariner followed, just to see what he would do, and was interested to note that Pritchard quickened his pace. There were a number of possible explanations. The simplest was that the recognition hadn't been mutual, or perhaps Pritchard just didn't feel like talking to Mariner. Being a policeman could sometimes have that effect on people. Mariner gave it up.

Tired of the crowds, Mariner sought refreshment in the beer tent, but after standing in a motionless queue for ten minutes he abandoned that idea and decided to go and find a pub. Being on the Bournville Trust, and therefore Quaker and dry, the nearest was going to be a drive away. The incident with Andy Pritchard was niggling at him, too. The more he thought about it, the more he thought Pritchard's behaviour odd. He glanced over to where the Manor Park stall was. Anna was in her element, hidden somewhere behind a heaving mass of people. She wouldn't miss him for an hour or so.

* * *

Mariner's first stop was Granville Lane. 'Tony Knox in today?' Mariner asked the duty sergeant.

'He was here earlier, but the miserable sod's done us all a favour and gone home,' was the terse reply.

Even so, it didn't take Mariner long to find what he was looking for up in CID: the information Knox had followed up on the indecent exposures. After plotting the incidents on a map Knox had rightly identified the pattern as being access to railway stations, but when he looked closely Mariner found another, more subtle pattern. Each of the attacks had also occurred close to a council park or open space; not on it, but close by. Andy Pritchard used his bike to get around and what better way of covering bigger distances across the city with a bike than on the train?

Mariner switched on his computer. While he was waiting for it to boot up he sorted through the phone messages in his in-tray. One was an urgent phone message to contact the forensic service. Mariner called back. Most of the scientists were off duty for the weekend, but the technician who was covering was expecting Mariner's call.

'The gaffer thought you might want to know that we've identified the type of wire that was used to strangle Yasmin Akram. It's a kind of annealed wire, coated with a chemical rust inhibitor.'

'Would it have a plastic coating?'

'Wouldn't need it.'

'So not an electrical wire,' said Mariner, disappointed.

'Electrical wire isn't normally left exposed like that,' the technician told him. 'It's a fairly soft wire, easily pliable but strong enough to withstand quite a powerful force, so it would be an effective murder weapon.'

'Any idea what it would be used for?'

'The clue to that may be in the other substance we found at the joint where the wire had been twisted. In the crook there was a tiny residue of claydium.'

'Which is what?'

'A type of nylon-reinforced clay. Specifically used for modelling. Add that to the wire and I'd say you were looking for someone who's a modelling enthusiast.'

Mariner thought about Pritchard. He could imagine him with his Airfix planes or battalions of model soldiers. Ringing off, he ran a check on Andy Pritchard but no criminal record appeared and there were no details on the database. Mariner thought about the man. How would he fare with women? Probably not that well. He wasn't particularly good looking, the skin problem saw to that. Helen Greenwood had mentioned the flasher's complexion. Sunburnt she'd said. Or could it have been acne? The way he'd looked at Yasmin's partly clothed body had seemed a little off-kilter too. And why had he taken so long to phone it in? What had he been doing in the forty minutes after he found it?

Suddenly Mariner remembered Croghan's remark about Yasmin's missing underwear. Had it been removed at the time Yasmin was killed or afterwards? Because Pritchard had discovered the body long after Yasmin disappeared and had no apparent connection with the disappearance, checking his alibi had been a formality. Yasmin's body was discovered in an obscure area of the park. What had prompted Pritchard to even look there? And most importantly where had Andy Pritchard been on the afternoon of Tuesday, 3 July? Mariner wondered what

Tony Knox was up to today. He couldn't imagine that it was anything much. Drinking himself into a stupor probably. The man needed saving from himself.

CHAPTER 29

When there was no response on the phone, Mariner drove round to Knox's house. He rang the doorbell at Knox's house several times and then hammered on the door a couple of times. There was no response, despite the car on the drive and, looking through the window, he could see that the place was still a tip. Christ, Knox was hopeless on his own. Mariner went round to the back of the house. The garden was empty and despite the growing heat the house still shut up. He peered in through the patio doors and a chill ran through him.

Tony Knox was slumped lifelessly in an armchair. Mariner could see the bottle of spirits on the floor beside him and lying on the sofa within arm's reach, another small, brown bottle. Mariner's mind raced back over Knox's behaviour over the past few weeks: the mood swings and the pent-up anger, along with that unprecedented reluctance to talk about anything, until his recent shame-faced revelation. Putting it all together with the scene before him, Mariner came to one unspeakable conclusion. He banged on the window, hard. Nothing. Being a policeman the house was like Fort Knox. How appropriate was that? The back door was the flimsiest and in the end Mariner smashed the glass to get in. He rushed in on Knox who hadn't moved a muscle. This wasn't good.

'Tony!' Mariner shook him, slapping his cheek with more force than he'd intended. Knox jolted back to life with a start. 'What? What's going on?'

Mariner sat back on his heels, weak with relief. 'Nothing, I thought . . . nothing. It doesn't matter.' He'd explain the kitchen window later. His gaze skimmed the brown stubby beer bottle on the sofa and after a split-second delay, Knox's face cracked into a smile.

'You thought I'd topped myself, didn't you?'

Mariner said nothing.

'Aw, I didn't know you cared, boss.'

'Piss off,' said Mariner.

'Listen,' said Knox. 'If I take that way out, it won't be quietly in my own living room. It will be off the roof of the Hyatt with the TV cameras rolling. And you'll be among the first to know. Anyway, where the hell have you been? I've been trying to contact you.'

'I was at Anna's last night.'

Knox raised an eyebrow. 'You talked?'

'We talked.'

'About fucking time. Anyway I think I've found something.'

'Me too.'

'Really?' Knox looked almost disappointed, but he listened patiently while Mariner ran through what he'd got. 'Pritchard sounds like he could be our flasher, but did he kill Yasmin?' he said, when Mariner had finished.

'He had every reason to be in the area,' said Knox. 'The park is just across the road from the reservoir. And he's definitely a bit weird. But it doesn't necessarily make him a killer.'

He was right. 'Okay,' said Mariner. 'So what have you got?'

'Come and have a look.' Knox took him back up to the little office and onto the Old Friends website.

'Is this to do with Theresa?'

'Not exactly.' He logged back onto the website to show Mariner the message he'd found. Mariner was doubtful. 'It's not much.'

'No. But then I started thinking: what would make a good teacher resign or get the sack?'

'Stealing? Embezzling the school fund?'

'—or having the wrong kind of relationship with the students.'

'Goodway doesn't fit the usual profile. He's got three kids of his own. Happily married man.'

'How happy though?' said Knox. 'Barbara Kincaid was pretty scathing to Shaun Pryce about her love life, which might indicate that her husband has other preferences.'

Mariner thought back to his visit to Brain Goodway's home. 'He made some comment about how young and glamorous Barbara *had been* when he met her. I thought then it seemed an odd way of putting it.'

'Maybe "young" is the operative word. And if he went off her as she got older, it might have left both of them looking elsewhere for gratification. He gets his from ogling the kids at school—'

'—and along comes Shaun Pryce, for her.'

'He could easily have been lying about his relationship with her. Which makes me wonder about what really happened to Barbara Kincaid?'

'We've no reason to believe she was murdered,' Mariner pointed out.

'It was a sudden, unexplained death.'

'Yes, but the suicide verdict is unlikely to be challenged. She was taking powerful anti-depressant medication and her GP at the time has confirmed that she was under a lot of strain.'

'Great cover for Goodway if he's found out that she's having an affair and decided to off her.'

'You've been watching too much crappy TV,' said Mariner. 'Where would Yasmin come into all this?'

'She could have seen Pryce with Barbara Kincaid and grassed on them to Goodway.'

'But that must have all erupted months ago. Why leave it until now to do anything about Yasmin?'

Knox couldn't provide the answer but luckily for him his phone trilled, temporarily letting him off the hook. He put it to his ear. 'Great. Thanks for getting back to me. Stewart Blake,' he hissed, over his hand, before embarking on a series of monosyllabic responses that left Mariner frustratingly in the dark as to what they were discussing. Ending the call Knox was smug and self-satisfied.

'We're on the right track, all right,' Knox said. 'Goodway's departure from St Martin's was sudden and unexpected. No official explanation was given, but rumour had it that he'd invited a sixth former to model privately for him — very privately. One thing led to another, until the kid blew the whistle on him. It didn't go down too well with the parents.'

'No shit.'

'Perhaps with his wife safely out of the way, he offered Yasmin the same opportunity.'

'And she threatened to tell someone. We need to ask Brian Goodway a few more questions.'

'Let's hope he's at home.'

'He isn't,' said Mariner. 'He's at the Bournville festival. He may be up for a prize. He's—' He broke off mid-sentence. '-the picture.'

'What picture?'

But Mariner shook his head. 'Goodway will be occupied all afternoon. Let's take advantage of that and pay a visit to his house. I just need to do something else first.'

'And what about Andy Pritchard?' said Knox.

307

'I agree with you. Pritchard is small fry. He's up to something, but he can wait.'

Knox waited in the car at Granville Lane while Mariner went in and picked up a camera. After that their first stop was the reservoir, Knox following like an obedient hound at the heels of its master. They walked round to the patch of crushed down grass that Shaun Pryce frequented and Mariner looked out across the water. It was as he'd thought. Moving in an arc of 180 degrees he began taking snaps.

'SOCO have already got all this,' said Knox. 'Now might not be the right time to be supplementing your photo album.'

'Call it a comparative study,' was all that Mariner would say.

* * *

From there they went to Brian Goodway's house. The door was answered by a white-haired elderly lady, Goodway's mother, and as Mariner had hoped, it seemed she was alone in the house.

'Do you think we could come in, Mrs Goodway?' Mariner asked, walking past her before she had time to protest.

'Is this about Barbara?'

'There are just a couple of things we wanted to look at again. We won't take up much of your time,' he assured her.

'Can I make you a cup of tea?'

'That would be lovely,' said Mariner. And keep her out of their hair for a few minutes while they checked over the downstairs rooms. The house comprised three floors of outsized rooms. This might take a while. 'We're looking for the wire and the modelling clay and anything else that might help,' he reminded Knox.

Mrs Goodway was back sooner than he expected, brandishing the same mug he'd been given before: a well-worn version of those on Eric Dwyer's stall.

'Does your son belong to the conservation group?' Mariner asked, wondering if she'd even know.

'He used to,' said the old lady. 'But I don't think he's been for a long time.'

Climbing the stairs Mariner brushed past pictures hanging on the wall. One in particular stood out. It was almost identical to the one he'd seen this morning in the festival exhibition. At a different time of year, with no leaves on the trees and more rain in the lake, it was an exact copy of the view in Goodway's picture.

'Tony.'

Knox came and peered over his shoulder. 'What have you got?'

'This drawing is almost exactly the same as the pen and ink Brian Goodway has entered for the festival competition.'

'So? It's a view.'

Mariner took the camera out of his pocket and held one of the photos beside the sketch. 'See any similarities?'

'Christ.'

'Strip the trees of their leaves and they're exactly the same. When I came to talk to Goodway after his wife's body was found, he denied even knowing about the reservoir's existence.'

'Maybe he sketched it from a photograph.'

'So who took the photograph? His wife, Shaun Pryce or him? I think Brian Goodway is very familiar with the reservoir. He was probably spying on his wife. Not that it proves anything, naturally.'

Knox shrugged. 'So we keep looking.'

They went from room to room opening drawers, scrutinising cupboards, searching under furniture, but found nothing.

'Maybe he does all his art work at school,' said Knox.

'There must be something. He told me this afternoon that he paints in his spare time. Where does he do it?' Goodway's mother was hovering in the doorway.

'Does your son have a studio or a workshop where he does his art work?'

'Yes, it's up in the loft. You have to open the hatch and pull down the ladder—' Mariner and Knox were already vaulting the stairs. 'He doesn't really like anyone going up there!' she called after them uncertainly.

'I'll bet he doesn't,' Mariner muttered to himself.

Though basic, the loft had indeed been converted into a fully equipped artist's studio. Two skylights provided the required natural light. The down side was the lack of evidence that any sculpting went on here, there were only easels and drawing and painting materials — everything strictly two dimensional. They were not going to find what was used to strangle Yasmin here.

An assortment of larger drawings stood stacked in one corner. Absently Mariner began to sort through them unsure of what he was looking for. Until he found it. 'Look at this.'

Knox came and looked over his shoulder. 'Jesus H.'

'Actually, Shaun P,' Mariner corrected him. 'This looks like some pretty close-range spying.' The pictures of Pryce were full-length pencil sketches, this time revealing his face, and beautifully drawn. He was also completely naked and in a considerable state of arousal. 'So that's why women throw themselves at him,' remarked Knox.

'And not just women,' added Mariner, as the final piece fell into place. 'We've been barking up the wrong tree altogether.'

A strident female voice rang out from below. 'Who is it, Gran? What's going on?' Chloe Goodway was home.

'It's the police,' they heard Mrs Goodway say.

'What are they doing here?'

'I'd better go and explain,' said Mariner starting down the ladder.

But Chloe wasn't in the mood to await explanations. 'You shouldn't have let them in, Gran. They can't just come barging—'

'But they're policemen, darling. I expect they're going to help us find out what happened to mummy.'

'They know what happened to mum,' Mariner heard as he descended the last flight of stairs. 'I'm going to call dad.'

'Miss Goodway, if you could just wait!' Mariner took the last stairs two at a time, but he wasn't fast enough.

'Dad? It's Chloe. The police are here. They're up in your studio. What's going on?'

Too late, Mariner snatched the phone from her. 'I really wish you hadn't done that.'

The girl was unrepentant. 'What are you doing here? We haven't seen a search warrant. You have no right—' But Knox was hard on Mariner's heels and, leaving the girl ranting behind them, they ran out to the car and jumped in. As Knox drove at breakneck speed, Mariner called for an area car to come and keep an eye on Goodway's house. Next he called ahead for Watson and Ellis to detain Brian Goodway in the exhibition tent at the festival. They arrived breathless to find Ellis waiting helplessly.

'We missed him. He'd already gone. One of the stewards saw him leave about ten minutes ago.'

'Let's get out a description of him and his car.'

The car was easy. As it turned out it was still sitting less than five hundred yards from where they stood, left where Brian Goodway had parked it that morning in front of the shops on Bournville Green. A lady who worked in the toy shop had a girl at the school and had seen Goodway come back to his car and retrieve something from the boot.

'He knew we'd be able to trace the car,' said Mariner. 'But if he's gone on public transport we don't stand a chance.' He looked across at the steady stream of traffic on the ring road. The festival grounds were at the centre of a public transport network, served by the railway station at the back of the factory works and major bus routes to the front and sides.

Knox was more optimistic. 'He won't get far. It may take a while, but somebody somewhere will recognise him.' All they could do was wait, but waiting wasn't Mariner's forte.

'We never found that wire,' said Knox, suddenly. 'Is it worth checking his classroom?'

* * *

The school seemed a desolate place without the noisy bustle of hundreds of students. Today even the caretaker's family had abandoned their house on the site in favour of the festival. Parking outside the locked reception area they walked round to the side of the building and found the door to Brian Goodway's classroom swinging open.

'He must have his own key,' said Knox, but any hope they might have felt was short-lived. The classroom and those around it were completely devoid of life. If he had been here, Goodway had long since made his exit. The classroom was as much of a mess as it had been last time Mariner was here, the forms of half-finished sculptures dotted about.

'He's left us plenty of modelling clay and wire,' said Knox, bagging up samples. 'So why was he here?'

'There's Lily's tan-coloured suit,' said Mariner, seeing the pristine brown overalls hanging on the back of the door, '—or at least the next generation of clean replacements.' It was then that the smell drifted in on the air; the faint, slightly acrid smell of burning. 'That's what he's here for.'

Following the smell they ran round to the rear of the building where they found Goodway standing beside the outsized refuse bins, black smoke billowing from the nearest.

'What are you doing, Brian?' Mariner called. Goodway reeled round, shocked to see them. 'It's all right, you don't need to tell me.' Mariner continued calmly. 'I know what you're burning and I know why. Burning won't get rid of all the evidence though. Even if the fabric is charred we can still get DNA. We'll still find Ricky Skeet's blood on those overalls, won't we?'

'And you've given us plenty of circumstantial evidence,' added Knox, 'the pictures of Shaun Pryce and the reservoir; the wire you used to strangle Yasmin.' Goodway's eyes widened.

'There might be a way out of this mess, Brian,' Mariner soothed. 'Why don't you tell us what happened?'

Goodway turned away, wringing his hands. 'I've nothing to say to you.'

'Why don't we start with St Martin's?' Mariner said, ignoring him.

Goodway couldn't help himself. 'St Martin's was nothing,' he said.

'So why did you resign in such a hurry? There were rumours. No smoke without fire, eh, Brian? What was the boy's name?'

'Boy?' Knox was totally lost now.

Mariner turned to him. 'We were only partly on the right track. When Stewey Blake said Brian here had approached a sixth former, we both assumed it was girl, because Brian here is a red-blooded, heterosexual family man. But that's not true, is it Brian? It wasn't your wife who was having an affair with Shaun Pryce, it was you.'

CHAPTER 30

Brian Goodway sank to the ground, burying his head in his hands. For several moments he said nothing then just as Mariner started to walk towards him, he spoke, his voice hoarse and trembling. 'I realised I was gay long ago,' he said. 'My whole marriage was a sham. I concealed it for years, satisfying myself with the occasional one-night stand. But it got more and more difficult, always feeling that I was living a lie and never being able to just be myself. I knew that eventually I'd have to give in to temptation.'

'Is that why you went to work at the girls' school, so that there couldn't be a repeat of St Martin's?'

'I told you, nothing happened at St Martin's.'

'—only because the kid ratted on you.'

'I'd done nothing improper,' Goodway insisted. 'It was a conversation, a careless gesture, that's all. But I did think working at Kingsmead would be easier. And for a while it was; everything was fine, under control. Then when I met Shaun that evening at our house, I knew what was meant by love at first sight. I couldn't get him out of my mind. Inviting him to model at school was really just a way of seeing him again. I never thought anything would come of it, especially when I saw him flirting so outrageously with the girls.'

'Afterwards I took him for a drink as a kind of thank you and that's when I discovered that he wasn't averse to male company either. I couldn't believe my good fortune. We began an affair. But this time it was a proper relationship and I knew I'd have to tell Barbara. She'd been suffering from depression for a long time, partly because of the state of our marriage. I thought we'd be able to work out something civilised between us. But when I told her she was devastated. She'd never guessed. She became very distressed and started talking about ending it all. Then suddenly she announced that she was going to tell the children. I couldn't let her do that. Not yet. I wasn't ready. So one night when she went out I followed her. She went down to the reservoir. It was somewhere we used to go together years ago. I would sketch and she would enjoy the peace and quiet.'

'Not that night though.'

'I caught up with her on the wooden bridge. I tried to reason with her, but she wouldn't listen. She said that I'd humiliated her and ruined her life and that now she would ruin me. In some strange way I even think she was jealous.'

'She'd made a pass at Pryce. Did you know that?'

Goodway snorted. 'No.'

'So you tipped her into the river.'

'It was an accident, I swear!' He glanced up. 'I had Barbara by the shoulders, trying to make her see sense. I was begging her not to tell the children. She just laughed at me. In my frustration I pushed her, the railings gave way and she fell. I went down to help her but knew straight away that she was dead. I was desperate, I didn't know what to do. I was going to pull her out, back onto the bank and get help, but then I thought about how it would look. It occurred to me then that the easiest thing was the drainage tunnel. We'd had a lot of rain, so the water was flowing fast, and it just carried her down. It was as if it was meant to be.'

Fate. Mariner was sickened by the self-justification. 'And Yasmin?'

'She was a lovely girl, truly talented.' A brief smile crossed Goodway's lips. 'I saw her flirting with Shaun but I knew it was harmless.'

'So what then?'

'She saw us together. Shaun and me. While the weather has been so warm Shaun persuaded me to meet him at the reservoir. I'd introduced him to it when he'd said he needed somewhere private to sunbathe. He talked me into going with him after school. It was thrilling.'

'So you were there on that Monday when Yasmin walked past,' said Mariner.

'She'd been to see that boy Everett and was taking a shortcut through the reservoir back to the station. The next morning she came to tell me. She was tougher than you think. She said "You're a queer, aren't you? I saw you with Shaun. It's disgusting." Actually I think she was quite shocked and upset herself, but she'd come to find out what I'd do to stop her telling anyone. But by then I guessed that she was meeting Everett and we came to an arrangement: I'd say nothing about Lewis if she would forget Shaun.'

'Cosy,' said Knox.

'I knew it wouldn't last,' Goodway went on. 'Everett was bound to let her down and then I'd never be able to trust the little bitch to keep her mouth shut. If she let it out I'd be ruined.'

This was the part Mariner didn't understand. 'What you and Pryce were doing is hardly illegal. You're both consenting adults.'

'There was my reputation though, the reputation of the school. I'd been lucky at St Martin's. It was the word of a young, impressionable boy against that of, as you put it, a heterosexual family man; the interpretation of a conversation. The head believed me and I was able to resign with dignity and take up another post, my record unblemished. If my sexuality became public knowledge now, all that could be dragged up again. Questions would have been asked about Barbara's disappearance. Besides, I have my children and my mother to think of. What would it do to them? I couldn't bear it.'

'So what did you do?'

'I started checking Yasmin's phone during lessons. I don't know what I hoped to find, I suppose knowing she was seeing Everett against her parents' wishes I thought there might be something more incriminating that I could use to buy her silence. When I saw the message from Everett cancelling their meeting at the reservoir I knew that was my chance.'

'Chance to do what?'

'Talk to her. During the lesson I took her travel pass, and before I left I dropped it on the classroom floor, knowing that she'd have to come back for it, which would give me time to get there ahead of her.'

'And what happened?'

'When she got to the reservoir I was waiting on the bridge. She told me there was nothing to say. Before I knew it she was lying at my feet, dead.'

'Do you always carry sculpting wire around with you?'

'I had it . . . just in case.'

'In case of what?'

'I don't know.'

'And the brown overalls?'

He had no answer.

'So what about Ricky Skeet?'

'I dragged Yasmin down to the drainage tunnel. The water hadn't released but I knew it would within a matter of an hour or so—'

'You took Yasmin down to where your wife was.'

'But when I climbed back onto the bridge this boy just rushed at me from nowhere, shouting and screaming that he'd seen what I'd done. He started hitting me with this chunk of brick, but it slipped out of his hand, so I grabbed it and hit him over the head. He fell but I had to be sure so I hit him again and then I found that I couldn't stop. I kept hitting him over and over.'

'Why didn't you dispose of Ricky's body in the same way as the others?'

'I was going to, but there was so much blood. Part of the stream flows down into the park, I thought someone might see it. And also there were already two bodies in the tunnel. A third could have caused some kind of blockage and drawn unwanted attention. I knew I needed time to think.'

'So you just dragged him into the long grass and left him?' said Mariner.

'Something made me look up. I thought I saw someone in the window of the nursing home. I needed to get away. I was going to come back later, after dark, to move the body, but when I came back he had gone. I looked around a bit but there was no sign of him, so then I thought perhaps I hadn't killed him after all.'

'Weren't you worried that he might turn up somewhere and report what he'd seen?'

'Of course I was. I even phoned round the hospitals to ask if an injured boy had been brought in. He hadn't been, so there was nothing else I could do.'

Mariner remembered how strung out Goodway had seemed on that first meeting. He must have been beside himself. 'And you didn't know that Yasmin had dropped her phone.'

'No.'

'It must have been a shock when that turned up. If it hadn't been for that our search would never have switched to the reservoir.'

* * *

While they'd been talking, the light had begun to fade. In the gloom Mariner moved towards Goodway. 'Come on,' he said. 'Let's get all this down on paper.' But as he moved forward he saw the glint of something in Goodway's hand, the razor-thin blade of a craft knife. 'Don't do anything—' he began, but before he or Knox could intervene, Goodway drew back the knife and slashed violently at his wrist. Blood sprayed out in a wide, crimson arc as over their heads the first dazzling scatter burst of fireworks lit up the sky.

'Call an ambulance.' Mariner sprang forward and seized the knife, just as Goodway collapsed to the ground groaning in pain.

EPILOGUE

DCI Jack Coleman stood surveying the building work going on two hundred feet below him when there was a knock on the door. 'Come.' It was DI Mariner. 'Tom.' Coleman moved forward and the men shook hands.

'Good to see you again, sir,' said Mariner.

'Seems you've done rather well without me these last few weeks; a high-profile killer and a potential sex attacker arrested within twenty-four hours of each other.'

'We nearly lost Goodway.'

'But you didn't.'

'No. A dozen stitches and some pretty comprehensive dressings did the job, although I understand they've got him on twenty-four-hour suicide watch at Winson Green while he's on remand.'

'And Andy Pritchard?'

'We found dozens of photographs at his place that he must have taken over years, students and young girls around parks in south Birmingham, and we can place him on or near the university campus at the times of each indecent exposure, along with a couple more in other parts of the city.'

'DCI Fiske seems to have left me with a lot to live up to,' said Coleman.

'With all due respect, sir, I'm not sure that Mr Fiske had much to do with either of the arrests.'

'You got him off the hook with Complaints though, didn't you?'

'I'm sure he's enjoying his refresher course on Risk Assessment,' Mariner smiled. 'It'll give him lots of opportunity to practise his vocabulary.'

'And Colleen Skeet's happy with that?'

'She's satisfied that we caught Ricky's killer, but I doubt Colleen will ever be happy again.'

'No. And I'm sorry about your mother, too Tom.'

'Thank you, sir. Welcome back.'

THE END

Thank you for reading this book. If you enjoyed it please leave feedback on Amazon, and if there is anything we missed or you have a question about then please get in touch. The author and publishing team appreciate your feedback and time reading this book.

Our email is office@joffebooks.com

www.joffebooks.com

DI TOM MARINER SERIES
DEADLY LIES
DEADLY INNOCENT
More coming soon!

56124669R00202

Made in the USA
San Bernardino, CA
08 November 2017